SILVER MISTRESS

CARLA SIMPSON

OLIVERHEBERBOOKS

1

MARCH 10, 1868, BOSTON, MASSACHUSETTS

"I will not allow it!"

Her uncle's response thundered through hastily closed double doors to the formal parlor.

In the music room across the hallway, eyes closed tightly against his tirade, Laurel Wentworth inhaled a long, steadying breath. When she opened her eyes, the gray-shrouded view beyond the paned windows seemed oddly unchanged.

Lies. So many lies. She fought acknowledging the truth as it became clear. Even her name was a lie. Wentworth was her mother's family name; she'd been denied her father's name because of old arguments and bitterness. For almost eighteen years she'd been sheltered from that bitterness. Now its ugly head had raised.

The weather added its own dreariness to this morning that still belied all traces of spring. A gray, vaporous blanket encompassed the city, clinging with desperation to roofs and windows, forming a fine sheen of droplets that thickened, then ran together. The glass was cold against her skin as Laurel pressed her forehead to the pane, and her thoughts were as vague and unnatural as the fine mist that seemed to reshape, to redefine itself with each moment, not lingering long enough for understanding.

Somewhere in the house a door slammed. There had always been such happiness and warmth within these walls. Now, in spite of the fire that snapped and crackled at the hearth, Laurel felt only the icy coldness of betrayal.

"Laurel?"

She felt a subtle pressure upon her arm, and her troubled eyes turned to the woman standing behind her.

"I tried."

Laurel nodded.

Yes. Aunt Cecile had tried. The taut lines of fatigue and tension about her mouth and at the corners of her eyes revealed her concern.

"I'm afraid, your uncle is quite determined in this."

"And I am equally determined." Her voice hardly seemed her own as she met her aunt's grave expression.

Aunt Cecile reached up to brush back wisp of pale, golden hair from Laurel's cheek. It was an endearing gesture carried over from her childhood.

"For all your differences, you are both so much alike. Try to remember that bee is more readily drawn by honey than vinegar," Cecile said as she drew her niece's slender arm lovingly through hers.

"He wants to speak with you."

"There's nothing more to say." Laurel couldn't bear to meet her aunt's gaze, knowing the pain it caused her. There had been so much pain, so many arguments over the past two days.

They walked arm-in-arm from the parlor, one silently giving strength, the other desperately needing it. Crossing the carpeted hallway, they stopped before the closed doors of the formal drawing room, and Aunt Cecile wrapped an arm about her shoulders.

"Words can wound. If we've learned nothing else in the past days, we've learned that. Please try to remember that in spite of the hurt you feel, he has made his decision out of love for you."

Bracing herself, she straightened as she placed a hand on the ornate brass door handle. Aunt Cecile followed her into the room, quietly taking a chair beside the fireplace. The position she'd chosen placed her at an equal distance from her husband and her niece. Giving Laurel a reassuring wink, she folded her hands in her lap. She would not be forced into taking sides.

Far too nervous to sit, Laurel remained standing, her hands inconspicuously clenched over the folds of her blue silk skirt, its shade deepening the sadness and determination in her eyes.

Her cousin Andrew stood behind his mother, trying to catch some of the warmth from the hearth. He met Laurel's gaze evenly, silently giving her support.

Across the room, Edwin Wentworth stood before the velvet-draped windows, staring into the same gray gloom Laurel had contemplated only moments before. Steeped in silence, one arm folded behind him, he abstractedly fumbled with the links of the gold watch chain anchored at his vest pocket. It was a solemn gesture Laurel had seen him make before, when he'd considered some matter of grave importance. The last time it had been directed at her she had been twelve years old.

Laurel had almost forgotten; it had been so long ago. In April. Laurel remembered the unnatural heat, the fragrant smell of the cedar tree that came through the windows as she painstakingly practiced her scales. Miss Lavell, her music instructor, was a prune-faced old harridan who exacted great effort from a pupil with merely an admonishing glance. But Laurel wasn't intimidated by her, and the woman knew it. Consequently, this child's lessons quickly became challenges of musical skill and of temperament. Laurel was always well prepared, and eventually achieved acclaim for her skill at the piano, but she took delight in deliberately reinterpreting the scores, much to Miss Lavell's exasperation.

On that warm, still afternoon, Laurel had quickly tired of the game, and her gaze had constantly strayed to the windows and to the painfully blue sky beyond. The sounds of carriage wheels on the streets below beckoned, and playmates' voices chanted challengingly, teasing her. She'd reinterpreted the score once more, then had sent Miss Lavell for a calming glass of lemonade, the poor woman proclaiming to all in the house that her charge was a hopeless pupil and Edwin Wentworth's money was ill spent. In that brief lapse of supervision, Laurel had escaped to the spring day. Crossing to the hallway, she had considered a hasty departure through the front doors before turning back to the windows.

The rapid clicking of Miss Lavell's black shoes on the gleaming wooden floor of the hallway had sent Laurel scurrying over the windowsill into the outthrust branches of the cedar tree. Its heavy green growth had concealed her, and had her hem not snagged on a limb with a loud, rending tear, the route of her departure would have gone unnoticed. But it had, and Miss Lavell's cry of alarm had scaled the musical spectrum as she'd reached the open window. Not daring a backward glance, Laurel had shinnied down the wildly swaying young tree into the waiting arms of her cousin.

Eight years older than Laurel, Andrew Wentworth had just returned from the office of Wentworth Shipping, located on the docks at Boston Harbor. He'd arrived in time to witness Laurel's hazardous flight from windowsill to tree, and he'd silently encouraged her escape. Throughout her childhood, Laurel had been his shadow, an impish bundle of flashing blue eyes and streaming golden braids, with a smile that could dazzle the stars in the sky. On the rare occasions when that smile had failed her, ingenuity had prevailed.

Andrew had been her protector, her friend, and on occasion

her co-conspirator. She could load a slingshot faster than any of his friends, and her aim was deadly. She wore mud and grass stains with as much aplomb as she had the demure dresses Cecile Wentworth lavished on her. And she'd sabotaged his romances without hesitation when the young ladies in question had seemed undeserving of his attentions, yet she'd encouraged his love for the woman who later became his bride.

Andrew had been married for three months. As he had always been like a brother to Laurel, his bride, Jessica, was now like a sister. Her soft, brown eyes reached out to Laurel, offering love and support.

"I want this matter settled once and for all." Edwin Wentworth sighed heavily, not yet trusting himself to turn around. To him, Laurel had been more like his own child than his sister's, but he knew his weakness for this young woman who bore such a startling resemblance to Rebecca Wentworth.

Dear Rebecca. Her death had been so difficult, so painful. And she had married in such haste, leaving this house nearly twenty years earlier for California. Jason Cameron... Laurel's father. Memory steeled Edwin's determination. He'd lost Becky; he wouldn't lose Laurel to an elusive dream.

"I, too, want it settled," Laurel declared. "I have the right to know about my father." Voicing the words gave her courage.

"Your right?" Edwin Wentworth whirled around, his face flushed with the anger he fought to control.

"Edwin, please." Cecile Wentworth started up out of her chair.

"I'll take care of this. I want no interference. I only agreed to discuss this before the entire family out of consideration for Laurel," her husband said vehemently.

Laurel's fingers tightened over the silk of her skirt. "Consideration? How can you say that after I've been led to believe lies all these years. Why couldn't you have told me the truth?"

"Because I knew you'd want to leave for California. I

wouldn't allow it then, and I won't now! He's dead! It's over! Finished! There's no reason for you to go there. Your life is here, in Boston." Struggling to remain calm, Edwin shoved his large hands into his trouser pockets and forced back a desire to shake some sense into his niece.

"There's nothing for me here, or anywhere, until I know about my father." Laurel's reply was almost a whisper, but she knew her decision had been made the moment she'd read the brief letter, written on legal stationery, delivered two days earlier.

Within a matter of weeks, Andrew was being sent to California to manage the San Francisco offices of Wentworth Shipping, and Laurel was determined to go with him and Jessica. At that very moment a sleek clipper, the *Waverall,* lay at anchor in Boston Harbor, taking on supplies and cargo for the voyage to Panama. A cross-country coach would then take them to a second clipper which would carry them to San Francisco.

His patience gone, Edwin turned to her. "Just what the devil do you think your inheritance is? Well, I'll tell you—nothing. Jason Cameron never had a penny to his name. I tried all these years to protect you from it. Your mother knew him only six weeks before he lured her into eloping with him and going to the gold fields of California. His promises were grand and absolutely worthless."

"She loved him." Laurel fixed her gaze on the portrait hanging over the hearth. The artist had managed to catch the spirit of Rebecca Wentworth Cameron, the young beauty who stared forth from the canvas almost challengingly. Blue eyes, the mirror image of Laurel's own, shone with an inner light, and though the tilt of Rebecca's head was aloof, a smile pulled at the corners of her lips.

Most portraits were fashionably austere, not Rebecca Cameron's. Without having known her mother, Laurel somehow understood the spirit with which Rebecca had embraced life... and Jason Cameron. Whatever had happened later, Rebecca had gone willingly to California in defiance of her family.

"Let me tell you exactly what I found in California!" Edwin wagged a finger at her as he crossed the room.

"Edwin, you promised." Cecile was out of the chair in a moment, laying a restraining hand on his arm. That simple, elegant gesture was more effective, than anything else in tempering her husband's anger.

"Please, try to calm yourself, you'll rupture something."

"Rupture something! I'll probably have heart failure because of this ungrateful child!"

"You're wrong on both counts," Cecile said soothingly. "Laurel is not a child, and she hasn't an ungrateful bone in her body."

The steam and bluster seemed to rush out of him. "If she loved us, she wouldn't be set on this. I refuse to allow it. But she's just like her mother—stubborn, single-minded, with more fancy than common sense. She hasn't listened to a thing I've said."

"Stubbornness would seem to be a trait she comes by quite honestly in this family," Cecile remarked pointedly.

"Family trait, my Great-aunt Matilda!" Edwin thundered. "It's Jason Cameron. She's just like him, all set to go traipsing off to San Francisco. And after what? Some pretense of an inheritance."

Cecile Wentworth poured a healthy draught of brandy and thrust it into her husband's hand. At his inquiring glance, she smiled.

"I think this might be just what the doctor ordered, " she said, then stood calmly behind him, placing light but restraining hands at his shoulders.

"Laurel... dear girl, " It was more a plea than a command, her uncle's voice full of emotion. "You can't begin to understand how it was when your mother left. Only a note left to inform us that she had eloped with your father.

"It was months before we received her first letter, telling us that Jason Cameron had used all his money to buy into a gold claim. My God, it seems like only yesterday."

"Those first letters were filled with happiness, news of the gold strikes, and hope for the future," Cecile interjected.

Edwin thoughtfully placed a hand over his wife's. "Then the letters became less frequent. There was a change in them. In her last letter Rebecca asked that I send her funds from our father's estate, but I refused to allow her to waste her money on some worthless mining claim.

"Then, when we didn't hear from her for nearly six months, I became worried. I learned from sources in San Francisco that Jason Cameron's mining claim had played out and he and your mother were living in a run-down cabin somewhere in a gold camp outside of Virginia City." The memory was obviously a painful one. Suddenly, Edwin seemed a much older man.

"When I arrived, your father was gone; Rebecca was alone in that small cabin. I didn't know she'd had a child. You lay in a cradle beside her bed. She was weak, she hadn't recovered yet from childbirth. Looking at her, I knew there was only one choice."

"So you took us away from my father." Bitterness sharpened Laurel's words.

"Your mother was ill, and you were so small. There was no food. Jason Cameron had been gone for days, and no one knew when he'd be back. For all I knew, he'd abandoned both of you. I couldn't just leave the two of you there to die."

Laurel met her uncle's gaze. "You couldn't have waited until he returned instead of taking it upon yourself to bring us back to Boston? And what about the years between? You told me he was dead. What about my father's letters?"

"What could Jason Cameron possibly offer you?" He replied. "The same existence he'd given your mother? Father in heaven, Laurel, if your mother had been strong, if she'd had proper care, she'd have recovered after you were born. As it was, she'd practically worked herself to death in that mining camp, living a life she wasn't prepared for.

"No! Right or wrong, I couldn't chance losing you the same way I'd lost her. I lied. It was wrong, but I'll not apologize for it."

"And I'll not apologize for what I must do now." Laurel's voice was cool, determined. "When Andrew and Jessica leave for San Francisco, I have every intention of boarding that ship with them."

Aunt Cecile paled, but remained silent. As she met Laurel's pained gaze, it seemed she'd known what her decision would be.

"I'll not allow it! Never!" Edwin Wentworth shot out of his chair. "Go to your room, this instant. We'll not discuss this matter further!"

Laurel bowed her head slightly in what passed for acceptance. She dared not meet her uncle's infuriated gaze, lest he see the truth in her eyes. As her aunt moved to restrain him, Laurel turned to leave. At that moment her room offered a calm haven.

Jessica rushed across to her and placed a restraining hand on her arm, sympathy in her dark eyes. "I'll come with you."

Laurel shook her head. "I want to be alone now."

Jessica nodded, misunderstanding the unnatural light that gleamed in Laurel's eyes. The afternoon had worn badly on everyone. She thought a little time alone would give Laurel the opportunity to better understand Edwin Wentworth's decision.

Closing the paneled doors of the parlor behind her, Laurel

released a shaky breath. Her legs were unsteady as she made her way to the landing, stopping just beyond the entrance to the music room. Thin shafts of golden sunlight shone through the clinging fog, sending the promise of light into the room. Beyond the paned windows, stood the cedar tree, strong and green. It beckoned as it had that spring day so long ago.

As the day of her cousins' departure drew closer, Laurel threw herself into their last-minute plans for the voyage.

She and Jessica spent long hours shopping for the items the couple would need, and she helped pack the wedding gifts, many still in their original boxes, that were taken to the Wentworth warehouse at the docks, from there to be placed in the hold of the *Waverall.*

Spring, with all its promise had descended on Boston, and the clear weather promised a calm sea. The long-awaited trip would not have to be postponed.

Laurel offered silent thanks. Whirling about, she gave Jessica a sympathetic smile. The dear girl was completely undone by all the preparations.

"I just don't think there'll be enough room. I'm going to need at least two more trunks, and Andrew already swears he'll throw any more overboard. But I need everything I'm taking. There's no telling how long we'll be in San Francisco." Jessica rolled her eyes heavenward in a silent plea for understanding.

As her gaze met Laurel's, she suddenly regretted not having chosen her words more carefully. Over the last weeks, everyone had carefully avoided talking of the trip, for fear of sparking another confrontation between Laurel and Edwin Wentworth.

Surprisingly, there'd been no further outbursts or arguments. Laurel seemed to have accepted her uncle's edict quite stoically. Jessica had laughed off her husband's doubts about that.

"I'm sorry," Jessica murmured.

"For what?" Laurel carefully folded another satin petticoat, then placed it carefully in the trunk that sat before her.

"I know how you wished to be going with us."

Laurel turned about to survey the remaining garments and linens yet to be packed. Her response was seemingly unconcerned.

"I really haven't given the matter that much thought. Uncle Edwin made his decision." She hadn't lied. Every word she had spoken was true. She just hadn't elaborated on the decision *she* had made. With genuine enthusiasm, she turned back to Jessica.

"We'll need at least another trunk from the attic. I'll have Jameson bring another down."

Returning, a thoughtful expression on her face, she directed the servant to take the cumbersome trunk across the hall.

"There's hardly enough room to move in here as it is. I've had Jameson place the trunk in my room. It will be close enough to pack these last linens."

Jessica crossed the room and wrapped her arms about Laurel's waist. "You're a dear friend, as well as my cousin now. You've been a great help to me these last weeks. I don't know how I could have done all this without you. But it's more than that." Tears appeared at her dark eyes.

"I shall miss you dreadfully."

"Nonsense." Laurel hugged her. "We'll see each other before you know it."

The maid announced the morning meal and Laurel walked with Jessica into the hall. Her eyes gleamed with excitement as she stopped beside the door of her own room, and a devilish smile pulled at her lips as she gazed at the trunk resting at the foot of her bed. Then, with a satisfied nod, she closed the door behind her. At least her plan had gotten this far.

Aunt Cecile was flushed with excitement and Uncle Edwin was trying his very best to carry on casual conversation, but appetites were sadly lacking, even though the cook had prepared a tempting breakfast. Laurel barely heard her uncle's remark, her attention was fixed on her carefully laid plans.

"You're hardly dressed for a send-off at the docks, my dear," he commented.

Laurel composed herself, her faint smile firmly in place as she turned to her uncle.

"We've already said our good-byes. I think you'll understand if I don't accompany them to the ship."

Edwin Wentworth cleared his throat. He had hoped Laurel wouldn't choose to vent her unhappiness at this last meal his family was sharing.

"Very well," he muttered gruffly. "I understand."

"Thank you." Keeping her eyes downcast, Laurel rose from her chair. "If you don't mind, the last few days have been exhausting. I would like to retire to my room."

"You are looking a bit pale. You're not ill?" Concern in her eyes, Cecile folded her cloth napkin as she rose to follow her niece.

Laurel waved her back. "Not at all. Jessica and I were up quite late last evening doing the last of the packing. I'll just rest till you get back." She rounded the magnificent dining table to embrace Andrew, and then Jessica.

"Have a safe voyage, and you must promise to write," she said, and before either could respond, she left the dining room and headed up the wide staircase to the second floor.

Gaining the upper hallway, she cast a glance into Andrew's rooms. The trunk Jessica had finished packing stood near the door, waiting to be loaded into the wagon for the trip to the ship.

Leaning out over the balustrade, Laurel called down to the servant who was crossing the foyer.

"When the men arrive, there are two trunks still upstairs, one in Andrew's room and the other in mine." At the servant's nod of acknowledgment, Laurel returned to her room.

Closing the door behind her, she opened the trunk, and muttering a silent prayer for forgiveness, she removed the elegant linens packed carefully within, part of Jessica's purchases for when they arrived in San Francisco. She vowed that she'd replace them.

She piled them all neatly inside her wardrobe. She then placed the neatly penned letter to her aunt and uncle on the writing desk beside the window. Finally, she lowered the lid of the trunk wedging a tortoise-shell comb into the latch to keep it from settling into place. Satisfied, she raised the lid and surveyed the trunk one last time.

The trunk would have to do. Thank God that she was small. Pushing back last-minute uncertainty, Laurel climbed inside and lowered the lid. She listened and then waited, holding her breath as she heard the men who'd been brought from the docks to assist, grabbed hold of the trunk and then carried it downstairs to be loaded onto the wagon that would take all of Jessica and Andrew's things to the dock.

When the thumping and bumping at last halted, Laurel was certain every bone in her body was broken. Inside the trunk, sounds were oddly muffled, so she heard no last-minute conversations or farewells but after what seemed an interminable amount of time, she felt the trunk being lifted and her stomach turned over at the swaying, lurching motion of the wagon that followed.

She'd seen cargo hoisted into holds on countless visits to her uncle's offices at the docks. Remembering one such afternoon, Laurel closed her eyes and offered a silent prayer for safe delivery aboard ship.

The rope used to transfer cargo onto the ship had snapped, sending everything, including a seaman, into the waters at the harbor. The man had been rescued. The cargo had gone straight to the bottom.

In spite of the musty heat inside the trunk, she shivered and wondered how long it would take water to seep inside if that were to happen this time.

She held her breath from the moment the trunk lurched, hovering between the dock and the ship until it scraped against a solid surface. The trunk landed heavily, and with sickening finality Laurel heard the audible snap of the comb wedged beneath the lid. The latch clicked into place and held firm. She was trapped!

Her heart pounded and breathing became difficult, but she tried to remain calm. Surely someone would return to the hold to check the cargo. She would simply wait until the ship was underway, then make her presence known.

Surrounded by complete darkness, she couldn't guess how long it had been since they'd left the house, and she feared lack of air was confusing her memory. She vaguely recalled that Andrew and Jessica had planned to leave the house no later than ten o'clock in order to be aboard and prepared to sail before noon.

Could a person die in two hours? What if it took longer for someone to check the hold? What if no one checked it until the ship docked at Panama? It would be too late then.

She grimly imagined her cousins' expressions when they opened the trunk in San Francisco to retrieve damask table-cloths and instead found her cramped body. One thing was certain. At that point, she wouldn't care.

SHE AWOKE SUDDENLY and tried as best she could to stretch her cramped legs and arms.

How long had she been dozing. A few minutes? Longer?

There it was again, a tapping.

Perhaps she was imagining it. No, there it was again, and from somewhere very close by. Something or someone was inside the hold of the ship. She beat on the sides of the trunk with both fists.

Please let them hear me! Please! she thought over and over.

The sound was barely audible over the creaking and groaning of the ship. Inspecting first one heavily reinforced crate and then another, the tall man bent his head and listened.

"Did you hear that?"

"I didn't hear nothin', boss, just the ship. You think we'll make New Orleans on time?"

"We'd better, or I'll be stuck with three hundred and fifty rifles. And right at the moment I don't know of any new wars or revolutions." The reply was guarded.

"Will we be stayin' at The House?"

His heavy-set companion didn't have the rolling gait of a seaman. Instead, he leaned on the crates for support each time the ship crested a wave. The taller man frowned slightly.

The House of the Rising Sun was a well-known gambling establishment and brothel. It was one of the few places in New Orleans where a man could get a drink during the war, no matter which side he served on, no questions asked.

He smiled with pleasure at the memory of the Creole girl he'd stayed with that last time. Had that really been over three years ago?

What a trip that had been, dodging Union soldiers, renegade Johnny Rebs, and a one-eyed blockade runner who'd claimed he'd been cheated at poker. War brought out greed in everybody, and greedy people made him cautious. He'd never crossed the line into that business.

He'd just done his job—somebody had to do it. His smile reappeared briefly at the thought. Well, maybe there was a little greed in him, just enough to make him want a small stake so he could get started in a more legitimate line of work. He was damned glad to be getting out of this business.

"You say somethin', boss?"

He shook his head and then looked up as the sound came again.

"Over there, those trunks tied down that came aboard last in Boston."

"Hey, you don't suppose... one of them smugglers got aboard?"

"We'll just find out," Ruel Delaney replied.

The sleek, blue-black barrel of a pistol slid silently from polished leather as he slipped carefully among the tightly stacked trunks. All except two had been secured to the sides of the hold.

The sounds came again, stronger and more urgent now—a thumping from inside the farthest trunk. He pulled back the trigger and reached for the latch with his other hand. He threw it back.

The soft glow of lantern light filled the inside of the trunk with shadows. As a rush of fresh salt air hit her, Laurel let out a startled gasp.

"What the hell?" Ruel exclaimed.

Laurel took another breath to clear her head. She wasn't going to die after all!

Gratitude at being rescued from the trunk turned into a strangled gasp as she was dragged from the trunk.

Her cramped legs gave way as she tried to stand and a powerful hand clamped over her shoulder. She clung to the trunk, raising uncertain eyes to the man before her.

Whoever he was, whatever he was, she'd never been so glad to see anyone in her life, not even Andrew when he'd broken her fall from the garden tree so long ago.

Her throat was parched from the long hours she'd spent inside the trunk. As the meager light from the lantern fell across her face, she could imagine what she looked like. She'd lost most of the pins from her hair, and her gown was badly rumpled. With as much dignity as she could muster, she pushed her hair back from her face.

A long, low whistle of surprise came from nearby, but the shifting shadows inside the ship made it impossible to see who was there.

The man who had pulled her from the trunk was not Andrew, and she realized her precarious situation at being discovered by two strangers, and one of them very tall, quite strong, and intimidating as he shouted at the other man.

"Close the damn crates." He turned to her, that dark gaze and the growth of beard on his face giving him a menacing look. He stared at her, those dark eyes narrowed. His hand tightened at her shoulder.

When she would have thanked him for rescuing her, his hand tightened at her shoulder, handsome features twisted with anger.

"What the hell are you doing here?" His voice was cold. His hand clamped over her wrist.

"Let me go!" She demanded, trying to twist away, only to be dragged across the floor of the hold. The other man she'd briefly glimpsed scampered up the wooden ladder with surprising a speed as her own numb legs gave way beneath her.

She managed to free one hand and struck out at the man who continued to drag her across the hold.

"You lying, thieving little whore. Did you really think you could sneak aboard this ship without anyone knowing? After San Francisco, I thought I was well rid of you. Couldn't you find some poor bastard to support your acting career?"

He was mad, absolutely mad! Her head spun crazily, the

deck beneath her feet slipping away. God only knew what he would do to her. It was a mistake, a dreadful mistake.

Had the trunk been brought aboard the wrong ship? Would there be anyone to help her? He shook her violently, until her head threatened to separate from her neck.

Teeth clenched, Laurel fought back but she was disoriented from the hours in the trunk, and she seemed to have no legs, at least none capable of supporting her.

She cried out, her knee scraping painfully against the corner of a crate as she was pulled full length against a very angry, very tall man.

"You really are something!" He buried his hands in her hair and twisted the gold strands around a fist.

His face was so close, the heat of his breath burned her, and the same time the expression in his eyes was cold as ice.

She was terrified, helpless, with no idea what would happen. The only weapon she had was the fear.

"Take your hands off me!" she demanded, then gasped as the air was crushed from her lungs. This madman was going to kill her, she was certain of it, and no one would know.

"What are you up to now?" he demanded, as Laurel tried to wedge her hands between them.

"You think you can come to me now, after what you've done and a few hours in bed will make everything all right. Well, I suppose that's how a whore thinks. No more. I told you!" he spat out.

Her thoughts spun. What was he talking about? Almost as if he knew her?

With a rending tear, Laurel's bodice gave way. She gasped as cold air touched her exposed skin.

Dear God, wasn't there anyone to stop him? Her fingers fumbled at tattered lace as she struggled frantically to hold the torn fabric together over her breasts.

"Now you'll see what it's like. I want you to know how it

feels to be used. I'll use you for what you are, bought and paid for. And, by God, I've more than paid for you."

Arms trapped Laurel cruelly, cutting off the air she'd been so grateful for a moment before, and she was forced down beneath his buckling weight.

"No! You don't understand!" Her broken sob was cut off by the assault of cruel, bruising lips. She struck out, raking her nails across his face.

Brilliant colors shot through her brain—fiery red, icy blue, stark white. Anger, fear, helplessness.

"I understand everything perfectly!" he growled. "Now, I want you to understand, once and for all." The air inside the hold was suddenly cold, damp against her bare flesh as he yanked at the bodice of her gown.

In the swaying light from that single overhead lantern, the roundness of her breasts was softly illuminated. Their fullness rose and fell with her labored breathing.

One of his hands wandered beneath her silk skirts, tracing the slender curve of a hip covered with lace. He frowned. As long as he'd known her, she'd shunned the more delicate garments of a lady's wardrobe in favor of convenience.

He hesitated. Revenge! Hadn't he told her? He'd always taken revenge against anyone who'd crossed him. Why did he hesitate now? He'd taken her before, for pleasure, they'd used each other, and then he'd walked away.

A muffled sob escaped her, and tears dampened his shirt.

The fear he'd seen in her eyes a moment before was genuine and surprised him. Now she tried to twist away from him in an attempt to free herself, and there was something in her voice, different, the fear there as well.

There were countless ways a woman used her body to promise and entice. Hadn't she shown him? Yet now, at this moment, he was convinced that she was completely unaware of the heat that exploded between their bodies.

She was different, changed—someone he knew, yet didn't know. Was it because she was trapped, completely defenseless?

Tears. Christ, he'd never known her to use that trick before. She strained away from him, as if his very touch terrified her. Yes, he'd wanted to hurt her, to make her cry. He needed to be cruel to cut her out of his life once and for all. Then, her lower lip trembled, vulnerable, when he had been convinced she was incapable of it.

He reached up, wrapping her hair around his hand. The soft gold strands clung to him. She was the same! People didn't change. But she wasn't the same and the difference, something that slipped just out of reach, tore at him.

He forced her to meet his gaze. God, she was beautiful, eyes the color of blue sapphire, and a mouth... that trembled.

He'd hated her, wanted to hurt her. "I'll hand you over to the captain, and see you thrown overboard for the stowaway that you are," he threatened. "If you're fortunate, maybe another ship will pick you up before you drown. Then you can spread yourself to save that beautiful neck of yours."

The scream caught in her throat. She was certain he meant to strike her.

Not waiting for her to gain her footing, he dragged her across the hold toward the ladder. His hand closed over the back of her gown as he climbed with amazing strength, pulling her along behind him.

Laurel could only try to keep herself from being more badly bruised as she dangled helplessly against the ladder. She twisted around, attempting to gain a foothold on the next rung.

But the effort was wasted. No sooner did she hook the toe of her shoe over a rung of the ladder than she was hauled up to the next. She'd die of a broken neck before reaching the top.

Blinding light cut painfully into her eyes. The sky above was mercifully, gloriously blue as her vision slowly cleared after the darkness of the ship's hold and the first face that took form after she was unceremoniously dumped onto the deck of the ship was undoubtedly that of the captain. Behind him stood Andrew, a horrified expression at his face. He sidestepped the captain, quickly removing his frock coat, and dropping onto one knee, he wrapped it about Laurel's shoulders.

"What are you doing here?" He demanded, his expression taut as he closed his coat around her against the stares of the crew.

"I think so, now that you're here. Please don't be angry." She forced a smile.

"That's gentlemanly of you," Ruel Delaney replied. "But believe me, she's accustomed to wearing a great deal less in front of most men."

Laurel cringed despite Andrew's protectiveness. The stranger's eyes were dark, filled with dangerous, glowing light. Fire and ice.

"Good God, man! Just what the devil is going on here?"

The captain of the *Waverall* stepped between the two men.

"I found this stowaway in the hold of the ship. I'm certain you'll want to take appropriate action."

"Mr. Delaney, I specifically warned you against making trouble on this trip. I trust you have an explanation for this."

"The *lady*, and I use the term loosely, has quite a reputation. If you'll check with the authorities once we reach New Orleans, I think you'll find that though she likes to call herself an actress, she's really an accomplished thief and whore. While I personally have no objection to the latter, I won't tolerate the former. She stole a substantial sum of money from me before she left California, and I'll be more than willing to bring charges when we put ashore. In the meantime, the best place for her would be in chains."

As the captain turned and spoke briefly to the young man beside him, Ruel Delaney took a long cigarette from his pocket and lit it. He squinted through curling smoke at the young woman. Then, he looked away and his frown deepened as he fought to hold onto the anger.

"Delaney, there's been a grave mistake," the captain said firmly. "I'm personally acquainted with Miss Wentworth and can vouch for her character. You will immediately apologize to her and Mr. Wentworth, for your behavior."

"Like hell I will!" Delaney took a threatening step toward her despite the captain's presence. He could almost feel the slender column of her throat beneath his fingers.

"Andrew, please. I would like to leave..."

But to where she thought, as she pressed back against her cousin. It wasn't as if she had a stateroom. But she didn't want to risk another confrontation with this man.

Andrew placed a protective arm about her, as he turned to the captain. "I demand that this man be put ashore. Be assured that I intend to take appropriate action." He escorted Laurel away from the openly inquiring stares of the crew.

"Do you mean to tell me that you're just going to forget the entire matter?" Ruel demanded. A head taller than the captain, he gave little heed to the seaman who approached with a club in hand.

"I'll have no further incidents on my ship, Mr. Delaney. You were allowed aboard only because of that other gentleman. I don't like carrying cargo I haven't previously inspected. As for your allegations against this young woman, let me assure you, you're mistaken and out of line. I suggest you give some consideration to your own reputation in such matters. Do I make myself clear?"

Ruel couldn't afford to be thrown in jail once they put ashore. And the captain was right about one thing—his reputation certainly wouldn't stand up to scrutiny at least not in any southern state.

"Mr. Delaney?" Not easily intimidated, the captain reminded him.

He nodded.

Satisfied that he would be obeyed, the captain turned his attention to the running of his ship.

Ruel Delaney's stared where the woman had disappeared below decks with the other man.

2

"You're angry." Laurel's gaze rested on her hands folded at her lap.

"Furious is more like it!" Andrew Wentworth didn't yet trust himself to say more.

"I know it was wrong to deceive you..." Laurel slowly began, carefully choosing the words she'd practiced over and over during those long hours in the trunk.

The only problem was, she hadn't known then the dramatic conclusion to her little adventure. Andrew was angry, and she supposed that he had every right to be.

Her cousin cursed, then muttered something else. After a long sigh, he regained some control.

As long as she could remember, she'd never known him to become quite so angry. They'd fought as youngsters, especially when she'd pulled childish pranks on him. But always that faint twist of a smile had appeared at his face, as if he secretly enjoyed her escapades. Now he stood beside the open porthole refusing to look at her.

Two trunks filled the space between two narrow beds. Laurel caught herself wondering if they would occupy both, or just one. Odd that she would think of something like that at a time like this.

Stranger still that she would think of it at all, for her newly married cousin's sleeping arrangements had never entered her mind. Now, she watched as Jessica approached Andrew and placed a gentle hand on his sleeve.

"I think you should feel relieved that we have her with us safe and sound, dear." Jessica's tone was soothing and reassuring. "Have you stopped to think about what would've happened if Mr. Delaney hadn't found her in that trunk?"

Dear Jessica, friend and champion, Laurel thought. Who else could so easily turn everything around and make it seem as if she were quite fortunate to have had such an encounter?

Dear God, if Jess only knew how terrified she had been, and what might have happened... Fortunate indeed! At least she was out of that trunk and they were well at sea, impossible to simply have her put off now that she'd been discovered.

Maybe Uncle Edwin was right. He was certain there was too much of her mother in her, that she possessed those same qualities that had Rebecca eloping with a young man unacceptable to her family and going to California.

"You'll need a cabin of your own," Andrew was saying. "Jessica can help you find clothes."

Laurel's head jerked up. She hadn't been listening to a word Andrew had been saying.

"I don't think now is the appropriate time to make any further decisions. It'll be several days before we reach New Orleans."

"Then you won't have the captain return to Boston?" she asked.

"No, there's a schedule to keep for the rest of the cargo that was brought aboard. I wouldn't want to explain to Father or the merchant in San Francisco, that we were delayed."

Since Andrew intended to allow her to remain aboard until

they reached New Orleans, she would have time to convince him to let her accompany him to San Francisco. She was certain she could change his mind. All she needed was a little time to allow his anger to cool.

Andrew shook his head. Delaney had a notorious reputation when it came to women, and his exploits in shipping were well known. Though he'd never been caught, and nothing could ever be proven, it was rumored that he was responsible for ships being sunk or diverted from Union ports during the war. A good deal of Wentworth cargo had been lost.

Little else was known about the man except that he'd refused to fight for either side. And he had accumulated substantial wealth, a pirate, according to some, masquerading in fine clothes.

"I'm sorry I caused you so much worry," Laurel apologized.

Andrew nodded. His wife stopped him at the door of the stateroom.

"Thank you, darling," Jess told him. "You know how I adore her. You'll be so dreadfully busy, and she'll be marvelous company for me." She kissed him lovingly. "Now, go. I need to find her something suitable to wear."

She meant until they reached New Orleans, Andrew thought. Or did she? Good God, if his wife took up Laurel's cause, he was lost. He'd once thought he'd married Jessica because she had such a caring nature, not given to gossiping or inserting herself into other people's affairs. What he realized now was that she was very much like the little imp who'd made his life so interesting when they were children. Well, if he wasn't going to have his cousin sent ashore immediately, at least he'd make certain she had no further encounters with Mr. Ruel Delaney. Andrew straightened the collar of his shirt as he went to find the captain to secure another cabin for the trip.

. . .

LAUREL PACED the width of the cabin. She'd lost count at three hundred ninety-one. The dark blue of the crinoline skirt rustled crisply against the edge of the bed. If she had to spend one more afternoon there, she would scream. At that moment, she'd gladly be tossed overboard as Ruel Delaney had threatened, just to break the monotony of the past three days.

Sighing resignedly, she plunked herself down on the corner of the small writing desk positioned directly beneath the porthole. She stared out across the expanse of blue-gray ocean to the verdant shoreline in the distance. One neatly booted foot poked out from beneath her hemline and swung distractedly back and forth, brushing rhythmically against the desk leg.

The cabin was sparsely furnished, but substantially more spacious than others on the *Waverall*. The captain had graciously relinquished his own private quarters to Laurel. Declaring that she could hardly be expected to sleep in the cook's storeroom, he'd removed his charts, maps, and log.

She was grateful for the cabin's size. It allowed for her daily ritual of pacing; Andrew had strongly suggested she remain in her cabin until she'd had time to recover from her *"ordeal."* But to Laurel's way of thinking, being confined to a cabin, no matter how spacious, was infinitely more of an ordeal than her brief encounter with Mr. Ruel Delaney.

She seized the pale lavender shawl Jessica had given her, along with the other garments she wore. The few clothes she'd thrown into the bottom of the trunk were still there, but she was certain Andrew wouldn't allow her to retrieve them. In any event, she and Jessica were very nearly the same size, and the dress fit well enough, if a bit snugly, across her breasts.

The first day had passed quickly enough, for she and Jessica had gone through a large trunk, dividing up the wardrobe it contained. The second day, they'd spent countless hours making an extensive list of the garments she needed to purchase once they reached New Orleans. They would be in that southern port for several days—before continuing on as Laurel planned to Panama and then San Francisco.

She wanted to go up on deck and join her cousins, to walk about in an area larger than eight feet by eight feet, to feel the salty air against her face, and to enjoy the warmth of the sun. And she couldn't deny that she wondered if she would encounter Ruel Delaney up on deck since he was obviously also a passenger.

Closing the cabin door behind her, Laurel wrapped the shawl snugly about her shoulders and then started down the narrow passageway.

The sunshine was glorious, as was the wind. Even Andrew's disapproving frown failed to dampen her spirits as she stepped out on deck.

"Jess went below to take you lunch." The reprimand was obvious, that he preferred that she stay in her cabin. She chose to ignore it.

"I'm not hungry. How could I be, when I haven't had fresh air or exercise in three days?" She refused to acknowledge the grave expression at his eyes as she tucked her hand through his arm.

"She went below over an hour ago. Haven't you seen her?" Andrew's disapproval quickly turned to concern.

"I haven't seen her since breakfast. She wasn't looking too well then. I don't think ship travel agrees with her," Laurel observed, grateful the conversation had turned away from her.

She had no problems at sea. She'd been five the first time Uncle Edwin had taken the family to New York aboard a schooner. Poor Aunt Cecile had been confined to her bed for most of the short voyage, but Laurel and Andrew had scampered about, playing hide-and-seek in all the wonderfully secret places to be found aboard ship. She could still see Uncle Edwin's horrified expression when he'd caught Andrew halfway up the main mast. Laurel had been encouraging her cousin from the bowsprit. Andrew was thirteen at the time and had never quite forgiven her for the dressing down he was given.

"I'll take you back to your cabin and check on her. I hope it's nothing serious." Andrew commented.

"Please let me remain here. I'll be fine. It's been dreadful being closed in that cabin for the last three days." She smiled at him.

"I'll only be gone a short while ..."

"I'll be all right. There's nothing to worry about. Check on Jessica. If she's up to it, we'll have supper together."

Objection was written all over his face.

"Go ahead, young man. I'll keep an eye on her for you." A matronly woman slowly approached them from the railing.

"I'm an accomplished traveler and quite capable of keeping her company. Adela MacMillan, if you've forgotten." She introduced herself as she approached, tapping her way across the deck with a magnificent, black walking stick. She navigated between Andrew and Laurel with amazing surefootedness in spite of the roll of the deck.

"Yes, of course, we met the first evening," Andrew responded.

Wentworth Shipping transported MacMillan Manufacturing's goods. Lawrence MacMillan had died two years ago, leaving a very wealthy widow. She'd taken up the management of her husband's diverse business interests, shocking society and, according to Cecile Wentworth, loving every minute of it.

Mrs. MacMillan was reputed to be a formidable businesswoman.

"If it's not an inconvenience..." Andrew hesitated.

"Not in the least, I've been dying to meet this young lady. "Go ahead and look after that wife of yours." She dismissed Andrew with a wave of her walking stick.

"I don't know how to thank you," Laurel said to the woman she'd heard so much about from her uncle.

"Don't thank me until you know me better. I have an insatiable curiosity about things. And of course, being female, I am called *nosey*. If I were a man, I would be called *inquiring*." She gave a good-natured shrug.

Laurel fell into step beside her as they walked the length of the deck.

"I'm simply dying to know how you came to be locked in that trunk in the hold of the ship. Of course, Ruel Delaney has the most dreadful reputation where women are concerned," Adela commented. "However, he's not usually the sort to accost a woman. He's never had the need for that, if you know what I mean.

"I've heard he has women waiting for him in every port up and down the eastern seaboard, and I wouldn't doubt it. He's devilishly good-looking, sinfully so, wouldn't you say?"

Laurel laughed at Adela's boldness. No wonder the woman had such a reputation. She was outrageous.

Sinfully good-looking. Yes. Laurel thought that was a fitting description for Ruel Delaney. He was indeed devilishly good-looking, a man to be avoided by a proper, well-bred young lady.

"You seem to know him well," she observed as they stopped beside the aft railing, both women delighting in the warmth of the sun that shimmered on the rolling expanse of sea.

"My husband had some dealings with him a few years back. I wasn't privy to the details, but I did meet Mr. Delaney. He's quite an unconventional man, mysterious, and a gambler I'm told. It sometimes gets him into trouble.

"Of course, when one has his looks and charm, one can get by with just about anything. Wouldn't you agree, Miss Wentworth, "Adela MacMillan tilted her head in her direction.

Laurel turned back to her *chaperone*. "I certainly didn't find him charming," she said.

"No, I suppose not, under the circumstances. Where did you say the two of you had met before?"

The question was casual enough, but Laurel recognized it as an undisguised attempt to gain information. Nosey indeed.

"I didn't," Laurel replied, a smile tilting the corners of her mouth.

"Ah, you're trying to be discreet. Actually, that's to your credit. That last little episode was publicized for days—the woman, poor distraught dear, ran practically naked through the streets of New Orleans chasing after him. Seems she was betrothed, and her fiancé caught them *en dishabille,* as they say.

"At any rate there was a dreadful scandal even by New Orleans standards," she continued. "The girl was *from* a prominent family. Seems she just couldn't help herself. The fiancé, poor fool, demanded satisfaction."

Laurel gasped. "A duel?"

She'd heard of such things, and even thought they were illegal, it was still rumored to take place in some areas of the South.

"Hmmm, yes. To Mr. Delaney's credit, he refused the challenge. He has a notorious reputation with a weapon as well. It would've meant the poor man's death for certain."

Adela sniffed. "I declare sometimes I think the French are completely lacking in all common sense. The man just wouldn't leave him alone, made quite a nuisance of himself. In the end Mr. Delaney concluded his business in New Orleans and departed."

"It seems he has quite a reputation on several matters," Laurel commented.

"Whatever the man's faults," Adela commented. "And God knows there are many, he's always been the soul of discretion. He's never been the one to flaunt a woman's company. At least not until now." Her meaning was unmistakable.

"Do you always say what you please?"

"Always." The older woman inhaled the salt-sea air with enthusiasm, closing her eyes with obvious delight. "This air reminds me of a young man I once knew. In many ways, he was a great deal like your Mr. Delaney."

"He's not '*my*' Mr. Delaney," Laurel corrected her.

Adela waved a hand through the air. "I was fifteen at the time. He had piercing blue eyes. A sea captain. Physically he didn't bear much resemblance to Delaney, but he had that same wildness about him, an attitude that said everyone could go to hell. I grew up a lot that summer before he sailed away."

"He left you?" Laurel felt an inexplicable sadness.

"I didn't see him again for eight years. I thought I'd get over him, but the memory remained. Every other man paled in comparison. If I couldn't have him, I didn't want any other."

"I'm sorry."

Adela's story reminded her too much of Rebecca's.

She laughed. "Sorry? Balderdash! I went after him. What a time that was. I asked him to marry me."

"You proposed to him?" She regarded Adela MacMillan with a mixture of incredulity and admiration.

"Of course! Remember one thing, my dear, if you want something, go after it. There's no one on God's green earth who'll hand it to you. Life, dear girl, is for the taking. I've always believed that. Maybe that's why I wish I were twenty years younger." She cast a meaningful glance down the length of the deck.

Following her gaze, Laurel caught sight of Ruel Delaney. The wind had caught his midnight-dark hair, whipping it back from his face. Long, powerful arms she remembered too well stretched before him, bracing himself against the rail, and his knuckles were white as his grip steadied him.

He was like some magnificent god sprung from the depths of the sea, leaning into the wind, challenging, taunting it. Only his eyes were not visible to her as he stared out across the ocean, those dark eyes that had seemed to pierce her soul, even in the darkness of the ship's hold.

She thought she'd forgotten the sheer power of him. But now his presence on the rolling deck only sharpened the images from that encounter.

True to her promise, she'd had no further contact with Ruel Delaney. But that didn't matter. She remembered everything about him, along with that searing kiss that had been terrifying in its intensity.

Almost as if he'd read her thoughts, he turned, and the memory was complete; dark eyes that seemed to look deep inside her, and the taut expression on his face.

She turned back at the rail, leaning far over it as if the wind that came off the water might clear her thoughts.

"Are you all right, my dear?" Adela asked.

"Yes, of course. I think the sea is a bit rougher today."

"Hmmm. Yes, I suppose. At any rate, you mind what I say. "The woman tapped her black walking stick emphatically.

"About Mr. Delaney's reputation?"

"Heavens no! If we steered clear of everyone with a so-called reputation, there'd be no pleasure in life. That's the spice, the recklessness that everyone else avoids. Remember what I said about seizing life, don't wait for it."

"My Uncle Edwin would argue with you about that."

"That's only because he's grown cautious in his old age." Adela gazed across the ocean, a mysterious smile crossing her face as she was lost to her own thoughts.

Ruel Delaney turned back to the open sea. He respected the merciless, unyielding, ever-changing power of it. He'd challenged the sea countless times, more than wise even for a fool.

He'd made a fool of himself with her. And she was beautiful. He frowned. If he hadn't known her so well, known the true actress she could be, he'd almost be willing to admit he'd made a mistake as she had insisted, playing her part perfectly.

There'd been so little light, only the one lantern. But the resemblance had struck him from the first moment, after he'd recovered from his first surprise at finding her hidden inside that trunk. He glanced back at her now.

The wind caught her hair. She brushed it back with a slender hand as the sails snapped on the wind.

She'd always used a trick of the French, dying her hair with a henna rinse that gave it bold, red tones. Its paleness now like spun gold made him frown. What game was she playing? Pretending not to know who he was? Pretending to be so innocent.

His gaze swept over her, taking in the delicate arch of her neck. In his imagination he could still see the luminous glow of skin drawn across her collarbone, could picture the faint indentation between the well of her breasts.

Even as they had struggled, he'd been aware of the slimness of her waist. His hands had easily closed around it, fingertips meeting fingertips, as his thumbs had caressed her through the gown she wore—different.

It had been over a year, but she hadn't been that slim the last time they'd been together—very few secrets remained when making love. There had been a gentle, tell-tale swell to her abdomen. She'd met his gaze coolly in response to his question about the child. Slipping from the bed, she'd pulled on a silk wrapper and stepped over to the dressing table. With maddening calmness, she'd pulled the brush through her henna-dyed hair as she'd told him not to be concerned.

Not concerned! His anger had been instantaneous, explosive. He'd wanted to know whether she carried his child. But as their argument had erupted, the answer had become lost in cruel words. Only later, miles away in Virginia City, over a bottle of brandy had he realized she'd never answered that question.

Within the month he'd returned to San Francisco. When

the rumors reached him, it was already too late. She'd not lied about them when confronted, she'd said she'd gone to an old Chinese woman. It was done, finished. Without so much as consulting him, she'd gotten rid of the child he carried. But was it his?

The doubt was there. God knows she made no pretense about other men when he was away.

"A girl needs to support herself." But the possibility that it might have been his child ate at him. It was the last time he saw her, until three days ago.

He'd learned to read people, in a business deal or across a card table. He'd seen the coldness in hers so many times. It was undoubtedly there now with the game she played.

Except that it wasn't.

He saw many things in that dark blue gaze. But there was no coldness, no anger, or deceit. Only confusion.

But even as he watched her, standing on the deck, the wind whipping at her hair, hatred fought a losing battle with desire.

She *was* different.

And there were questions that needed answers. Andrew Wentworth be damned, he intended to have them.

Laurel forced herself to stare out over the ocean. It was much safer to ignore Ruel Delaney's disconcerting gaze.

"Eccentricity!" Adela boomed with delight. Punctuating the air with her walking stick, completely oblivious to the sudden paleness of her young companion.

"Eccentricity is a luxury of the rich. You see, my dear, if I were poor and said the sort of things I've said to you, I'd be considered quite mad. People would look at me strangely, avoid me, cross the street in order not to associate with me.

"But, I am very wealthy," she continued. "So that same madness is considered eccentricity. People cluster about me, fawn over me, and, God knows, they dare not criticize."

"I think that you're neither mad nor eccentric," Laurel

replied, a bit of color returning to her cheeks. If she concentrated very hard, she could almost forget the tall, brooding man at the far end of the deck.

"You take great pleasure in putting people off, undoing them."

Adela MacMillan laughed uproariously. "You've found me out, my dear. Now what do you say to some food? I'm absolutely starving. Must be the sea air. A female trait I've never been fond of is starving oneself in order to be more appealing to a man. I pride myself on my rather well-padded form, there's more there for a man to enjoy."

Seizing Laurel by the arm, Adela navigated her in the direction of the open hatch and the companionway below, tapping her walking stick threateningly at any of the crew who wandered across her path. Following Laurel below decks, she left her in front of her cabin.

"Refresh yourself, my dear. Then join me in my cabin."

Laurel headed down the passage to Andrew's and Jessica's cabin. There was no response to her knock. Evidently Jessica had recovered from her bout of seasickness, and they'd gone to eat in the small dining room.

She moved past the ladder that led to the deck. Overhead lanterns swung and sent halos of light against the wooden walls. Stepping into the light, Laurel gasped and drew back abruptly as a figure moved out of the shadows.

"Miss Wentworth, is it?" The greeting was insulting "If you're looking for the crew's quarters, you're going in the wrong direction. I'm certain they'd be delighted by a little visit. After all, that's what you do best."

Words failed as Laurel stared into that angry dark gaze. How had he gotten down there without her seeing him? And was there no limit to what the man would say or do? She recovered, indignation surfacing as she drew back her hand and slapped him.

Ruel stared at her as he rubbed his cheek, his expression filled with both surprise and amusement. The little fool could pack a wallop. He thought she'd learned her lesson about striking him a long time ago.

In the cool expression in those striking blue eyes, now darkened with anger, there was that subtle difference again that had nagged at him ever since that encounter in the ship's hold.

"I didn't mean to frighten you."

"Didn't you? I think you specialize in frightening people." Laurel coolly replied. "Now if you will please stand aside."

They were alone in the passage. Adela hadn't come out of her cabin, and Andrew and Jessica were already gone.

The darkness in the passageway reminded her of the hold. Trying to remain calm, she tried to control the sudden nervousness in her voice.

"What do you want?"

"The truth," he replied. "Who are you?"

"You already know that. The captain and my cousin told you who I am."

Ruel watched her with growing fascination. In the past, in all their arguments, all their confrontations, she's always tried defiance first, then lies. But coolness was completely out of character, and it occurred to him that he was probably looking at the best imitation of a real lady that he'd ever seen.

"They told me," he replied. "They both seem to think I've mistaken you for someone else, but you've always been a good liar."

He slipped a long thin cigarette from his shirt pocket and lit it. The tip glowed, and the flare caught at those dark eyes.

"What do you say?" His gaze narrowed in the fragrant haze of smoke.

"I say you're a fool with no manners and even less intelligence. I've never seen you before in my life, and if I never see you again, it will be too soon."

Blue eyes flashed. He had to be completely mad. No one in his right mind would follow her down here after Andrew's warning.

"No one has lied to you, Mr. Delaney," she continued. "You made a mistake." Her patience slipped another notch.

"Why can't you just accept that?"

"I don't make mistakes. They're dangerous."

"There's a first time for everything," she coolly informed him. "Now, let me pass."

Her nearness was unraveling strands of tightly restrained anger. In the past, she'd always matched his anger, using words meant to wound. This was a new side of her.

"Please step aside or I'll ..." Silk skirts gathered in one hand, Laurel tried to get by him, but the passage was narrow permitting only one person to move through easily at a time, and as soon as she'd taken a step forward, Laurel realized the mistake she'd made.

Ruel Delaney calmly leaned back against the far wall of the passage. He braced his weight on one leg and set his other boot against the near wall, blocking the passage. It was impossible to pass him without brushing against him.

It was there again, that illusive quality that made him think he didn't really know her at all. How could she be the same, and yet so different? The eyes, the face, the voice that he remembered too well.

Stunned, she halted. She'd been certain he'd let her pass. She was wrong. He wasn't the least concerned that they might be seen. His left leg was now braced to prevent her retreat. In the narrow passage, her body was wedged intimately against him. She tried to shove him back. Her hand was suddenly trapped in his.

"Your hand is cold." He stroked her fingers, watching the expression at her face.

"Stop that!" Laurel tried to free her hand, but she might as well have tried to hold back the sea.

"Stop what?" His voice was low, too close.

"Stop that!"

"You've never been afraid before."

That voice was frightening and fascinating at the same time.

"I'm not afraid," she informed him.

He leaned in close. "You're trembling."

"I'm not trembling!" Laurel tried to snatch her hand free. "You're a scoundrel and I don't like you," she told him, remembering Adela's advice. "Let me pass or I'll call out."

She wanted to strike him, right between those dark eyes.

Anger turned to fascination. "A scoundrel?" He slowly stroked her taut fingers. He would play her little game, and he would break her down. He'd break her this time, he decided. By God, he would.

He made small, circling motions across the palm of her hand. That simple touch was feather-soft, warm, and sent currents of heat spiraling through her.

"I prefer nice men. You're not a nice man," Laurel informed him as she strained to free herself.

His fingers were having a disturbing effect on her. It was the simplest contact, yet it brought back memories of that kiss, of its demand as they'd struggled in the darkness of the ship's hold.

"No, you don't. Remember, I know you too well."

Know her? Who had he mistaken her for?

The words were achingly soft, confusing, persuasive. She should have been insulted. She wasn't, she was fascinated.

"You're dangerous, Mr. Delaney, or whoever you are." Laurel clamped her eyes shut tightly, as his lips brushed her cheek. "I don't know who you think I am, but I've never met you before in my life!"

He kept talking, ignoring it. This was madness.

"Not if you know the rules," he whispered.

Rules? What was he talking about?

There was no running from this man. The madness that drove him was pulling at her. His head bent toward her. Then his mouth teased hers.

"I think you make your own rules," she whispered. It was impossible not to breathe in his scent as he leaned against her, feel him, tasting him unlike anything she'd ever felt before.

He wanted revenge, wanted to hurt her with her own cruelty.

"Haven't you heard? Rules are made to be broken." The coldness in his voice made her shiver.

She pushed at him, but her arms felt weighted. He was so close she couldn't see his face. She'd thought him some sort of demon in the darkness of the hold. Now she was certain of it.

Wrenching herself free, Laurel spun away from him and managed to escape. A moment passed before she trusted her voice.

"Can you be broken, Mr. Delaney?"

"Every man can be, but that could be dangerous for you." His voice was mocking, challenging. "You always liked a little danger."

She wanted to scream. She had no idea who he thought she was, but it was frustrating and frightening. She pitied the woman, whoever she was.

"With you, I think there's no such thing as a *'little'* danger," she replied. "It must be like falling in love. A risk one must take."

"And you have a great deal of experience with that, don't you?" Bitterness edged his words. "Falling in love. Who is it now?"

She wanted to scream at him.

"I've never been in love, Mr. Delaney," she replied. "I can live my life quite nicely without it." And without you, she thought.

Without another word, she whirled around. She wouldn't give him the satisfaction of knowing his words had unnerved her.

She swept past Adela MacMillan's cabin, driven by anger and the sheer desperation to be as far away from him as possible.

THEY CONTINUED on a southerly course down the eastern seaboard. Blue sky churned to ominous gray as the sky darkened on the fourth day at sea. The warm spring, which days earlier had promised only fair weather, now seemed as changeable as Laurel's mood.

The porthole in Jessica's and Andrew's cabin was closed to keep out sea spray, and overhead the lantern swung as the ship cut through yet another wave. Straining timbers creaked and groaned, and hatches remained closed as waves washed over the bow, sending sheets of water onto the decks.

Laurel had spent most of her waking hours with Jessica, while Andrew had discussed business with the captain, or had sat in the corner at the small desk, making countless entries in his journals.

She sighed as she waited for Jess to play her next card at the game they'd begun. They'd decided that a game of cribbage would relieve the monotony. Glancing up, she saw Jessica nervously bite her lower lip and then cast a worried glance at the porthole.

"Uncle Edwin insists that his captains are the finest seamen," Laurel reminded her. "He's never lost a ship to weather. We've nothing to worry about. And it is your turn."

"I don't know how you and Andrew can remain so calm. It

sounds as if the ship is breaking apart." Jessica threw down her next card without paying attention.

Laurel frowned at the card she'd laid down, giving herself another win as she counted out the score.

"Everything will be fine. If Andrew thought we were in any danger, he would have the captain put into port," she assured her.

"Do you really think so?" The deep frown lines between Jess's dark eyes eased.

"Of course," Laurel assured her. "If you don't pay attention to the game, I'll win another game."

"You might as well. You've won every one so far. If I didn't know better, I'd swear you cheated."

"It's skill, my dear." Laurel scooped up Jess's cards and handed them to her as she sat down on the bed opposite.

"Does that include persuading Andrew to let you continue to San Francisco?" Jess asked.

Laurel smiled.

The ship crested yet another wave, seemed to wait, then shuddered and slipped slowly down the next wave.

In spite of Jess's dire predictions, she was certain the storm was no worse than it had been when she'd joined her cousin an hour earlier to await the evening meal.

A rough sea did not deter many appetites. Crew and passengers must be fed, and the cook aboard the *Waverall* had done a commendable job of providing ample fare.

"I remember a story Andrew told me about your escaping your governess by way of a tree in the garden." Jess braced herself against the side rail of the bunk.

"I was escaping my music teacher, Miss Lavell. And I did climb down a tree." Laurel smiled as she dealt another round.

"Do you really think he's accepted the idea?" Laurel asked. Andrew had refused to discuss it further with her.

"I'm certain of it. His only concern is explaining everything to his father." Jess groaned as she looked at her cards.

Both young women looked up as Andrew entered the cabin. Crossing the small space, he kissed Jess and then gave Laurel an affectionate peck on the cheek.

"How's the game?"

"She has absolutely no mercy. I've lost every hand." His wife laughed, some of her earlier fears disappearing now that her husband was there.

"In spite of the squall, the captain assures me that we will make New Orleans by tomorrow afternoon. He's asked everyone to attend a last supper this evening. If we can keep the plates on the table, he's promised an excellent meal," Andrew announced as he crossed the cabin. He removed his gray day coat and replaced it with a dinner jacket.

"I shall definitely be the envy of every man aboard this ship in the company of two lovely young women," he added.

"Since we are the only women under the age of sixty on board, that's certainly a safe statement," Laurel pointed out as she set the cards aside.

"But true." Andrew added. Opening the door, he extended both arms to escort them to the small dining room at the end of the passage.

Jessica smoothed her hair into place at the small mirror at the wall above the cabinet, then accepted Andrew's arm as they stepped out into the narrow passage.

The rolling motion of the ship sent Laurel against the wall at the side of the passage. When she reached a hand to steady herself, strong fingers closed about her arm as Ruel Delaney stepped into the soft circle of light from the overhead lantern that swung back and forth.

"You need to be careful about dark passageways." That dark gaze caught hers. Before she could demand it, he released her.

"Good evening, Mrs. Wentworth," he greeted Jessica Wentworth.

His pretense at anything close to manners was insulting as he inclined his handsome head toward Andrew's wife. His greeting for her was considerably less cordial, even arrogant.

"We were just departing for supper, Mr. Delaney." The coolness in Andrew's voice was as unmistakable as his obvious dislike of the man.

"Then, we'll be dining together." Delaney replied. "The captain was good enough to extend an invitation."

Without waiting for a response, Ruel stepped past Laurel and extended his arm to Jessica.

"Allow me to escort you to the dining room, Mrs. Wentworth, with your husband's permission of course." He turned briefly to Andrew.

Not that he waited for permission. With maddening and unexpected politeness, he tucked Jessica's arm through his and led the way to the dining room.

"Of all the ...!" Laurel whispered. "Aren't you going to say something?"

"I know you had a dreadful experience with the man, but it does seem that he realizes he made a mistake," Andrew replied.

"We'll be in New Orleans tomorrow, and that will be the end of it." He took her hand and guided her in the direction Ruel and Jessica had gone.

"I'm told that Delaney is getting off in New Orleans. We will continue on to California." He guided her around the corner of the passage. Only a few feet ahead, Jessica and Ruel Delaney had stopped before the dining room. As he leaned around to open the door for her, Jessica laughed at some comment he made.

He might have fooled Andrew, but he hadn't fooled her, Laurel thought. There'd been nothing gentlemanly in his eyes in that brief moment in the passage. Ruel Delaney didn't think he'd made a mistake. Not for a moment.

Their last supper aboard the *Waverall* was unexpectedly pleasant. There was a lull in the storm, but not her emotions. It was completely unnerving to feel that dark gaze resting on her each time she looked up.

Even more disconcerting, upon entering the small dining room, he'd carefully maneuvered Jessica down the opposite side of the table to two vacant chairs, forcing Andrew to take the seat beside her. Laurel was forced to take one of the two remaining chairs, and Ruel Delaney had casually slipped into the one beside her.

The only saving grace had been their proximity to the captain. Across from her, Adela MacMillan gazed at her with amusement, as if she might have had something to do with the seating arrangement.

There was absolutely no reason why she should have felt so distracted and unsure of herself, yet she felt as unsettled as she had that first time Aunt Cecile had insisted she wear a white lace dress for a formal dinner attended by several important guests.

She'd been eight at the time and remembered it vividly. Andrew, older and should have known better, had rolled several green peas toward her from across the table. She'd retaliated by pouring salt in his drinking water. But when a plump blueberry from Aunt Cecile's dessert was flung at her and made a colorful path down the front of her gown, Laurel had emptied her water glass on him. Aunt Cecile had been furious.

The ship rolled as she reached for her wine glass and nearly upset it. Her head came up as Ruel Delaney's fingers closed around hers as he steadied the goblet, a dangerous smile in those his dark eyes.

He was dressed simply in gray breeches, white shirt, and a black coat that darkened the depths of his eyes. His face was tanned, filled with an almost animal leanness that made a lie of the courteous smile. Everything this man did was a contradiction.

The other men about the table, including the captain, had dressed formally in deference to the occasion of their last supper together. But Ruel Delaney had dressed like the gambler she had heard he was, almost as if he were flaunting his profession.

Yet his manners were flawless. He could pretend anything he wanted, she thought, make the others believe his little game, but Mr. Delaney was a very dangerous man.

She took a calming drink of wine. False courage?

She didn't need it. After tomorrow Ruel Delaney would be out of her life once and for all.

3

NEW ORLEANS

R uel Delaney leaned against the marble mantel.

He'd always liked this room. Perhaps because Dominique had decorated this one herself, and in colors that proudly announced her French heritage. He'd known the house should be hers the moment he'd seen it. That was the reason he'd bought the stately, columned dwelling on Esplanade Avenue for her years ago.

He'd seen it and bought it that same afternoon without telling her. Then, with great ceremony, he'd moved her from the small house on Dauphine Street in the Vieux Carre, the French Quarter.

In the elegant parlor, brilliant blue-and-gold velvet portieres were draped across the tall windows, and a Persian rug dominated gleaming wood floors. Set at intervals around the room were pieces of a matching set of Belter furniture, brought from New York before the war. The seat cushions were of the finest satin with a deep blue fleur-de-lis pattern. Like the woman who lived there, the room was elegant.

He turned at the faint rustling of silk skirts. Her rich auburn hair, pulled back from the soft oval of her face, cascaded in glistening curls down her back, and her large dark eyes seemed to fill her face. Dominique's smile was an intimate greeting.

She carried two cut-crystal wine glasses shimmering with a liquid as deep burgundy in color as the dressing gown she wore. Reaching up, she caressed his cheek, kissing him before handing him the glass.

"How is it that some man hasn't swept you off your feet and married you while I was away?" he asked, a familiar question.

Her eyes darkened to smoky gray. "I have loved only one man, you know that. All others are, shall we say—companions, for a while." She changed the subject glad to see him once again after the ship arrived the day before.

"Have you been to The House yet?" her voice was deep, husky with that familiar sensuality.

"Not yet. I wanted to see you first." His smile deepened. It was always the same between them.

"Ah, *mon cher,* you mustn't tease. But you will be pleased when you meet with Paul. He was an excellent choice as manager, and business has been good, even with this dreadful Reconstruction.

"All of civilization may crumble, but certain things never change," she continued. "Men still want good drink, women, and a game or two to divert them from their everyday cares."

Ruel slipped an arm about her waist. "I have you to thank for that."

"I was only following your instructions to make it the finest sporting house in New Orleans." She sighed, then hugged him. It had been too long.

It was true, he thought. The House of the Rising Sun on Royale Street had gained the reputation as one of the finest gambling houses in the world. Neither war nor the Reconstruction had curtailed their clientele, and judging by reports from Paul and Dominique, the past year had been their best yet.

"Not only beautiful, but talented." Ruel's lips lightly brushed her hair. The scent that was hers alone filled the air.

"Was it dangerous this time?" she asked.

He downed the wine, handing her the glass as she offered the stronger brandy which he preferred.

"No more than usual. This will be the last shipment. I'll see that the cargo reaches its destination. Then I'm out. The captain of the ship wasn't too pleased about taking on '*unidentified*' cargo. It seems my reputation precedes me."

He chuckled as he thought of the business venture that had kept him busy the last few years. Too busy. But it had been extremely profitable.

"You mustn't worry," he admonished her with a smile.

"I always worry. With all the Federal agents in town, it's more dangerous now than during the war. I hear they're at The House all the time. Do you really think your man in Washington would do anything to help if you were caught?" Her eyes flashed passionately.

"No!" she answered her own question. "They would deny ever associating with you. You take too many chances. Stay, out of it. I fear for you."

"I am out of it, I promise. Don't worry your pretty head." His tone was light, but it was an end to the conversation.

She knew from past experience he'd wouldn't discuss it further. At least not tonight. But there would be other opportunities. She had to be certain he was telling her the truth.

He'd been born with more good fortune than any ten men she knew, yet luck could run out. Dominique poured him another brandy.

"Will you be staying tonight?" she asked.

She watched his handsome face. It was usually carefully masked, but she noticed a subtle change in him tonight as if he his thoughts were someplace else.

Her hand rested gently on his arm. His visits were few and

far between, yet she knew nothing would ever change between them.

"I think I'll go over to The House and check on Paddy," he replied. "I'll have dinner there." He reached up and gently ran the back of his fingers along her cheek.

"I'll see you in the morning."

She walked with him through the open doors into the courtyard. The fragrance of blossoms of the magnolia trees was thick on the warm night air.

"Does this restlessness of yours have anything to do with the young lady aboard the *Waverall?*" She inquired, and at Ruel's surprised glance, she laughed.

"I have my sources, and they are usually very accurate."

Ruel stroked her hand reassuringly. "I will see you in the morning. Be ready early. I intend to take you to breakfast at Maxim's. Does he still serve that magnificent shrimp omelet you're so fond of?"

"You're changing the subject, but yes, he does."

Ruel bent down and pressed a kiss to her cheek. "I'll have Paul send a carriage. Ten o'clock?" He added. He knew that she hated early mornings and wondered who might be sharing the night with her, then let it go.

Dominique groaned disapprovingly. "You know that I hate rising early."

Then he smiled. "Afterward, I'll take you shopping." He laughed as she brightened.

"Have I told you lately that you are a very beautiful woman?"

"Not lately, *mon cher,* and not nearly enough." Her heart filled with desire as she stared up at him.

"Then, I'll have to do something to change that." Taking her hand, he pressed a kiss against her fingers.

Dominique raised her hand and waved as he disappeared through the wrought iron gate. Carriage wheels clattered on the brick drive, then grew fainter. She sighed as she turned back to the house. Her time with him was always so short. But if that was all she could have of him, so be it.

LAUREL STRETCHED, curling her toes deeper into the soft bedding. It was heaven to be able to turn over without hitting her head on a wood railing or scraping her knees against the wall in the narrow bunk aboard the *Waverall.*

Three days in New Orleans, and she'd spent them at the St. Charles Hotel, eating, sleeping, and thoroughly enjoying having a real floor beneath her feet, one that didn't roll and lurch.

After the first day, she'd felt amply rested, but in consideration of the news that Jessica had shared—that she was going to have a child, she'd remained at the hotel, keeping her company while Andrew attended to business.

At dinner the evening before, Jess had proclaimed herself completely rested and she'd declared that they would visit the dress shops that lined Canal Street. Andrew had objected out of concern for his wife's condition, but he had agreed when Jessica had pointed out that her waistline would be changing over the next months and she needed new gowns.

Laurel rose from the bed. Her room was enormous with a private bathing alcove adjoining it. An elegant framed silk screen cut off the dressing area, though with the few gowns she'd borrowed from Jessica, she'd had little need for it. Now, she stepped behind the screen and slipped out of the thin nightgown.

After she'd dressed, she brushed her hair then wound it into a thick knot, pinned at the back of her head, leaving some strands loose about her face.

"Do you intend to waste the entire morning in front of that mirror?"

She looked up as Jessica swept into the room. She hadn't heard her come in from the adjoining room.

"I think I've gained weight on all the delicious food I've eaten the last three days. I could hardly close the hooks across the back of the gown. Although I do appreciate your lending me the gown."

Jess laughed. "I think, my dear, the plain and simple truth is you have developed far better than I in certain areas. As for me, by the time we reach California, I shall be fairly bursting out of my own gowns."

"You're certain you feel up to shopping?"

"Absolutely! After all, you can't go about New Orleans in only the three dresses I gave you. What would people say? "And," she looped her arm through Laurel's, "the sooner we purchase your new wardrobe, the sooner Andrew will have to face the fact that you are going to California with us."

"Has he said anything more about it?" A worried frown clouded Laurel's face.

"I've been doing all the talking and I think that I have him convinced."

Jessica's expression was smug.

"I keep reminding him that it will be very difficult for *me* in California when the baby comes. He'll be at the office all day, and I'll be in a strange city with no friends and a new baby."

Laurel laughed. "You're terrible."

"I'm honest. And he's wavering." She smiled triumphantly. "This morning over coffee in our room, he even went so far as to suggest that you would be needing several new gowns to wear. And," her eyes gleamed, "he mentioned that he would send a telegram to his father informing him that you are safe with us. He mentioned nothing about informing him of your return." She clasped her hands together.

"So, you see, he's already accepted that you're continuing on with us."

"You're wonderful," Laurel told her. "You're the best and dearest friend anyone could have, and cousin. You know how much this trip means to me."

Jess patted her hand. "Now, are we going to waste an entire day talking about this new wardrobe, or shall we purchase it?"

The small, unpretentious shop was called simply—*Juliette.*

Laurel soon discovered that it was the name of the proprietress of one of the most renowned dressmaking shops in New Orleans.

Tucked away amidst discreet residences that faced onto Chartres Street in the Vieux Carre, the courtyard opened in back to reveal several rooms along the rear of the house.

In each room, a seamstress was busily applying chalk or pins to precisely cut fabrics that would eventually become gowns for the *crème de la crème* of New- Orleans' society.

Juliette had been recommended by Adela MacMillan. With two servants hurrying to match her pace, the older woman had emerged from the printer's just as Laurel and Jessica left the milliner's, where each had purchased one of the wide-brimmed straw hats popular in the warmer, sunny climate of New Orleans.

Greetings exchanged, Adela had bestowed on them a freshly printed invitation to her grand soiree, to be held in exactly two weeks. Begging their forgiveness for such short notice, she had insisted they absolutely could not leave New Orleans without meeting her circle of friends. Then she had invited them to join her in her private box at the Metairie Race track the following Saturday.

Upon learning they were shopping for Laurel's wardrobe, she'd heartily recommended *Juliette*, proclaiming discreetly that she, of course, purchased all her gowns from the well-known French seamstress.

Thinking of Adela's penchant for vivid colors and wildly draped fashions, Laurel had suppressed a fit of laughter over this discreetly given advice. Then, patting Laurel's cheek and making an elaborate gesture, Adela disappeared down the street, servants in tow. The signature feather in her hat, dyed to match her dress, dipped and swayed as she bobbed her head in the direction of one acquaintance after another.

In spite of Adela's decidedly bold taste in clothes, Laurel soon discovered *Juliette* was a genius with measuring tape and fabrics. After spending the greater portion of the morning in the small fitting room, selecting designs and appropriate fabrics, Jess had retreated to the center courtyard to enjoy the cooling breeze and a refreshing glass of lemonade beneath the spreading umbrella of a mimosa tree.

Inside the small shop, Laurel turned first one direction and then the other as her measurements were quickly taken. She glanced up as Anjanette, Juliette's young assistant came into the small room, closing the curtain discreetly after her.

"Madame thinks this gown would be most suitable. It is very near your measurements, so it needs little alteration. You may take the gown with you later this afternoon. And three others can be altered in the same time."

"In that case I'll take all four gowns."

The slender girl curtsied, then gathered up the gowns Laurel had tried on.

"If you would care to wait, I will make the alterations myself."

Laurel pulled on the lace-edged dressing gown. Obviously, ladies lingered at the shop until their purchases were ready. Thinking of the last gowns she and Aunt Cecile had purchased, Laurel agreed—the new sewing machines were indeed a wonder.

She stepped out into the shop to escape the confines of the airless dressing room. In several glass-topped counters a vast array of ribbons, laces, and assorted trim were displayed, and in one long case, several silk undergarments were delicately laid out.

She listened to the conversations being carried on in the shop. Another customer was being attended in the draped dressing room across from her. The curtain parted, and an elegant woman with auburn hair stepped in front of the arc of mirrors set against the far wall. Arranged at precise intervals, they afforded a full-length view from every angle. The conversation was softly muted, only a few words in French reaching her.

"Madame Dominique, it is most elegant. You shall be the envy of all the women at the *bal masqué*."

Most certainly the beautiful woman would be the envy of every woman, and the object of every man's attention, Laurel thought.

Dressed in a gown in a shade of apricot, Dominique adjusted the fall of the skirt to her satisfaction. The satin clung to her like a second skin, accentuating the fullness of her breasts. The skirt was styled fully to accommodate the crinolines currently in fashion.

"Please have Mr. Delaney come back. I'd like him to see the gown."

Laurel froze as the young seamstress curtsied.

Suddenly she was ice cold, when only a moment before she'd been certain she would faint from the cloying heat inside the shop. She quickly returned to her own dressing room, but as reached to push aside the curtain she was brought up short.

"Good morning."

A smile twitched at his lips.

She stood like a frightened doe, perfectly still, the soft folds of the dressing gown draped over her slender body.

He'd only caught a glimpse of whirling blue fabric and golden hair, but it had been enough. He'd never known anyone else to possess quite that same pale, shimmering hair, the richest gold at one moment, then almost silver.

Heat spread across her cheeks. Didn't he realize how humiliating it was to be singled out in a lady's shop. She slowly released the breath she was holding. Of course, he did, the cad. He'd said it himself. He didn't give a damn what other people thought, not about himself and obviously not about anyone else.

All right, she thought. For the two weeks that remained of her stay in New Orleans she could play his game. But she'd be damned if she'd allow anyone to think their acquaintance was anything other than a proper one. She'd prove to Mr. Ruel Delaney that he meant nothing to her, that she hadn't given him a single thought since their parting three days earlier. Relaxing her hold on the curtain, she slowly counted to three.

"I beg your pardon?" she asked. Her response had just the effect she'd hoped for. "Have we met before?"

She was perfect, proper, and completely in control. At least she made it seem so. Beneath her cool words and equally cool manner, Laurel's pulse leapt as her gaze met his dark one.

He was watching her with a mixture of amusement and something else she didn't recognize. His gaze slowly lowered, taking in the full length of her before it returned to meet hers. It was as if his glance had stripped the dressing gown away. His smile deepened.

"We met aboard the *Waverall*, if you remember." The response was perfectly proper, as he joined in her little game.

Laurel was aware of the sudden subtle interest the mention of the *Waverall* aroused in the woman, Dominique.

Dear God, who was she? His mistress? And how much had he told her of their meeting aboard ship?

There was no turning back. She would just have to see her little charade through.

"Of course." She might have said it was nice to see him again, but she didn't want to give him that satisfaction.

"Captain Delaney," Jess greeted him as she joined them.

Captain? Where on earth had she gotten that? Laurel thought. Turning to her cousin, she gave a small shake of her head in an attempt to discourage any conversation.

"Mrs. Wentworth," he replied. "How very nice to see you again."

Laurel groaned inwardly. Must he be so maddeningly charming? As it was Jess had had nothing but praise for his many kindnesses aboard the ship. The entire situation couldn't be more awkward, and Jess seemed completely oblivious to her feelings.

"I don't believe we've been introduced." Dominique joined their small circle, curiosity in her expression.

"May I present Mrs. Andrew Wentworth, and her cousin, Miss Laurel Wentworth. Ladies, Dominique de Beauvoir."

From the moment she'd first turned in response to his greeting, Laurel had been aware of the scrutiny of the Frenchwoman. She met the woman's inquiring gaze.

Dominique's dark beauty was mysterious and alluring, and she had the sort of bold maturity that could come from nothing else but experience where men were concerned. Her golden skin and her sculpted cheekbones accentuated the tilt of her eyes. She was tall in comparison to the other women, and her height gave her a regal bearing and made Laurel more conscious than ever of her lesser height.

Silently cursing all the times she'd avoided practicing her French lessons, Laurel realized the time she'd been certain would never arise was sorely at hand. She felt awkward as a schoolgirl beside this more worldly beauty. What she wouldn't give to be able to converse fluently with this woman in her own language. She was jarred back to reality by her warm greeting.

"I am most pleased to make your acquaintance, *mademoiselle*. Ruel has told me much about you."

Laurel felt all color drain from her face. Dear God, what had he told her? Mumbling a faint response, she turned gratefully as Anjanette bustled into the salon, an altered gown draped over her arms. Taking it, Laurel quickly fled into the dressing room.

The gown was made of light blue silk and had a sheer overskirt that was hand decorated with dark blue flowers. The skirt, gathered and pleated for fullness fell softly just above the toes of her shoes. A wide satin ribbon accentuated the narrow span of her waist, and more of the ribbon was interwoven down the lengths of both sleeves, which were made of the same transparent fabric for coolness in the warm New Orleans climate. The blue silk of the bodice was overset with a panel of the sheer fabric, a chain of tiny blue flowers setting off the neckline that was cut squarely across the swell of her breasts.

It was a little daring to wear such a gown during the day. Laurel was startled to find herself wondering how this gown might compare with those worn by Dominique de Beauvoir. Straightening the sleeves, she decided she hadn't the slightest interest in the Frenchwoman, or Ruel Delaney.

Emerging from the dressing room, Laurel thanked Anjanette and asked her to have the other gowns sent to the St. Charles when they were finished.

She turned to find him only a few feet away, that dark gaze fastened on her.

"A beautiful gown," he told her.

It was there, the desire to say more, to tell her that she should always wear that color that matched her eyes. But he didn't.

"You may find this surprising, Mr. Delaney," she replied coolly. "But I didn't select the gown because I thought you might approve. I dress to please myself."

There was something in his expression—a question? Or possibly something he would have said and for a moment, Laurel was certain he would touch her.

"There you are," Jessica reminded her. "We really must be going. Andrew will be expecting us."

She ignored Jess's surprised expression. She hooked her arm firmly through her cousin's and propelled Jess through the door. She didn't slow their pace until they reached the corner where she intended to wave down a public carriage. In her desire to leave the shop and be rid of Ruel Delaney, she hadn't noticed the darkly dressed man who suddenly took great interest in their departure and followed them.

"Laurel, what has gotten into you? Your manners were absolutely appalling back there. I will admit that Captain Delaney is a bit mysterious, but certainly handsome and quite the gentleman. Anyone would think you don't like him."

Laurel exploded. "Gentleman? The man is an overbearing, arrogant..." she struggled for just the right word, and finally settled on the one that came to mind. "Cad! And why do you call him Captain? The man as the reputation of a thief, a pirate, probably worse. Honestly, Jess, how can you tolerate the man?"

"I heard his man Paddy call him Captain Delaney when we were aboard ship."

"Jess, really. I do think you've gone round the bend. Either that or you 're quite taken by the man. A married woman, and in your condition." Laurel shook her head in dismay.

"At least I admit I find the man attractive, in a rakish sort of way," Jess replied. "He's not at all like Andrew, of course. A girl would certainly have to be careful around his sort, or she'd be swept right off her feet. But he's always been a perfect gentleman around me."

"You don't understand," Laurel argued.

"Good heavens, you act as though the man attacked you. It

was all a mistake, a case of mistaken identity. He thought you were someone else. I think you're being unreasonable."

"Unreasonable?" her control was slipping. He seemed to have that effect on her. "The man has the worst reputation, yet you treat him like a long-lost friend. I just don't see how you can be so foolish."

"Good heavens, Laurel, it isn't as if the man has tried to take advantage of you," Jess reasoned, unaware of how close she'd come to the truth.

"Of course not!" Laurel's response was unnecessarily sharp.

Mercifully a public carriage pulled up before them at that moment, and gratefully accepting the driver's assistance, Laurel settled back onto a cushioned seat. Jess took the seat across from her.

"I wonder if she's his mistress." Fascination danced in Jess's eyes. "I've never met such a woman."

Laurel groaned. Those had been her same thoughts. "I couldn't care in the least," she replied.

Jess rode across from her. Both young women were oblivious to the carriage that followed theirs at a discreet distance.

"She's very beautiful," she commented.

Laurel groaned.

THANKING the young seamstress who'd assisted with her fitting, Dominique slowly approached Ruel. He stood with his back to her, looking out the window of the shop. She followed the direction of his gaze.

"What is it?"

He turned. He'd watched the man follow Laurel and her cousin. He'd have to be more careful, about her and a great many things. Mentally making a note to have Paul check the man out, he fastened his gaze on Dominique and complimented her on the gown she'd selected.

"You're beautiful."

She appreciated the compliment, but she wasn't fooled. "Whenever I ask questions, you change the conversation. You don't realize how much you say without words, my love."

A dark brow lifted. "I have no idea what you mean."

Dominique smiled. "You have never been so attentive to another young lady's attire," she added. "It is different with this one, I think. You say much with your eyes. I know." Dominique smiled with a hint of satisfaction. Then, placing her slender hands on the lapels of his day coat, she smoothed an imaginary wrinkle, her dark eyes softening.

"I know there have been many women for you, my love. Here, in New Orleans. I have seen them, the women on Royale Street who offer themselves freely to you. I am certain there are more I do not know of. But this is different I think."

Ruel closed his hands over hers. "You know as well as I, there can never be anyone like that for me."

"When will you stop punishing yourself? The past is past." She touched his cheek, her eyes moistened. "You don't need to prove anything to anyone."

Ruel gently took her hands in his. "The sins of the father?" he said.

As she'd tried countless times, Dominique tried to ease his pain.

"You must let old anger go."

4

Ruel blew a faint stream of smoke into the air. It lingered, pungent amidst the smell of fine leather and fine whiskey.

Dominique was right. Whole civilizations could disappear, but as long as man survived, greed and temptation would remain. He closed the bound ledger, satisfied with the entries of the past six months.

In a way, civilization in the South, at least as most people remembered it, had disappeared. It had been trampled under the boot of an invading army, and further destroyed by carpetbaggers and Federal occupation troops. The last were only the token signs of war and defeat.

Sheer stupidity, greed, and arrogance had fed the seeds of the conflict—politics. Ruel had never cared for it, and did his best to avoid being sucked in by it. He was a businessman, though his dealings might be a bit questionable at times.

The House of the Rising Sun had survived war and occupation, and was making an exorbitant profit during Reconstruction. The color of a man's uniform didn't matter, his needs were the same: whiskey, women and gaming. And Ruel Delaney didn't mind supplying those needs.

He looked up as Paul Chandler opened the door to the office.

"You need a break from those numbers?"

"I'm done. Come in and join me for a drink," Ruel invited.

He rose from the mahogany desk, crossed to the round, claw-footed table, and lifted an elegant crystal decanter. Here, too, Dominique's subtle presence made itself known. Splashing hefty draughts into two glasses, he offered one to his manager.

"You've done well, Paul. I'm pleased. I know this is one of your busiest seasons, what with Mardi Gras, but when you have a chance, I'd like to discuss that buy-out."

Paul Chandler was also a man of dubious background. Perhaps that was the basis of their mutual trust. They'd never had a written contract outlining the specifics of the operation of The House, for Ruel had learned long ago not to trust the written word.

Clever people wrote contracts; equally clever people broke them. Better to know the true nature of a man, to bind him to you with loyalty so he'd never turn on you.

In the beginning, Paul Chandler had been a man without family, without a name. A near victim of shanghaiing. But Ruel had intervened. That night a crew had been short one man on their quota list. The man Ruel had rescued had had no name, or at least none he would give, so Ruel had dubbed him with the name on the handbill nailed to a warehouse. He'd asked for nothing, except the man's loyalty. Paul had possessed a sound business head and a keen sense of people. He'd been working at The House ever since.

The two men relaxed in leather-covered chairs, their feet propped up on opposite sides of the desk.

"You still intent on selling out?" Downing a portion of the

finest whiskey in all New Orleans, Paul swirled the amber liquid remaining in the glass.

"That's always been my plan. I can't stay here, you know that. And it's getting harder all the time to keep control of the business. You're the one who puts in all the time. It might as well be yours."

Ruel contemplated the man he'd known for ten years, yet never really known at all. In that, they were much alike. There were certain boundaries to their friendship. They never referred to their lives before that night on the docks.

"Is Dominique in agreement?" Paul asked.

"She'll do as I ask. I've tried to get her to consider leaving, but that's another issue. At any rate she'll be well taken care of."

"Personally, I can't see her leaving New Orleans. This is her home. It's in her blood." Paul tossed back the remainder of the whiskey, frowning slightly.

"You still in love with her?" Ruel's eyes, dark as obsidian, hooded, carefully probed the facade of the man across from him.

Startled, Paul Chandler met that dark gaze. It was like staring into the eyes of a dangerous snake that was coiled to strike. He knew feelings between this man and Dominique ran deep because of a past bond neither spoke of. A part of his own life fit that same pattern, so he respected it.

"There's nothing between me and Dominique."

"That isn't what I asked." The words were knife-edged.

"I don't discuss my personal life." Paul Chandler's reply was equally sharp.

Glass in hand, Ruel swirled the last swallow of whiskey.

"Dominique is very special to me. Don't ever do anything to hurt her. Whatever business agreement we strike, she must be free to go her own way. My decisions do not include any arrangement concerning her. Understood?"

Steel gray eyes narrowed as Paul considered Ruel Delaney.

Their friendship had always been tenuous at best, perhaps because they were so much alike. But their respect was mutual. "Dominique has always made her own decisions."

"Good." Ruel finished the whiskey, and set down the glass as the door to the office opened. King Donovan, the bartender, poked his head around the door.

"That fella you wanted to see is here, Mr. Delaney. He's losing pretty good at the craps table."

"If he's losing, he'll be eager to earn some money. Let him lose one more roll, then send him to me." Ruel waved Paul back into his chair as he rose to leave.

"You can stay. This won't take long."

It didn't. The only predictable thing about gambling was losing. The odds were always stacked in favor of the house. Maybe that was *why* Ruel liked an evening on the town once in a while, just to try his skill. He liked changing the odds. Now the odds were in his favor and he soon had the man he sought in his office.

"Well, Mr. Delaney?"

"I hope you didn't lose too badly."

The man called Brady smiled, exposing a gap where teeth had once been. Several days' stubble covered most of his face, and his longish hair was in desperate need of soap as was the rest of his body. Ruel discounted appearances. They could be deceiving. He knew that well. Hadn't he been deceived by a golden-haired little witch with breathtaking eyes? And for this job he didn't need a finely groomed gentleman of quality. Not in postwar New Orleans.

Such a man would have stuck out like a twenty-dollar whore at one of Adela MacMillan's afternoon teas. No, what he wanted was someone who could blend in with the thieves and riffraff who'd descended on the city like a plague of locusts after the Union Army had left.

Brady squinted. "I think maybe you got those dice loaded,

Mr. Delaney. I got me a system, but it never seems to work in your place."

Equally comfortable among thieves, Ruel laughed. "Did it ever occur to you that everyone else loads their dice, and ours are clean?"

"Probably some truth to that. At least you make no pretense at bein' a gentleman, unlike some of them high and mighty dandies."

Paul winced at the sudden, perceptible change in Ruel.

Eyes as black as jet hardened as he regarded Brady. "I have work for you."

The pleasantries ended, Ruel tossed a small leather bag across the width of the desk. The unmistakable rattle of coins brought a gleam to Brady's eyes, and he reached for the bag. Ruel cut him off.

"You can count it later. There's five hundred in it, in gold."

A low whistle cut the tension in the room. He had Brady's full attention. Gold coin was hard to come by since the war, and Confederate currency was worthless.

"A hundred can buy a man's life. What's so all-fired important that you're offering five hundred?"

Ruel shifted in the chair, unwinding slowly as he stood up. He towered a good six inches over Paul, with a lean, animal intensity. Even Brady seemed to sense it, lowlife that he was. Danger hovered about Delaney.

"Two things. And you'll be paid for each. Five hundred now, and another five hundred when the job is done."

"Name it, boss." Brady's tongue greedily licked his lips.

"That's just what I want."

At Brady's confused expression, Ruel came around the desk. Leaning a hip at one corner, he lit another cigarette and slowly exhaled. "I want a name."

"For five hundred in gold, I'll give you a whole list of names."

"I've already made some inquiries, the man's new in town.

He's been following a young lady." There was a softening in Ruel's voice.

Paul had been concentrating so hard on being unobtrusive, he'd almost missed it. His eyes narrowed as he peered over his steepled fingers. Delaney never gave anything away. This was completely out of character. Except for Dominique, Delaney didn't bother with ladies. And as for the prostitutes down on Bourbon Street, he'd never known the man to pay for their favors.

Word usually got around when you were in the business they were in, and there just wasn't any word about Ruel Delaney. His interest piqued, Paul frowned slightly. Who was the lady that was so important to Delaney he'd pay for Brady's services?

"She's staying at the St. Charles." Ruel gave Brady a physical description, bare details, and then Laurel's name.

"You can't miss the man—dark suit, a hat, watchful. Bring me his name, and mind you, I don't want Miss Wentworth knowing about this. Keep your distance, but get the information. Give me what I want, and there's another five hundred for you."

"Gold?"

"Gold."

"Right you are, Captain. Ole Brady'll get that information. How often do you want me to report back?"

"Each day. Miss Wentworth will be attending the horse races on Saturday."

Brady nodded. "Keep that gold safe. The name of the man is as good as yours. You want me to do anything to him?"

"No, just get the information."

Tipping the floppy brim of his hat, Brady rose, stuffing the leather pouch inside his grimy shirt. "I wonder if my luck has changed."

"I am your luck, Brady. Stay away from the tables."

The threat was subtle.

"Right."

As Brady slipped out the door, Paul turned to Ruel.

"Can you trust him?"

"I can trust his greed. That's all I need."

"Isn't New Orleans marvelous?" Laurel exclaimed as she leaned far over the wrought-iron railing of the balcony outside Andrew's and Jess's suite at the St. Charles.

Situated on a corner, the hotel faced one of the busiest streets in the city, while a quieter, tree-lined avenue lay below their bank of windows.

Reminders of the war still lingered. The St. Charles had once housed Union occupation officers, and Andrew had explained that the entire city had been ransacked, New Orleans being a strategic port. But the heart of the city, its people, had survived, and in the three years since the end of the war, they had struggled to bring their city back to life.

Andrew had described his earlier visits, before the war, depicting a city more European than any other in the United States. Yes, the war was over, but scars remained. New Orleans was like a lady once vibrant and beautiful. The beauty was still there, but the lady had matured and because of what she'd endured she was perhaps a little sad but a little grander as well.

Fascinated, Laurel watched the street below. A tall woman, dressed in a brilliant red cotton dress, a spotless white apron tied around it, walked to the opposite side. Her head was wrapped with a cloth of that same red cotton fabric and upon it she carried a wide straw basket, perfectly balanced. She was statuesque, almost regal in her bearing as, with her street song, she peddled *cala*, a delicious pastry.

Not far away another woman, dressed much the same,

carried a basket filled with fresh blackberries. The day before, Laurel had rushed into the street, eager to sample both women's wares. Always possessed of a healthy appetite, she found the cuisine of New Orleans intriguing and wonderful.

Even now, in the late morning, aromas from a nearby restaurant filled the warming air—jambalaya, trout, oysters, bouillabaisse. She'd finished dinner the evening before with an extraordinary dessert called cherries jubilee. It was her favorite. While she usually enjoyed an equally healthy appetite, Jess had turned absolutely green at even the mention of food.

"I'm to meet Adela MacMillan for luncheon. I wonder where we'll be dining?"

From inside the room, Jess groaned. "How can you even think of food?"

Laurel turned to her. Jess looked absolutely terrible. If this was what a woman was forced to endure to bear a child, she decided she could do without having a child.

She wondered if Jess and Andrew made love every time they went to bed together, and she almost laughed. Surely not. And yet, if the man were Ruel Delaney, he would expect it, she was certain of that. If the man were Ruel Delaney, she would expect it. Mentally shaking off that train of thought, she gave Jess a sympathetic smile.

"Didn't the doctor, say this was all very normal?"

"Just because it's normal doesn't make it any easier." Jess moaned and buried her face underneath a damp cloth as another wave of nausea took hold. "You've been the best company for me, but shouldn't you be getting ready?"

"I suppose you're right." Laurel rose reluctantly. She felt almost guilty over enjoying the stay in New Orleans when Jessica was so miserable... almost. Dampening Jess's cloth, she pressed a kiss against her cousin's cheek.

The bellman informed them that Adela's carriage had arrived. She checked on Jessica one last time before leaving and found her dozing soundly in the cool darkness of the shuttered room.

Sweeping down the large staircase of the hotel, Laurel glanced about for Adela's driver. The lobby was crowded, businessmen were meeting acquaintances, guests were leaving, others were arriving. She stopped beside the spreading fronds of a huge fern.

As she glanced up, her gaze momentarily fell on the man, dressed in a dark suit seated nearby. He seemed absorbed in his newspaper, but there was something oddly familiar about him. She frowned slightly, thinking she'd seen him before, but she was unable to remember where. Catching sight of Adela's driver, Laurel crossed the marble lobby and stepped into brilliant midday sunshine.

They dined in the Garden District at the outside patio of the Commander's Palace, seated on wrought iron chairs painted white. Adela told vivid tales of her youth in New Orleans. Laurel soon learned that although Adela had spent the war years in the North, because of her husband, few of her Southern acquaintances held it against her. All seemed delighted to find she'd returned to New Orleans and had reopened her house on Granville Avenue.

As Adela finished yet another story of her wild and somewhat colorful youth, Laurel went into fits of laughter, then took another sip of champagne. It was light, bubbly, and warmed her blood. Her cheeks glowing, she sat back in her chair.

"Tell me about Ruel Delaney," Adela said casually.

Laurel blinked and sat straighter in her chair. She shook her head as the waiter offered her more champagne.

"There's nothing to tell."

"And you've met Dominique," Adela probed as she accepted a fresh glass. At Laurel's gasp of surprise, she waved her hand nonchalantly.

"I haven't been spying on you, my dear. But word does get

around, especially when the people involved are so... fascinating. At any rate, Anjanette came to the house to make the last alterations on my gown for the soiree. You are coming, of course."

"Yes, of course," was all Laurel could manage.

"What do you think of her?"

"She's very beautiful," Laurel replied. Somehow recalling seeing Ruel Delaney with Dominique de Beauvoir had made the afternoon a little less bright.

"She's Creole, from a very old Louisiana family," Adela replied. "Her father was Claude de Beauvoir, titled and all that, with vast land holdings. There was also a son, but not much is known about him. He died some years ago.

"And for all the family wealth, Dominique ended up with very little," she continued. "She left New Orleans, then returned about ten years ago. Her father was ill, and she'd come home to see him. But there was some bitterness between them. Even when he was dying, he refused to forgive her."

"For what?" Laurel asked.

"It seems Monsieur de Beauvoir arranged a marriage for her. It's quite the custom, you know, much as it is among the royalty. Parents choose partners according to property and title. It's not clear whether Dominique refused her father's decision or the gentleman in question changed his mind.

"At any rate, the wedding was called off, and shortly thereafter Dominique left for France. Not much is known of those years. Since her return, Ruel Delaney's been with her, except when he's traveling about."

"Is she his mistress?" Laurel idly asked.

An amused smile twitched at one corner of Adela's mouth, as if she'd discovered something very interesting.

"That would seem obvious. They're always together. And she is stunning, although I would guess a few years older than Ruel. I've never objected to such age differences myself, or to such arrangements. And it's quite true, he's never shown an interest in any other woman. At least not until recently."

Catching Adela's meaning, she swallowed back a sudden dryness at her throat, and when the waiter next offered to refill her glass, she gratefully accepted.

It was late afternoon when she returned to the St. Charles. After Adela bid her farewell, reminding her of their plan to attend the races together on Saturday, she stopped at the flower stand outside the hotel and purchased a bouquet of fragrant blooms, thinking they might lighten Jessica's spirits. Then, turning about, she nearly collided with a short, ragged man whose clothes seemed to contain more dust than the streets. Sharp, beady eyes bore into hers for a moment before the man dipped his hat to her and brushed past, blending in with the people on the sidewalk.

Saturday morning, Laurel rose early. She was starving. Deciding it must be the tropical climate, she downed a shamefully large breakfast, disposing of four beignets, several pieces of fresh fruit, and several cups of coffee.

Just after ten o'clock she knocked on Jess's door. The doctor had suggested that Jess remain in bed for a few more days, so her cousin had insisted that Andrew accompany Laurel to the races.

"How do I look?" Laurel swept into the sitting room in which Jess reclined on a chaise, an open book at her lap. Adela had mentioned that she wanted to introduce her to a certain young gentleman, so she'd taken great care in dressing.

"Absolutely stunning. Juliette was right about the white and black gown," Jess responded.

Laurel had been highly skeptical. Made of white silk taffeta, the dress was fashioned along the lines of a riding costume. The form-fitting bodice was almost masculine in its simplicity of cut, ending in a long V that extended down from her waist, and the collar was wide, cut much like the lapels of a man's coat. A single row of buttons ran down the front. They were small, and set close together, adding a feminine touch.

The sleeves, designed for comfort in the warm Louisiana climate, ended just below the elbow, but the skirt was a departure from the customary long, trailing ones. It clung with form-fitting tightness over her hips then spread into several pleats, all in white moiré silk. The buttons, covered in black, starkly contrasted with the gleaming white bodice, and black piping was set around the armholes and sleeve edges.

For a further accent black satin cording, worked into an exquisite floral pattern, decorated the front panel of the skirt, ending at the hemline just above the toe of her gleaming black boots. In a season favoring soft pastel colors, the combination of white and black was eye-catching.

The cut of the dress accentuated Laurel's slenderness, making her seem more fragile and delicate. Her thick hair had been swept high atop her head, exposing her throat. And a small, white silk riding hat, trimmed with black satin, sat atop her head, sheer, black netting trailing from it. All in all, the effect was striking.

"You don't think it's a bit..."

"What? Breathtaking?" Jess commented. "Yes, I do. And it's just perfect. Southern gentlemen have always prided themselves on their Southern belles. I think it's about time they saw what the North has to offer." Jess smiled at her reassuringly.

Light danced in Laurel's eyes. She felt light-hearted, excited. She loved New Orleans, and she would hate leaving it, though a part of her yearned to be on the way to San Francisco. It had been nearly two weeks since they'd arrived, and Andrew had finally acknowledged that she would continue on with them.

He'd sent off several telegrams to Boston, explaining she was well and was determined to go to California. Laurel had become nervous during their stay in New Orleans. She feared her uncle might board a ship and come after her. She did not want a confrontation. And she had convinced herself she'd soon have no further contact with Ruel Delaney.

She bid Jessica farewell and looped her arm through Andrew's. She was greeted by a marvelous spring day as they emerged from the St. Charles and walked toward the carriage. While Andrew gave the driver instructions, Laurel concentrated on the people that passed by.

Her gaze froze at the sight of the darkly dressed man, leaning on the lamppost at the corner. For the briefest moment their eyes locked, then he quickly glanced away, shifting the brim of his hat to conceal his eyes. It was the same man she'd seen in the lobby of the hotel. She watched him move down the street and signal for a carriage.

She smiled briefly at Andrew as he slipped into the carriage beside her. As they pulled away from the hotel, she strained to catch sight of the second carriage, but had lost him in the crowded street. She shivered in spite of the warmth of the spring morning.

Was it her imagination or had that man been following her?

Shrugging off the uneasy feeling, she turned her attention to Andrew as he pointed out the sights of interest along the way to the racetrack.

The Metairie Race Course was much more than its name indicated. As Laurel quickly learned, it was laid out in an oval in front of a massive grandstand. They entered through an archway and proceeded to a grassy area where other private carriages stood, the horses tethered and the drivers adjusting their hats in the warming sun.

The grandstand was a wooden structure built above the level of the track to allow all patrons an excellent view. Its wide roof was supported by massive posts set at regular intervals, and each tier was enclosed by a carved wooden railing. The best seats were in the boxes that lined the center area. Behind them, row upon row of wooden seats rose to accommodate those not fortunate to have box seats. Across the track in the center of the green stood a wooden structure, much like a gazebo. Andrew informed her this was the judge's box, where races were started and winners were announced.

Smaller buildings lined the back side of the grandstand. Laurel quickly learned these were where bets were placed. Across from them and separated by a wide green, was a long row of stalls. Horses stood in several stalls. On a small knoll set apart from the grandstand, and connected by a brick walkway with the Metairie Club House, was a large open pavilion. Here patrons could enjoy an exquisite luncheon or refreshment between races.

Proceeding quickly to find Adela MacMillan's box, Andrew escorted Laurel up the wide stairs leading to the second level. Adela's was number twelve, just to the right of the starting line.

"How delightful that you could make it," the woman greeted them. "It's an absolutely perfect day for racing. Not a cloud in the sky and just a breath of wind. It'll be a fast track today."

Adela introduced her to the other occupants of the box. The young man seated immediately to her left, Laurel quickly learned, was Etienne du Villiers.

He was handsome. His light brown hair was precisely cut and smoothed back, and he had a sophisticated manner. Bending over her hand, he lingered, then raised inquisitive dark eyes to hers. When his own smile deepened beneath the thin, clipped mustache that ended just at the edges of his mouth, he conveyed a more silent, intimate greeting.

"I am indeed enchanted, Mademoiselle Wentworth. You add grace and beauty to our city."

Completely taken aback by the boldness in this man's eyes, Laurel pulled her hand away and turned to Adela.

There were six seats in the box, three rows of two each, Adela sat in the top row much like a queen holding court. Indeed, she resembled a monarch in the brilliant jade green

silk gown she'd chosen. Etienne moved so that he might take a
seat beside Laurel, and Andrew was forced to take the seat
beside Adela.

They quickly fell into discussion over some business matter
involving MacMillan Manufacturing and Wentworth Shipping.
As there was still quite some time before the first race, Etienne
offered them all refreshments, and Adela graciously accepted,
giving Laurel a meaningful look as he slipped through the
crowd.

"He comes from a very fine family, and they seem to have
weathered the war quite well. They've only just returned from
abroad," she explained.

She smiled as Adela recited Etienne's various assets, the
long peacock feather adorning her hat punctuating her conversation. But as the seats in the boxes around them were beginning to fill, she fastened her gaze on the horses emerging from
the exercise yard.

"Have you placed your bet?"

Her heart almost stopped. Ruel Delaney seemed to block
out the brilliant blue afternoon sky.

"Ruel Delaney, you sly fox," Adela saved the awkward
moment. "I was wondering if you'd make it today. Dandy's Run
is the horse to beat," she offered boisterously.

"I'm a betting man, but I might disagree with you.
Dominique has entered her horse, and he looks very good."
Turning slightly to the side, Ruel drew Dominique into the
conversation. Her gown was soft apricot, the one Laurel had
seen her in at Juliette's. Its color accentuated her bronzed skin
and auburn hair. Smiling a warm greeting to Adela, the Frenchwoman turned to Laurel.

"You've taken the day with your fashion, *mademoiselle*," she
complimented her. "The rest of us are now but a sea of muted
color, while you are quite striking."

Her comment completely unnerved Laurel. The last thing

she'd have expected from Ruel's mistress was a compliment. In spite of herself, Laurel smiled.

"You didn't answer my question," Ruel commented. "Have you bet on any of the horses?"

"I know very little about horse racing," Laurel admitted, hoping to end the conversation. She didn't want to talk to him. She didn't want to see him again. Folding her hands together at her lap, she tried to ignore him.

"At least you haven't forgotten our meeting." Ruel smiled softly.

Forgotten! The word struck Laurel. Forgotten him? Dear God, she'd tried. She'd almost thought she had. Until today.

"You must teach her, Ruel," Dominique offered, a genuine smile lighting her dark eyes.

"Yes, of course, you must join us, though your box is far better than mine. However, we shall be having champagne any moment now." Adela thought the afternoon suddenly promised to be very interesting.

"It has arrived," Etienne announced with a flourish as he approached the box, a steward bearing an elegant silver tray and glasses in tow.

"Champagne sounds delightful. Etienne, so good to see you again," Dominique gracefully moved into the box. Taking one of the glasses she held it aloft as Ruel slipped his long frame into the box's narrow confines.

Bending low over Laurel, his hand went beneath her arm and drew her to her feet, leaving Etienne to serve the champagne. He chose to ignore the man's obvious dislike of the change in seating arrangements. Dominique would keep him occupied, and he hadn't the slightest intention of sharing Laurel with that fawning idiot.

"You can see the field much better from here."

He drew her to the railing in front of the last two seats. Below them at least a half-dozen fine horses paraded out onto the open field. He recited their names and the names of their jockeys.

Laurel's panic dissolved as she listened to his voice. There was nothing threatening or malicious in his tone. Only his eyes betrayed him when she caught him looking at her.

"How do you pick the winning horse?" she asked, certain there was more to it.

After all, he was a gambler by reputation. He could win or lose a fortune based on skill. She wanted to know more.

He smiled. That first moment, when she'd turned and looked up at him, he'd thought she'd jump right out of her skin. Now he saw a spark of genuine interest in her magnificent eyes. Dominique was right, in the elegant white satin dress trimmed in black, she was absolutely breathtaking. His hand ached to reach out and stroke the single golden curl that rested on her shoulder.

As he drew her into conversation, he realized he'd longed for the sound of her voice, soft and a bit breathless. He pointed out yet another horse and rider listed on the betting card he held.

The sheer black netting that trailed down her back, caught by the breeze, veiled her face momentarily as she turned to ask him another question, and he felt he was seeing her through the veil of night, golden light exposed in darkness.

Ruel realized more than his hand ached. His longing for her had remained, yet it was a longing of the past, a passion he'd known and then destroyed.

Who was she? He'd asked the question a hundred times, and a hundred times there was no answer. He'd been mistaken, he could accept that now. But there were moments, expressions on her face when she turned to him, and the memory returned. Then it was gone.

He'd learned to close himself off emotionally to people.

He'd had to in order to survive. But this was something different and he didn't like it.

Laurel laughed, and then caught herself. She'd thought before his eyes were darkest ebony, hiding secrets. The secrets were still there, masked, but there were also warm, dancing lights.

"Make your choice." Ruel offered her the betting card.

"I wouldn't know how." Laurel drew back, smiling in spite of the warnings she'd given herself. At least now that she was ashore, she was no longer trapped by the confines of the ship.

"You now know the names of the horses, and I've told you who their jockeys and owners are," he reminded her. "You even know their histories and their bloodlines. Go ahead make a choice. I'll place the bet for you." He watched her, wondering if she'd accept his offer.

Laurel studied the betting card carefully, going over each horse in her mind, recalling the facts Ruel had given her. She eliminated ten of the twelve horses. Clearly the last two were the odds-on favorites, as Ruel had pointed out. One was Dandy's Run, the other was Dominique's horse, a steel gray by the name of Bellage.

Her attention came back to one she'd eliminated based on facts alone. Fire and Brimstone. He was jet black, with an elegant mane and tail. He danced about on long legs, hooves pawing at the ground. Ruel said he was young, untried against the other horses. His dark eyes rolled defiantly as the groom held him to keep him from bolting down the field. He wanted to run.

"Fire and Brimstone," Laurel announced.

A dark brow arched at her choice. It wasn't the one he'd anticipated. He'd expected the logic Dominique usually exhibited or sheer fancy, picking a horse by its name. If she had picked this one by its name, that raised all sorts of interesting questions.

"Why this horse?"

"Maybe I'm a bit of a gambler," she replied.

"All right, lady gambler." His smile deepened. "Let's just see what Fire and Brimstone can do." He marked the card, then waved down a steward to place the bet. The horn sounded across the track, and the signal brought the horses to the starting position.

"Would you like to sit down to lose your money?" Ruel asked with amusement.

"No, I want to watch him win." She flashed him a challenging smile.

"And if he should, I suppose you'd want all the money," Ruel teased.

"Of course," she replied."

A wicked light leapt into his dark eyes.

Fire and Brimstone came from far behind, dark and magical, straining, stretching against the odds. He fought the man atop him and the race course beneath him. He was a wild animal, out of place among the tried thoroughbreds. But as if he understood that he must win this race, his distance-eating strides brought the crowd in the grandstands to their feet. It was there in the bunching and stretching of lean, powerful muscles, in the thrusting reach of his powerful neck. He wanted to win.

It didn't matter that he was untried. It didn't matter that his past was obscure. Fire and Brimstone was a champion. He had only to prove it to himself. He swept past eleven thoroughbreds to receive the winner's flag.

Laurel shrieked with joy. "I knew it! I knew it!"

Her joy was contagious. She was like a child who'd just discovered presents under the tree on Christmas morning.

"He won!" She couldn't believe it. Then, the moment slipped away.

Laurel smiled, her fingers curled inside his warm hand.

"It's late," Andrew reminded them. "We should be going. I did promise Jess we'd be returning early." He made his way down through the narrow seats.

"Yes, of course." Laurel glanced down at her hand, still firmly closed within Ruel Delaney's hand. He slowly released her. Her eyes met his briefly. Even as she stepped away, she still felt his touch.

5

J ess had recovered. That morning she'd downed a breakfast that amazed Laurel. Afterward they'd taken the advice of the hotel maid and had visited the French market, then had lunch with Andrew at a restaurant near the Merchant's Exchange.

Adela MacMillan's party was to be held the following evening, they were to sail for Panama the day after, and she'd hear no more from Ruel Delaney.

Luck had been with Laurel at the races, so their agreement had been canceled. She'd been able to enjoy the last days in New Orleans without fearing he'd arrive at the hotel to collect on it. She should have been ecstatic, but she had to admit that she was disappointed that he hadn't pressed the matter. She didn't think it like him to accept defeat so easily. But, of course, he had Dominique de Beauvoir.

Laurel paid the driver of the carriage when they arrived at the St. Charles. As she turned toward the entrance, she was brought up short by a man in a dark suit.

"Good afternoon, Miss Wentworth. I was wonderin' if I might have a minute of your time."

An uneasy feeling slipped down her spine. He knew her name, but she didn't know his.

"I'm sorry ..." she attempted to sidestep the man. He was standing within arm's length of her and his eyes were only now visible beneath the brim of his hat. They were set in a square face with a grim mouth set off by a long, waxed mustache. His hair just reached a collar that had once been starched, but was now limp due to the heat and the humidity.

"This will only take a moment." There was something in his manner, his voice almost a whisper, that seemed strange, somehow threatening.

"Is something wrong?" Jess asked.

"Not at all," she assured her, not wanting to alarm her. "This gentleman has made a mistake." Looping her arm through Jess's, she stepped past him and walked toward the entrance of the hotel.

"No mistake, miss." His gruff voice halted Laurel before she could reach the door.

"I'd like to ask you a few questions about that ship you came in on."

Jess's hand closed over hers. Laurel squeezed her fingers reassuringly as she turned back to the man who'd followed them.

"I don't know you, sir, and I don't think I can be of any help to you." Laurel fought back a twinge of panic.

Andrew had warned them both that New Orleans was a Reconstruction town, full of every kind of hustler and two-bit con artist imaginable. The dregs of humanity were drawn to it like locusts to summer wheat. This was the aftermath of war, a stark contrast to the safety of her proper upbringing in Boston.

"Name's Bodine, Sam Bodine." The man tipped his hat in a gesture that was almost mocking.

"This letter will identify me and my reasons for bein' in New Orleans." Handing Laurel the letter, he waited while she read it.

"I've never heard of William Rawlins," Laurel informed him as she read the signature on the letter.

"Now, Miss Wentworth, if you'd just answer my questions," Bodine said.

Folding the letter Laurel put it back in the envelope and shoved it at Sam Bodine. She didn't like his manner, and she didn't like him.

"All I need is some information about the ship you came in on. I believe it's owned by Wentworth Shipping. That would be the firm of your cousin, Mr. Andrew Wentworth." Bodine slipped the letter into the inside pocket of his jacket. "Maybe I should take this up with him."

"If you're so curious about this particular cargo, I suggest you contact the captain and ask to see his manifest."

Passing a hand over his whiskered chin, the man nodded in agreement. "I tried that. He wasn't accommodating."

"If he wouldn't give you the information, I fail to understand how you think I can be of any help."

Bodine's smile sharpened. "I understand you spent some time down in that hold. I'd like to know what you saw down there."

Whoever his source was, evidently, he knew something about the episode aboard the *Waverall*. Laurel's thoughts raced. That letter had been sent by a congressman named Rawlins. She'd never heard of him, or this man.

The moment he approached her, she realized he was the man she'd seen on several occasions since they'd arrived in New Orleans. He'd obviously been following her. Whoever he was, she owed him nothing. Less than nothing. Her eyes locked briefly with Jess's, and she saw a faint warning at her eyes.

"I'm afraid you're going to be disappointed, Mr. Bodine. There's nothing to tell," Laurel announced flatly.

"What do you mean?" he growled.

"I mean exactly that. I saw nothing in the hold of the ship

except trunks, barrels, and boxes—nothing I haven't seen on other ships."

"I'm talking about wooden crates, long ones."

Laurel met his gaze with forced calm. The crates! He was after information about those crates Ruel Delaney had been guarding so carefully when he'd found her in the trunk.

What was it Andrew had said about Ruel? A known smuggler. A privateer who'd gotten wealthy during the war?

It was obvious this man was extremely interested in the contents of those crates.

Gold perhaps? Not likely. Now that the war had ended and normal shipping had resumed, what could possibly be of such interest? If, that letter was authentic.

She couldn't have said what it was that influenced her decision. Considering what had passed between her and Ruel Delaney, she had no reason to protect him.

Perhaps it was Mr. Bodine's arrogance or his attempt to frighten her into giving him the information he wanted. Maybe it was the uneasiness she'd felt the last days when she'd turned around to find him only a few feet away, calmly watching her. In any case, she wasn't about to tell this man anything.

"I'm sorry, Mr. Bodine." Her tone was polite but firm. "I have no idea what you're talking about." Gathering up her skirt, Laurel whirled about, with Jess behind her. Not until they were in the hotel lobby did she release the breath she held.

"Is he following us?" she whispered to Jess.

"He wouldn't dare. There're too many people here. Let's go straight to our rooms." Jess propelled her toward the wide stairway.

Once she was in her room, Laurel slumped down onto a chair.

"I wonder who that man was?" Frowning, Jess pulled off her gloves.

"Sam Bodine." Laurel collapsed against the back of the chair, her heart only now slowing its frantic pace.

"No. I mean who he really was. That sort of man doesn't work for any congressman. At least not legitimately."

"What do you mean?" She had Laurel's full attention.

"Mr. Delaney has quite a reputation. Why did you lie about what you saw in the hold?" Her curiosity piqued, Jess removed her hat, and a smile curved her lips.

"It's quite simple," Laurel replied. "I didn't like the man. He was arrogant, too sure of himself, as if he were certain I'd tell him anything he wanted to know."

"Arrogant, self-assured." Jess considered her explanation. "I seem to remember your using those same words to describe Captain Delaney."

"What are you saying?"

"Only that it would seem this Mr. Bodine and Ruel Delaney are cut from the same cloth. Andrew insists that he's a smuggler. He told me a shipment of Union gold disappeared en route to Washington during the war. Everyone was convinced Captain Delaney had something to do with it."

"Jess, honestly. Rumors?" Jess pointed out. "Why are you protecting him?"

"I wasn't protecting him. I merely didn't see any reason to give information to that weasel. I didn't like the looks of him, and I certainly didn't care for his manner."

"I have to agree with you. Ruel Delaney is far better looking and he does have impeccable manners," Jess teased. She watched Laurel carefully for a reaction. "I'm beginning to think you're completely taken with the man," she added. "He is terribly attractive, in a roguish sort of way." Jess smothered laughter behind her hand when Laurel glared at her.

"I don't want to talk about Ruel Delaney!" She pointed to the long, garment box on the bed. "What's that?"

"This is your room," Jess commented. "It's obviously for you.

"My gowns were all delivered yesterday. There must be some mistake."

"Open it. Perhaps they forgot to send something over. "Jess pulled a pillow from beneath the satin coverlet and propped herself against the carved headboard, and waited eagerly, like a child anticipating Christmas.

Slipping the ribbon from the box, Laurel lifted the lid. After removing the tissue wrapping, she just stared.

"What is it?" Jess asked.

Laurel lifted the gown from the box. It was exquisite, midnight blue velvet, an elegant whisper of a gown that hardly seemed to contain enough fabric. How different it was from the voluminous gowns she had purchased the day before.

"There's a card from Juliette's," Jess exclaimed, producing a small envelope from the top of the box. The ornate letter *J* was embossed on the upper left-hand corner.

"It's a beautiful gown," she commented enviously. "You must try it on to be certain of the fit so that you can wear it to Adela's party tomorrow evening."

Laurel was baffled. She was certain she'd seen no sketch of this gown when they'd been at Juliette's, yet here it was, and her name was neatly lettered on the envelope.

She wondered if the gown would fit, so slender was the style. She slipped it over her head and held out her arms as Jess helped pull it down over her hips. Then she held her breath as Jess fastened the satin-covered buttons at the back. When Jess came around to gain a better view, Laurel finally released her breath.

"Oh my!" was all Jess said.

She crossed to the full-length mirror beside the armoire and found herself in complete agreement. The fit of the gown was perfect—in the areas that it covered.

The neckline, if it could be called that, was cut dramatically low, exposing the swell of her breasts, with rows of small tucks gathered down the center. The cap sleeves rode low at her shoulders.

It clung daringly and the seam at the front opened to reveal her legs at the front of the gown as the hem pooled at the floor.

She'd never seen anything so beautiful or extravagant. If this gown had been shown to her at Juliette's, she'd have remembered it.

"This is to be worn with it," Jess pulled the long wrap from the box. It was made of the same midnight blue velvet. She wrapped it around Laurel's shoulders.

"You must wear this tomorrow night," Jess told her.

Laurel reached for the envelope with Juliette's initial on it. Breaking the seal, she read the simple message:

You must always wear blue.

Anger shot through her. How dare he! The audacity, the arrogance...

"I'm not wearing it," she announced flatly.

"But you have to."

"I'll wear the yellow satin, just as I'd planned." Stripping off the wrap, Laurel tried to unfasten the buttons at the back of the gown.

"The yellow is nice. But this is absolutely extraordinary. What's gotten into you? This gown is perfect. Why wouldn't you want to wear it? Anyone can see it's probably one of Juliette's finest creations."

She groaned. Damn him! Her arms dropped to her sides and she turned to Jess. She could admit who had sent it even though there was no name at the bottom of the note, but that would bring even more questions. There was usually only one reason a man bought a gown for a woman—either he was her husband, or...

Damn and double damn!

She supposed she could give the excuse of an illness—the

long trip, the weather..." But looking at Jess, she knew that she'd see right through it.

She'd wear the gown, but that didn't mean she'd like it.

It was a masked ball, requiring all attending to wear some form of covering over their faces until midnight. The designs of the masks were varied and elaborate. As Laurel scanned the huge ballroom, she noted many full masks, depicting certain characters or animals. One woman wore a bird mask with extravagant feathers in her headdress. A gentleman who walked by her was disguised as a wrinkled old man, but his smooth hands belied the disguise.

Laurel smiled faintly as a man tilted his head admiringly. Sensing the focus of his gaze, she vainly tried to shift inside the gown, hoping to cover more of the daring neckline.

She dared not turn about quickly, and she was in mortal fear of dropping a glove or the small satin reticule she carried, certain she would fall out of the gown if she had to bend over. And drawing a deep breath was unthinkable. The small silver mask across her eyes helped to conceal her embarrassment. And the anger.

Jess had been supportive as they left the hotel. But Andrew had looked at her askance. It'd been too late for him to ask her to change, although she would gladly have done it. As it was, he'd mumbled some vague compliment and had tried to keep his eyes averted from the plunging neckline.

Adela bustled across the elegant ballroom as they arrived. She'd forgone a mask. What disguise could possibly conceal her colorful identity?

"My dear, how enchanting you are this evening," she told Laurel. "And the gown—*magnifique!* How I wish I were your age. But you mustn't hide here in the salon," she scolded playfully.

"There are several interesting gentlemen about, and Etienne arrived a short while ago. He's already been asking for you. I think that young man fancies himself in love, be careful about walking without a chaperone in the garden this evening; it could be a problem in that gown. Come, let's find some champagne."

Glancing back over her shoulder, Laurel saw Jess and Andrew disappear amidst a crowd of young couples.

By the time Etienne found her, she'd consumed three glasses of champagne and had forgotten her inhibitions about the gown. Her eyes sparkled from behind the mask, reflecting the deep midnight blue of the gown. She danced twice with Andrew, three times with Etienne, and then with the older gentleman Adela had introduced as a "special" friend.

Laurel wondered if they were lovers. Given Adela's outrageous unconventionality she thought it entirely possible and marvelous.

Etienne whirled her about the ballroom with a light hand and a perfect manner. The fragrances of scented candles and blossoms filled the air. The champagne was intoxicating, the air was intoxicating. Etienne drew her closer.

"You are the most beautiful creature in the world."

Laurel laughed as she spun away from him, his words lost in a dizzying whirl of light, warmth, and champagne. The dance was new to her, but she'd picked it up quickly. The ladies formed a circle and the gentlemen formed another about them.

Everyone started out in couples, moving through several steps in a set pattern before returning to their places. With the second set, positions changed for the ladies, and they found themselves with new partners. The dance continued until, the ladies were returned to their original partners, then the music ended.

She had already danced with several partners, her gaze

sweeping the large ballroom. This was her last night in New Orleans, and she was determined to enjoy it.

Then, she felt that inexplicable feeling that slipped across her skin, like a breath of a warm, spring air. Or a warning? *He* was here. She was certain that if she turned her head, she would see Ruel Delaney. His presence seemed to fill the room —along with whispers, speculation, and the admiring glances of several women.

She whirled through the steps, turning once, then twice. She was breathless, and her cheeks were flushed from the champagne. The pressure on her gloved hand was firm, warm. She turned back to greet her new partner, but her eyes widened as *he* pulled her into his arms.

"Good evening, *mademoiselle.*"

She would have known his voice anywhere, deep, rich, thrilling as thunder.

He was devastatingly handsome in the black formal jacket that was waist length in front with tails at the back. Its black satin lapels, wide near the collar, narrowed to a V as they tapered to his waist. The vest he wore was also black, and it contrasted with the stark white of his shirt. His black trousers were decorated with a satin stripe at the outside seams.

For a mask, Ruel Delaney had chosen the hallmark of a pirate, an eye patch worn over his left eye. Although dressed in the elegant finery of a gentleman, he looked every bit of one. He was absolutely the most arrogant man she'd ever known. Who else would flaunt his illegal profession at a masquerade?

"I knew the gown would be exquisite." There was a different timber to his voice. Gone was the arrogance.

And he was handsome, Laurel silently thought. Without being consciously aware of it, she realized that she had been watching for him all evening.

"I didn't wear it to please you."

His mouth turned down for the barest instant. "I thought perhaps it meant you had accepted my peace offering."

"Peace offering?" she replied.

"We didn't get off to a very good beginning. I thought we might start over."

His frown turned into a devastating smile.

"I'd hoped that you might accept the gown as a token of my esteem and admiration, Miss Wentworth." The mocking tone had returned.

Why couldn't he understand that she wanted nothing to do with him?

"A true gentleman would never force a lady to accept a gift. You knew perfectly well Jess would see the gown, and I would have to wear it."

"You could have told her the truth about who sent it," Ruel suggested. He liked the anger in her eyes. At moments like this, her resemblance to another he'd once known, was uncanny.

"Oh! You would like that," she replied. "A bit of scandal? I would think that you have enough following you around!"

Ruel threw back his head and laughed. Then his hand closed over hers. There was no way she could escape him without causing a scene, and he was certain she realized a scene wouldn't matter to him.

Laurel flashed a convincing smile as Adela MacMillan and her escort danced by.

"Please let me go. Everyone will be talking."

"And what will they be saying? That you're the most beautiful woman here and that I'm most fortunate to be dancing with you." Ruel's eyes swept over her, then lingered on the dramatic sweep of the bodice.

He'd been right when Juliette had shown him the blue velvet. It had been meant for some matron's Sunday dress and would have been made into a cumbersome and concealing gown. A complete waste.

He'd decided it would not be draped on some old *grande dame* of New Orleans society. For a hefty price he'd persuaded Juliette to sell him the fabric. Then he'd given his requirements for a design. He wanted something form fitting and low cut, a simple but elegant gown to display a woman's charms.

Juliette had raised a questioning brow at the time but had said nothing when he'd instructed that the gown be delivered to the St. Charles hotel. Her questions had all been answered when he'd told her to make the gown to the exact measurements of Miss Laurel Wentworth.

Laurel groaned. He was absolutely impossible. Maddeningly impossible.

"If you wanted to offer an apology, it could have been done quite nicely on paper."

"I said I wanted a new beginning. I don't think I mentioned apologies." He smiled faintly as her startled eyes met his. There was no mockery in his dark gaze.

"I haven't the slightest intention of apologizing for our first meeting, Laurel. I apologize only for the circumstances."

She swallowed what she would like to have said. He was everything she'd called him, everything she'd thought of calling him. And more.

"Now that you've said what you came to say, please be kind enough to leave me alone. I don't accept your apology, and if I'd had any choice in the matter, I'd never have worn this gown. It's not the sort of gift a gentleman gives a lady. It's the sort of gift a man would give his..."

Laurel caught herself, realizing what she'd been about to say. She'd gone from anger, to icy coolness, closing him out. She was hurt, and lashing out at him was the only retaliation her proper upbringing would allow.

"Yes?" His dark eyes twinkled as he played with her, enjoying her reserve, her calm, and the spark of something more at her eyes.

"You know very well what I mean." Laurel's cheeks flamed.

"I don't think I do."

She groaned as he whirled her through the next steps. "It's the sort of gift a man would give his... mistress!" Having blurted it out, she quickly glanced about to see if anyone might have overheard their conversation.

"You're afraid that anyone who knew about the gown would assume you were my mistress?"

Laurel was completely, totally mortified. She wanted to crawl behind her thin, silver mask. She wanted to run.

"You needn't worry about that. I won't tell anyone. I'll be the soul of discretion." He drew her closer, breathing in the scent of her hair. He wanted to drag her to some dark corner, wanted to take the pins from her hair and let that mass slip through his fingers. And... he discovered, he wanted more.

"Aren't you afraid of what Dominique might think?" She hadn't intended to be so outspoken. Why did he provoke her to say such things?

"Now *you're* being indiscreet."

"You should know," Laurel replied tartly.

"Are you insinuating I'm not a gentleman?" The corners of his mouth twitched a smile. He liked her anger almost as much as her smiles, rare though they were. At least as far as he was concerned.

"I think we both know what you are."

"Ah, yes. I think the word you used was *scoundrel.*"

Behind the mask, her eyes sparkled like blue ice.

"Do you still, think that, Laurel?" His arm tightened, pulling her against him.

They'd stopped dancing. They were standing at the edge of the floor, his one arm around her, his other hand at her waist, holding her against him.

She didn't know what to think. The champagne and warm night air were having a devastating effect on her senses. Her legs suddenly felt weak, and she closed her eyes to stop the room from spinning, and to block him out.

She failed miserably, and as she slowly opened her eyes, she realized a truth she'd been denying. She wanted him to kiss her. She wanted to feel his mouth, hot and demanding, against hers again.

"You need to be kissed," Ruel whispered. "And God knows I need to do it. But not here, not this way." Cursing mildly under his breath.

The music had ended. Laurel stared at him as common sense returned. Damn him! What was he trying to prove? That she was someone else?

Cheeks flaming, she realized several people were staring at them. She heard her name spoken. Glancing up, she saw Etienne making his way through the crowd.

"Here you are." Then a look at Ruel Delaney. "Are you all right? You look distressed." He took her hand and tucked through his arm.

"It's nothing," she assured him, praying there wouldn't be a confrontation. "It's just the heat of the evening."

Etienne had turned his gaze on Ruel. "Or perhaps the company?"

The atmosphere was intense, charged. Laurel placed a restraining hand on Etienne's arm.

"I would like something to drink."

"Perhaps a glass of champagne," Etienne offered as a servant approached with a tray, the glasses on it tinkling with false merriment.

Ruel seized two glasses before Etienne could reach around her. Handing one to her, he saluted, a dark light leaping into his eyes.

"To new beginnings." Ruel's toast excluded their companion. "And to their conclusion."

Then, draining his glass, Ruel bowed formally to them both.

"You must take Laurel for a walk. Perhaps the cool air in the gardens will calm her." Bidding them both good evening, he crossed the room and rejoined Dominique.

Laurel stared after him. One minute he was promising new beginnings, whatever that meant, and the next he was practically pushing her into Etienne's arms.

Very well, Mr. Delaney, she thought. Giving Ruel one last withering glance, she graciously accepted Etienne's invitation.

Ruel watched the French doors that led into Adela MacMillan's prized garden. Etienne du Villiers had a certain reputation with women, well-bred ladies in particular.

Discretion. Perhaps it was the only thing that distinguished him. Du Villiers was the sort of man who liked to make certain his paramours weren't aware of any competition. Ruel, on the other hand, had always believed in laying his cards on the table, no matter what the game was.

He waited a few minutes and wasn't surprised to see she returned abruptly, alone. He was standing nearby when she collected her wrap some minutes later as her cousin and his wife made their farewells to their hostess.

"Was your walk in the garden refreshing?" he asked as he came up behind her, also to bid farewell to Adela.

Refreshing indeed! She had to fend off Etienne's groping. But she'd learned a valuable lesson about Frenchmen and their amorous intentions. In fact, she'd learned a great many lessons lately.

"Quite refreshing," she replied, giving him a sideways glance.

"I hope the cool, night air wasn't too much for du Villiers." Ruel eyes slowly swept over her, then came to rest on her sapphire eyes. She was still angry with him, but there was humor in the turn of her lips.

"I think the lily pond might have assisted in that."

"The lily pond?" he asked.

"At this very moment, I suspect he's trying to figure out how he's going to leave without being seen," she explained then added. "Good-bye, Mr. Delaney."

Ruel burst into laughter as he watched her bid Adela farewell and then follow her cousins to their waiting carriage.

He would have given a good share of that stolen Union gold to see Etienne du Villiers sitting in the middle of the lily pond.

"Here you are, *mon cher.*" Dominique slipped an arm through Ruel Delaney's, drawing his attention away from the departing carriage.

"Paul has been looking all over for you. There's been some trouble at the warehouse," she whispered discreetly. A moment later, they were standing in Adela MacMillan's library.

"What happened?"

"One of the men found me at The House. There was a raid on the warehouse tonight." Paul Chandler braced himself for the anger the news would bring.

"Brady reported in just after you left this evening. He saw the Wentworth woman talking with that man outside the hotel. He caught the name Bodine." Paul chose his words carefully.

"Sam Bodine!" Ruel slammed a fist down on the desktop.

"Do you know this Bodine?" Dominique lifted worried eyes to him.

"We've had a run-in or two. He's a henchman of Congressman Rawlins. Damn! How did they find out about the shipment?"

Paul twisted the brim of his hat thoughtfully. "Must have been the Wentworth dame. Brady said they had a pretty good talk."

Ruel's eyes narrowed. So, Laurel had found a way to have her revenge. Her cousin's ship, access to the warehouse through Wentworth shipping. It had been so simple.

"How did you get here?" His eyes were hard as obsidian.

"I brought my carriage."

Ruel nodded. "Take Dominique home."

"Where are you going?" her gown rustled softly as she grabbed his arm.

"The warehouse."

"You must not. Those people will be waiting for you. Don't you understand? They wanted that shipment, but they also want something else—you." Her words sliced through his anger and forced him to see the logic of her words.

"I'll be careful," Ruel promised. He gently stroked her cheek before turning to Chandler. "Give me your gun."

Dominique watched until the carriage disappeared around the corner. When a shiver went through her, Paul wrapped an arm about her shoulders. "He'll be all right. Isn't he always?"

RUEL STEPPED from the carriage before it came to a complete stop.

"Where's Paddy?"

"Here, Captain." Wiping his hands, Paddy emerged from the side entrance of the warehouse.

Ruel gave him a hard look.

"I'm not hurt. I was down the line, makin' that connection with the man for the shipment to be delivered when I heard all the commotion. By the time I got here it was all over but the shoutin'. Loomis and Foley were on duty. They slit Foley clean up the middle. Loomis took a blow to the head," Paddy informed him grimly.

"Have you sent for a doctor?"

"Old Doc Wills down on Bourbon Street. He keeps his mouth shut about these things. He's with Loomis now. Wasn't much he could do for Foley."

"Did Foley have any family?"

"I don't even know if Foley was his real name. Most of these men don't want nobody snoopin' around in their past."

It was a hard fact Ruel understood. It didn't make the deaths of good men any easier.

"What did they get?"

He and Paddy walked together through the shadows, then stepped into the faint light of the lanterns hanging inside the warehouse.

"They got everythin', tore the whole place apart."

Ruel nodded as he kicked aside a broken packing crate. Barrels of molasses had been split open, grain sacks ripped apart. On the far side, several bales of cotton were askew, their bands clipped. He crossed to the small office.

The desk had been shoved against the far wall, the floorboards had been ripped up. Below them, in a sub chamber, lay the remnants of the shipment, the crates splintered and scattered. It was a mess, and a complete total loss. And something about it nagged at him, but he was still unable to put his finger on just what it was that bothered, him.

"Get back in touch with Captain Suarez."

"What am I gonna tell him, boss? They're expectin' that shipment."

"We'll get it to them," Ruel said grimly.

"You know who did this?"

Ruel cut Paddy off. "I know who ordered it. and I know who gave them their information."

"Sounds dangerous, Captain. Want me to come along?" The excitement in Paddy's voice was unmistakable. He sounded like he'd just found a rainbow and wanted to go after that pot o' gold.

Ruel nodded. There were people he knew he could trust. Others?

"We'll wait a few days and let things calm down. Meanwhile, I don't want word of this to get out. As far as others are concerned, it's business as usual here. Get some men down here in the morning to clean up."

"Yes, sir! Say, boss, where you goin' now?" When Paddy turned, he was gone.

LAUREL PLACED the last of her garments inside the trunk Jessica had given her to use. Then she stepped behind the silk screen and began to unbutton her gown.

It was late and she was exhausted, from the dancing and the champagne. She'd bid Jess and Andrew good night upon returning to the St. Charles. Struggling to undo the gown, she sighed and wished she'd thought to have Jessica unbutton it for her.

"Maybe I can be of help." The voice came out of the shadows. It made Laurel whirl around in stark terror.

She gasped as she turned around.

"What are you doing here? How did you get in here?"

"Don't scream. Don't even think about it." The menace in his tone reached her.

Wide-eyed, she watched as Ruel Delaney's shadow lengthened and separated from the darkness. Anger glowed at his eyes.

"Please continue... take it off."

Not yet understanding his meaning, Laurel's gaze dropped uncertainly to the gown.

"I said, take it off!" he repeated.

She stared horror-stricken at the long, shiny barrel of the revolver now pointed at her.

With lightning swiftness, Ruel reached out and grabbed the bodice of the gown. He jerked downward and the fabric separated down the front.

Laurel bit back a scream, and her hands flew to cover her naked breasts. Dear God, he was mad!

If she'd feared him before, that was nothing compared to what she felt now. She cringed, as he waved the gun at her.

"Take it off."

When she hesitated, he repeated it. Biting her lower lip, Laurel reached for the ties of the chemise she had worn underneath the gown with trembling hands. Slowly she drew out the bow. Her lowered head shot up as cold steel touched the swell of her breasts.

"Unlace it."

She raised anguished eyes to him. "Don't do this."

His only answer was a wave of the revolver. Slowly, Laurel drew the ties out of the lace of the chemise. Breathing raggedly, she stood frozen when the last chemise gaped open.

"Your hair—take out the pins—all of them."

A single tear slipped down her cheek.

"Tears won't save you, Laurel. You see, I know. I know all about your little meeting with Sam Bodine. Do it!"

One by one, she pulled the pins from her hair until it tumbled over her shoulders.

Bodine? What was he talking about? Her thoughts collided as she felt the heat of his hand against her bare skin. She gasped at the contact. With agonizing slowness, he drew her against him.

"Didn't anyone ever tell you, there's a price for everything?"

She trembled violently. "I don't know what you're talking about?"

"Don't you?"

"No!"

"Think about a conversation with someone on the street."

She tried, but her thoughts were scattered.

"I don't know anything about a conversation..."

"Lies are so easy, aren't they?" He leaned over her. "Until they catch you. You were seen."

She was shaking, trying to think what he was talking about.

"What lies? What conversation? I don't even know anyone in New Orleans..."

"Do you know how easy it would be to snap your neck?" He asked, stroking that silken column. "Just so." His fingers closed around her neck. Her eyes were wide and dark, her breathing ragged. She was terrified. He would use that against her.

He wanted to hurt her, but his own body betrayed him. He fought the passion, but it was there, spinning out of control, violent, ravenous.

He trapped her mouth, burying a hand at her hair. Anyone else... if anyone else had betrayed him, he would have killed them.

"Damn you!" He cursed her, then cursed himself.

"I don't understand." Tears were wet at her cheeks. Confusion was etched on her face.

The crates in the hold of the *Waverall*! And that disgusting man who had approached her on the street with his questions. That's what this was about. She was shaking so badly she could hardly get the words out.

"I never told anyone anything."

Standing there almost naked, tears wet on her cheeks, he believed her. He knew how to read people, knew when they lied. She was telling the truth.

The shaking threatened to send her to the floor. It was ridiculous, insane. He caught her, his hand tight in her hair. Then he was gone and she was alone.

THE GRAY PRE-DAWN was smoky from cooking fires across the harbor, and heat already shimmered across the water. Still wearing the dress suit from the evening before, Ruel let himself inside the warehouse.

Plans had to be made. He stopped, warily sensing someone

else inside. Drawing the revolver, he circled low around a cluster of large barrels. Then he aimed the pistol directly into the shadows where he saw a slight movement.

"Hey, it's me. Brady. You're liable to hurt somebody with that thing."

"How the hell did you get in here?" Ruel growled. He was in no mood for congeniality or small talk.

"Paddy said you might be back this mornin'. I heard about the raid."

Reaching inside his jacket pocket, Ruel drew out a cigarette. The match flared briefly as he touched off the tip, inhaling deeply.

"I paid you for your information."

"Ain't money I'm here for. We had an agreement. I may not be a real smart fella, but I always keep a deal, especially when a man pays as good as you do."

"Get on with it," Ruel snapped.

"Well, I got to thinkin' about what I told Mr. Chandler. Last night. I wasn't certain he got all the information to you."

"What are you talking about?" Ruel's eyes narrowed through the haze of smoke.

"He was real interested when I told him about that Wentworth gal talkin' to that government fella. Got all excited and said you'd be real happy to hear about it. Only thing was, she didn't tell the fella nothin'."

Ruel eyes narrowed. "What did you say?"

"I told Chandler she met with this Bodine fella outside the hotel. Only thing was, she refused to tell him anything. He kept questioning her about some kinda crates inside a ship. She told him she never saw no crates. I couldn't understand why Mr. Chandler got so all fired up over that."

"Are you certain about this?"

"Positive, Captain. As sure as I'm standin' here. She's sure a looker, that little gal."

Ruel forced his thoughts to clear as he scanned the warehouse. He'd been certain of it in her room at the hotel, now he had even more proof. Whatever the reason, she hadn't said anything about the creates in the hold of the ship.

In the early morning light, barrels, boxes, and bales of cotton were broken and scattered. But other than the crates in the sub chamber, nothing had been taken.

Why? And why had Paul lied about Laurel's conversation with Bodine? Unless he wanted him to think she'd passed the information along.

HE SAT in the elegant office, fingers drumming on the small leather-bound journal. He'd found it earlier, beneath the fake bottom in one of the desk drawers in the office at The House of the Rising Sun.

The double sets of entries over the last two years explained a great deal. One column matched the entries he'd reviewed in The House ledger, the second showed the actual profits. The House had, indeed, done well, had made a great deal of money as the war ended. A great deal of it had come from the girls operating out of the rooms at the top-floor.

God knows, he was no saint, but the percentages Paul Chandler had demanded from the girls who worked the rooms over the gambling house were exorbitant.

Ruel had never actively promoted prostitution. It had gone with the territory when he'd opened The House ten years ago. If girls wanted to work, he gave them the opportunity, but he'd always been fair about splitting the money and when one of the ladies had a difficulty of one kind or another, he took care of it.

The entries he'd found indicated they'd been treated like slave labor, but none of that had been reflected in the books he'd been shown. Clearly Paul Chandler had been skimming from the business—a lot and for a long time.

But why? Ruel had paid him damned good wages and had given him a percentage of the profits. They'd discussed a complete buy-out only days earlier, under conditions that were almost ridiculous. After ten years, Ruel had established other business ventures. He no longer considered New Orleans home. He wanted out. It seemed Paul Chandler also wanted him out.

It was early. There'd been no one about except King Donovan when he'd come in through the back two hours earlier. King was more than bartender. He had a small apartment upstairs, and kept track of the girls, made certain none of them got into any trouble with a customer.

He'd been polishing glasses when Ruel had come in, and had given him only the barest nod. That was the way it had been in the old days, when Ruel had been a working owner, putting in eighteen to twenty-hour days while pushing to make The House of the Rising Sun the best gambling hall in New Orleans.

Donovan poked his head inside the door. "He's comin' in through the front, boss."

His feet on the desk, Ruel nodded. Mentally, he forced back the dull ache that had begun at the back of his head and slipped the ledger into the center drawer. Sleep would ease the pain, or one of those magical powders Donovan kept behind the bar. But he didn't want to get rid of the pain. It set him on edge, sharpened his senses and heightened his awareness.

"What the hell are you doin' in here so early?" Paul asked as he came through the door. "If I'd known, I'd have come on down and we could have met for breakfast." He stopped just inside the doorway.

The surprised look on his face told Ruel that King hadn't told him he'd be waiting. Some loyalties remained. He swung his feet off the desk and turned to face Paul.

"I've been up a long time." Ruel watched him, searching for

any sign of uneasiness. He had to hand it to Chandler, the man was cool.

Paul laughed and threw his hat onto the hat rack. "Must have been one helluva party. Do I know the lady?"

The remark was casual enough, the offhand kind of remark any man might ask another. He chose not to answer.

"There was trouble down at the warehouse. But then I suppose you wouldn't know anything about that."

"I hadn't heard. I was down on Bourbon Street." Paul slipped into the leather-bound chair that sat across the desk. There was a trace of a frown on his face, then it was gone.

Ruel nodded. He knew the address. Dominique had supplied him with that information. There was a girl there, a quadroon. Dominique had also informed him that the girl had found herself pregnant last year. Chandler had ordered her to get rid of it, had even taken her to the house of an old woman who could do it. That grated on Ruel. Responsibility was responsibility, no matter how it happened.

Unknown to Chandler, Dominique had intervened, and Chandler's child now lived in a small cottage in Crescent City. The mother still hoped to bring Chandler to the altar. Until a few hours ago, Ruel might have believed it possible. That was before he'd learned some interesting information about his manager.

Taking the small, leather ledger from the center drawer, Ruel tossed it down onto the desk. There was only the slightest response.

"You've been so busy the last days, we haven't had a chance to go over all the entries."

More lies.

"There was plenty of opportunity. Tell me, which set of figures were you going to use to establish the net worth of The House for the buy-out?"

"You're jumping to the wrong conclusion."

"Am I?" Ruel challenged. "I haven't found the other entries, but I'm certain they're somewhere."

"What are you talking about?"

"I'm talking about all the cargo I delivered to those other locations over the last seven years. I want to see the entries for those."

"I don't know who you've been talkin' to, but there are no other entries. Did King say somethin' to you?"

"King didn't say a thing. I had a little talk with Brady this morning. He gave me some interesting information, but then, that's what I paid him for. At least Brady tells a person when he's going to steal from them."

Ruel inhaled at the cigarette. The smoke seared his lungs.

"I also had a long talk with the warehouse foreman. After a little *persuasion* he was able to give me a lot of information about certain cargos that were brought in under cover of darkness and then split up."

Ruel rubbed a bruised fist. "You ordered the cargos split, had part of them delivered to the original destinations, then shipped the rest to another location up near Baton Rouge. I'll bet there're people who can give me a whole lot of information there."

A fine sheen of moisture had formed at Chandler's upper lip.

"Now wait just a minute. I admit I had those cargos moved. But I did it for safety. Even now, we've still got Federal troops snoopin' all around. It just wasn't safe to leave it at the docks, even in that lower vault you had built."

"Rail travel was dangerous during the war. Did you work out some arrangement with the local military?" Ruel blew out a stream of smoke. "Have you ever heard the old saying, where there's smoke there's fire?"

Paul was now sweating profusely. He stepped to the sideboard, poured himself a whiskey, and downed it in one swallow.

"It's all on paper. I planned to lay it all out for you. It's just that you've been gone so much the last year. You have no idea what the end of the war was like. I was the one taking all the risks."

A deadly light glinted in eyes as dark as jet. It was all starting to unravel. "What about Laurel Wentworth?"

"I gave you Brady's message," Chandler stammered, running his fingers nervously through his hair.

"You gave me part of the message. You neglected to tell me she refused to give Bodine any information. I suppose I played into that. If your men hadn't been caught at the warehouse, and if Brady hadn't come back to tell me what he knew, it would have worked."

Opening the side drawer, Ruel pulled out a pistol. He laid it on top of the desk.

"You made one big mistake," he continued.

Chandler's eyes were fastened on the pistol. In the sudden silence, he raised his gaze.

"You misjudged Brady." Ruel added.

"I didn't misjudge him," Chandler snarled, shoving aside the chair and leaning across the desk. "Every man has his price. It's just a matter of finding it."

"There's no price you can put on a life, Chandler."

"What are you talkin' about?"

"You didn't know your man. There's something Brady values beyond a few gold coins. He likes living. He figures if he can keep from getting himself killed, he'll be able to cheat a few more coins out of the next guy who comes along. And he knows I'd kill him if he ever lied to me." Ruel caught the slight flexing of Chandler's fingers, the way he glanced down at the pistol.

"I know you carry a revolver inside your coat. I'm a gambling man." Ruel's smile was cold, deadly as he continued.

"Tell you what. I'll leave the pistol on the desk. You draw from where you're standing."

Chandler laughed bitterly. "You're a fool, Delaney. You'll be dead before you reach across the desk."

"Maybe," Ruel drawled, throwing the fragrant cigarette into the brass spittoon beside the desk. "Or maybe you'll be dead before you reach inside your coat. The question is, are you a gambling man?"

The roar of a single blast shattered the early morning quiet and startled the customers who liked to gamble early at The House of the Rising Sun.

6

SAN FRANCISCO

Laurel bit at her lip she shot a glance at Jess's reflection in the full-length mirror.

"Let me help you." Jess rose from the straight-backed rocker near the window and came to assist Laurel. Brushing her cousin's nervous hands aside, she tied the narrow silk ribbon on Laurel's collar with deft fingers.

"Your hands are cold as ice, and all of San Francisco is suffering a heat spell."

"I never could tie those things. How can anyone be expected to? You can't see them. And when you use a mirror, everything is backward." Laurel released a sigh of frustration. She caught the humor in Jess's eyes as she gave the bow a final inspection.

"Maybe I am just a little nervous."

"Maybe." Jess's mouth twitched with the strain of holding back laughter.

Then they both burst out laughing at the ridiculousness of two grown women struggling to tie a silk ribbon.

"Are you certain you don't want me to come with you?" Jess asked.

Laurel seized her hands and squeezed them gently.

"Through all of this, you've been more than a sister to me. It means so much, but I want to do this alone."

"All right. I understand. Andrew said he would drop you off on his way to the office. We'll all meet for luncheon afterward."

"I'd like that." Laurel pressed a kiss against Jess's cheek. Already a slight roundness could be detected beneath her more confining gowns, and for comfort she'd taken to wearing the Empire styles she'd purchased in New Orleans.

Andrew was waiting patiently when Laurel descended the staircase of the house he'd rented in South Park.

The main offices of Wentworth Shipping were located on Sacramento Street, with the warehouses situated down on Long Wharf where they'd docked over a month before. But Laurel was going to the offices of Hiram Turnbull, her father's attorney.

He'd been called down to Monterey just after their arrival from Panama and had just returned. The day before he'd sent a messenger to advise Laurel that he'd be free to meet with her promptly at ten o'clock this morning.

Since she'd gotten that note, Laurel had tried to reassure herself about this meeting. It was important to her, so important she'd lain awake practically the entire night going over all the questions she wanted to ask Turnbull about a man she'd never known.

Now, she sat beside Andrew in the carriage, twisting and knotting the linen handkerchief Jess had reminded her to take with her.

"Relax." Andrew patted her hand comfortingly. "Everything will go well. I can still accompany you if you like. It would be easy enough to rearrange my morning appointments."

"No," Laurel flashed him a grateful smile. "I would like to meet with Mr. Turnbull by myself. There's so much I want to ask him about my father."

"Laurel, you must bear in mind that there might be little he can tell you. Jason Cameron seems to be a man with a shadowy past."

"Shadowy?" She thought the word an odd choice.

True, she knew nothing about her father, but that wasn't her father's fault. No, 'shadowy' wasn't the word she'd have used to describe Jason Cameron. It brought all sorts of possibilities to mind. It suggested an illegal, secretive past. That sort of image suited someone else she knew—Ruel Delaney.

In the weeks since they'd left New Orleans, she fought to forget her humiliating last meeting with him. No, *shadowy* wasn't the word to describe her father. It was appropriate for a cad, a criminal... A scoundrel!

"Here we are," Andrew announced.

He stepped out first, extending a hand to her. Laurel hesitated, letting her gaze sweep the impressive two-story building that housed Turnbull and Associates. The name of the firm was neatly lettered in brass to the left of the main entrance. Taking a firm, grip on herself, she extended her hand and stepped down.

"You're certain?"

Laurel stopped Andrew with a quick kiss on the cheek.

"Absolutely positive. I'll send word to your office when the meeting's over."

Andrew took her hands in his. For a moment they seemed to have stepped back in time. He had caught her at some prank and was attempting to explain the consequences to her.

What were the consequences now? Laurel thought, as she squeezed his hands.

Waving briefly at the departing carriage, she turned and entered the office of Mr. Turnbull.

She squinted in the cool, dim light of the musty outer office, her eyes adjusting slowly to the light that came through the paned windows along the east wall. A cheery, feminine voice reached her, just before a smiling, primly dressed, middle-aged woman rose from behind a mahogany desk.

"Good morning. May I be of some help to you?" the woman asked.

"I have an appointment with Mr. Turnbull. My name is..."

"Good heavens!" the woman remarked, her gaze sweeping the young woman before her. She blinked uncertainly, then looked bemused and coughed nervously behind her hand.

"I beg your pardon. It's just that for a moment..." She peered at Laurel again, more discreetly, and then as if suddenly remembering her position, she straightened and motioned Laurel to follow her.

"I didn't mean to frighten you." Laurel wasn't certain why she was apologizing.

"It's not that." The woman gave her an odd smile. "For a moment, you reminded me of someone else."

She preceded Laurel through, the double doors that opened into a massive office filled with row upon row of desks and chairs. Behind each desk a man was poring over papers, and along the entire west wall of the room were glass-enclosed bookshelves. At the far end of the room, a young man dangled precariously from a ladder that had wheels at its base. Replacing a volume, he pulled himself along, the wheels riding on the narrow track that ran the length of the bookshelves. When he'd reached the location, he desired he stopped and climbed a few feet higher to select a book.

"Bascomb, this young lady has an appointment," the woman said to the balding young man seated at the front desk. In response to his quizzical expression, she turned back to Laurel:

"I'm sorry, I didn't get your name."

Laurel emerged from the shadows in which she'd stood in awe of the impressive law offices.

"Laurel Wentworth. I have a ten o'clock appointment with Mr. Turnbull."

The young man adjusted horn-rimmed glasses across the bridge of his rather long nose. They seemed to fit perfectly in a dip just behind a large bump.

Laurel remembered that Andrew had once broken his nose in a fight with Jonathan Parker. In the studious quiet of the office, she found herself wondering whether, this young man's nose had also been broken.

He certainly didn't seem the type who would fight. He looked like an officious little mouse sitting behind a too-large desk. He folded the papers before him as if he were gathering in a prized chunk of cheese. Even the small, straggly mustache resembled a rodent's whiskers when it twitched as if he'd just caught the scent of a cat.

"Wentworth, Wentworth... Ah yes, here it is." He scanned the calendar in front of him. Then with a self-satisfied nod he gave her a smile. The smile and the whiskers drooped as his mouth fell open.

"Good heavens! I mean... Oh, my, Miss Wentworth?"

"Yes." He was staring at her with the same incredulous expression the woman had given her only moments before. She wondered if she'd suddenly sprouted another head, so odd was his manner.

"I do apologize," he stammered.

Maybe Andrew was right. Maybe she should have allowed him to come with her. So far, she managed to elicit a "*Good heavens*" and a "*Good God!*"

She hoped this wasn't an indication of the response she'd receive from Mr. Turnbull.

Since it was obvious that both the woman and the young law clerk had taken leave of their faculties, Laurel decided it was better to take matters into her own hands.

"Please inform Mr. Turnbull that I'm here, I would like to see him immediately."

"Miss Wentworth?"

Laurel turned as her name echoed across the vast expanse of the office.

As if they were all joined by an invisible cord that someone had pulled, those seated in the office suddenly looked up and all eyes locked on the short, wiry-haired man at the far end of the office.

"Please come on back to my office, Miss Wentworth." Meeting her halfway down the aisle that divided the two halves of the large office, Hiram Turnbull reached for her hand and cordially escorted her into the cavernous room from which he'd emerged. Clearing his throat, he then turned back to the those that still gawked and stared.

"I'm certain, gentlemen, you can find something to occupy your attention. But if you lack work, I most assuredly will find something for you to do."

Papers rustled and chairs scraped against hardwood floors as the clerks returned to the matters at hand. Hiram Turnbull motioned Laurel into his private office.

"I apologize for my staff. I'm afraid their work is a bit tedious, and a distraction as lovely as you is quite rare." Mr. Turnbull looked at her thoughtfully for a moment as he rounded his massive desk.

"May I offer you coffee, or perhaps tea?"

Laurel smiled graciously. "No, thank you. I would like to get to the matter at hand." When he continued to watch her with unusual attention, she paused.

"Mr. Turnbull?" First the secretary, then Mr. Mouse outside, and now Mr. Turnbull. Why was everyone staring at her?

"Forgive me. It's just that you bear an uncanny resemblance to... Well, there will be time enough for that later. I understand your eagerness to learn more about the letter I sent you, but I must confess, after all these years I didn't really expect a response."

"Mr. Turnbull, until I received your letter over three months ago, I had no idea my father had been alive all these years. I was told... I was allowed to believe he died when I was only a baby." Laurel began slowly.

How could she possibly explain the parents her childish imagination had invented and loved? The images that had been fed by lies. She wasn't bitter, she understood her aunt and uncle had reasons for keeping the truth from her. But she regretted not knowing her father had tried to contact her while he'd lived. It was sad that in death the contact she'd hoped for had finally happened.

"I understand this must be very difficult for you." Hiram Turnbull coughed nervously. He rounded the desk, poured a glass of water, and handed it to his client.

He knew her history. When the letters he'd continued to send for Jason Cameron had been returned unopened, he'd begun to think Cameron's daughter had as much substance as his dreams of a strike in the Comstock Lode. Now, this young woman sat before him.

Laurel smiled at him. She hadn't cried when she'd received that black-bordered envelope from Mr. Turnbull's office, and she wouldn't cry now. A great deal of time had been lost. She would never have the opportunity to know her father, but she could know the man that he was.

"I want to know everything about Jason Cameron."

"Dear child, I wish I could tell you. For years he was my client, but I can't really say I knew the man."

Noting Laurel's puzzled expression, he continued. "Years ago, your father bought a modest house here in San Francisco, but he was rarely there. His dreams, his hopes were in the gold hills. That was what brought him and your mother here during the strike of forty-nine.

"Many fortunes were made. And eventually, Jason did well. He wasn't rich, but he could support himself. Then he and another group of miners moved up to the Comstock."

He drew a map from a desk drawer. Spreading it out, he indicated California and the neighboring area of Nevada, then pointed to the star marking Virginia City.

"The first substantial silver strike occurred here, on Sun Mountain. Most of the big gold mines were already played out by then. As soon as Jason got word of this new strike, he packed up and left for Virginia City. Before I knew it, he'd filed assay reports on a piece of dirt he'd purchased.

"He contacted me and had me draw up all the legal documents," he continued. "I saw him only once after that. He came back to San Francisco about eight years ago. That's when he bought the house. He didn't stay more than two or three weeks, and early in January I received word that he'd died up on that mountain of his, mining his claim, the Rebecca."

"The Rebecca?" Laurel's eyes widened. He'd named the mine for her mother!

Mr. Turnbull sat on the corner of the desk, his wiry gray hair fringing his balding head like a bristle brush.

His eyes were kind, and the smile beneath the sweep of his mustache, also liberally streaked with gray, was genuine.

"I know very little about the details of your parents' marriage. I only know that your father must have loved your mother very much. He spent a great deal of money trying to find both of you. He once told me it was the only thing that mattered to him—he wanted to have his family together again. The most difficult thing I ever had to do was tell him about your mother's death. For a long time, he blamed your uncle. The reasons aren't clear. Jason wasn't the sort of man who discussed personal matters. I only know, her death was the hardest thing he ever faced."

"Did he tell you anything about her?" Laurel asked.

"Very little," he replied. "You probably know more about her from your aunt and uncle."

Laurel's shoulders sagged. She'd hoped for so much and learned so little.

"I know how disappointed you must be. But please believe your trip is not wasted. Jason provided for you, though the circumstances are a little different than usual."

"What do you mean?" she asked.

"Jason Cameron had no will. Instead, he executed two contracts. On his instruction, I was to carry out the instructions of those contracts. I assure you, it's all quite legal."

"You mentioned two contracts?" Laurel was beginning to feel there was something he hadn't mentioned.

"Yes." Turnbull released a slow, measured breath as he chose his words very carefully. He realized his young client had experienced quite a surprise upon learning that her father had been alive until six months ago. But this...

"I'm not quite sure how to tell you this," he began.

Laurel gave him a confident smile. "I assure you I'm not weak kneed, or given to hysterics or swooning. I've traveled over three thousand miles in the hope of learning about my father. Whatever you have to say, I assure you I want to hear it."

Turnbull took the chair behind his desk and contemplated Laurel Wentworth. She was the same, hauntingly the same, and yet different.

He'd noticed it the moment she'd swept into his office with the quiet, yet elegant bearing of a lady, and a very determined young lady at that.

Resting his hands on the arms of the chair he decided the best approach was a direct one. And an important issue had been avoided for far too long.

"There is another matter you must be made aware of." He hesitated, making certain he had her full attention.

"If your uncle had allowed you to see the letters your father sent over the years, there would be no need for this. As it is ..."

He often had a difficult task where a client was concerned, but this one was most unusual.

"When your uncle arrived in California to take your mother back to Boston, he found the two of you in a small cabin outside of Sacramento," he began with what he knew.

"What he didn't find, and probably never knew was that you had a sister." He paused, watching Laurel for any sign that she already knew of this. There was none, only the slow fading of her smile into an expression of complete surprise.

"Sister?" Laurel struggled with the idea as the word came haltingly.

"I think it's an easy assumption that, had your uncle known, he'd have taken her back to Boston as well. At the time, your mother was very ill. Delia, your sister, was with a friend of your mother's to keep her from contracting the fever that she had come down with. That's as much as I know.

"Jason never saw a need to tell me anything more. She was the reason he bought the house here in San Francisco. He didn't think a mining town was the proper place for a young girl to grow up."

"Delia?" Laurel whispered, struggling to understand.

Hiram Turnbull leaned forward in his chair, watching her carefully. "I know this has been quite a shock."

Laurel rose. She paced the width of the office, trying to sort out her jumbled thoughts. A sister! She had a sister! It was incredible.

"Is my... Is she here in San Francisco? Does she know about me?" Laurel's disappointment vanished. Her father was gone, lost without her ever having known him. But Delia had known Jason Cameron. There was so much she'd be able to tell Laurel about him.

Her reaction was hardly what Hiram Turnbull had expected. Surprise? Yes. Perhaps even anger. But what he saw in the expression at her face was excitement.

"She knows. She's had a bit of an advantage. Delia's known for some time that you existed."

"Known for some time? And she never tried to contact me?"

Turnbull coughed uncomfortably.

"When I received word about Jason's death, I contacted Delia regarding the second contract I mentioned to you."

At Laurel's puzzled expression he realized she hadn't been the least interested in the contract or in its importance to her. Such a difference. She'd come hoping to learn about the father she'd never known. In that he'd had to disappoint her. Now, he feared her sister would be an even greater disappointment.

Laurel's brilliant blue eyes sparkled with excitement and color spread across her cheeks. Turnbull hadn't the heart to tell her everything just then. If he knew Delia Cameron at all, she'd find out the truth soon enough.

"One contract made Delia a gift of fifteen thousand dollars and it turned over the title to the San Francisco house to her," he went on to explain. "The second contract, the one in your name ..." He hesitated, not at all certain how this beautiful, refined young lady was going to respond to what he was about to tell her.

"Jason left you sole title to the Rebecca."

Laurel stared at him—the Rebecca. A silver mine?

"I don't understand."

"I assure you I'm not at all certain I understand either. But those were his wishes."

How could he tell her that he thought the entire arrangement completely unfair? To do so would have been a flagrant violation of his obligation to Jason Cameron.

Delia had been absolutely jubilant over the turn of events. She had calmly proclaimed that day in his office nearly six months earlier, that she hadn't thought old Jason had anything of value, and she certainty wasn't interested in a "*worthless*" mining claim. At the time he'd been inclined to agree with her. But looking at Laurel, he realized she was hardly disappointed.

"Mr. Turnbull, I never knew my father. I can't pretend to understand his decision. The only reason I came to San Francisco was to learn what I could about him, yet I find I know even less than when I left Boston. What I have learned is that he must have loved my mother very much. Please tell me about the Rebecca."

For the next hour Hiram Turnbull pulled out maps, assay reports, and the few letters Jason had sent over the last ten years. They provided a scant profile of a man's elusive dream. That dream had become his legacy—the Rebecca.

Laurel wearily sat back in the chair as the clock struck the noon hour. Her head was swimming with facts and figures, none very hopeful, yet none dismally disappointing. Jason Cameron had spent the last ten years of his life living a dream. She had a sister. She also had an unproven silver mine.

"May I offer you luncheon, Miss Wentworth?" Turnbull rested his hands thoughtfully on his desk. He hoped she would agree to join him. She was beautiful, poised, and intelligent. The questions she'd asked during the last hour showed a keen grasp of figures and terminology that were completely foreign to her. If her startling beauty and striking features hadn't been sufficient evidence of her heritage, that alone would have convinced him that she was Jason Cameron's daughter.

"Thank you. I'm joining my cousins for lunch," Laurel announced as she rose from her chair.

She needed time to think, to absorb everything she'd learned over the last two hours.

"I'd like to see my... sister." She hesitated, savoring the word. It sounded strange, yet oddly comforting. She actually had family! Not just the memories of her aunt and uncle, but family... a sister!

Hiram Turnbull frowned. There was no avoiding the

moment. Sighing heavily, he opened a bound ledger, copied an address on a piece of paper, and handed it to Laurel.

"This is the last address I have for Delia. Right after your father's death, she left for New York. I'd heard, unofficially, that she was back in San Francisco. But I've had no contact with her." Coming round the desk he seized Laurel's hands in both of his.

"Miss Wentworth, a word of caution. Delia is... quite different from yourself. Her younger years were spent in a series of gold camps. It was a meager existence. I suppose she naturally felt some..." he searched carefully for the correct word..." *resentment* of your father for all the time he spent away working the mine."

She had noticed Mr. Turnbull's hesitation more than once. What was it he was trying to say?

"Surely she can tell me about our father," Laurel began enthusiastically.

"If you should decide to go to Virginia City, you'll find a man who might be able to tell you more about Jason. His name is Cappy Burnett. He and your father were partners in another mine near the Rebecca. They knew each other for years, since the first gold camp on the Sacramento. Cappy knew Rebecca too. It's not an easy journey, but I have associates there and from time to time I make the trip myself. As a matter of fact, I'll be leaving again next Tuesday. I'd be more than happy for you to accompany me. It would give you a chance to see the mine."

Laurel smiled. "Thank you. You've been a great help to me. I'll let you know my decision." Extending her hand, Laurel bid him good day.

"Sister! My God, I had no idea." Andrew's amazement confirmed what Laurel had suspected. Neither Andrew nor her aunt and uncle had known of it.

"She's lived here in San Francisco for the past several years. Evidently my father thought it better for her than a mining camp."

"And a silver mine!" He shook his head in disbelief, no longer interested in the food the waiter had set before him.

"An unproven silver mine," Lauren added. "There are assay reports but the most recent is more than ten years old. There's nothing to prove that it's worth anything."

Andrew reached across the table and took her hand. "I know you're disappointed in not learning more about Jason. I'm sorry Mr. Turnbull knew so little about him. It seems Father may have been right about your making this trip."

"Oh no," she exclaimed. "Don't you see? Mr. Turnbull may not have been able to tell me very much about my father, but if I hadn't made this trip I'd never have known about my sister. She's alive, and probably here in San Francisco. It's so much more than I expected."

Laurel was too excited to pay much attention to the food spread before her, but Jess was not distracted. She savored another bite. During these weeks in San Francisco, she'd rapidly made up for her loss of appetite at sea.

"When are you going to see her?" Jess set down her fork and fixed her eyes on Laurel.

She knew how much this trip had meant to her. Now it seemed Laurel would learn something about her father, finding out she had a sister was an entirely different matter.

"I have her last address. She left for New York several months ago, after learning about Father's death. It seems she's an actress. I just don't understand why Uncle Edwin never mentioned Delia. Surely mother must have written about her."

Andrew squeezed her hand reassuringly. "There's so much we don't know about those early years. Father certainly had no reason to keep this from you."

"He had no reason to keep from me the fact that my father

was alive all these years. Unless he was afraid, I might want to come to California." Laurel fastened compelling dark blue eyes on her cousin.

"If the decision had been mine there'd never have been any question about your coming with us to San Francisco. Tomorrow we'll take the carriage and find that address. Perhaps a landlady or a neighbor can tell us when she'll be back. Now, ladies, I have to return to the office. I'll tell the driver to take you back to the house. Remember, I'm escorting you both to the theater this evening."

"And we're dining afterward at Baldwin's," Jess reminded him.

"Baldwin's, of course." He bent over and pressed a kiss against his wife's forehead as he rose to leave. He turned to Laurel.

"All she can think about these days is food. I wouldn't be at all surprised if she has twins."

Jess gave her husband a withering glare that quickly turned into a loving pout as he disappeared out the door of the restaurant.

LAUREL TIED the wide sash at the back of Jessica's Empire gown. Glowing with good health and a new softness, Jess was radiant.

"I don't know why you didn't want to wear the blue velvet. It's absolutely breathtaking on you. And Baldwin's is the most fashionable restaurant in San Francisco. I understand all the most important gentlemen dine there. Andrew mentioned that John MacKay is a regular customer. He has his own table. It's reserved every evening."

"I'm beginning to think you're trying to marry me off!" Laurel laughed, carefully sidestepping the issue of the blue velvet.

How could she possibly explain that it had been torn by Ruel Delaney that last night in New Orleans? Even now the gown lay carefully folded inside the matching stole at the bottom of her trunk. She dared not even unpack it for fear Jess would see the damage.

"John MacKay might not be available, but I hear he has a circle of wealthy and influential friends. They've all made millions in the Comstock." Whirling about, her eyes sparkling with a sudden idea, Jess seized Laurel's hands.

"Maybe your mine's worth a fortune. Wouldn't that be wonderful?"

"I sincerely doubt there's a fortune in the Rebecca. If there was, my father would have found it years ago. From what Mr. Turnbull told me, except for the house my father bought for Delia, he lived the life of a penniless recluse the last years."

"What are you going to do with the mine?"

"I haven't decided." A mischievous gleam sprung into the depths of her sapphire eyes. "I may work it myself."

They both dissolved into fits of laughter, their merriment covering the momentary seriousness that filled Laurel's eyes.

The dress Laurel had chosen to wear that evening held no memories for her, except perhaps of the afternoon when she'd selected the fabric and the design in Juliette's small shop in New Orleans.

As she slipped into the pale blue silk, Ruel's words washed back over her—"*you should always wear blue.*"

Now, she stared at her reflection, searching the face that stared back at her, looking for some outward sign of change. There was none.

The face was the same, if a bit thin. Her high cheekbones, more clearly defined now, and emphasized her eyes. She drew the cap sleeves over her shoulders, then reached to fasten the hooks of the bodice, adjusting the neckline that allowed ample exposure of her breasts. She inhaled sharply. She could almost feel his hands, the taste his mouth on hers. Closing her eyes, she fought the unwanted feelings inside her.

Jerking at the pale blue fabric, she forced those thoughts from her mind. There was no point in dwelling on things that should never have happened. If she'd learned one thing about Ruel Delaney, it was that he was a man of few virtues. And she was absolutely certain regret wasn't among them.

7

L aurel rose early the following morning. She'd slept little the night before. Having returned late after an evening at the theater followed by dinner at Baldwin's, the restaurant in the hotel built by Lucky Baldwin, a man of scandalous reputation, she'd pondered Hiram Turnbull's revelation that she had a sister.

For some time after the downstairs clock had chimed four in the morning, she had still been awake, so she'd decided to go to the address the attorney had given her as soon as possible.

Now, she sat before the rosewood dressing table. There were faint circles beneath her eyes from lack of sleep, but there was nothing to be done for them except to apply a little tinted face powder.

The gown she'd carefully selected was a soft shade of lilac. It had black lace trimming on the bodice, sleeves, and skirt; and black braid accented the hem. The sleeves were decorated with small black rosettes. The pleated skirt panel that ran from waist to hem at the front was trimmed in black satin. At the high neck and at each wrist was a frill of white lace. As was the recent fashion the skirt was full so it would allow for the stiff crinolines.

Laurel had chosen the gown for its simplicity. Although she knew her sister had inherited a substantial sum of money, she had no idea what Delia's exact financial situation might be, and she didn't want to give offense when they met... if they met.

Hiram Turnbull had mentioned that Delia had returned to San Francisco, but he had no further contact with her after their father's death.

Jason Cameron. It was the name of a man who'd lived and loved and dreamed. A miner. According to many, a ne'er-do-well who'd chased elusive fortunes at his family's expense.

The name didn't yet match the image she'd carried in her head an entire lifetime. There were still too many gaps in the details of his life. She knew only the stories told by her uncle and his attorney. The essence of the man still eluded her. Until she learned more about him, she would never be satisfied.

Delia could help her. She'd be able to fill in some of the missing pieces, to answer questions Laurel had from childhood.

She laid down the hairbrush, listening as the downstairs clock chimed ten o'clock.

It was Andrew's custom to leave early enough to arrive at his office promptly at eight-thirty. In spite of the late hours, he'd kept the preceding night, he'd followed his usual custom, leaving the house quietly. Jess, she knew, would still be sleeping. At this hour only the maid, Tilly, a sweet-faced Irish girl, and the housekeeper, Mrs. Handley, would be in the house. Neither would question her leaving at such an early hour.

She slipped quietly down the angled staircase, treading softly. Tilly was nowhere to be seen, but she heard Mrs. Handley busily humming to herself as she disappeared into the kitchen.

Seizing the black, lace trimmed parasol from the hall tree, Laurel quickly stepped out into the bright morning sunlight, closing the door quietly behind her. The decision to visit her sister alone hadn't been a conscious one, but as the previous evening had progressed, she'd been subtly aware of Andrew's disapproval, though he'd kept his misgivings to himself. Nonetheless, this was a matter she wanted to handle herself. She'd come a long way and wasn't about to be put off now.

The morning sky was an exotic shade of robin's egg blue, and a crisp fresh breeze swept off the bay. The house they occupied was situated on a hill, and below it, Laurel could see a maze of cobbled streets lined with shade trees.

Most of the houses were clapboard, but occasionally there was a red brick. All were built straight up and had narrow facades. She smiled as she adjusted the parasol, remembering Jess's words of the day before about the heat wave. The mornings were fog-shrouded until this time of the day when the breeze drove away the fog.

The day before the temperatures had soared. The humidity that accompanied such a temperature in New Orleans would have left clothes damp and clinging. But here, the morning and afternoon breezes were cooling and refreshing. Laurel loved San Francisco.

Hailing a public carriage at the corner, she gave the driver the address Hiram Turnbull had provided the day before. Then, seeing the driver's hesitation, she leaned forward in the seat.

"You are familiar with the address?" she asked.

"Oh yes, miss," he assured her. "It's just that..."

"What is it?"

"Well, I just thought... you being a lady of quality and all. Well, you see ..."

"Yes?"

"I just thought you might want an escort. That's all."

She gave him a reassuring smile. "It's quite all right. My sister lives at that address. Please drive on."

The ride across town took little more than half an hour. Her driver had taken the self-appointed task of tour guide, and was pointing out one building after another, that included the Crocker mansion that occupied the entire block of Nob Hill bounded by California, Jones, Sacramento, and Taylor streets.

Boston had many lavish residences, some more than one hundred years old. But for size none of them could rival the Crocker home. She recalled Andrew mentioning Charles Crocker the evening before over dinner. He'd said Crocker and several other prominent San Francisco residents were backing the construction of the western portion of the transcontinental railroad.

She thought of the weeks of ocean travel she'd endured, not to mention the four-day trek across Panama and she silently applauded the man's ambition. It was predicted that in less than a year the railroad would be completed. Already massive construction crews were working round the clock, laying down miles of track every day.

As they rounded the corner of Sacramento Street, Laurel realized they would be passing very near Andrew's office. She pushed aside a twinge of misgiving at her decision. Andrew knew her better than anyone. Surely, he wouldn't fault her in this. Her carriage passed a streetcar drawn by horses along tracks that angled down one busy street and then climbed another.

The buildings in this area were impressive as any in New England. But it was the streets that fascinated Laurel. Andrew had explained that the city had been built on a series of hills that rose sharply from the harbor when San Francisco was established as a major Pacific seaport.

In the downtown district the driver followed Market Street, turned down a side street, then turned again, onto O'Farrell. He reined the horses in before an impressive four-story brick building. The gleaming wood sign to the side of the entrance, in gold block letters, proclaimed this the *Golden Empress, Private Club*.

The building's facade was understated elegance, causing Laurel to wonder what sort of private club this was. Thinking the driver might have made a mistake, she leaned forward.

The driver shifted uncomfortably in his seat, anticipating her question. "One hundred forty-three O'Farrell, miss. Just as you said." He pointed to the gold numbers and letters beneath the club's sign.

Stepping down from his seat, he offered Laurel his hand. "Would you like for me to wait, miss?"

She gathered up her skirts and alighted from the carriage, her gaze fastened on the building. Dozens of questions raced through her mind.

Private club? Perhaps it was some sort of home for young ladies. But why had her sister chosen to live here when Jason had bought her a house?

She shook her head, reached inside her reticule so she might pay the driver. She missed the uncertain expression on the man's face. Having paid him, she turned toward the entrance to the club. If her sister wasn't here, someone might be able to provide information about her.

The massive wooden double doors opened into an elegant, long foyer. Its crimson carpeting was the finest she'd ever seen. Surprisingly, this area was flooded with light, and Laurel's gaze was immediately drawn upward to the source.

Six stories overhead, a massive glass dome revealed the brilliant morning sky. At the back of the large foyer was a wide mezzanine enclosed by a half-railing over which the fronds of several lush ferns were draped. A huge, gilt-framed mirror ran the length of one wall, and before it stood a long, narrow, mahogany table.

At each end of the table and in its center stood a cut-crystal vase filled with freshly cut flowers, a decidedly feminine touch in an otherwise masculine room. Beyond the table were double doors, closed. Obviously, they led to the rooms beyond. Opposite the table and the mirrored wall were two pairs of double doors. One set was closed, the other stood open. Through the opening, Laurel could hear the tinkling of glass and muted conversation. Realizing she'd been standing in the foyer for several minutes and no one had come to greet her, she headed toward the sounds.

As she descended three steps, Laurel's gaze widened. She had entered a massive room with gleaming wood wainscoting. Several tables were set about it, each draped with spotless table linen. The wall coverings, of brilliant blue silk, were highlighted by gaslights gleaming from crystal globes.

"May I help you, miss?"

She turned. "Are you the owner?"

"I'm the manager. We're not open for business at this time of day, as you can see." He made a sweeping gesture with his hand, and at that moment an impeccably dressed Chinese man entered, carrying a silver tray laden with crystal stemware.

"Oh, I'm not here to ..." Laurel couldn't think of an appropriate word. She wasn't here as a customer, and she wasn't exactly certain what sort of establishment this was.

"I'm looking for someone. I've been told she lives here, although I really think there must have been some mistake." Laurel gave the young man an uncertain smile.

He extended his hand. "I'm John Palmer. Perhaps I can help you locate your friend." He watched her carefully.

Laurel drew her hand back. He seemed kind enough. His manners were impeccable, as were his garments. His stylish dress coat was black, as were his trousers. A starched, white shirt, a black satin vest, and a bow tie completed his attire. It might have been a bit elegant for midmorning, but it seemed appropriate in the elegant room. He was a short man, barely taller than Laurel, but he moved with confidence.

"I was told that my sister lived here, but there must have been a mistake about the street number. I'm sorry to have bothered you."

"Not at all." John quickly stepped in front of Laurel. "It's been no bother. I am new here. I've only been in San Francisco for three months, but the owner has lived here for some time. He might be able to assist you."

"I would appreciate any help you could offer."

"If you'll wait just a moment, I'll see if he's in his office."

"Thank you."

Mr. Palmer left the room, and within moments he returned.

"He'll see you now. Perhaps he can give you more information about your sister." Leading the way through the doors, he preceded Laurel into a large office.

Light filtered through leaded glass panels that faced onto a courtyard, and from beneath a green glass shade, a lamp glowed down onto the desk on which several ledgers lay open. The chair behind the massive desk was pushed back.

"This is the young woman I told you about."

A long shadow separated itself from the others, and the man moved along the shelves of books lining a wall. Half-hidden in the muted light, he waved his manager from the room.

Moments passed as Laurel waited for the owner of the Golden Empress to acknowledge her. Finally, she could stand the delay no longer.

"I don't wish to intrude. Actually, I think there must be some mistake ..." Laurel hesitated, for a moment uncertain whether there was anyone else in the room.

At the sound of her voice, the man's head snapped up from the volume he'd been perusing. He turned slowly, his eyes fastened on her.

"What are you doing here?"

An uneasy chill slipped down Laurel's spine. "I... I'm looking for my sister."

Hearing an audible intake of breath, Laurel felt her color rise. The owner of the Golden Empress had a decided advantage.

"As I told Mr. Palmer, I must have been given the wrong address." The one-sided conversation made Laurel feel awkward.

"My father's attorney said I might find my sister here. This was the last address he had for her."

Even as he came to stand behind the desk in the light cast through the windows, other shadows seemed to move with him.

He was dressed all in black, except for the gleaming contrast of his white shirt. But it wasn't his attire that caused Laurel's breath to catch in her throat. She stared disbelieving at a lean angular jaw, dark skin warmed by the sun, wavy black hair, and equally dark eyes.

Impossible! Choking back a strangled gasp, she turned to leave.

"Laurel, wait!"

JOHN PALMER quickly strode across the gaming room, cutting off the woman in the crimson silk gown, her head shot up and she met his gaze. Her wide-brimmed hat only partially concealed her titian hair.

"I'm sorry you can't go in there. Mr. Delaney has someone in his office."

Eyes the color of ice bore into his. "And just who might you be?"

"John Palmer, manager of the Golden Empress," he introduced himself. It was amazing. No, it was unbelievable. The resemblance...

A slow, self-satisfied smile dimpled the woman's cheek. "We haven't met." A sultry purr replaced the arrogant tone she'd just used.

"You're new." She pushed past him, not the least intimidated.

A hand closed over her wrist and halted her in front of the door to Delaney's office.

"Simon always let me pass. No questions." Her eyes may have been pure ice, but the fire behind them was lethal.

"Perhaps that's why he's no longer manager." Palmer's grasp tightened.

He'd seen many women like her. Some of them worked the upstairs suites of the Empress. But he'd been warned about this one.

There was no mistaking the color of her hair, her style of dress, or those cold eyes. Paddy had given him the details, and Mr. Delaney had left clear instructions. Her reputation had preceded her.

Delia smiled sweetly, then twisted out of his grasp and burst through the closed doors.

"Darling!" she exclaimed.

Two pairs of eyes fastened on her.

"Mr. Delaney, I tried ..." John Palmer raised his hands in a gesture of frustration.

Ruel shook his head. "I'll call if I need you," he said abruptly.

Delia paraded around the room slowly, enjoying her little performance. "Well, well, well, isn't this the most pleasant little reunion?"

Ruel stared at her. It was impossible. Yet, as he stood across the room from both women, he realized it wasn't.

"My God!" Laurel whispered, completely taken aback. The anger that had sent her toward the door a moment before, suddenly drained from her.

"I really think she'll recover after she gets over the initial shock. It is a little disconcerting to meet someone so like oneself."

"Delia?" Laurel asked, her mind struggling to understand.

"It seems that I have the advantage." She pulled off one glove and then another as she crossed the room.

"I seem to be the only one who knows everyone here, except for your manager, of course. Is he new, darling?" Delia wound her way around the desk, then stood in front of Ruel.

After everything that had passed between them, after all the angry words, she knew she was taking a chance. But this entire matter just might work out in her favor if she played things right.

Delia smiled as she looked directly at her sister and tucked her arm through Ruel's.

"Darling, don't be rude," she said. "You seem to be acquainted." Angling her head, she cast him a sideways glance filled with meaning.

"Introduce us. It's so awkward to meet one's sister for the first time."

If any man had described this situation, Delaney would have called him a liar, but the truth was standing before him— two women so incredibly alike they could easily be confused for each other.

"Laurel..."

He tried to imagine what her thoughts must be. Reaching across the desk, he tried to touch her. But she took a step back and the look on her face told him her shock was as great as his.

He recalled their few conversations. She'd been so desperate to reach San Francisco, though she'd given him no reason. Because of the Wentworth name, he'd never made the connection.

That was a mistake, a horrible mistake. From the moment

he'd seen her down in the hold of that ship he'd been certain she *was* Delia Cameron. Because of that...

His hand fell to his side. What comfort could he possibly offer her? How could he explain that he'd caused her pain in order to get at someone else?

When he'd arrived in San Francisco weeks earlier, he'd known they might eventually meet again. He'd planned on it. Now, his stomach muscles knotted at the thought of that last night in New Orleans, the memory of the pain and humiliation in her eyes when he'd left her.

He'd used her badly over a mistake. But he was determined to change that. Something about Laurel Wentworth had burrowed deep inside him and stayed. But now everything had changed. Once Laurel knew about his relationship with Delia, no words or new beginnings would make her trust him. He knew he deserved nothing but her hatred, yet he wanted so much more.

Frowning at the absurdity of it all, Ruel made the formal introductions. It seemed ridiculous, almost laughable, even to him. But he could see the conflicting emotions reflected in her eyes. She'd been given this address and had come looking for her sister, obviously a sister she'd never known. It wasn't in her to be deceptive.

Delia clearly had the advantage, and he was certain she meant to use it. That was why she had come to the Empress in spite of everything that had passed between them. In the years he'd known her, kept her as his mistress, she'd never mentioned one word about having a sister. Clearly Laurel hadn't interested her, until now.

"I came here as soon as I learned of father's death, I'd always believed he died years ago." The pain in Laurel's voice cut through him. Her grieving was so genuine, he wondered how he could have mistaken her for Delia. Their features were the same, but there was a vast difference between the sisters.

"Ah yes, Jason Cameron, our dear, departed father," Delia commented. "What he couldn't accomplish in life; he finally managed in death. At least he did something right, even if it is a bit late. He made several attempts over the years to contact you. I must have been eleven or twelve when I heard the story."

Delia nonchalantly came round to stand before Laurel. "He and mother were living outside of Sacramento in a gold camp when I was taken from him."

"We were born there. In that filthy, wretched place. There was always an epidemic of some kind. It's a wonder anyone survived." Delia had lightened her tone to disguise her contempt.

"Uncle Edwin came from the East to get Mother." Laurel's initial shock was beginning to ease. Now, she stared, fascinated, at her sister. The past night, unable to sleep, she'd imagined their first meeting. Delia Cameron was her sister, a link to a past she'd never known, to a father she'd never met. She supposed it was only natural they were both a bit awkward, but she couldn't shake off the feeling there was more to this.

She sensed that they were all playing at some game. Certainly, Delia's shock was as great as her own, even though she'd had the advantage of prior knowledge, but there was something almost resentful in Delia's manner, some indefinable wariness beneath her smiles. It was in the forced ease of her speech, and in the watchfulness in her eyes.

Uneasy with Laurel's sudden scrutiny, Delia fussed with a strand of reddish hair, then glided across the room.

"It was my misfortune I was gone at the time. It seems you and mother were ill with fever, and Father was afraid I would come down with it, so he'd made arrangements for me to stay with friends of our parents. When he returned one evening, you were gone." Delia sliced the air with a casual wave of her hand.

"All those years I never knew," Laurel whispered.

And I never knew. Dear God, Laurel, I swear, I never knew. Ruel watched her face. Twins. Identical twins. Except for the artificial differences—the abundance of Delia's makeup, the reddish tint to her hair, they were exactly alike.

"You certainly seem to have done quite well for yourself, but I must admit, anything would be preferable to living in a damned gold camp."

"Father bought you a house here in San Francisco," Laurel replied. "I thought this was the address."

"You thought this ...? Good heavens, no!" Delia slowly ran her fingers over an elegant mahogany sideboard.

"But Mr. Turnbull gave this as your address," Laurel replied.

"This was my address before I left for New York, to pursue my acting career." Delia did not bother to explain that failure had sent her back to California, nor did she mention that a prominent New York businessman had died of a heart attack in the midst of one of their meetings at the Dorchester Hotel, at which he'd set her up in a suite of rooms.

For the first time, Laurel dared to glance at Ruel.

Privateer, thief, gambler. Her eyes widened with understanding. Now she knew the exact meaning of the words beneath the name on the sign beside the entrance. She'd heard stories about places like this—gaming halls, more discreetly labeled private clubs. Men went to them for an evening's relaxation, to drink, dine, gamble, and seek out a woman.

That explained the additional floors above the mezzanine. They contained private rooms where a man could purchase the favors of the woman of his choice. Ruel Delaney owned this place, just as he owned the one in New Orleans. She struggled to recall the name Adela MacMillan had whispered with a knowing wink.

Delia smiled. "Good heavens, you don't think that I ...? Sister dear, you've jumped to the wrong conclusion. Ruel and I were business partners in a number of enterprises. I hated that dingy little house, and he was kind enough to offer me the use of one of his private suites. When I decided to pursue my theatrical interests in New York, it just seemed logical to sell the house."

Ruel shot Delia a warning glance. She'd very conveniently omitted telling Laurel the circumstances under which they'd parted almost a year earlier. He wanted to keep it that way. He also wanted to make certain she didn't give her sister any details of their prior relationship.

"It seemed ridiculous to maintain two residences, when I was never home. Oh, dear me, I suppose Ruel hasn't had the time to explain all that to you. He can be such a devil at times."

"Delia!" The warning in Ruel's voice caused both women to look up.

Deciding on a different tactic, Delia smiled. "I just arrived in San Francisco a week ago, on a Wentworth ship of all things! My dear, you are certainly most fortunate to have been raised by our mother's family." She simpered. "The second mate just couldn't take his eyes off me. It seems he'd been on another Wentworth ship that sailed from Boston earlier this spring. He noticed the resemblance between us, and he told me the most fantastic story about how you two met."

When Laurel paled suddenly, Delia knew what she wanted to know. Fighting back a sudden twist of jealousy, she deliberately sweetened her words.

"It's actually quite humorous when you stop to think about it."

Ruel cut her off. "It's none of your business."

"You're right, darling. It's just that I was curious. The poor man went on and on about how you confused Laurel with someone else.

Giving Ruel a knowing glance, Delia smiled. "And you've always been so discreet, darling."

"Enough!" Ruel warned.

Laurel hastened to explain. "That has nothing to do with us. We have so much to talk about. I'd hoped ..."

This wasn't how her first meeting with her sister was supposed to be. Laurel clenched her fists as she struggled to hold onto her composure.

"What had you hoped for?" Delia turned on her. "A loving reunion perhaps? I don't even know you." She ignored Ruel's earlier warning and continued her assault.

"Did you hope to bed her as well?"

Now Laurel understood why Ruel had mistaken her for someone else. Dear God, he and Delia had been lovers!

It was painful to acknowledge, yet true. And she'd been caught up in all of this by a simple mistake aboard the *Waverall*.

The past had left her sister bitter and angry. The love Laurel had hoped for wasn't to be found here.

All her life she'd dreamed of her lost family. In that respect Delia had been the more fortunate one, she'd known their father. Laurel clutched her arms tightly about herself, as if she might squeeze out the pain, and she shivered uncontrollably.

Ruel started across the room, his fury barely suppressed. "Shut your mouth, Delia, or I swear, I'll shut it for you! You've been in the gutter for so long, you don't know anything else."

He'd often thought he'd take great delight in seeing some other emotion in Delia's cold eyes. He wanted to see it there now. She was causing pain. God knows, that was all they'd ever brought each other. Lying and deceit were second nature to her.

He almost laughed recalling that, as she'd swept into the room, he'd been fool enough to think she might have some feeling for Laurel. And she had to be desperate to come back here like this. What the hell was she after? It certainly wasn't sisterly love; she'd done her level best to destroy that.

"Darling, you must learn to get that temper of yours under control. It will get you into trouble someday. Why, I'd almost suspect you're trying to protect her." Delia's eyes glinted maliciously. Have you suddenly developed a preference for virgins? In the past, you would have chosen a woman of experience. You must be very careful with inexperienced lovers. There are those nasty little complications to consider. Of course, there are remedies for such matters." She traced the line of his jaw.

"It's not what you think," Laurel replied. But Delia continued as if she hadn't heard her.

"Poor dear, it must be true. I do hope you made Ruel promise he would accept responsibility for any complications. A woman does have to protect herself. Certainly, you aren't that naive. Although, I suppose only someone naive would come all this way to claim a worthless mine."

She winced as Ruel's hands closed over her arms and forced them away. A vengeful light gleaming in her eyes, she deliberately brushed the curve of her hip against him.

"Actually, I'm quite pleased with my part of the inheritance. It's a lot more than I ever thought old Jason had, and cash is better than some worthless hole in the ground. That, dear sister, is your inheritance." Delia no longer bothered to disguise her contempt.

"I'm sorry you feel that way," Laurel whispered. "I didn't come here because of the inheritance." She bit at her lower lip, drawing on some last measure of strength.

She glanced over at him. She expected to see ridicule, perhaps even disdain, in his dark eyes. Instead, she saw something unreadable, something that seemed to reach out to her.

Delia laughed, a hard, cruel sound. "Our father wasted every penny he ever earned and poured good money into worthless mining claims. He was always searching for a bonanza, always coming up empty-handed! Believe me, you'll be better off if you sell that mine.

"I suppose it's fortunate our mother died when she did. She

didn't have to live through the hell of those filthy mining camps."

"Don't say that! She loved him." Laurel spoke calmly. "She willingly followed him to California, in spite of her family's objections, and she'd never have left if she hadn't been so ill."

"Love? He loved her so much he brought her out here from Boston and then abandoned her in one of those godforsaken camps. Hold onto your illusions, little sister, but I know he killed her just as surely as if he'd held a gun to her head."

Laurel turned on Delia, her shock giving way to anger.

"I don't know why you're so full of bitterness. Right or wrong, at least you knew our father. I never knew either of our parents."

Ruel watched her, fascinated. It wasn't the first time he'd seen it. Courage. That was something Delia couldn't begin to understand because she'd never possessed it.

"I don't even have the luxury of your anger," Laurel told her.

She refused to look at either of them. She felt she was being torn apart. All these years she'd envisioned the parents she'd never known, creating her version of them from things she'd been told. Now what she had imagined was being shattered by Delia's bitterness and anger.

As she turned to leave, Laurel hesitated. "I'm sorry it couldn't be different between us," she said, her eyes were fixed on Delia's, eyes so like her own yet so- different.

The door closed behind her.

"Damn you!" Ruel turned from Delia and started after Laurel.

"Let her go." Delia caught at his arm and gave him a disarming smile. But the coldness in his eyes cut clear through her. She drew back her hand as if she'd touched ice.

"For God's sake, she's your sister. Isn't there one ounce of caring in you?"

Delia glared at him." She's the one who has led a privileged life. Look at the dress she was wearing. Never in my entire life did Jason Cameron see fit to provide me with that kind of gown.

"Care? Why should I? She thinks she missed something in not knowing the old bastard? She's better off not knowing the truth about him."

"You consider yourself an expert on truth?" Ruel's fingers snaked around her wrist.

It would be easy, so easy, to snap her bones. During the war he'd killed a lot of men. It still haunted him. But he'd never killed a woman. At that moment he was tempted. He wasn't about to let Laurel suffer to give Delia satisfaction.

Delia's wild laughter tore through him as he went after Laurel, nearly colliding with John Palmer outside the office.

"Where is she?" Ruel demanded.

"She just left. What the hell is going on?"

"Did she have a carriage?" When John shook his head, Ruel reached inside his vest pocket. He pulled out a handful of one-hundred-dollar bills and he thrust them into his manager's hand.

"Get a carriage! Find her! And make sure she gets home safely." Fear now took over his anger. San Francisco was a raw and wild town, a seaport, and no place for Laurel to be unescorted. There were men who would like nothing better than to find a beautiful young woman alone. Such a prize would command a high price on the white slave market.

"Maybe you should go after her," John suggested. He had overheard the argument, and he knew the young woman, whoever she was, meant a great deal to Ruel Delaney.

"At this moment, I'm the last person she wants to see." Ruel's voice softened. "Make sure nothing happens to her."

John nodded as he headed for the front door of the Golden Empress. He'd known Ruel Delaney a long time. They'd met in prison and had eventually broken out together. Under those circumstances, you never knew when your time might be up and men opened up to each other. But Ruel Delaney hadn't. He could be a cold sonofabitch, ruthless. John had once accused him of having ice in his veins. Yet he asked only for loyalty. He, too, was a man with secrets, with a past he refused to discuss, and it was the first time John had known him to care about anyone.

8

"You 're absolutely certain about your decision?" Hiram Turnbull, Attorney at Law, considered his young client. "I assume you've discussed this with Mr. Wentworth."

Laurel nodded, not wishing to discuss Andrew's reaction.

"I'll trust you to make all the necessary arrangements."

There was a subtle authority about her now, different from the young woman who'd caused such a stir in his offices four days earlier. Turnbull sighed heavily, deeply regretting the offer he'd made. He'd never for a moment considered she might take him up on it.

"Miss Wentworth... Laurel." He smiled gently. "Surely there's no need to make this trip now. Within a few months, a year at the most, the railroad will be completed, and it will be a much easier journey. At best the overland route is nothing more than a wagon road right now."

"I understand your concern, Mr. Turnbull, but you will be making the journey." Laurel wanted to end the conversation. There were more pressing matters to see too. She had to tell Andrew and Jessica about her sudden change in plans.

"If I had any choice in the matter, believe me, I wouldn't be going. But, I have urgent business in Virginia City."

"As do I, Mr. Turnbull," Laurel informed him. Throughout their meeting, she'd had the unsettling feeling that he was trying to dissuade her from going. Now his fingers drummed on the surface of the desk.

"It's just that you have family here, and San Francisco is a beautiful and civilized city. And there's the matter of your sister. You'll want to see her of course."

A frown pulled at the corners of Laurel's mouth as she slipped on her gloves, then rose to leave. She'd chosen not to mention her meeting with Delia. What was there to say? She'd been so hopeful and she had come away painfully disillusioned.

Delia and Ruel Delaney! Her frown deepened. She was tired. She'd slept so little the last few nights. Even upon arising, the weariness had been there, but she'd sent a note round to Mr. Turnbull's office informing him of her desire for a meeting.

"I, too, have business in Virginia City." She smiled faintly. "And there are many things I must see to before we leave." Reaching across the desk, she shook hands with him.

Refusing to relinquish her so easily, he bent from the waist and brushed a kiss across the back of her gloved hand. If he couldn't dissuade her, perhaps he could make the most of this unexpected turn of events.

"If you will not change your mind, then I shall look forward to seeing you again three days from now."

Laurel withdrew her hand. She was already anticipating her conversation with Andrew.

She'd decided to go to Virginia City after that painful meeting with Delia, but she hadn't acted on that decision right away.

Now, walking through the austere outer offices of the law firm, Laurel ignored the stares that followed her. She understood the curiosity that had left poor Mr. Mouse befuddled and confused.

She'd been angry because Hiram Turnbull had failed to mention that she and Delia were identical twins. Of course, he'd had no idea they'd meet under such circumstances, and Laurel didn't intend to reveal they had. It served no purpose.

Clearly, Delia wanted nothing to do with her. Any hope she had of learning about their father was in Nevada. When she got to Virginia City, she'd look for an old miner by the name of Cappy Burnett.

As Laurel stepped out onto Sacramento Street, into bright mid-morning sunlight, she drew a steadying breath. Now, she had to convince Andrew of her decision.

Across the busy street, Ruel Delaney stood before the men's haberdashery. Smoke rose from his thin, black cigarette to encircle his head and then drift on the morning breeze. He waited until Laurel boarded a horse drawn car, then cut through the carriages and wagons that clogged the streets at that time of day. He wasn't interested in new hats or shirts, and he had no need for legal services. He wanted information.

LAUREL PACED her sunlit room for a while, then she helped Jessica arrange the new pieces of furniture that arrived just after lunch. She had sent the girl Tilly to the bottom of the hill to purchase fresh-cut flowers from the vendor who passed that way each afternoon, pushing a hand cart that carried a profusion of brightly colored blossoms. As she arranged and rearranged those flowers in two vases, she had practiced what she would tell Andrew about her decision.

"I do hope you won't be displeased, but I must go to Virginia City." No, that was all wrong. Laurel stuffed a purple iris into a vase that was too short. She began again.

"I realize you will probably be upset with my decision, but I hope you'll understand my reasons for wanting to go to Virginia City." The stem of the iris snapped.

Cutting it above the break, Laurel placed it in the shorter vase. She then stared at her floral arrangement with a critical eye. Jess was far better at this. She simply didn't have the patience for flower arranging or stitchery. And Aunt Cecile had so wanted a daughter accomplished in those skills. However, Jess possessed all the talents required of a proper, young lady. She even played the piano.

Her interest in the flowers waning, Laurel realized she'd be better off allowing Tilly to finish arranging them. No, she thought with sudden determination, I mustn't sound apologetic when I talk with Andrew.

He'd surely know she had doubts about going and would undoubtedly make every objection he could think of. The direct, simple approach was better. She seized another iris. Its blossoms were deep purple, almost black.

Thrusting the iris aside and swearing under her breath, Laurel called Tilly and asked her to finish the task.

By late afternoon, she'd discussed with Mrs. Handley the menu for the evening meal after Jess had begged off to take a nap.

"Andrew, I'm going to Virginia City," she rehearsed as she heard his firm tread in the hallway. Then she fixed a smile on her face and went to greet him.

"You're what?" Andrew's words fairly crackled in the air.

She'd tried to prepare herself for this, but the sleepless nights had worn her down. She jumped as he laid down his knife, the silver clinking against china.

For several moments there was only silence and his disapproving glare, broken only by Mrs. Handley who returned from the kitchen with a water pitcher. He waited until she had gone.

"My father lived and died in Virginia City," she argued.

"Everyone who knew him is there. His attorney could tell me almost nothing about him."

"Laurel, have you thought this through?" Andrew struggled to remain calm. "What about your sister? Surely, you want to contact her."

"I really can't wait. I won't be gone long, just long enough to settle the details about the mine." How could she possibly explain her disastrous meeting with Delia? It would bring too many questions that she wasn't prepared to answer.

"I think Laurel's right."

Surprised and dismayed, Andrew turned to Jessica. Undaunted, Jess pressed ahead.

"She's never known her parents. We can't begin to fully understand the feelings she must have. And she's already come such a long way."

"Which, I might add, she did against my better judgment," Andrew added.

"But you did agree to let her join us." Jess smiled at her husband. "Jason Cameron lived and died in Virginia City. I think it's understandable that Laurel would want to go there. And there is the matter of the mine."

"The sale could be handled very easily from here," he informed them both. "It's done all the time."

"But, until she actually sees the mine, speaks with people who know about these things, how can she know what it should be sold for?"

Laurel was fascinated by Jess's subtle manipulation of her husband. She'd never discussed the Rebecca with her, but Jess had struck on an important reason for her planned trip to Virginia City.

"I suppose this means I'll have to fight both of you if I disagree," Andrew replied.

"Darling, I have no intention of arguing with you. Oh dear!"

Jess exclaimed, her eyes widening as she pressed a hand to the swell of her stomach concealed beneath the folds of her gown.

Andrew was out of his chair in an instant. "What is it?"

Laurel poured a fresh glass of water. Dabbing a dinner napkin in it, she took Jess's hand, then pressed the cooling cloth against her temple.

Jess smiled her gratitude. "I think it was just the excitement. The way this baby moves around, I sometimes think he's turning somersaults, either that or there are two of them in there."

Laurel inhaled sharply at Jess's comment. Twins.

It was a possibility. She'd heard they were born with great frequency in some families.

She smiled sadly, wishing things might have been different for her and her sister. But there was no point in telling either of them about Delia.

"I'm much better now. Thank you." Jess squeezed Laurel's hand.

"There'll be no further discussion about Laurel's trip to Virginia City. It's obviously too upsetting for you." Andrew kept a watchful eye on his wife as he returned to his chair.

"I quite agree, there'll be no further discussion," Jess happily announced. "The only distressful part was your arguing with her about it. There, it's all settled. In the morning, we can begin to pack. I'll supervise."

Andrew's fork clattered onto his plate. He'd been outmaneuvered and hadn't even seen it coming. Now, by his own words, there'd be no further discussion of the matter. His eyes narrowed as he caught the fleeting glance that passed between Laurel and Jessica. He shook his head. The man who'd said a man's home was his castle and he was king of his domain, had failed to mention the power of the queen.

· · ·

"You're absolutely certain you have everything?" Jessica asked worriedly for the third time since they'd left the house.

"Positive. I couldn't possibly get anything more in the valise. And Mr. Turnbull has assured me I can take only the two pieces. There isn't room for more on the overland coach." Laurel indicated the small trunk sitting beside her. As she did, she noticed Andrew approaching with Hiram Turnbull.

"Good morning, Miss Wentworth. Fine day," Turnbull glanced over at Andrew as he tipped his hat to Laurel. She wondered what had passed between the two men.

They stood beside the gangway of the riverboat, while passengers who'd boarded earlier meandered on the upper and lower decks. The final whistle blew, shooting a plume of steam high into the cool morning air.

Jess hugged Laurel fiercely. "You must promise to be back by the time the baby arrives."

"I promise." Laurel pressed a kiss against her cheek and conveyed a silent thank you with a loving glance.

"Mr. Turnbull will be returning before the end of the month." Andrew added meaningfully. "I'll expect you to be with him."

"I'm certain that will allow me enough time." Laurel hugged Andrew as he gave her a last embrace.

Enough time for what? she thought. To sell the Rebecca? She turned wistfully away from Andrew and Jess, but she heard Andrew's last instructions to Hiram Turnbull as she boarded the steamboat that would take her upriver to Sacramento. From there they would take the Sacramento Valley express train to Auburn, the end of the line for passenger travel. Then, they would continue by overland stage to Virginia City.

"Send a wire as soon as you reach Sacramento, and I'll expect to hear from you as soon as you reach Virginia City," Andrew reminded her.

Once Laurel was aboard the *San Rafael,* a steward quickly

showed her to her stateroom. Mr. Turnbull was to occupy the one directly across the companionway. Reluctant to set foot on another ship, given her condition, Jess had chosen to wait for Andrew on the dock. Her husband set Laurel's trunk against the wall, then placed the small valise on the bed.

"I still don't approve," he said to Laurel.

"I know." An impish gleam sparkled in her eyes. Andrew had been forever disapproving and then looking the other way since she was a child, so as not to witness her endless pranks. Although on more than one occasion he'd rescued her from one mishap or another.

"Be careful."

"I will," Laurel answered dutifully.

"Send a wire the minute you get to Sacramento, and again when you get to Virginia City," he repeated.

Laurel sighed patiently. "Yes, of course."

"Don't talk to strangers."

She giggled at his reluctance to leave. "Yes, yes, and yes." She responded.

"What!" Andrew looked up in alarm at the third 'yes'.

"Yes, I won't talk to strangers. After all, I have Mr. Turnbull to chaperone me."

Andrew shook his head doubtfully. "I'm not at all certain of the wisdom of that. I've heard the man drinks, that he always carries a flask with him. Just don't stay out late at night." Retreating to the louvered door to her compartment, he inspected the lock. "And..."

Laurel finished for him, "Lock the door. I will. Now go, or you'll be making the trip with me, and Jess will be left waiting on the dock."

Andrew crossed the room one last time and brushed a strand of hair from her forehead as he had when she was a child. For once he had nothing to say. Pressing a kiss against her cheek, he turned and left.

The *San Rafael* was long and low with two enormous steam-driven paddle wheels positioned on either side of the huge pilot house. Railed decks ran the length of the craft, open both forward and aft of a midsection enclosed by large panels of glass.

On this warm, summer day, as the *San Rafael* prepared to leave the pier at the ferry house on Market Street, her open decks provided a breathtaking view of the bay and the coastline, including the town of Marin across the water. On foggy or rainy days passengers could view the same panorama from behind a protective barrier of glass.

Excitement surged through Laurel as the *San Rafael* bumped gently against the dock. The huge paddle wheels churned briefly, stopped, then reversed. Slowly, the riverboat drew away from the dock, then turned northwest into the wide expanse of San Francisco Bay.

Laurel's stateroom was on the main deck as were those of the other passengers traveling all the way to Sacramento. On the second deck were the pilot house, more staterooms, a solarium, a dining room, and a common room.

Having made the voyage several times, Hiram Turnbull explained that the common room, open to passengers during the daytime hours, afforded a magnificent view of the bay and channel. At night, parties or celebrations were often held there, a small dais being situated at the far end for an orchestra. On occasion, tables were set up for card games, but many passengers preferred to relax and watch the coastline drift by.

Laurel smiled politely, remembering her promises to Andrew. She would have little time for onboard celebrations. Late the following day, they would be in Sacramento. And if proper arrangements had been made, she would board the eastbound train for Auburn the morning after.

She chose to spend the remainder of the morning on deck, enjoying the salt air from a deck chair. The breeze off the ocean was cool and the spray it carried made her cheeks tingle. After luncheon, she returned to her stateroom. Pulling several old letters from her valise, she lay across her bed and untied the faded rose-colored ribbon that bound them. Nearly twenty years before, her mother had written these letters to her aunt and uncle from California.

Laurel had read them countless times, trying to understand the woman her mother had been. The lettering—small and precise—was written in an elegant hand. The first letter contained descriptions of the magnificent California coastline.

Skipping over the passages she knew by heart, Laurel searched through the letters written months later. There was mention of her parents' move to a gold field outside Sacramento, and a vague description of the small cabin they'd been living in.

The next letter postmarked almost two months later, happily announced that Rebecca was going to have a child. It was not the letter of a sad, impoverished woman who regretted her choice of a husband. The words flowed easily, providing details about the small cradle Jason had carved, the countless garments Rebecca had made for the baby.

She only indicated uncertainty in mentioning that they hoped to save enough money to work another claim. With the help of a man by the name of Cappy Burnett, they planned to start working the new claim after the baby was born.

The next letter, dated almost four months later, briefly mentioned the fever in the camp, but Rebecca didn't seem concerned. She went on to write that a neighbor woman with several grown children had offered to help when the baby arrived.

Re-reading the letters one more time, Laurel failed to see why Edwin Wentworth had hastened to California to bring her mother home. She silently wondered if there had been other letters.

She put the letters away. It was warm inside the stateroom, and sleepless nights caught up with her as she drifted off to sleep.

Laurel stirred in response to the faint knocking at her door. Hearing Hiram Turnbull announce that dinner would be served promptly at six o'clock, and that he would return to escort her in half an hour.

An hour later, they were enjoying a delicious supper in the main dining room. After dinner, she decided to stroll on the forward deck of the riverboat, but Hiram Turnbull excused himself, saying he intended to visit the common room. Laurel smiled faintly, remembering Andrew's warning.

It was only nine o'clock, and she had no intention of retiring to her stateroom on such a magnificent summer evening. The huge paddle wheels churned rhythmically through the water, the light in the common room shone brightly, and the music the orchestra was playing drifted through open glass panels.

Couples walked past her, or chose to lean against the rail and enjoy the magnificent view of the lights along the river-bank. How many of them would continue on to Virginia City?

Looking back at the common room, she noticed several men seated at one of the far tables. The fancily dressed one took something from an inside jacket pocket. He then spread his hand in a fanlike motion across the table. A gambler.

She stared at him, fascinated, wondering at the character of a man who chose to make his living on a game of chance.

The players placed their bets. The cards were shuffled and dealt. Each man checked his hand. Then one player glanced toward the gambler who'd dealt. Uncertainty was clearly written on his face. The gentleman beside him smiled briefly, then assumed a somewhat bored expression. The fourth card player immediately threw more money into the center of the table.

Without knowing anything about the game they played, Laurel already knew much about the players. The first man had received a bad hand and was wondering how best to play his cards. The others had undoubtedly received better ones, but their enthusiasm was evident. She glanced to the gambler. He'd been unobtrusively watching the other players.

She watched the men play two more hands. The gambler won both. He obviously knew the game exceedingly well, but while his opponents' responses had been obvious, the gambler had not indicated what sort of hand he held. His emotions were carefully concealed behind a mask of indifference, and he hadn't spoken more than a couple of words throughout the course of the three hands.

Cool and calm. She was reminded of Ruel Delaney. His thoughts were always hidden behind dark eyes.

She knew so little about him. She tried to make herself believe she wished she knew even less.

Turning away from the salon, Laurel continued along the deck, then stopped by the rail at the point where they'd boarded earlier that day. The section of rail had been set back into place and latched. Leaning against it, she stared out over inky darkness as water swirled past the ship's hull.

Looking up, Laurel picked out the five points of the cluster of stars named Cassiopeia. Andrew had taught her the constellations the same summer he'd taught her how to navigate with a sextant. Uncle Edwin had disapproved, insisting that there was absolutely no reason for a young woman to have navigational knowledge. But Andrew had finished her instruction in secret.

As she gazed at Cassiopeia now, Laurel wondered if her father would have objected to her learning such things. Fascinated by the twinkling glitter of the distant constellation, she leaned far over the rail, feeling she could almost clutch the stars in her hand, so clear was the sky. Finally, she looked down into the inky darkness below, watching as white crests of water appeared and then rolled away in waves until they disappeared into darkness. The gate rattled loosely.

She gasped as the gate shifted, then caught on the guard chain. Her instinctive backward lunge, the momentary release of her weight, caused the gate to shift at an even more sickening angle and to dangle away from its mooring. The murky darkness of the river rose sharply as Laurel clawed for something to hold on to.

The wind whipped at her hair and tugged at her skirts as if it were trying to suck her out into the void between boat and water. Her leather soled shoes slipped on the wooden deck, and her feet went out from under her.

She was suddenly pulled back to the deck, an arm around her waist, her face buried against the soft worsted wool of a jacket. Hands stroked her hair.

A softly muttered curse reached through the terror of moments before and she felt herself being lifted in strong arms.

"Laurel?"

She stared up into the black-pearl depths that had haunted her dreams.

"What the hell were you doing out here alone?" Ruel Delaney's dark eyes blazed, his fingers bit into her skin as he gently shook her back to reality.

"I..." Laurel inhaled sharply. "What are you doing here?"

He tightened his grasp on her arms to calm his shaking. It was like her to answer with a question.

"Rescuing you from a plunge in the Sacramento River, it appears." A smile lifted the corners of his mouth. "I didn't know you were fond of moonlight swims."

"I'm not... That is, I didn't... I've never ..."

"I see." His hands relaxed, slipped down her arms, and closed over her hands. "You're cold as ice."

Laurel shivered. "You didn't answer my question," she said shakily as he pulled her back against his chest.

Ruel tucked her head beneath his chin. She fit so perfectly against him, and she was so soft.

"What are you doing here?"

He smiled ruefully at her indignation. She'd scared him badly, but he much preferred the anger to the horror he'd seen in her eyes only moments before. If he hadn't been there... But then he'd had every intention of being there.

"I have business in Sacramento," he answered. "I stepped out to have a cigarette and saw the gate give way."

As a couple walked by and gave them a curious stare, Laurel stiffened. She pushed away from him.

"I'm all right now."

Much to her surprise, she was abruptly released. Ruel's hands steadied her as he helped her to her feet, then dropped to his sides as he rose to stand beside her.

"You had quite a scare."

"I'd hardly expect you to be concerned with such matters," she replied. Then, aware of the sharpness in her voice, "I'm sorry. I am grateful. If you hadn't come along when you did ..."

"I might have had to go in that water after you," he finished the thought. "And I would hate to ruin a brand-new suit of clothes. Amusement teased at the corners of his mouth.

"You needn't have been concerned," she declared. "I'm an excellent swimmer."

"You're angry with me." The humor remained, but it was shadowed by the change in the expression at his eyes.

"Not in the slightest." Laurel missed the change in his voice. "I don't feel anything, one way or the other about you." She turned to leave, but Ruel caught her arm and gently restrained her.

"Since we have met again, it's important that you believe I didn't know Delia was your sister. I'd heard she was back in San

Francisco, but I had no idea she'd come to the Golden Empress that morning. She and I didn't part on the best of terms."

Laurel stiffened, fighting two very different feelings. She'd never known his gentleness. It was disconcerting, completely unnerving, and she had no idea how to respond to it.

Damn! Why couldn't he just be himself, the scoundrel that she'd first thought him to be. She knew that Ruel Delaney. This man was unfamiliar to her and more than a little frightening, and more dangerous? And he was apologizing to her.

Not in so many words, but it was there. The memory of that painful morning returned, and with it, her shock and surprise at meeting Delia face-to-face for the first time. And there was the memory of his reaction—his anger at Delia, his attempts to make her understand that he hadn't known they were sisters, and then dispatching John Palmer to make certain she reached home safely.

"I accept your apology," she finally told him, but she didn't dare turn around for fear he might see something other than the coolness in her voice. "The circumstances of your relation-ship with my sister hardly matter to me. Good night." She pulled her arm from his grasp.

"Goodnight," he whispered, as his fingers slowly slipped from her arm, gently releasing her.

If an acceptance of his apology was all he could have, it would have to be enough. For now.

9

Laurel stepped from the front porch of the Kinmont Hotel, shielding her eyes from the glare of morning sun. It was shortly after eight o'clock in the morning, but already heat shimmered above the street separating the hotel from the stables. Clouds of dust billowed and swirled around the hooves of a passing horse and rider, then settled. She waited a moment and then crossed the street.

Auburn, California was the end of the line for passenger service aboard the Central Pacific Railroad. She'd learned the day before that the line extended farther, but only for the work crews who laid track up the grade of the Sierra Nevada range.

In the brilliant light of early morning, those distant, jagged peaks were a purplish blue. She recalled the station master's odd expression when she'd informed him that this was her first trip across the mountains to Nevada. His cordial smile had slipped into a frown. So much for encouragement.

She stepped onto the porch spanning the front of the office of the Overland Stage Line. As she waited for Hiram Turnbull, she contemplated the scorching day to come, the meager breakfast she'd had, and her poor choice of clothing for this trip.

Sighing heavily, she realized there was nothing to be done about her clothes. She gave an envious glance at the messenger boy from the telegraph office as he sprinted past wearing blue pants tucked into high boots and a white shirt open at the collar, sleeves rolled back the length of lean, brown arms.

As another rivulet of perspiration slipped between her breasts, she heartily wished she could take off the heavy silk jacket of her traveling costume.

Why were men allowed to wear far more comfortable and practical garments while women were expected to suffocate under crinolines, heavy silks, and row upon row of muslin?

The train returning to Sacramento had pulled out earlier, but nearby she could hear a harness jangle and a man curse as teams were led out of the stables and hitched to the Concord coach.

There were to be four passengers for Virginia City. Since they'd arrived in Auburn last evening, and everyone had to find accommodations for the night, Laurel had no idea who the other two passengers might be.

"There you are. You're up bright and early this morning." Hiram Turnbull stepped onto the porch just as the coach was brought around in front of the stage office.

"I woke early," Laurel replied. Then she glanced away from his heavily veined and blood shot eyes and concentrated on the coach that hardly looked big enough to accommodate four passengers.

Adjusting his hat against the glare of the sun, Hiram winced painfully. "Beastly hot. But you'll have plenty of opportunity to rest once we're underway. There's nothing else to do between stops. I don't suppose you know who our fellow travelers are?"

"Perhaps they changed their minds," Laurel suggested as the driver of the stage checked the large watch in his vest pocket.

She and Turnbull had been told to be at the stage office promptly at eight o'clock.

The driver gave them a brief nod of acknowledgment, and Hiram escorted her to the waiting coach. Drawn by a team of six horses, the coach was made of leather and wood and appeared to offer little in the way of comfort.

Seizing her skirts in one hand, Laurel mounted the two steps into the coach. To her left, behind the driver, and to the right were bench seats that spanned the width. Laurel chose the seat to her right, and Hiram sat across from her.

The long panels of leather that served as protection against dust and blistering sun had been unrolled and lowered over the open spaces resembling windows, plunging the interior of the coach into stifling shade. Only one leather panel remained rolled. It rested over the small doorway to the coach. Laurel released a long breath as beads of moisture slipped down her chest and back.

Their luggage was secured at the rear of the vehicle, along with two heavy wooden boxes marked Wells Fargo. In addition to the driver, a relief man would be accompanying them. Laurel gave him a long sidewise glance as he hoisted himself to his seat atop the coach. As sunlight glinted off the steel barrel of a long rifle, she frowned slightly and wondered if the contents of those two boxes necessitated the guns. Her frown became a polite smile as a third passenger poked his head into the coach.

"Good morning." The young man's high-pitched voice had a nasal twang. He tipped his hat politely as he waited for his pale eyes to adjust to the darkness of the interior. Mumbling apologies, he avoided their feet and slipped into the long seat opposite, taking a handkerchief from his coat pocket and drawing it across his forehead as he removed his hat. He was more limp than the sodden cloth.

"I can't imagine what the day will be like if it's already this warm. I'm Darby Cullen," he announced, observing them congenially from behind the wire-rimmed glasses perched precariously on the bridge of his incredibly thin nose.

Laurel smiled at him as Hiram made the introductions.

"I ride this stage frequently, but it's not often we have such lovely company." Cullen's voice cracked causing him to flush with embarrassment. Despite his youth, he didn't appear to be a well man.

"Do you have family in Virginia City, Miss Wentworth?"

"My father ..." she caught herself. "No, I have no family there. I'm going on business." Laurel clasped her hands and rested them on her lap.

"It seems we're all bound there on business. So's the fella I met earlier in the dining room over at the hotel. But that's about all there is to Virginia City. Nobody goes there to live. The climate is beastly hot and dry."

Laurel gave him a polite smile as she turned to glance casually out the open door. A man was crossing from the hotel, but she couldn't make out his features as the sunlight glared painfully off a shining object in the mercantile window.

"Good morning. I'm sorry I'm late, I had to send a telegram."

The fourth passenger had stopped beside the coach in order to apologize to the driver. His voice cut through the stifling heat, then his imposing frame filled the doorway—Ruel Delaney!

"We're all here now. Just climb aboard, and we'll get underway," the driver said.

It couldn't be! Laurel leaned forward, then drew back as a dark gaze met hers across the shaded interior of the coach.

Ruel Delaney smiled like a satisfied cat. Then he took hold of the doorframe, pulled his long body inside, and settled into the only space available, the one across from Darby Cullen and beside Laurel.

Laurel shifted uncomfortably in her seat. How was it that this man seemed to turn up where she was?

"I suppose you're going to tell me you have business in Virginia City?" she coolly commented.

His smile deepened. "So it seems."

THE COACH TURNED SHARPLY up the steep grade that ran alongside the railroad track they'd followed for the last three days. Dust and rocks rolled out from under its steel-rimmed wheels as the driver pulled the team to a stop in front of a long, low building. A large corral stood behind it, framed by oaks and the giant pinon trees that thrust into the darkening night sky.

A young man darted out from the barn across the wide yard. He secured the team of horses, as another boy ran out of the house and began to unload the rear compartment.

Then a small woman stepped from the opening of the house, a rifle balanced on one hip. She wore a man's work shirt, the sleeves rolled back and tail tucked into tight-fitting pants, men's boots, with dark hair bound back with a length of ribbon that framed pretty features.

She exchanged a few words with the driver and then came around to greet the passengers. Peering inside the coach, she drew back, a smile of pure delight on her face.

"That you, Delaney? I heard you were back in San Francisco. Figured you'd be headin' up this way before too long."

"How've you been, Cass?" Ruel replied.

"Can't complain. Got my oldest boy back from the gold fields. He decided there was more money to be made here from the railroad and the toll road than grubbin' for a stake. Told him you'd probably be comin' through any day. He's all hot to head out for Virginia City."

Ruel stepped down from the coach.

Cass Driscoll was no bigger than a flea, but she had that insect's energy. Widowed over ten years earlier, she'd raised five boys in these hills and had turned a remote way station into a profitable enterprise.

She'd come from Dutch Flat two years ago when the railroad had selected their Sierra route. The main house had been nothing more than a cabin then, but with the help of five strong boys she'd added on to the original structure and had built a barn. She'd also set up corrals and fenced in some pastureland.

He swept her into a tight embrace, swinging her and the rifle around as if she weighed no more than feather.

"Put me down you big, handsome devil!" Cass laughed heartily. "Or I'll get Sandy after you."

Ruel set her down gently. Cass had always been one of his favorite people. More than that, she was one of the few women he trusted.

There'd been a time when she'd carved a bullet out of him after he'd been left for dead. She and the boys had brought him here and had cared for him until he was strong enough to travel. Since then, he'd made two or three trips a year across the Sierras, always stopping at her place for a few days.

"How's business?"

"Oh, you know how it is. I'm always fightin' them damned railroad people so they'll pay me for the horses and food I supply the work crews."

"Who's trying to cheat who?" Ruel chuckled.

Cass was known to be a shrewd horse-trader. She'd had to be, raising five boys on her own. The youngest, Tyrell, bounded around the corner of the house, a large black dog racing after him.

Cass, circled Ruel's waist with an arm. He was the only man she'd ever considered asking to stay on with her and the boys, and the one man she knew never would. Whatever might have been between them had begun and ended one night two years ago when she'd gone to him.

Before that he'd been found half-dead, shot up by outlaws.

After two weeks he'd been well enough to travel, but he'd delayed returning to Virginia City. There'd been an instant bond between her youngest and this man with black waving hair and dark haunted eyes.

She'd figured a man who loved kids as much as he did couldn't be all bad. And she'd also figured she'd been alone long enough. A woman could get mighty lonely in the hills, trying to raise a houseful of boys. She'd had needs and those needs had sharpened the moment she'd stripped the blood-soaked clothes from his lean body.

In the days that followed, her needs had intensified. And so, she'd gone to his room that last night, slipping quietly beneath the covers and molding her body against his. Even in sleep, he'd responded, but as he'd come awake, she'd seen something in his eyes that had made her stop—pain, the deep pain that rode his soul. And anger, anger at someone else for something done in another place and time. Too many secrets. And she hadn't wanted to cause him more pain.

He'd have taken her if she'd asked, but in the taking both had known something might have been lost—their friendship. Afterward there was an indefinable barrier that neither had wanted to cross or tear down. In the end, she'd lain with him till almost dawn, taking what pleasure she could from feeling a man's arms around her, and then she'd left him, slipping back to her room at the front of the house just as quietly as she'd come to him. When he'd mounted the horse she'd given him just after dawn, neither had spoken of what might have been. They'd parted friends, and their friendship had remained to this day.

"Seems like some of the other passengers were a bit eager to get inside. Come on up to the house," Cass invited. "The stove's fired up and I got steaks an inch thick, a pot of beans, and fresh-baked bread." She was glad to see him.

Whenever too much time passed between visits, she got the

nagging feeling that he'd caught another bullet, and this time he hadn't been so fortunate. Danger clung to him like a well-worn pair of boots. She glanced back as Ruel hesitated outside the coach.

Turning and peering into the darkened interior, Ruel smothered a twinge of humor as Laurel remained stubbornly in the far corner. Darby Cullen had already gone to seek a cool drink of water, and Hiram Turnbull had been the first out when they'd reached the way station at Dutch Flat.

"There somebody else in there?" Cass pushed around him, peering inside.

Having watched the entire exchange, Laurel could only guess what might once have passed between them. How very convenient for him to have women waiting at every stop!

At that moment she'd rather have remained in the coach, but hunger nagged at her, as did other pressing needs. Sooner or later she'd be forced to join them, better to do it now.

Forcing a polite smile, Laurel seized the doorframe and started down the two steps. If she hadn't been concentrating quite so hard on avoiding Ruel's amused gaze, she might have noticed the toe of her boot catch in the hem of her skirt. But she didn't. The fabric was jerked underfoot, causing her to stumble, and Laurel fell out the door of the coach into the waiting arms of Ruel Delaney.

If he hadn't been so certain it was the last thing she wanted, he'd have thought she'd planned to fall into his arms. But what he'd suspected was confirmed when she came up gasping and fighting to remove his arms from her waist and regain her footing.

Something had to give. It was the fabric of her skirt. With a rending tear, it separated from the band at her waist.

"Oh, you! Of all the ...!" Laurel slapped at Ruel's hand as he tried to steady her.

"Please, Laurel, not here." Amusement glinted at his dark eyes as he held firmly onto her waist.

"This is Cass Driscoll. She owns the way station here at Dutch Flat. She can out cook and out sew any woman I've known—and outshoot most men." Ruel quickly got through the introduction.

"Most everyone around calls me Ma. That's `cause I got five boys. And somehow I always seem to be collectin' an extra one or two along the way." She gave Ruel a thoughtful look when his arm remained around Laurel's waist.

"You'll meet them all later on, after they've finished their chores. Right now, I'd say we best be gettin' on inside. Gets a mite cool up here at night, even in the summer." Cass tilted her head, a knowing light springing into her warm brown eyes.

She'd heard Ruel had taken up with a pale-haired gal, a real beauty but she'd also heard it had ended badly. Still, the way he was holding onto her, it didn't look ended at all.

"I'm very pleased to meet you, Mrs. Driscoll..."

Giving Ruel a withering look, she threw off his arm and extended her hand to the slender, attractive woman who was about her own height.

Cass smiled to mask her curiosity. The description fit, but not the manner. This young lady was just that, a lady. She had manners and fine speech. And at the moment, she looked as if the three-day coach ride from Auburn had just about done her in.

She probably had no idea what she was in for. Just like some soft, Eastern lady to get herself into something and then expect everybody to get her out of it. But even as she gave Laurel a thorough inspection, Cass had to smile as Laurel twisted out of Ruel's grasp and headed toward the house. The little gal had spirit. Cass was certain there weren't many women who wanted to walk away from Ruel Delaney.

After fresh hot apple pie had been served with slices of

cheese, Hiram Turnbull retreated into his cups before the crackling fire and Darby Cullen opened one of his large traveling cases, revealing a variety of books. The boys were intrigued by the latest book written by Mark Twain. Ruel tilted back in his chair, stretched out his long legs, and let tendrils of fragrant smoke encircle him as he gazed contentedly about the room.

Cass sent Tyrell out to the smokehouse to bring in a fresh ham and threw one last stick of wood into the stove to keep the embers alive for the morning fire. As if it were the most natural thing in the world, Laurel removed the last of the dinner plates from the long table. Stacking them beside a metal tub filled with hot, soapy water, she began to scrape the scraps onto one plate. Ruel watched her perform this basic task. Whenever she wasn't angry or running away from him, he learned something new about her.

Tyrell returned from the smokehouse and handed his mother the ham. Then, taking a chair beside Ruel, he produced the piece of hand-tooled leather he'd been working on.

"Sure missed ya." Tyrell had his mother's easy way with words.

"And I've missed you." Ruel rumpled the boy's sun-streaked hair. "You've put in a lot of time on that bridle."

Tyrell sighed. "It never looks as good as the piece you showed me. Ma says I'm too impatient. But I got my brother, Rowdy, to bring me a new cuttin' tool from Sacramento the last time he was there." He looked up, following Ruel's dark gaze to the golden-haired girl who'd also arrived that evening.

"She sure is somethin." Tyrell sighed. "All that pale hair, just like silver light. And I swear I ain't never seen eyes like hers. They're so blue it almost makes you ache to look at 'em. And she's nice. Not like some of them fancy ladies that come through. Ma won't let me even talk to 'em. But Rowdy, he says he talked to one of 'em in Sacramento."

Ruel smiled knowingly at the boy. His older brother had probably done a lot more than talk. But Tyrell wasn't even ten yet. There was plenty of time for him to find out about women who could be bought—and women who couldn't. Looking over the boy's head, his gaze fastened on Laurel. Then she looked away and concentrated on the dishes.

First John Palmer, then Darby Cullen, not quite a man. Laurel seemed to have an effect on men of all ages.

"You don't have to do that. I got plenty of help." Cass motioned to the stack of dishes Laurel was submerging in the steaming water. "Since I often do a man's work around here, I think it's only fair the boys help out in the kitchen once in a while. It's good for 'em."

"I don't mind. It's good to have something to do after riding in that coach the last three days. I don't think I'll sit for days after I get to Virginia City." Laurel smiled as she rinsed a platter in a bucket of water. Steam rose and warmed her cheeks, already reddened from the heat inside the house.

"Aren't exactly dressed for this kind of trip, are you," Cass commented.

Laurel brushed back a wisp of hair that had fallen over her forehead. "I didn't realize it would be this hot. Silk isn't very practical out here, is it?"

Her gaze wandered to where Ruel sat with Cass Driscoll's youngest. Their heads were bent over some project, one a tousled honey blond, streaked by the sun, the other silky black.

The boy listened intently, working the metal-bladed tool as Ruel quietly instructed. She stared at him, fascinated by this part of him she'd never glimpsed before.

Except for that moment when she'd found him watching her, his attention had remained on the strip of leather that lay on the table before him. She'd never have thought him to be the kind of man who'd take an interest in such a skill, much less have the patience to teach it to a young boy.

The heavy washcloth slipped from her fingers and plopped into the metal basin, splashing bubbles of soap onto her silk skirt. Laurel shook her head, and a smile lifted the corners of her mouth.

Cass laughed. She hadn't expected, a high-class lady to be so easily amused, or to wash dishes as if she'd done it all her life.

"I got some extra shirts and pants, and maybe a pair of boots Tyrell has outgrown. I swear I can't keep anything on that boy's feet. Instead of growing tall, he's just growin'."

When she returned a short time later, she sat down scuffed boots, faded blue pants, and an equally faded work shirt. She eyed Laurel critically as she spread the shirt across her shoulders to check the fit.

"That should do. The pants are mine, but the shirt's one of Rowdy's. You got a bit more up front than me. You'll be needin' these when you get to Virginia City. They'll be a sight more comfortable than all those skirts tangling about your legs."

"How much do I owe you?" Laurel wiped the soap suds from her hands.

Cass waved her off. "You don't owe me nothin'. I'd folded these away. Weren't nobody small enough to wear them around here anymore."

"Then we'll trade." Laurel seized her by the hand and scooping up the valise Tyrell had carried in for her, she led Cass to one of the back rooms.

Cass's eyes widened at the sight of the blue muslin gown Laurel pulled from the valise.

"I've never seen anything so beautiful in all my life." Cass sighed wistfully, then drew back. "I can't accept that."

"Of course, you can. Every woman needs a pretty dress, something to make her feel extra special," Laurel insisted.

Cass spread the voluminous gown across her arm. "It's so delicate. I never had anything like it."

"Then, now's the time. We're almost the same size. With just a tuck or two, it'll fit you perfectly. There must be someone you'd like to wear it for."

"There was, once." Cass sighed meaningfully. "But things just didn't work out."

Laurel's surprised gaze met hers. At first, she'd been certain Cass was talking about the boys' father, but she remembered Rowdy had said Jake Driscoll had been dead for a long time. Another man had brought that light to Cass's eyes. Laurel could well understand that. And though her oldest boy was twenty, she probably wasn't more than thirty-five, very near Ruel Delaney's age.

Her eyes darkened as she remembered their greeting earlier that afternoon and wondered if Ruel Delaney might have been the special man in Cass's life. Whatever had passed between them, they were still friends. She held back a frown as Cass grasped her hands.

"I'm good with a needle and thread."

"Then it's settled, the dress is yours. And I think I have the better bargain."

They were laughing as they returned to the main room of the house. The fire had burned low, and Hiram Turnbull was dozing in a chair, his head slumped down on his chest. Every once in a while, his rhythmic snoring changed abruptly, he paused then snorted, all without waking. By the light of a kerosene lantern, Rowdy and Darby Cullen were looking through a book, and Tyrell was just finishing the dishes.

"See, what I told you. They're good boys." Cass went to stand beside her youngest, planting an affectionate kiss on his cheek.

"Ah, Ma!" he complained, trying to slip out of her embrace.

"He's the only one I can still kiss, and it's gettin' harder all the time." Seizing a cotton towel, she gestured toward Laurel.

"It's mighty pretty up here this time of night, and you look a bit flushed from the heat. I'll finish up here while you go on out and get a breath of fresh air." She motioned her from the kitchen.

Laurel stepped out onto the porch.

The horses in the corral picked up her scent and nickered a greeting. The fragrant pine needles provided a soft carpet underfoot as she walked to the corral. Reaching through the rail fence, she stroked a velvety muzzle thrust toward her.

"The Indians have a legend about the stars."

Laurel whirled around as he emerged from the darkness— Ruel Delaney. She hadn't heard him approach.

"And I suppose you're going to tell me all about it." She was aware of the sharpness in her words and felt a twinge of guilt.

For the last three days she'd fought the feelings he stirred in her. The thought of spending four more days so close to him left her feeling vulnerable and uncertain.

He continued, apparently unaffected by her sarcasm. "Legend has it that each of the stars represent the spirit of a great Indian warrior. The brightness of the star is symbolic of his courage and strength. When a brave warrior dies, his light is forever reflected in the heavens so that others may look to the sky and see his courage."

She watched him as he stared into the night sky. "And what of the falling stars? Have those warriors lost their courage and strength?"

"Once an Indian warrior died in a great battle. His light reflected brightly in the sky at night as his family mourned the loss. The falling star was his journey back to earth, to take up the lance once more."

Laurel stared at Ruel's profile, visible in the moonlight.

Who was this man who charmed women and small boys? What filled him with such tenderness at moments like this, when at others he was capable of such brutality? And why did his path continue to cross hers?

"I'd better go back to the house," she whispered haltingly, unable to understand.

"Please, stay." His hand closed gently over hers as she turned to walk away. "There's so much I have to explain."

There was something in his voice that stopped her, something different.

"There's nothing to explain."

Ruel pulled her against him. "I swore I wouldn't come near you..." he touched her.

She pressed her hands against him. He trapped her mouth beneath his, crushing her protest.

"I can't do this!" Her hands flattened against his chest, forcing distance between them.

"Delia...!"

The name sliced through him like a blade, cutting deep until it seemed every part of him lay exposed and raw. He slowly released her.

She stood a safe distance away, her back toward him, her breasts heaving with the effort to suppress the emotions that twisted inside her. She fought to bring those emotions under control.

"Don't come near me again. I don't want to know what passed between you and Delia. I only know that I won't be your whore." Laurel's voice trembled.

If he touched her again, she was certain she'd never have the strength to walk away from him, and she had to. He was far too dangerous for her. The feelings he aroused in her were far too dangerous.

Slowly, she took a step toward the house, then another until she reached the porch.

The door closed softly behind her.

The others had long since retired for the evening to the rooms Cass had shown them. But she lingered in the main room, staring into the soft glow of the embers that were all that were left of the fire at the hearth.

"There isn't any walkin' away from a man like Ruel Delaney."

Laurel looked up, the rocking chair creaked faintly. Cass Driscoll watched her from the shadows near the hearth. How much had she seen from the window facing the open yard?

"The man's got a hunger deep down inside, like he's starvin' for something he can't have. And a man like him doesn't live by other men's rules. He'll keep right on 'til he gets what he wants."

Laurel stared at her. *"A man like him"*. A dangerous man.

"It doesn't matter," she finally replied. "The only thing that matters is that I reach Virginia City."

"And after that?"

"I have family in San Francisco. I imagine I'll be returning, there." The chill spread from her fingers to deep inside.

"And what about him?"

"Nothing," Laurel whispered passionately, yet as she did, she heard the unconvincing sound of her own voice.

"Not likely! But I'll tell you what. You're a fool if you don't give in to it."

Wasn't that what she feared the most? The desire she desperately wanted to keep at bay. She laughed softly.

"He doesn't want me. It's just an illusion. Like looking in a mirror and seeing an image." She saw Cass's confused expression.

"I can't be what he wants."

He wants Delia, she thought, someone who fit into his world. "I'm tired. Good night." She walked quietly down the dark hallway and closed the door, taking her troubled thoughts with her.

"You little fool," Cass whispered into the shadows as she rose from the rocking chair.

She stopped at the window to watch the man who leaned against the corral gate, the tip of his cigarette glowing brightly.

Two years ago, she'd have given anything to have him look at her the way he'd looked at Laurel Wentworth.

True, but only half true. Two hours ago, she'd have given anything. And his answer would have been the same, only for a different reason this time.

Ruel Delaney was in love, possibly for the first time in his life, and it was with someone else.

10

"I thought you might want a drink of water, Miss Wentworth." Darby Cullen smiled sheepishly.

Shading her eyes from the sun, Laurel took the cup he offered and smiled gratefully. They'd been on the road since daybreak and the driver had chosen to stop briefly so they could stretch their legs, take care of other needs.

It was three days since they'd left Dutch Flat. On the first day they had managed to cover more than thirty miles, easily making the next way station by nightfall. But the last two days they'd been making the twisting climb through the Sierra Nevada mountains, and their pace had slowed considerably.

The day before they'd left the railroad work crews behind. The next way station was almost twenty miles ahead at Donner Lake. They were now alone in the wilderness.

"I want you to know this trip has been a real pleasure, Miss Wentworth." Darby toyed nervously with his cup, then offered her more water from the canteen.

"Women don't usually make the trip. I understand that your business in Virginia City concerns your father's estate. My condolences on your loss."

Conversation didn't come easily for Darby Cullen. He seemed to labor over every thought. Yet when she'd seen him talking to Cass Driscoll's boys about his books, he'd seemed at ease. He was obviously more comfortable with books than people.

Her gaze wandered across the clearing where Ruel stood beside the driver. Since the evening at Dutch Flat, he'd stayed away from her. And yet, even though he had honored her request, Laurel felt a tremor of uncertainty each time she found him looking at her.

She remembered Cass's statement that he didn't live by other men's rules. She'd known that long before. Darby Cullen was a simple, unpretentious man that a woman could be certain of, but Ruel Delaney was a contradiction.

"You were saying..." Laurel realized Darby had been making an effort to keep up the conversation.

"I was saying that I hoped when we get to Virginia City you will allow me to call on you."

Call on her? Oh, dear. He was so shy; she could only guess what it took for him to make that statement.

"That's really very kind of you..."

Across the clearing, the driver checked the harnesses and made adjustments while the horses drank water from a creek they had crossed. Nodding curtly to him, Ruel turned and started toward her. Laurel stiffened.

Ruel crossed the distance in long, easy strides and, without so much as a word, seized her by the arm.

"I want to talk to you." Abruptly drawing her to her feet, Ruel pulled her in the direction of the coach.

"Mr. Delaney..." Darby Cullen's protest was silenced by the dangerous look Ruel gave him.

"Well, I suppose it's all right if Miss Wentworth doesn't object."

Of course I object, Laurel thought, but that made absolutely no difference.

"What do you think you're doing? I told you..."

Ruel cut her off. "I know exactly how you feel, but for the time being everything's changed."

"Changed? What are you talking about?"

What was he up to now? Well, whatever it was she was having no part of it.

"Outlaws." Ruel glanced around the small clearing. "They've hit the stage route twice in the past month."

"What are they after?"

He could tell by her tone that Laurel hadn't fully grasped what he was trying to tell her.

"Payroll shipments for the mines. Two men have already been killed."

Laurel swallowed to ease the knot of fear in her throat. "Why are you telling me this?"

"Two reasons. Both the drivers have rifles, but Hiram Turnbull is so drunk he'd probably end up shooting himself if he tried to use one. And Cullen over there wouldn't shoot himself, he'd faint first."

Laurel's anger returned. What right did he have to criticize Darby Cullen?

"You have no right to say those things about him. He's not like you, he's kind and thoughtful."

Ruel held up his hand. "At the moment, that's not the issue."

He reached into his jacket and drew out a small, short-barreled pistol. "I want you to carry this."

She shoved the pistol back at him. "I don't know anything about guns."

"Lesson number one—watch where you point it. Even an unloaded gun has been known to kill. This one is loaded." Seeing her bewildered expression, he showed her how to unload and then load it. Then he flipped the chamber closed and placed it in her hand.

"Aren't you afraid I might decide to use this on you?" she asked. She fixed him with that blue gaze.

"What's the other reason?"

Dragging his gaze from hers, his mood shifted, and the edge to his words softened. She had a way of reminding him of too much—promises, memories, the past. His eyes locked with hers.

"You said there were two reasons for telling me this," Laurel reminded him.

The second reason—she'd only throw the words back in his face.

"In spite of what you think of me, I don't want anything to happen to you." He turned and walked back to the coach to help the driver secure the team.

THEY'D BEEN BACK on the road for hours, everyone on edge because of the robberies.

Laurel squinted as the late afternoon sunlight slanted through the window opening at the door. Something was wrong. She braced as the coach lurched around the next bend in the trail at unusual speed.

There was a gunshot, then another. Across from her, Ruel had drawn a pistol from inside his coat and he moved toward the door. Beside her Hiram Turnbull grumbled as he was jostled from his stupor and attempted to focus his reddened eyes.

"Aren't we going a bit fast? Just what is that driver trying to do to us anyway?"

Darby Cullen started up out of his seat, as if he meant to follow Ruel's lead.

The coach lurched around another turn, sending them back against their seats. Everyone except Darby. He seemed to hang like a suspended puppet for a moment.

Regaining her seat, Laurel stared at him. An expression of surprise and shock was on his face. His eyes gaped and his mouth dropped open. His lips moved, but he made no sound.

Laurel reached out to him, but he didn't seem to hear her. As if the strings that held him up had suddenly been cut, he tumbled forward in the coach, crumpling at the floor. A darkened stain spread across his back.

"Good heavens!" was all Hiram Turnbull could manage.

Ruel leaped across Darby's fallen body.

"Get down!" He shoved Laurel to the floor of the coach as more shots cracked outside the coach. Grabbing Hiram Turnbull by the collar of his shirt, he pushed him down beside Laurel.

"Stay down!" Ruel told her. "And use that gun if you have to!"

"Gun? What gun? What the devil is going on?" Hiram Turnbull demanded as Laurel pulled him back down to the floor.

Crawling across the seat, Ruel peered out of the lurching coach as more shots were heard. He fired twice. One man fell from his horse as they rounded another bend, the coach now wildly out of control as the horses charged into a downgrade at the road.

Ruel hoisted himself out of the window at a lull in the gunfire. His hands closed around the metal railing at the top of the coach and he pulled himself on top of the coach.

The relief driver was nowhere in sight, probably been picked off after he'd managed to get off that first shot. The driver lay slumped across the bench seat. The reins dragged between the wildly racing horses as the coach careened down the slope of the road.

A shot sliced through the air inches from his head. He ducked, then fired two rounds before reaching for the rifle pinned beneath the dead driver. Freeing it, he turned and took aim.

It was almost impossible to get an accurate shot off because of the swaying of the coach. They hit a bump in the road, and Ruel was forced to forget the outlaws and concentrate on staying aboard. He had to get the horses under control or none of them were going to live through this.

There was just one way to do that. He threw himself from the driver's seat and landed on the nearest horse. Twice he very nearly lost his grip as the motion of the horses threatened to send him beneath the coach. He held on and pulled himself up to the lead horses. There he was able to grab the reins, lost when the driver was shot.

At first there was no response from the team, then they gradually slowed, and came to a full stop, sides heaving. He dropped to the ground and ran back to the coach. He grabbed the rifle where he'd wedged it at the driver's box.

Hiram Turnbull slowly rose from the floor of the coach. Coming to an upright position, he rubbed his bruised head.

"What the devil is going on?" he demanded coming up off the floor.

"Wait!" Laurel called a warning.

He raised the leather drop shade, then stiffened, the dull crack of a shot sending him back into the coach.

Ruel ran to the rear of the coach at the sound of gunfire. He took aim and fired at the departing rider.

He pulled the door of the coach open. Laurel sat on the floor the revolver pointed at him. Turnbull lay at her feet, blood staining the front of his shirt.

A brief glance at Cullen, he knew without checking that he was dead. He reached into the coach, and his fingers closed gently around her wrist.

"All quiet now. They're gone." He told her, slowly taking the revolver from her.

She pulled away from him. "Darby's wounded...?"

He forced her to look at him. "There's nothing we can do for him now."

For a moment, the light in her eyes wavered.

"Look at me," he told her. Don't leave me now, he thought desperately, shaking her to make her feel anything except the numbing horror of death. Then he stepped back out of the coach, pulling her with him.

Keeping a careful eye on the rim of the hill behind them, he led her to a nearby rock and sat her down. She stared at nothing as he returned to the coach for the canteens of water. Returning, he twisted the cap off one and washed the blood from her hands.

"Mr. Turnbull?" she asked.

"Dead." Ruel gently dried her hands with a strip torn from her petticoat.

"We've got to get out of here," he said finally.

Replacing the cap, he set both canteens down beside her. Then he went back to the coach and took her valise and a pair of saddlebags from the rear storage compartment, continuously glancing to the crest of the hill with the eye of a man who'd learned early that to stay alive he had to keep a careful watch over his shoulder.

He set Laurel's valise at her feet; he took her by the shoulders. Death was never easy to face, but some people were stronger than others. If they were going to make it out of here alive, she had to be strong. He'd seen her flashes of determination and defiance, He prayed she had strength.

"What about the driver and the guard?" Her fragmented thoughts started to come together.

Unable to bear the pain in her eyes, he busied himself reloading the pistol he'd tucked into his belt that he always carried.

"The driver's dead. The guard is gone. He was probably the first one they shot."

Laurel glanced uncertainly at the top of the coach, seeing the driver's lifeless body slumped over the seat.

"Maybe he's only injured."

Ruel's gaze met hers, and he knew he'd never convince her to leave until he'd gone back to check the driver. Shoving the pistol into his belt, he muttered an oath.

Crossing to the horses in quick strides, he started unbuckling the harness. The outlaws would be back. They wanted two things—the leather satchels with the payroll and the horses. Pulling one horse from the team, he quickly mounted and circled to Laurel. He handed her the small revolver.

She took it, with more confidence than the first time. Her eyes were wide and dark.

"We can't help the driver. Stay in these rocks. Don't go back to the coach, and don't hesitate to use that gun." He whirled the horse around.

Her hand closed around his boot. She was terrified, he saw it in the expression at her face. Along with something else. He brushed her cheek with his fingers.

"I'll be back." He found the guard several hundred yards back up the trail. He was dead.

If they were lucky, the outlaws had ridden off a safe distance, but they would be back. He hoisted the guard's body across the front of the horse and was headed back to the coach when he heard gunfire.

Ruel pulled the horse to a stop beside the coach. One of the outlaws, wearing a long coat lay on the ground. He poked him with the toe of his boot to make certain he was dead.

He looked up and his gaze fastened on Laurel a half dozen steps away. Her face was drained of all color, her eyes wide and dark as she stared at the man on the ground. He stepped between her and the body of the outlaw sprawled at the ground. She was shaking but there was no blood on her.

Her voice broke. "Is he dead?"

He took the revolver from her and pulled her against him.

"He's dead."

She nodded.

"We have to go before the others return," he told her.

She pushed away from him. "We can't just leave them!" She glanced at the driver then at the guard slumped across Ruel's horse.

"Mr. Turnbull... And Darby?"

"You're not leaving them, I am. I can live with that if it means I get you out of here alive."

"We have to bury them!"

"Take a good look at them." Ruel told her. "They're no position to care about a burial."

He winced as he saw the light in her eyes waver. He'd gone too far. She'd been through a lot and somehow held it together until now.

"The next station we come to, I'll send someone back for them," he promised.

Gazing sadly at the coach, Laurel nodded. She knew he would have his way no matter what argument she made.

He freed the other lead horse from the harness. He then picked up her valise and led her to the waiting mount. He had shortened the harness and handed it to her.

"Do you know how to ride?"

She slowly nodded. "What about the coach?"

"The axle's broken. I'll turn the other horses loose. We'll travel faster and it'll be a lot safer if we don't keep to the main road." He gave her a leg up, then went back to the coach.

Laurel turned away as he lifted the driver down, hoisted him over his shoulder, and gently laid him inside the coach. Then he unharnessed the other horses and turned them loose. He retrieved the two canteens of water, and flung them, along with the leather satchels over the back of his horse.

He pulled himself up onto the horse and laid the rifle across his lap. The sun cast long shadows across the clearing as they left the road and headed into the forest, leaving death behind them.

LAUREL SWAYED ATOP HER HORSE, then forced herself back awake.

She'd lost all track of time and she had no idea where Ruel was taking them, only that they were going deeper into the forest, tall pine trees towering over them into a moonlit sky.

Then, they had stopped.

Hands reached for her and she slumped exhausted against him. He tucked her head into the curve of his shoulder as he carried her to the outcropping of rock he'd found. He carried her through a narrow opening and gently laid her under the outcropping.

He returned for the horses, and led them, one at a time, through the niche in the rocks then made his way back to the overhang. She snuggled against him as he joined her. He wrapped the woolen blanket he'd taken from the coach.

"It's cold," she murmured wearily, and was asleep almost before the words were out.

HE ROSE BEFORE first light and left her sleeping. He had only dozed from time to time, watching, listening. Now, he wanted to check the trail behind them to make certain they hadn't been followed before leaving the safety of the rocks.

Laurel slowly wakened, then she sat up as everything that had happened suddenly came back. She was alone.

She found the horses tethered nearby. If he was gone, he would have taken one of the horses. She turned, hating herself for the relief that she felt.

"Are you all right?" he asked.

"Yes, it's just that... I thought that you might have..."

"What?"

"I thought that you might have left."

He shook his head. "I'm a lot of things," he told her. "But I would never leave you out here alone."

"I'm sorry. I didn't mean..." she apologized.

"Yes, you did, and we'll leave it at that."

She slowly nodded. "Is there some place where I can...?" At the station there was a privy where she could see to her needs, but out here...

"Through that break in the rocks. Don't go beyond that. And you need to change into those clothes Cass gave you."

She nodded. Two day's growth of beard shadowed his face. It made him look like the scoundrel she'd accused him of being.

"There's water and... water but no food," he told her. "Until we reach the next station or an outlying farm," he told her when she returned.

She didn't complain. She simply nodded as she accepted the canteen.

He winced as he reached for the leather bags he'd thrown over his horse at the last minute before leaving the coach the day before.

"What is it?"

He shook his head, as if to say it was nothing, then rotated his shoulder as if he was loosening a tight muscle.

Laurel's eyes widened when she saw the gaping hole at his jacket low at his side.

"You're wounded!"

"It's not bad. I didn't get out of the way soon enough."

"Take off your jacket," she told him and reached for a canteen.

"That's not necessary."

"Take off your jacket," she repeated.

There were times, he thought, when the most surprising things came wrapped in small packages. He slipped out of his jacket and unbuttoned his shirt.

"Do you know what you're doing?"

"I can manage." She lifted the edge of her gown, seized the petticoat underneath and tore off a wide strip. She soaked it in water from the canteen then turned to him.

He saw the hesitation. He reached to take the cloth from her.

"I can take care of it. It's not the first time."

"Why am I not surprised?" she replied.

He smiled to himself as she refused to hand over the cloth. The expression on her face was worth a thousand words—hesitation, uncertainty, then grim determination. That was the only word for it as she gently began to clean the dried blood at his side.

"I'll have to remember to get shot more often." Ruel told her.

"Your luck could run out," she said, a frown at her mouth.

She wiped around wound as best she could. She knew nothing about bullet wounds, but common sense told her that what went in had to come out. Except there was no exit wound low at his back. She swallowed hard at what that meant—that the bullet was still in him.

He sucked in a breath at the pain her cleaning caused, but didn't complain.

"Next time," and she was certain there would be a next time as she put on a brave face, "you might want to get out of the way."

"I was busy at the time."

She looked up and found that dark gaze watching her. She tore another strip from her petticoat and folded part of it into a bandage.

"Hold this in place."

"Yes, ma'am."

She angled a sideways glance at the sarcasm, then took the rest of the strip of her petticoat. She started to wrap it around his waist over the bandage, then hesitated. Cleaning the wound was one thing, wrapping the bandage required coming into too close contact—very close contact.

"I can manage," he told her.

When he would have taken the cloth from her, she slapped his hand away and proceeded to reach around him to secure the long strip over the bandage.

"It's a wonder you've survived to... whatever age you've managed to survive to."

His skin was warm, dark silky hair dusted across his chest, then narrowing to a thin line that disappeared below his belt.

She quickly wrapped the cloth around his waist. She looked up and found him watching her.

"Why are you looking at me that way?" she asked, trying her best to ignore him, which was a little difficult with him only inches away and... without that damned shirt.

"I was thinking, you're not the person I thought you were," Ruel admitted.

"Oh really," Laurel replied.

He smiled at her reply. He liked that about her. She was no bigger than a child, but she gave as good as she got, not the least intimidated by him or what had passed between them. And he very much liked the touch of her hands.

He wished things were different, that they had met under different circumstances, except that he had to admit the chances of their paths crossing in the usual way—a proper introduction, courting her, and then... what?

What would have followed? Would they have become lovers? Would she have become his mistress? He knew the answer.

That wasn't for her. It would have been impossible considering what he was, and what she was—a lady. She deserved someone who loved her, who wanted to build a life with her... family.

Impossible. But there was that other part of him...

She tied off the bandage and sat back.

"Thank you," Ruel told her and saw the surprise at her eyes.

"You're welcome." She made a nervous gesture as he pulled the front of his shirt together and buttoned it. He smiled to himself again as she put distance between them.

Not impossible, he thought. Virginia City was a long way from Boston, and he was used to getting what he wanted.

11

Ruel glanced back as Laurel guided her horse down through the brush behind him.

Her shoulders sagged and it seemed that it was all she could do to remain upright in the saddle. She'd changed into the clothes Cass had given her earlier, the pins were gone from her hair, and she had pulled it back and tied it with another strip of cloth torn from her petticoat. She had no hat to protect her from the sun, her nose and cheeks bright pink.

He'd pushed them hard since they'd left the place where they'd spent the night, stopping only to water the horses. That was hours earlier.

There had been only one question—how far were they from the next stage stop? He didn't lie or sugar-coat it. At the time they had at least ten hours ahead of them, if they didn't stop, if one of the horses didn't come up lame, if...

There was no complaint from her, no constant requests to stop and rest, just that quiet determination when her gaze met his and she nodded when he asked if she was all right.

Then when he would have stopped at midday, she hadn't

asked how much farther but insisted that he didn't need to stop for her... That they should keep going.

He thought of Delia. How could two women look so much alike and be so different? Delia would have fussed and complained about ruining an expensive gown. The clothes Cass had provided would have been tossed aside. But Laurel had simply packed away the gown, the pants, shirt, and boots made riding astride easier and more practical.

They climbed a steep rise, then rested their horses at the crest of the grade. Below them, lay Donner Lake in a small valley between tall mountains. Its shimmering water reflected the fiery ball of the setting sun.

"The stage stop is at the base of that mountain. Can you make it?" he asked.

She simply nodded wearily.

"They'll have food and hot water for a bath."

"At the moment, I'd settle for a warm fire."

Something simple, and again he was struck by the difference in the two women. Delia would have insisted on the finest restaurant, a new gown, and champagne.

"We should be there before dark."

She nodded again and tucked her horse in behind his as they rode down the mountain.

Sunset came and went, the trail ahead steeped in darkness as they reached the bottom of the hill.

"I'll ride on ahead. You stay here. I want to check everything out first." He led her horse over to a towering pine tree.

"You don't think those men might have come here...?" Laurel began uncertainly.

"I want to make sure everything is all right before we ride in. Stay here."

She heard something in his voice, something different, cautious and nodded, then slipped wordlessly from the back of her horse. Her legs ached and shook from long hours in the saddle.

When he hesitated, she told him to go. "If you're not back by the time I count to one hundred, I'm heading for that lake."

Another side of her so different from Delia, who would have demanded a fine hotel and room service.

He was back before she had a chance to count to fifty.

"We need to go on around the lake." He announced his voice tight.

"What is it? What did you find?"

"The settlement has been burned out, the horses are gone." He didn't tell her the rest of it—that the couple who ran the station had been inside the house when it was torched.

She didn't question, she didn't argue, she simply climbed on a nearby fallen timber and dragged herself onto the back of her horse.

They passed the settlement as they headed around the lake. She glanced only once at the still smoldering timbers of the house, all that remained of the way station.

He continued around the perimeter of the lake, long after complete darkness settled around them, the stars winking overhead through the canopy of trees.

She had no idea how much farther they rode, only that he seemed to follow some invisible path. She prayed that he knew where he was going. She nodded off, caught herself, then fought to remain upright on the back of her horse.

How much farther they rode, she had no idea, only that they eventually stopped. It was completely dark; she couldn't see her hand in front of her face with only a few stars shining through the tree cover overhead. Then, she felt him reaching for her.

"Are we stopping?"

"We can't go on tonight. We have water for the horses, and I found a place where we can bed down for the night, then continue in the morning."

She didn't argue or protest, but simply nodded as she leaned into him.

He hobbled the horses, then returned where he'd left her sitting in front of a downed log. She'd nodded off, coming awake suddenly as he laid a hand at her shoulder.

"I made a place where you can sleep in a lean-to in case it rains. It's the best we've got." He pulled her to her feet.

She swayed slightly but managed to stay on her feet. He picked her up and carried her to the lean-to. There he pulled the lap blanket over her, then dragged several more downed branches and laid them over the lean to, then crawled under the crude shelter with her.

Her breathing was low and even with sleep, still she curled toward him, her head resting at his shoulder. He pulled the blanket over both of them, the rifle at his other side.

EARLY MORNING LIGHT penetrated the branches overhead.

Turning, Ruel gazed down at Laurel. He drew the blanket up over her shoulder as she shivered from the chill of the morning air and then snuggled further into the warm cocoon they'd made.

Twins. Incredible! Thinking of the first time he'd seen her on board the *Waverall,* it was still hard to believe. Yet, he understood how he'd been fooled. They were almost identical—the same blue eyes, the same slender height, the same high cheekbones, and that full mouth. But it ended at the physical resemblance.

He also understood the subtle differences that had nagged at him and wondered if he'd chosen to ignore the obvious because he'd been so angry.

Once, he'd thought himself in love with Delia. The thought

almost made him laugh out loud. But the laughter froze. How could one sister be so cold, bitter, and ruthless?

Pushing back the blanket and standing abruptly, Ruel knew exactly what had goaded him these last days—twins. Two who looked alike; mirror images of one another.

Were their emotions reflections of one another? If so, which was real, which the illusion? Looking down at Laurel, her lips slightly parted in sleep, he remembered similar moments with Delia. Finally, saddlebags thrown over his shoulder, he headed towards the shore of the lake.

Reaching the water's edge, he squatted, plunging his hands into the icy depths. Dousing his face, he shook droplets of water from his hair. He looked back at their crude camp. He should never have let it happen.

Something else had driven him to her, and it hadn't been the desire for revenge. Somehow he'd known, even as he lashed out at her, that she was different—softer, innocent, not at all like Delia for all that they looked alike.

"We need to leave as soon as you're ready," he announced when he returned.

She struggled up out sleep, squinting into early morning sunlight. Instinctively she reached out, her hand finding only the empty twist of blankets now cold beside her. She raked her fingers through her hair.

"This isn't Boston, and you're not being served breakfast in bed," he snapped at her.

Laurel's deep blue eyes widened as she watched him disappear through the trees in the direction of the tethered horses.

She struggled with the brass-button closure of the denim pants Cass had traded her. Finally, tucking the tails of the blue cotton work shirt into them, she forced the last button through the hole. Even with the thickness of the shirt, the pants gaped at the waist and threatened to slip down over her hips.

"I'm ready," she told him when he returned.

"Good. Take this and slip it on the black like I showed you." He handed her the headpiece and harness.

Laurel swallowed uncertainly as he handed her the leather. One hand clutching the waist of her pants, leather in the other, she eyed the gelding skeptically. She felt more confident astride the big horse than approaching it on foot, especially when she wasn't quite certain of how she was going to manage to get the headpiece on the gelding without letting go of her pants.

"Silver Butte is about thirty miles up ahead. I'd like to make it before nightfall. There's an old cabin there where we can spend the night." Glancing over the back of his own mount, Ruel checked to see if she needed any help.

After trying for the third time to get the leather over the black's head, Laurel cursed in exasperation.

"Damn, your rotten hide! Stand still!" The last thing she wanted was to make Ruel angrier than he already was. She'd had far too much experience with his anger to want to risk that. At the moment, she still needed him to help her reach Virginia City.

Astride, the gelding didn't seem so big, but now, as Laurel again attempted to approach him, he sidled away, pulling back his massive head until he was jerked up short by the tether.

"I'll bet there's at least one jackass in your family!" She muttered. Her patience fast disappearing, she hitched up her pants.

"Not that I recall." Ruel frowned trying not to notice the curve of her bottom. He'd never given much attention to women who wore pants, but he could have a new appreciation.

"Need some help?"

She glanced up, the leather hanging from her hands. "No, thank you."

"Apparently you do." He took in her firm grip on both leather and pants.

Stepping back warily, Laurel indicated the extra width in the waist. "What I need is a belt."

Ducking under the head of the gelding, Ruel shook his head. She was such an independent, stubborn, willful... The list was growing.

He always ended up yelling at her, cursing her! There'd been the times when he'd actually thought he might kill her! No, not her! Delia!

Yanking his belt off, he reached around her slender waist, jamming it through the loops. At the touch of her, his anger slipped away. Squinting up into the early morning sun, he found those remarkable blue eyes fastened on him. When had Delia ever looked at him that way?

"You and Cass don't fill these out quite the same," he announced. "This should help." He cinched the belt in snugly, then let his hands ride on either side of her waist. Her gaze met his.

This wasn't Delia, he told himself. Here was a beautiful young woman with more courage than a lot of men he knew. She'd left a life in Boston that was safe to face an unknown future. And without so much as a complaint, she'd shed silk skirts and donned sturdy pants, because, as she'd said at the time, they were far more practical.

Laurel held her breath as his fingers pressed into the curve of her hips.

"Thank you," she murmured, glancing down to avoid the scrutiny of his dark gaze.

"You're welcome." His hands still rested on her waist. She was trembling. He could feel it beneath his fingers.

Unwilling to meet that dark gaze, Laurel tried to bring a casual tone to her voice. Deep inside she couldn't draw an even breath. "We'd better go if you want to make that cabin by nightfall," she broke the contact as she moved away from him.

Ruel watched her struggle atop the black gelding, refusing to meet his eyes as she took a firm hold on the reins.

Ruel jammed his hat down low over his eyes as he turned and headed for his own horse. Delia had once called their relationship convenient—no strings, no obligations, no expectations.

Jerking the bay around and sending him through the sparse trees at the perimeter of the lake, Ruel set a hard pace. No strings, no obligations, no expectations, the words set him on edge.

The wind came up steadily through the long silent hours of the morning, scattered puffs of clouds into an angry, churning mass above distant peaks by midday. Towering pines bent like reeds as the wind came up, and the blue sky overhead faded to gray as the afternoon wore on. Finally, the first heavy spatters of rain soaked both horses and riders.

Cold, wet, and miserable, Laurel strained to keep Ruel in sight, desperately hoping he'd stop. But he pushed on through the thickening storm. She huddled into the blanket, thankful that numbness was setting in.

She jerked upright. Somewhere up ahead she'd heard a shout. Shielding her eyes against the stinging rain, she shouted his name. Unable to see him, she hauled back on the reins. The black slid to a halt in the mud, his head sawing back and forth. Spotting a dark form moving in the distance, Laurel eased the gelding forward.

Two dark shapes moved closer until they merged, and the gelding snorted wildly as the reins were jerked from Laurel's hands. She screamed as she felt the horse going down under her. From somewhere up ahead, she heard a gunshot. Then pain burst at her head and light exploded, and she was falling.

"Hey, Emmett, that one over there's beginning to stir. Seems the fall didn't kill him after all."

The voices were a faint buzzing sound, gradually slowing

until the words became more distinct. Laurel opened her eyes, painfully fixed them on the glow of a fire. She moved slightly as memory returned. They'd been riding and Ruel had grabbed her horse. No. It wasn't him. There'd been two of them. Her eyes slowly focused so that she saw things clearly. She moved her legs, then her arms. Something was wrapped around her. The blanket. She shivered, aware now of the clammy, cloying dampness of musty wool. Her movements had pain pounding in her head. Relaxing, she waited until the room stopped spinning about her.

Somehow, they must have reached the cabin. But who were the men she'd heard talking, and where was Ruel? Struggling against the weight of the blanket, Laurel sat upright. Immediately she felt faint, but it passed. Opening her eyes once more, she stared straight into the blue-steel of a gun barrel. Her head throbbed, every muscle in her body ached. Pain overrode caution as she swiped at the barrel of the gun pointed directly at her.

"Get that out of my face! Who are you? And what have you done ...?"

Scanning the crudely furnished room, Laurel's eyes widened upon taking in a second man. He was warming himself in front of the fire, his face indiscernible for a tangled mat of hair and beard that covered it. Steam rose steadily from his heavy, wet coat. Across the room, someone lay slumped in the corner.

Starting up from the dirt floor, Laurel again met the ominous sight of steel. Whoever these men were, if they'd wanted to kill her, they'd have done it already.

'*That one over there's beginning to stir... The fall didn't kill him after all.*'

Him? They thought she was a man!

She'd been bundled in the blanket, and no one had bothered to check. Wrapping the blanket more securely about her,

Laurel pushed past the younger man with the gun. As she crossed the cabin, she wondered what it felt like to be shot.

"Hey, just what the hell does the kid think he's doin'?"

The man in front of the fire rose to his feet and started toward her.

Kneeling down beside Ruel, Laurel pressed shaking fingers against his chest. His pulse was faint but steady. But he felt feverish, even through his shirt. Realizing that her fingers were warm and sticky, Laurel pulled back, then stared at the dark blood on her hand.

"Don't get yourself all excited. He's alive. He put up a fight, even with that bullet hole in him. Now just get yourself away from there!"

The one called Emmett ordered as he seized Laurel from behind, his meaty fist closing over the wool blanket. As she was pulled back, the blanket fell away, her hair tumbling past her shoulders.

"Lord almighty, it's a woman!" The younger man breathed, awestruck.

"Sure is." Emmett's lips drew back to reveal blackened teeth. "And a might pretty one at that, even if she is a bit pale. Look at all that gold hair." His fist tightened in her hair.

Laurel glared at him. "Take your hands off me!" she demanded.

"Oooeee, if she isn't just full of fire, too."

"Laurel." The sound of her name brought her up short. Despite Emmett's powerful grasp, she twisted around to find Ruel's dark gaze fastened on her.

"Now that's a mighty pretty name," Emmett commented.

He hauled her back against him, the rancid smell of his damp clothes now mixed with wood smoke, almost gagged her.

Tightening her fingers into a fist, Laurel jabbed her elbow back into Emmett's stomach. With a loud exclamation, he released her. Taking advantage of her freedom, Laurel fled across the cabin to Ruel's side.

Emmett cursed as he descended on her.

Laurel flinched, waited for the blow that never came. All eyes turned as the door to the cabin was blown back on its stout hinges to reveal a third man silhouetted in the frame.

"Leave her alone."

"But, Dawson," Emmett whined, "you didn't see what she did to me." He ran a paw of a hand over his midsection.

The one called Dawson strode into the room, rain coursing down his slicker to form puddles at his feet. His face was almost completely obscured by the hood yanked low over his head. Removing a heavy bundle from his shoulder, he tossed it onto the wooden floor—the leather satchel Ruel had carried from the coach.

"See what's in there," Dawson growled, as he went to stand before the fire and extended a rain-soaked hand covered with scars toward its warmth.

"I already searched him." The younger man gestured toward Ruel. "Want me to search the girl?" he asked, starting toward Laurel. A powerful arm shot out, stopping him.

"Leave her be for now. We got other things more important. Besides, you can see she's nothing more than a child. Help Emmett with those bags. See if there's anything to eat. And I want all guns on the table."

Laurel's eyes widened at Dawson's last order, then met Ruel's fevered gaze. His mouth was pressed into a tight line as he shook his head.

"The pistol," he mouthed so that only she could see.

Laurel's hand went to the belt at her waist. The small derringer was still safely concealed by the shirt inside the waistband of her pants. Ruel nodded as Laurel reached to unbutton his shirt. He winced as she drew back the cloth.

The wound had started to bleed again. They exchanged a look. He shook his head.

She was tired, hungry, and scared. She tore off another strip of cloth.

"You never did tell me how you and Delia first met." She needed to talk about something, anything, to keep herself from falling apart.

He inhaled sharply as she pressed another pad of cloth against the wound, his head going back, eyes closed.

"Oh no, you don't!" she threatened. "You can't die on me and leave me out here with..." she lowered her voice. "I've survived nearly being suffocated in a trunk, shot at by outlaws, and..." She caught herself just before blurting out what she wanted to say.

"If you expect me to keep bandaging you up, the least you can do is live long enough to get us out of here," she said as she tied off the bandage.

Ruel reached up, his fingers closing over hers as she tucked in the ends of the ties. Her words touched something inside him. She trusted him—not in so many words, but it was there. It was a beginning.

"You wouldn't understand about Delia," he whispered, so low she had to strain to hear.

"You're wrong. I do understand." She forced a smile. "And my misfortune to be caught in the middle. Now, do you any ideas for getting us out of here?"

Her gaze met his. His smile was almost boyish.

"Just keep your hand on that gun," he replied.

"You don't mean... There are three of them, and only two of us."

"She's beautiful and she can count."

"You can't be serious." There was that smile that she'd learned meant she was probably in trouble.

"I figure you can handle two of them. That raises the odds."

"Obviously you can't count," she whispered.

"What the hell you two talkin' about?" Emmett demanded. "Get away from him. And don't look at me like that. I still got a mind to teach you a lesson about how to talk to your betters." He started toward her as she helped Ruel to his feet.

"You don't strike me as being stupid," Ruel told Dawson. "But you let this sonofabitch touch her, and I'll have to kill all three of you."

"What are you doing?" Laurel whispered. He had to be delirious.

His arm about her shoulder, Ruel leaned on her a bit more heavily than necessary.

"Running a bluff, to see who's willing to play his hand all the way to the end of the game."

This was no card game. Someone could get killed, Laurel thought, as she helped him across the single room cabin to the woodstove.

"The first guy that moves, shoot him," he told her. "Only don't shoot me instead."

She helped him sit down on the small bench beside the stove. Then he sent her back to the corner with a single nod.

"You just sit yourself down and shut up." Emmett's eyes narrowed as he pointed a finger at her. Turning back to Ruel, he drew the back of his hand across his mouth.

"I think you're just a bit confused here, mister. You could just be the one to get yerself killed."

"Not unless you're in the habit of throwing away thirty thousand dollars," Ruel replied. "That's what you lose if I die."

Laurel sat back in the shadows, grateful that she could sit and watch everyone else. Her hand brushed over the comforting bulge of the pistol tucked at her waist, then she wrapped her arms around her knees for warmth.

The leather satchel Ruel had brought with them lay on the

table. She frowned at the sight of the contents spread across the surface. There were only a few items, but none of the payroll for the mine that the driver and the guard had supposedly carried.

Ruel sat at the table and pulled out one of his long, dark cigarettes that he preferred. She stared at him. What was he doing?

He leaned back from the table and pulled the oil lamp toward him. He touched the tip of the cigarette to the chimney at the lantern and slowly inhaled. The tip caught, glowing as he gazed around the room. He slowly exhaled.

Laurel was convinced that he was either mad or delirious from the wound.

Emmett laughed, then looked at Dawson and the boy. The boy laughed uncertainly as he gazed from one man to the other. Dawson didn't share their amusement.

"What the hell you talkin' about?"

Gesturing toward Laurel, Ruel played on their curiosity but more on their stupidity. "Ten thousand dollars. That's what she's worth at the white slaver's market in San Francisco," he announced, so slowly that even the dullest person could understand.

Ten thousand dollars! White slave market? My God, Laurel thought. He is insane. How could any of this talk get them out of this mess?

"Ten thousand? For her?" Dawson turned to stare into the corner where Laurel sat. "Now that's real interestin'." He rubbed a dirty hand across his grizzled chin as he considered Ruel's words, and an evil gleam sparkled in the depths of his beady eyes as he turned to Ruel.

"Seems you're forgettin' just one thing. We got the guns. What's to stop us from killin' you and takin' her?"

Laurel's mouth dropped open, and she came out of the corner. "Now wait just a minute!"

"Be quiet and get back in that corner," Ruel ordered, the gleam in his eyes flashing a deadly warning.

"Can't we talk about this?" Laurel whispered urgently. He was up to something. But what?

Couldn't he at least have told her what he was going to do? His eyes fastened on her, the expression in them dark, cold, terrifying. She retreated to the corner, Dawson's jeering laughter taunting her.

He was playing a very dangerous game, and she didn't know the rules. Her head. She watched him. Something he'd said before came back to her.

'I make my own rules.'

Dear God, she hoped he knew what he was doing.

"There's a man called Big Jake Malloy," Ruel forced a lazy calm into his voice. Only the crackling and popping of the fire broke the silence.

Big Jake Malloy? She hugged her knees tighter against her chest to keep from running to the door. Instinctively, she knew the slightest movement could get them both killed. She had to trust him in this.

Shifting a thick wad of tobacco from one cheek to the other, Dawson nodded. "I heard of him."

Gambling on the reputation of a man he'd met once and never wanted to meet again, Ruel rolled the cigarette slowly between his fingers. "He's my partner, owns half-interest in the girl."

Laurel's eyes widened.

"So what?" Dawson jeered between stained teeth.

"You said you'd heard of him, so you know he's not the sort to take kindly to having something stolen from him, or damaged. Big Jake may be a thief, but he won't tolerate anybody else taking what's his." Ruel inhaled the cigarette.

Dawson nodded. "He hasn't been in this part of the country

for a while. Rumor had it he'd gone south to Mexico." Across the room, the boy laughed.

"Shut up!" Dawson growled. He leaned against the table, resting his hand on the long-barreled pistol under his coat.

Laurel caught the gleam of satisfaction that leaped into Ruel's eyes. Whatever he was up to, it was working.

"Like I said, being a thief himself, Malloy has no tolerance for them. But Big Jake fancies himself a sportin' man. He likes a bit of gamblin' every once in a while. Are you a gamblin' man, Dawson?" Ruel tossed his cigarette into the fire at the woodstove, then calmly spread his hands on the flat surface of the table.

"I've held a hand or two," Dawson acknowledged.

Ruel leaned forward. "If I were to lose my interest in the girl in a card game, that could be a lucrative investment."

"You'd be willing to bet the girl in a game of poker?" Wetting his lips, Dawson didn't even bother to hide his enthusiasm. "Against what?"

Ruel sighed heavily as if forced to make a bad decision. "If you win, the girl's yours, and I clear out in the morning."

"What about Malloy? What's to say you won't tell him we stole the girl?"

"I'll sign over a bill of sale for my interest," Ruel offered. "It's up to you to deal with Malloy and his half."

Dawson smiled, his satisfaction deepening. He smiled. "You got yourself a deal, Mister... You didn't say what your name was."

Ruel gave Dawson a long look, ignoring his last comment. "If I win, the girl stays with me, you and your men ride out."

"Beats spendin' the night holed up here with these two jackasses," Dawson replied. "Guess it's a lucky thing I didn't kill you. What do you bet with?"

"I've got a couple of gold pieces," Ruel nodded at the leather pouch beside the oil lamp.

There was a great deal more in that leather pouch, Laurel thought of the payroll shipment. Unless?

"We start even. The one who ends up with the most at the end of the game, wins."

Dawson drew out the long-barreled pistol and leveled it at Ruel's chest.

Laurel drew in her breath sharply, and started out of the corner, but Ruel warned her back.

"If you kill me, all you have is stolen property," Ruel explained. "Malloy doesn't take kindly to stealing. He's got a certain reputation about that."

Beyond the cabin, the wind filled the trees. The seasoned timbers of the rafters creaked and groaned, and occasionally a gust of wind stole beneath the sagging door, swirling the dust at the dirt floor. That single oil lamp provided the only light other than that of the fire at the woodstove.

In the center of the room stood the table, one leg replaced by a stout log on its end. The man, Emmett, and the boy sat on a bench across the cabin while Dawson and Ruel sat opposite each other at the table.

"I just happen to have a deck of cards," Ruel announced.

Watching from the shadows in the corner, Laurel hoped this part of Ruel Delaney's reputation wasn't merely rumor. If he lost...?

"Give me what's in yer pockets," Dawson told the other two.

There was some complaining, but both laid down several coins when Dawson aimed the revolver at first one then the other. Then, he called the game—five card draw, and smirked as he waited for Ruel to cut the deck.

She watched as Ruel took the cards then handed the deck back to Dawson.

"I think I remember how this is played," he said.

He *thought* he remembered? What was he doing? The man

owned gambling houses. Was it possible he didn't know how the game was played?

The first two cards were dealt face up, the next two were face down, the last card face up. Then, each was allowed to draw up to three cards to replace three in his hand.

"Ante up."

Dawson placed his bet and Ruel matched it, then called for three cards. Bets were made again and raised. Apparently not receiving the cards he wanted, Ruel tossed his cards across the table. With a smirk of satisfaction, Dawson scooped his winnings toward him.

"This is gonna to be quick and sweet." He chuckled. Then, suddenly struck by an idea, he turned toward the corner of the room.

"Hey, missy. Get yourself over here. Right over here in that chair by the fire," he commanded. "I want to see exactly what I'm winnin'."

Ruel nodded as alarm sprang into her eyes, and she slowly rounded the far end of the table toward the woodstove.

Seizing her by the arm, Dawson shoved her into the chair.

"Sit right there. That way you can see this here fella lose his bet." The gleam in Dawson's eyes sharpened. "I just had me a thought. I want to take a good look at the prize."

"Leave her alone," Ruel said, almost indifferently.

"You leave be, mister, or I might just decide to try her out first," Dawson replied. "After all I got no guarantee she's worth ten thousand dollars."

"And here I was looking forward to a game of cards. My daddy must have been wrong." Ruel drummed his fingers at the edge of the table. "He always said you could judge a man by the way he played a game of cards."

"What the hell you talkin' about?" Dawson turned back around.

Ruel had his full attention. The game had just started. He

needed to lose a few more hands, and he needed Dawson to stay in the game.

"My daddy said only a coward would back down on a bet."

Laurel's eyes widened as Dawson's eyes narrowed.

"What kind of a man would go and lose all his money? You tell me that!" Dawson taunted.

"He may have lost, but he was always able to walk away from the table without wondering whether someone was going to put a bullet in his back." Ruel's dark gaze never wavered.

"You saying you'd kill me if I just wanted to sample a little first?"

"A bet is a bet. You win, she's yours. But not until then."

Dawson slammed down his cards. "All right, I'll stick by the bet, and I'll win. But the next hand I win, she takes somethin' off."

The game continued. As Dawson took the next three hands, Laurel was forced to shed both boots and one stocking.

Her cheeks stung with the humiliation. How could Ruel do this to her? How could he be losing? As panic and anger collided in her, she pressed her hand against the gun concealed at her waist. If Ruel hadn't the skill to beat this lowlife at a game of cards, she'd make certain Dawson never lived to collect his bet.

Her nerves were taut, and only a few more coins remained on the table in front of Ruel.

She understood betting and raising a bet, though she had little idea of the strengths of certain cards. All she knew was that Ruel had thrown in the last three hands, and her panic rose. Now, they had played one last hand, winner take all. She couldn't bear to see the satisfaction gleaming in Dawson's eyes.

"Full house," he announced with satisfaction and laid down his hand. "Let's see that last card."

Laurel held her breath, and her hand closed over the steel of the pistol hidden under the tail of the shirt. For a brief moment, Ruel's eyes met hers. Then his gaze flickered briefly to the revolver only inches away from his fingertips.

Dear God, was he bluffing? If he didn't have the card he needed... If she lived through this, she'd kill him for doing this to her.

Elbow at the table, a hand propped at his chin, Ruel turned over the last card with his other hand. Firelight glinted off red markings and the gold glinting in the lady's crown. The queen of hearts.

"You sonofa... !" Dawson slammed down a meaty fist. But before he could reach for his gun, Ruel's right hand dropped over the pistol, the steel sliding comfortably into his fingers.

"I believe a royal flush beats a full house."

"You cheated!" Dawson roared. He turned to his men. "He cheated; you saw him."

The younger man shrugged. Across from him, Emmett coughed nervously. "I watched him the whole time, Dawson. I never saw nothin'," he nervously muttered.

"Well, I say he cheated. Give me your gun!" he thundered. Then he suddenly became aware of the gun barrel thrust against his forehead.

"The game was fair. But if you want to argue about it..." For emphasis Ruel shoved the pistol against Dawson's head.

Dawson blanched and pulled back. "No! It was a fair game! You keep the girl!" He raised his hands.

"And the coins that you bet on that last hand," Ruel said coolly.

Laurel held her breath. The scowl on Dawson's face was deepening. A moment before she'd been angry enough to be brave. Now, staring into that whiskered face with that leer pulled back over those stained teeth, she fought back a wave of nausea.

"A man always pays his gambling debts. Isn't that right, Dawson?" Ruel asked.

"I suppose so." Dawson grabbed for his coat. Without batting an eye, Ruel squeezed the trigger and a loud roar filled the cabin.

Laurel cried out, her hands clasped over her ears at the deafening sound in the small cabin. Dawson's coat lay on the floor, the long rifle it had hidden exposed, Dawson cradling his right hand as blood oozing between his fingers.

"Get the rifle," he told her.

As she scurried around the table and brought the rifle to him, Ruel shifted in his chair.

"Gentlemen, according to our little wager, if I win, the girl stays with me, and you leave."

The boy protested. "You wouldn't send us out in that storm."

"Gentlemen, I'm far too tired to stand guard over you till sunrise. Guns on the table and leave now, or not. Either way, I'll be rid of you," Ruel said coldly.

Laurel's eyes widened. Surely he wouldn't... *His own rules.*

"Move and get out while you still can!" Ruel's tone was quietly threatening.

In a wild scurry, the three reached for coats and hats.

"Empty your pockets. You leave on foot, your horses stay here."

"But we'll die out there without our horses and guns," Emmett complained.

"That's your problem," Ruel said. Motioning them to the door with the pistol, he sent the youngest out first.

They did as he said, including knives, extra load for the rifle, and two smaller revolvers.

"Now, get out. And if I so much as hear a suspicious sound, I'll shoot first and ask questions later."

Exchanging uncertain glances, the three started out the door.

"I won't forget this, mister," Dawson threatened.

"Make sure you don't," Ruel told him. "You'll stay alive that way."

The young man turned in the doorway. "There's only one man in these parts plays cards like you, a fella by the name of Delaney."

Ruel smiled faintly. "I'll say hello for you when I see him." He motioned to Laurel, instructing her to drop the bar across the door as Dawson followed the others out into the blinding storm.

"Will they go?" Laurel turned large eyes on him.

"If they know what's good for them, they will."

"Damn you, Ruel Delaney! You could have lost that game, and I was the bet!"

He saw the anger at her eyes. "A half interest was the bet, and there was never any danger that I would lose."

"You mean, you played that game exactly the way you wanted?" She stared at him. "And who is Malloy?"

"An old friend."

"You lied, cheated, and..."

"I didn't lie. Malloy would be more than happy to have a half interest in any investment with me. But I don't share."

12

"How are you this morning?" she asked. He'd been restless through the night, between watching out the shutter at the window and putting more wood in the woodstove to keep the fire going. She wasn't certain he'd slept at all.

"I've felt worse."

He leaned heavily on one of the chairs at the table. She was beside him in an instant, her arm going round his waist.

"You need to be careful or the bleeding will start again."

He lowered himself into one of those chairs. "Would that matter to you?"

She gave him a long look. "Of course. I'm running out of petticoat," she added. "And I need your help to get to Virginia City."

"I'll try not to die on you before we get there."

She hoped that he was joking. "I am grateful."

"Smells good. What is it?" Ruel watched her go to the wood-stove. He gestured to the pot simmering on top.

"Something Dawson left behind. I found it in one of the saddle bags. It looks like dried meat of some kind."

"You cook?"

She caught the surprise in his voice. "I don't think warming some beans and strips of meat is considered cooking," she replied. "But it's all we have, and it smells better than it looks."

She was full of surprises.

"How soon will that be ready?" he asked. Considering neither one of them had eaten the past two days, anything would have been welcome.

"We should leave as soon as possible." Ruel grimaced as he slowly came to his feet. "I want to put as many miles as possible between us and here."

It was a reminder that there was still danger out there.

"You won't do anyone any good in your condition." She wondered what might have happened the day before with Dawson. She gently pushed him back down into the chair.

"I'll saddle the horses while you eat."

A dark brow angled sharply. She was beginning to know his expressions and the words behind them.

"You're going to saddle the horses?"

She heard the doubt in his voice.

"I always saddled my own horse back..." she started to say 'home', but Boston seemed less and less like home every day and more like a place she was from.

"It's pretty much the same," she added.

He was surprised, and it irritated her considering what she'd been through the last several days. It raised more questions about her sister, the sort of person she was, someone she didn't know at all.

"I can manage," he told her.

"Maybe, but if that wound starts bleeding again, neither one of us will make it to Virginia City. And I don't like the thought that Dawson and the other two are out there somewhere."

"Take this with you." He was still skeptical as he handed her the pistol.

The sun was just slanting through the trees as she pulled

herself up into the saddle of one of the horses that had been left behind. He checked the cinch of the other horse she'd saddled for him. His gaze met hers as he checked the cinch, then stepped up into the saddle.

She smiled to herself that he didn't need to tighten the cinch. But as much as she'd learned some of his expressions, the one at his face now was unreadable.

They trailed the other horses behind them, leaving no possibility that Dawson or his men would be able to follow them. He was determined they would make Virginia City before dark.

At the bend of a stream some hours later, he reined in his horse.

"We'll rest the horses here, before moving on," he announced. He swung a leg across the saddle and dropped to the ground, his pain evident from the lines at his eyes and mouth.

Laurel tethered the horses and brought the two rifles and one of the saddlebags over. She frowned at the sight of fresh blood at the front of his shirt.

"We could stay here and continue in the morning," she suggested, tearing another strip of cloth from what was left of her petticoat.

He shook his head as he took a drink of water. "The sooner we reach Virginia City, the better it is. I don't like being out here..."

She finished the thought for him. "With a woman?"

That dark gaze narrowed on her. "I need to get you where it's safe from the likes of Dawson."

She didn't bother to point out that she'd done fairly well until now, all things considered.

"What about your father?" she asked. "Was he a gambler too?"

He shrugged. "I never knew him."

"But you said..."

"I said he was a gambler. I didn't say that I knew him. He worked the riverboats, and had quite a reputation. Everyone it seems, knew Chance Delaney. Everyone, except... "

She heard the hesitation in his voice. "Except you." They had a lot in common in spite of how they'd met.

He took another drink of water, heartily wishing he had something stronger to dull the pain, and he carefully avoided the haunting blue eyes resting on him. "When there are empty spaces in your life, you can make up anything you want."

She smiled a little sadly. "When the other children used to tease me about not having a mother or father, I made up all sorts of stories. Once I said my parents were part of a traveling circus. Another time, I made my father a diplomat.

"His work took him and my mother to other countries, so it never seemed strange that they were never there." She changed the bandage at his side, frowning at the heat that came off him.

"My aunt overheard me tell one of my stories. I'll never forget the hurt in her eyes. Both she and my uncle tried hard to make me feel welcome. But there was always something missing. I didn't realize until then that there's much more to the words *mother and father*."

"Why did you come to California?" he asked.

"I had learned about my mother from my aunt and uncle. But no one ever spoke about my father. I was only told that he'd died when I was a baby. A letter arrived informing me of his death only a few months ago, and I realized I'd been allowed to believe a lie all of my life. I wanted to know the truth." She finished tying off the bandage.

"What about your mother?" she asked.

He shook his head. "She was from a pretty important family. She suffered a lot for loving my father." His expression tightened. "Her family didn't approve of a gambler."

"But if she truly loved him, perhaps it was worth it to her," Laurel thought of her own mother and father.

He pushed to his feet and buttoned his shirt. "She loved him too well, and he didn't love her enough. And when she went to him and told him that she was going to have a child, he ordered her to get rid of it. He provided her with the name of an old Creole woman who could give her something to get rid of the child."

Laurel stared at him, horrified. "But she didn't."

She tried to imagine the young woman who chose not to destroy her child, what she must have faced.

"No, but I've often thought it would have been better if she had. I was sent to the Catholic nuns after I was born. I was six years old the last time I saw her. She came to the school to bring clothing for the orphans and foundlings.

"We talked until the reverend mother found out. I never saw her after that. I left the school when I was twelve." The words were cold, hard, as he turned and walked from the stream.

"I tried to find my father on the river." He shook his head. "I never found him, only rumors and stories, most not the sort a child wants to hear. An old gambler took me in and taught me the cards. At least, I had a way to survive. I owed him a lot—a complete stranger who cared more that my own father."

She heard the bitterness. And in spite of that he'd used that skill to build a life for himself. It explained a great deal.

"We need to go," he said sharply. "We've got a few more hours of light. We should be able to make Virginia City by dark." He moved stiffly toward the horses, jerking the bay's reins sharply, then pulled himself into the saddle, the rifle in one hand.

~

Virginia City lay in a small valley, the lights from the buildings glowing.

He led them down a street. A dog barked in the distance, and laughter rose to greet them. They passed businesses closed for the day, the proprietors long gone to their evening meals.

She had heard stories about the mining town. That it was wild and raw, in the middle of mining country, and drew all sorts from miners to merchants, and outlaws. But she hadn't expected ornate brick structures, there were elegant restaurants with paned windows with lace curtains hung, side-by-side to a Chinese laundry. She saw a man assist a well-dressed woman from a carriage in front of the Opera House that sat across from the Royal Gambling house with more shops, saloons, the smell of stables, and the noise that spilled out from the gaming houses.

They rounded a corner and the soft glow of lamplight at the side of a building reached out to them as Ruel reined his horse before an impressive brick building. Laurel's gaze was drawn up, six full stories to the top floor of the stately International Hotel.

"Sorry mister, you can't leave those horses here." A voice cut through the night, then a lanky youth came down the steps. "There are stables down the street."

"You're supposed to be efficient, Cal, but don't overdo it," Ruel said as he stepped down from the saddle.

"Mr. Delaney?" That same voice was attached to a youth who stepped into the light from the lantern, followed by a smile.

"We heard you were on your way. Got the wire from Jim Palmer in San Francisco. But that was eight days ago."

"We ran into a little trouble. This is Miss Wentworth. Let Soon-Li know that we've arrived and then see to the horses. The extra ones belong to Wells Fargo."

"Yes, sir!" Cal came forward to tether Laurel's horse and then waited to help her down.

She slipped from the back of her horse, painfully aware of her odd attire. Then Cal bounded up the steps ahead of them and disappeared into the lobby of the hotel.

"Your reputation precedes you."

Ruel's gaze held hers briefly. "A disadvantage at times."

Laurel thought she caught the faint trace of a smile as she moved past him through the etched glass doors, but she couldn't be certain. More secrets?

She was painfully aware how she was dressed along with the fact that she hadn't had a proper bath other than mountain streams the past several days as she stepped into a hotel that easily rivaled any in San Francisco for opulence.

Without so much as a sideways glance despite all the attention they were attracting, Ruel approached the front desk, manned by a bespectacled man in an impeccable black suit, a stiff white shirt, and a string tie. Upon seeing Ruel, the desk clerk flushed with excitement.

"Good evening, Mr. Delaney. This is a most pleasant surprise. We were quite concerned because you were overdue. There's been some trouble on the overland route. Welcome back to Virginia City."

He fixed Laurel with a cool gaze, and his smile quickly vanished. "Good evening, Miss Cameron."

"Oh no, my name is ..." Laurel's eyes widened with sudden understanding. It had happened again—he thought she was Delia! So simple, so easy. The man hadn't been mistaken. At least not as far as appearances were concerned.

Laurel felt the color rise in her cheeks. Why hadn't she realized people would mistake her for her sister? Obviously, Delia had been to Virginia City. Hiram Turnbull had spoken of Jason Cameron's meager existence up on Sun Mountain, about his mining the Rebecca. There would have been no money for Delia to stay in a hotel as grand as the International. The only way she might have been here... was as Ruel's mistress.

"Tibbits, this is Miss Wentworth. She will be staying in the Parisian suite," he explained.

"I shouldn't have come here," she told Ruel. "I should have gone straight to the Rebecca." Laurel fought back a wave of uncertainty.

Once again, she'd been confused for Delia. The mistake was natural. On the surface she understood that. But beneath the man's error, she'd seen more. Mr. Tibbits disapproved of Delia. Why?

"There's no way for you to get up there tonight. It'd be far too dangerous to attempt it by yourself. There'll be plenty of time in the morning to make inquiries," he added wearily.

"And mining camps can be rough, at best. Accept the rooms for the night." Then, without waiting for her answer, he turned to the clerk.

"Tibbits, the key," Ruel said with quiet authority.

"Yes, sir. Of course." He coughed to hide his embarrassment at his mistake, his confusion evident as he checked the ledger, made a brief notation, and then turned to the panel behind him. A few keys remained on it. Taking down one from the top row, he gave Ruel a questioning stare.

"And for yourself?"

"The office will be fine."

"And a physician," Laurel added.

Ruel nodded, then signed beside the notation on the ledger.

He was full of surprises. By the way everyone had greeted him, it was obvious that he spent a great deal of time in Virginia City. Of course—gambling. A boomtown. The silver mines undoubtedly attracted a lot of people.

Andrew had given her a brief education on the fortunes already made on the Comstock by cunning San Francisco investors. Virginia City was a paradise for a man who made his living by his wits and a deck of cards.

Ruel handed Laurel the key.

"It's made of silver?"

"Silver plate. The real stuffs too soft to be used for keys. A German fellow plated all the keys," Ruel informed her. Leaning across the elegant mahogany front desk, he informed Tibbits that he wanted a bath and fresh clothes, and to send for the doctor.

"And where is Soon-Li?"

"I believe she's in the dining room. Cal has already informed her of your arrival."

He nodded and turned to her. "An attendant will see you to your room. It's on the third floor."

He noted the weary sag in her shoulders. "You don't have to use the stairs." He angled his head toward the gleaming brass and mahogany elevator cabs across the lobby.

"The owner had them brought over from Europe."

Laurel sighed with relief. She'd been tempted to ask Mr. Tibbits about the possibility of sleeping in the lobby.

"What about the driver and the others?"

He nodded. "I'll speak with the manager of the Wells Fargo office in the morning."

"Thank you," Laurel replied. "You need to see a physician about that wound as soon as possible," she reminded him.

"And I need to send word to Andrew that we arrived safely. He'll be worried when he learns about the attack."

Ruel nodded. "Tibbits can see that a message is delivered to the telegraph office in the morning."

A hotel attendant was now standing expectantly at her elbow, her dusty valise in his hand.

"And the contents of this will need to go into safe until morning." It took some effort, but he lifted the leather satchel he'd taken from the stagecoach onto the counter.

Mr. Tibbets opened it. He looked up in surprise.

"It's the payroll shipment for Chollar Mining," Ruel told him.

"I'll see to this right away."

"You had the payroll shipment all along?" Laurel said with more than a little surprise.

"There is some honor among thieves," he replied.

"I didn't mean... that is..." she started to explain.

"I know what you meant."

Everything had changed the moment they'd ridden into town. She was a lady, beyond his reach. She had come here because of her father, not because of him. He regretted that and he'd long ago refused to regret anything.

The invisible barriers between his world and hers had reappeared along with the trappings of society, raw as it was in Virginia City.

She was stronger, finer, more beautiful than any woman he'd ever known. But she was not for him, and she had what she wanted. He'd brought her safely to Virginia City just as he'd promised.

"The physician?" she reminded him. One corner of his mouth lifted in a faint smile.

"Soon-Li will take care of it. She always does. Tibbets will see that you have everything you need," he added. "And he can put you in contact with someone who will help you with the Rebecca."

The woman he'd asked about when they first arrived.

"I appreciate everything," she replied.

After all, what had she expected? He'd delivered her just as he promised, and that was the end of it. But for just those few days, she had glimpsed someone far different from the man she had first encountered aboard the *Waverall*.

He had shared things about his life with her, protected her

—aside from betting her in that ridiculous poker game. But even then... *"I never lose."*

Now, he walked away, as a young Chinese woman greeted him. There was no mistaking the small, slender hand that rested against his shoulder or the soft look of brown eyes filled with warmth and concern. This could only be Soon-Li.

She was dressed in a floor-length tunic made of pale blue embroidered satin, her hair worn in a single braid down her back. The richness of her costume set her apart from the more simply dressed Chinese men, and the ample swell of her waist set her apart from the other women.

She stared as they talked, the expression on Ruel's face attentive, the lines of his frown the last days disappearing. Without regard for the hotel patrons, as if no one else was about to see it, he reached out, his hand gently patting the roundness of her stomach so obviously swollen with the child she carried. His child?

"Miss Wentworth?"

She turned and followed the young attendant to the elevator at the end of the lobby.

LAUREL EASED herself slowly into the tub of steaming hot water. Slipping deeper, she let her thoughts drift as soothing heat eased her bruised body and strained muscles. Yet even as she let her thoughts wander, they kept coming back to Ruel Delaney.

She removed the braid at her hair and slipped completely beneath the surface of the water, as if she could wash him from her thoughts as easily as she could wash her hair.

She would have preferred to remain just where she was all night, but the water was rapidly cooling. Turning suddenly at the click of the latch on the door to the suite, Laurel reached for the towel on the nearby stool. She wrapped it about herself and stepped from the tub just as a Chinese girl entered the room.

"I hope everything meets with your approval. Mr. Delaney requested food to be sent." A soft, accented voice greeted her.

Soon-Li, the same Chinese girl she had first seen in the lobby, bowed her head slightly.

"Good evening." Laurel stepped back, remembering that she was dressed only in the towel. Soon-Li smiled and gestured toward the massive bed with a sweep of her arm.

"I have brought clothes. Mr. Delaney spoke of the difficulty of your journey. Please accept whatever you wish."

Laurel stared clothing that had been provided—a dressing gown, a walking skirt, shirtwaist, and undergarments.

How convenient it had been for Ruel to send up a few garments! They weren't in the style favored by the delicate Soon-Li. Just judging by appearances, Laurel was certain the fit would be perfect. Undoubtedly, they had belonged to Delia.

She grabbed the dressing gown. "You can tell Mr. Delaney that my own clothes will do just fine, and as for his generous offer, I'm certain the one they belong to will be looking for them."

Soon-Li stared at her in complete amazement. "Mr. Delaney went to great trouble to have a dressmaker bring these clothes to the hotel at this late hour."

Laurel whirled around. "These don't belong to someone else?"

"They are yours, to wear or not as you choose. Mr. Delaney assured me the fit would be perfect," Soon-Li explained. "If there is anything else you need, it can be provided. And I will have your other clothes washed."

Of course, they would fit. He knew her body—or Delia's body well enough. She smiled apologetically.

"I'm sorry. It's just that the last few days have been so diffi-cult." Laurel reached for the dressing gown. She had only the barest necessities in the small valise. Her meager wardrobe had been reduced by one traveling outfit after the attack on the coach raid, and the shirt and pants Cass had traded her lay in a heap on the floor. She slipped on the dressing gown.

"Please, take the rest of the clothing back. My own clothes will do just fine."

Soon-Li bowed her head again. "I will have them washed for you. But first..." She gestured to the chair before the dressing table.

Drawing the sash of the dressing gown tight about her waist, Laurel silently obeyed, though she stared uncertainly at Soon-Li's reflection in the mirror.

Taking up a brush with a silver inlay, the girl began to work the tangles from her wet hair.

"It's not necessary. I can do this." She felt uneasy having the young woman attend to such things.

"But it pleases me. It pleases me, because it would please Mr. Delaney." Soon-Li smiled and continued stroking.

Realizing it would do little good to argue, Laurel relaxed and quietly contemplated the young Chinese woman.

"How long have you known Mr. Delaney?" she asked.

"Two years now. I am most fortunate." Soon-Li smiled again and continued to brush her hair.

"Fortunate? How?"

"Many on the boat coming from Canton had no family, no work. My mother and father die at sea."

Laurel understood loss. Soon-Li had been orphaned and alone in a strange country.

"How did you meet Mr. Delaney?"

"He buy me at slave auction. I owe him much, too much to ever repay." Soon-Li separated Laurel's hair in fanlike motions so it would dry more quickly.

Stunned, Laurel whirled about. "He bought you?"

"Oh yes, and most fortunate. I might have been sold to one

of the fancy houses in San Francisco. Many end badly there. I have much to be thankful for." She gestured to the room. "I have fine home, good work, and soon a fine son to make his father proud." Soon-Li beamed.

"How can you be certain he will be pleased?" Laurel whispered heavily.

Soon-Li gazed at her with quiet patience. "Because he has told me. He has long awaited a son. He is most pleased with the child I carry. If we are fortunate there will be many more sons."

Dear God, she thought. Ruel had bought the girl, then brought her here and found her work. And he kept her here, seeking her out on his occasional visits. And Soon-Li believed herself to be fortunate.

She remembered what Ruel had said—he had not implied about his own lack of legitimacy. He'd been very bitter about it, yet he'd placed Soon-Li's child in that same position.

She remembered Adela MacMillan's warning aboard the *Waverall*. Obviously, the rumors that Ruel Delaney had lovers in every port on the eastern seaboard were incorrect. They failed to include his mistresses in New Orleans, San Francisco, and Virginia City.

Casting a sideways glance at the Chinese girl, she smiled. In spite of the man who'd brought them together, she liked Soon-Li. She seized her hand and squeezed it gently.

"Thank you. You've been very kind. If I can help you in any way..."

Soon-Li smiled. "You are most generous, Miss Wentworth. It is my pleasure to know you." She gazed at Laurel thoughtfully, as she stroked her hair.

"You are like the sun. Such fine hair should be worn long. These are a gift." She pulled two perfectly carved black combs from the pocket of her tunic.

"Black jade, highly prized among the people from my province. When worn in the hair, like this." She scooped Laurel's hair back at either side and secured the combs, "they reveal all of a woman's charms. The hair is worn loose when the woman awaits her lover."

Laurel's hands stopped hers. "You don't understand... There is no one that I would wear them for."

Gazing into Soon-Li soft, almond eyes she instinctively knew that she could not refuse the gift. She smiled.

"I accept the combs, but you must allow me to give you something in return."

She was afraid that money would insult the girl. She reached to the back of her neck; she unhooked the chain to the locket Andrew had given her for her sixteenth birthday.

She opened it and revealed the places for pictures on either side. "It is for a picture of someone you care for, so that you always carry it next to your heart."

Soon-Li smiled. "I will treasure it always. And may you always have sunshine and happiness at your door."

Leaving Laurel to silently contemplate her words, Soon-Li crossed the room and opened the door into the hallway. As she did so, a young Chinese boy pushed a wheeled cart to the center of the chamber. A command softly spoken in Soon-Li's language sent the boy from the room.

"I hope you will like." She gestured to the domed platter and then removed it. It contained roast chicken and vegetables. Another one contained strawberries in cream.

Laurel's astonished gaze widened. Having eaten only dried strips of beef and water the last three days, it was a feast by comparison.

"It's perfect." She inhaled the aroma of the chicken, suddenly ravenous.

Soon-Li turned to leave.

"Please stay," Laurel invited. "I can't possibly eat all of this."

"Mr. Delaney is waiting," Soon-Li replied and then left.

After she had eaten, Laurel pushed back the velvet drapes

and opened the glass doors that looked out toward the distant mountains. In the street below a single carriage passed by. A silver moon hung high overhead, its gleam revealing the hills in the distance.

Sun Mountain was covered with glistening campfires dotting its sides, and she wondered about the men and women who warmed themselves before those fires, the strength it took to come here leaving everything behind.

Even on this summer night the air was cool and dry. Sun Mountain, Jason Cameron's mountain. Near one of those campfires lay the Rebecca, her legacy, and the key to her past.

RUEL CRUSHED out the cigarette he'd lit, holding the fragrant smoke in his lungs, needing the heat against the probe of the slender blade Soon-Li wielded with an expert hand.

She worked quietly, quickly, found the bullet, then removed it, blood flowing from the open wound. The only sound was the clink of metal against the porcelain of the wash basin as she dropped the bullet into it.

There was no criticism, no chatter, only that quiet way that reminded him of another even though they were as different as they could be.

"What about the clothes?" he asked.

"She did not want them."

He frowned. The truth was, he wasn't surprised. He winced as she spread a salve, something from the Chinese market in San Francisco, over the neatly made stitches.

"Do not make such a face," she playfully scolded him. "It is not the first time."

"No, it's not." He pulled on a clean shirt, then took Soon-Li's hands in his.

"I am grateful for your care."

"You should rest, give your body a chance to heal."

He nodded, taking another long pull on the cigarette. But he was restless, in spite of the salve, in spite of the tea she made him drink—foul stuff. She swore it would heal him from the inside out... if it didn't kill him.

Still restless, he stepped away from the long bar. Across the room, a dealer signaled a game to him.

His manager, Tom, looked up from his conversation with the bartender, and approached him.

"You should get some sleep. Soon-Li said the wound isn't bad, but you did lose a lot of blood. I can take care of everything here."

Ruel flashed him a quick smile, the anger lines about his eyes easing briefly. "You always do."

"One of the staff mentioned he saw Miss Cameron earlier," Tom commented. "Should I make the usual arrangements?"

"Not tonight," Ruel replied, then made a comment about managers overstepping their boundaries as he slowly approached the gaming tables. Several card players looked up. The dealer glanced up briefly, but only nodded his acknowledgment. One seat at the table was empty.

"Deal," Ruel told him.

13

"Get outta my way! Where is she?"

The door to the suite was sent crashing back on its hinges.

Awake since dawn, Laurel had long since eaten. She whirled around as the voice echoed through the elegant rooms. When the door to her bedchamber opened, a young Chinese girl bravely guarded the threshold as a bearded giant of a man thrust his head into the suite.

"Are you her?" He squinted through silver-streaked shaggy brown hair that grew so low over his eyebrows little else was visible except the inquisitive gleam of blue eyes.

Gathering her dressing gown tightly about her waist, Laurel drew herself up to her full height, a good foot shorter than the dusty giant's. "That depends on who you're looking for."

The man grunted appreciatively as he pushed the young Chinese girl aside. "Go on, get out." As the girl scurried out of harm's way, babbling wildly in Chinese, the man swung a booted foot in the direction where her backside had been a moment before.

"I got no use for squawky women." He turned on Laurel, his

eyes narrowing. "Reckon you are her. Just about what I expected," he acknowledged gruffly. "Wouldn't have thought it possible, after all these years. These are for you. That little Chinese
gal was bringin' 'em in to you when I came along." He thrust
freshly laundered pants and shirt into Laurel's arms, then
jerked a thumb over his shoulder.

"I'll wait out here till you're ready."

Laurel stared at him in amazement. "Ready? For what?"

"To head on up to the Rebecca." He turned back as if he'd
forgotten something. "You can ride, can't you?"

Laurel slammed the door in his face. "I can ride."

No name, no greeting, nothing. Just plain rude. Yet she was
certain she'd just met Cappy Burnett, the man she'd come over
five thousand miles to see. She stuffed the tail of her shirt into
the pants and pulled on boots. Having looked at Sun Mountain
from her window the night before, Laurel had a feeling they
wouldn't stay that way long. She seized Ruel's leather belt and
threaded it through the loops at her waist.

Her excitement grew. Cappy was gruff, crude, and
completely overbearing, but in spite of it all, she liked him. At
least he hadn't turned right around and walked out after
meeting her.

Laurel secured the combs in her hair. She wasn't wearing
them for Ruel Delaney, and she didn't give a fig about the
Chinese custom Soon-Li had told her about the evening before.
They were practical and they were a gift from someone she
liked in spite of the circumstances. With any luck at all, a
second friend waited in the sitting room outside her bedchamber. But she'd better hurry. By the looks of him, Cappy had little
patience. She seized her valise and opened the door.

"You always so fired up to go off with the first man that
walks through your door in the mornin'?" Cappy turned back
from the window that looked out on Sun Mountain.

"This may come as a surprise to you, Mr. Burnett, but men

don't usually barge into my bedchamber. Now, where are those horses?"

Cappy Burnett's eyes narrowed for the second time as he scrutinized the slender girl, from Boston according to rumors he'd heard. He'd expected silks and frills, and fancy manners. The manners were there but little else of what he'd expected.

His mouth softened beneath the thick beard that practically covered his face. She was a beauty. Something about the way she stood there, all proud and faintly defiant tugged at his memory. The hair was lighter, but the tilt of the chin the same, and the eyes. Her eyes were as deep blue as the far oceans, innocent and fearless at the same time. And her hair was almost as light as the silver hidden in the distant hills. Not a bit like that other one. He cleared his throat.

"You just might do," he said, and turning on his heel, he threw the door open wide and disappeared down the hall, leaving Laurel to stare after him. Quickly recovering from the strange meeting, Laurel went after him.

RUEL CALLED for Soon-Li as he passed through the massive dining room of the International Hotel and entered the kitchen.

At eight in the morning a full staff worked over steaming kettles and two hot cast-iron stoves. Breakfast was served from six until noon, which meant the day began at five for the cook and six for his staff. Ruel was irritable from having spent a restless night and his temper climbed another notch when he failed to find either Soon-Li or his manager awaiting the day's instructions, though from experience he knew neither needed them. Both Soon-Li and Tom Chin had been with him long enough for his requirements to be understood.

"Soon-Li!" His voice cut through the cacophony of banter in the kitchen. The staff, mostly Chinese, chattered their native language or in a mixture of pidgin English.

At a light pressure on his arm, Ruel whirled about.

"There is no need to shout," Soon-Li said softly, giving him an inquisitive look.

"Why the devil do they insist on speaking that gibberish?" Ruel complained as he led the way from the kitchen to the dining room.

"It would be more correct to ask why you insist on visiting the kitchen when you have ugly temper." Not the least intimidated by his black mood, Soon-Li arched a delicate brow.

"I am not in a bad mood."

Soon-Li bowed her head obediently, but not soon enough to conceal the teasing smile that danced in her eyes.

"And don't do that," Ruel told her. "You know how I hate that."

"Of course."

Ruel groaned and ran a hand through his hair. Soon-Li always knew exactly how to bring him down a notch. She was aware that he detested the feudal system that had forced many Chinese to come to California. In his opinion any man or woman who did a good day's work should earn a good day's wage and a person's respect.

"That bad?" He groaned.

"Bad," she replied. "You're like cat with thorn in paw. You frightened poor Wing May when she went to collect the receipts from last night for Daniel. She said you growled at her." Soon-Li carefully hid her amusement.

"I'll apologize."

Soon-Li watched him carefully. "What is the thorn in your paw this morning?" she asked.

"I'm looking for ancient Chinese wisdom." He rubbed his neck against the unaccustomed constraint of the starched collar and tie he always wore when he was at the International.

"Have you seen Miss Wentworth this morning?"

He walked beside Soon-Li as she straightened the linens on

the tables. She was as much a perfectionist about the appearance of the hotel as he was. Perhaps more.

"She is gone," Soon-Li answered simply.

"Where?" he demanded and in doing so caught the knowing smile she gave him.

"A man came early this morning. Big man, a miner. Went right on up to Miss Wentworth's room."

"And she left with him?"

Soon-Li watched Ruel carefully. "Yes, they leave together."

"Did she leave any message, maybe a note?" Ruel asked.

"I will ask Mr. Tibbets. He was on duty at the desk when they left."

Ruel nodded, knowing if there'd been any message, Tibbets would have already told him.

"What was he like?"

"Big. Tall, like you. Dirty." Soon-Li sniffed disapprovingly. "Need bath and haircut. Wore pants with ... red straps."

"Suspenders," Ruel translated.

"Yes, suspenders. And big, dirty boots. He didn't smell so good. Must have come right off the mountain."

Standing at the paned windows that faced onto the main street, Ruel nodded. "Cappy Burnett."

"Didn't give name and didn't use elevator. Just walk right up all three stairs."

As if he knew exactly what he was after, Ruel thought. And he had the courage to walk right through her door, like I should have done last night.

"You know this man?"

"I know him." Ruel frowned. His gaze swept the distant line of Sun Mountain. "Have Tommy bring a drink to my office. And take the rest of the morning off. You need to rest."

Soon-Li smiled, her eyes softening. She wasn't fooled by his dark anger or his even darker eyes.

"Baby is very strong. But still almost three months before he come, and work makes me stronger. Come, I look at those bandages. You don't need drink, you need work." It was a simple philosophy, and she used it on him all the time.

"You think so?"

"Know so!" She nodded emphatically. "Then you can make plan to see Miss Wentworth again."

"That doesn't bother you?" Ruel asked. "You didn't like Miss Cameron."

"That one is evil. She has cold eyes, cold heart," Soon-Li replied as she pushed open the office door and motioned for Ruel to sit in a chair. She waited patiently as he unbuttoned his shirt.

She brought a basin of fresh water from the adjacent bathing chamber, then slowly peeled off the bandages from the night before.

"They're twins, Soon-Li. The same. They look the same, talk the same." He winced as she pulled the bandage away. She made some comment, impossible to understand, then applied more salve—an old Chinese herbal cure, as she explained it, frowning at him like a disapproving mother.

The 'same'.

"Not the same," Soon-Li insisted, her hands stopping and her almond eyes meeting his for a moment before she continued. "Not the same."

"How do you know? I just got through spending eight days in the wilderness with her, and I'm not sure," Ruel argued. He glared at her as she pressed that pungent salve into the wound.

"You're sure." Soon-Li smiled softly.

"What are you babbling about?"

"Not babbling, you teach me good English. She's not the same, and you know it. Appearance is the same. But when she speaks, the words are not the same."

"She's from a place called Boston." Ruel was unaware that his voice softened.

Soon-Li smiled. "I know Boston—Massachusetts. One of the original thirteen colonies."

"That's right."

"Not accent," she informed him emphatically.

"What do you mean *'not accent'*?"

"Her words are gentle, kind, softly spoken. "It is more than that."

Ruel hid a smile. Soon-Li had labored long and hard over the books he'd provided, improving her English and her understanding of geography, history, and mathematics. She was bound and determined to be well educated. And she wanted those same things for her child.

"All right, no accent. Just gentle words."

"Yes, and her eyes are different. They are soft, open."

"What do you mean *'open'*?"

"Old Chinese proverb says the eyes are mirrors to the soul. They show the feelings one carries deep inside. We talk last night when I take the clothes you send. She is very proud, would not accept the dress. But there was a certain light in her eyes when she knew you had sent them, and the combs."

His head came up, his dark gaze locking with hers. "She accepted the combs?"

Soon-Li applied a fresh bandage. "She accept, even after Soon-Li tell her the legend of black jade. But her eyes say much more. Someone has touched her heart, but she is afraid. Her fear makes her vulnerable She is not same as the other one."

He took her hand and kissed it. "Thank you. You've helped more than you know."

~

"YOU WANNA STOP AND REST?" Cappy twisted around in his saddle, a dark frown making his brows converge beneath his shaggy mane of hair.

Wiping her arm across her forehead, Laurel waved him on. They couldn't have been riding for very long, but already the sun was high in a dazzling sky and heat shimmered across the hillsides. It promised to be an extremely hot day, yet this heat was far different from that of Boston or New Orleans. It was a dry heat that she'd first noticed on that long ride with Ruel Delaney.

"How much farther?"

Muttering under his breath, Cappy fought back irritation. He had to hand it to her; she hadn't complained or asked to stop a half dozen times. In fact, she was the one who suggested they keep going.

"Not long," he called back, fully expecting to hear some complaint. But there was nothing. She just straightened her back as she adjusted herself in the saddle. Cappy had deliberately mounted General Grant, the larger and more easygoing of the two mules he'd brought down off the mountain, leaving the more cantankerous Lucille for her. But he had to admit, there'd been no objections, no emotional outbursts, only that determined look in her eyes as she guided the mule over the trail he followed.

A bead of sweat slipped down Laurel's spine, dampening the denim pants, and for the fifth time in as many minutes, her mule halted, ears twitching. Giving Lucille a good, firm kick in the flanks, Laurel spoke to her softly.

Up ahead, Cappy was fast disappearing into the shade around the bend of the trail. Sweet Lucille. Well, if she didn't get her going pretty soon, Cappy would do one of two things— he'd either go on without her, or he'd come back and he'd take her back to Virginia City.

Dismounting, she kept a firm hand on the reins as she offered the mule water from the canteen he'd had her carry. Lucille proceeded to make a belligerent noise and then slop water down the length of her pants. If it hadn't been so oppressively warm, she would have been tempted to punch the mule right in the nose. A determined light gleamed in Laurel's eyes. She knew if she didn't do something quickly, Lucille would have the upper hand, and she'd never get the animal to do anything for her again.

The silence on the mountain, was calming. The pungent aroma of greasewood was carried on the hot air, and occasionally locusts broke the silence. A shadow streaked overhead, and Laurel looked up. She'd heard about the buzzards that roamed the skies looking for hapless animals or travelers, then swooping down and picking their bones clean. Instead, she saw the elegant arc of powerful gleaming wings. The hawk was majestic as it soared on the warm breeze.

"If I could fly," Laurel murmured, her wide blue gaze—once more contemplating Lucille. "But I can't, and it's hot, and you're the only transportation."

Lucille snorted, blowing out hot air.

"And the longer we remain out here, alone and without food, the greater the chance our next visitor will be a buzzard," Laurel argued.

Receiving no response, she twisted the reins firmly about her left hand, and looked around for something that might be used as a switch. But the landscape was almost barren. Glaring at the spot where Cappy had disappeared, Laurel turned back to the mule.

"Last chance. Then we do things my way." This time there wasn't even a faint twitch of an ear.

"All right, you asked for it."

Pulling up any slack in the reins, Laurel jerked on them.

The mule responded with an indignant huff and a rolling of the eyes, but her feet didn't move. That did it. Doubling her fist and drawing back her right arm as far as she could Laurel connected with Lucille's nose. The result was instantaneous. In a stunned whoosh of air, the mule exhaled. Her eyes rolled and her ears went back immediately, Laurel jerked on the reins as hard as she could.

"Now that I've got your attention, let's understand who's boss." The mule pulled back trying to get the reins from her hand.

Since she obviously couldn't win a game of tug-of-war, she decided on a different strategy, and loosed her hold on the reins. Lucille blew out more air, and her ears came forward in a gesture of capitulation. Before the mule had a change of attitude, Laurel scrambled atop her and, reins firmly in hand, and gazed up the trail.

"Not bad," Cappy muttered, as he sat calmly astride General Grant and watched her. "First time I ever saw anybody punch out a mule. Although I've had the notion several times," he said as Laurel drew up alongside him.

"It's the first time I've done it," Laurel admitted ruefully.

She rubbed the bruised knuckles of her hand. Cappy reached out and his large hand enclosed hers. Turning it and inspecting her slender fingers and pale palm, he saw a half-dozen blisters.

"Must have been a rough trip over the Sierras."

"It was." Laurel gently freed her hand. "Shouldn't we be going?" she suggested, eager to reach the Rebecca before Lucille had a change of attitude.

Cappy turned his mule about and rode beside her. "Just in case Lucille decides to act up again," he said.

Laurel's eyes narrowed slightly as she contemplated the man beside her. Why couldn't he have done that before? The answer came more easily than the question. He was testing her —first by barging into her room at an ungodly hour of the morning, then dragging her up this barren mountainside through insufferable heat, and giving her this damned mule.

She smiled herself. She didn't doubt that if she failed to meet Cappy's expectations, he would send her back to Virginia

City. Well, he hadn't done it yet. As a matter of fact, they were still headed up the winding trail to Sun Mountain.

There was, of course, one thing he hadn't considered. She had no intention of leaving Sun Mountain until she was good and ready. She'd come too far and been through too much, to turn back because of a mule as cantankerous and ornery as he was.

Finally, cutting through the entrance to a ravine, Cappy reined in his mule.

"Gold Hill." He indicated a long line of buildings strung along the ribbon like twist of road that followed the contour of the ravine.

"Why do they call it Gold Hill?" Laurel kept a firm hold on the reins while she dampened the collar of her shirt, finding cooling relief as a faint breeze plastered the shirt front to her body.

"'Cause it's located at the base of Gold Canyon Ravine," Cappy replied stoically.

Laurel chose to ignore his obvious contempt for her lack of knowledge of the area. "Are there Indians?"

"There haven't been any Indians hereabouts for over ten years—just miners, hoity-toity rich people from San Francisco, and them Chinese." Cappy contemplated her through narrowed eyes. Maybe he'd been wrong. Could be she wasn't any different. Still, even when she was asking about outlaws, she didn't seem scared, just curious.

"I was just wondering why you circled past this entrance to the ravine once before. It seems like a waste of energy and time." Laurel replaced the cap of her canteen. If she was right, she wondered what his answer would be. It was a loud snort that resembled the sound Lucille had made earlier when she'd been punched in the muzzle.

"You don't say?"

"Just observant, Mr. Burnett. Now, if you don't mind, why

don't we move on? I want to see the mine. How far is it from here?"

Well, I'll be damned, Cappy thought, rubbing a gnarled hand across his bearded chin. This little girl had more spunk than anyone he could easily remember.

"Up that ridge. You can see the surface buildings."

Shading her eyes with her hand, Laurel turned in the saddle. A long, wooden building was barely visible. A smaller building stood in the shade of the hill. A short distance below the slope, ran an intricate framework of flumes.

She'd done some reading and had asked Ruel a few questions. Now, upon seeing the Rebecca, she was even more curious.

"What are the flumes for?"

Cappy urged his mule through the mouth of the ravine. A series of buildings lined the entrance—a small general store, a telegrapher's office, stables, a corral, and a saloon.

"Devil's Toll Gate." He mumbled as they passed through.

He nodded to a man, rifle butt balanced on his hip as they passed through. "There's a river up there behind the Rebecca. A group of us built the flumes two years ago, to take the ore to Virginia City."

In the space of a moment, he'd managed to answer one question and to raise at least a half-dozen more.

"Do you have to pay a toll?"

"Wagons are charged toll fees; riders pass on through. They know me here. They don't like me, but they know me."

"Why don't they like you?" Laurel urged Lucille to a brisker pace until she was practically shoulder to shoulder with Cappy's mule.

He gave her long look. "Because of the flume system. It passes them by."

Turning so that she could follow the line of the distant flume, Laurel realized what he was saying.

"You don't pay a toll because you have no wagons. Everything is shipped down the flume."

Cappy smiled to himself, keeping his gaze straight ahead. "Ah, yeah, that's about it."

"It *will* be shipped down the flume? Do you mean you haven't used it yet?"

"Others have. I been waitin'."

"Waiting for what?"

"Waitin' for you." Cappy cut across in front of her, leading them along a wagon path that gradually ascended the mountain. As they climbed, they wound their way around to the shaded side of the hill. Come afternoon, the entire mountain would be ablaze with shimmering heat that withered everything that attempted to grow, be it animal, vegetable, or human.

Cappy was beyond earshot, obviously not interested in further conversation at the moment. Laurel wondered about his answer. He owned ten percent of the Rebecca according to Hiram Turnbull. He could certainly have continued mining operations after her father died. Obviously, he hadn't.

Just before midday, they reached the smaller of the two buildings. Notched into the side of the hill, it was actually a sturdily built cabin. Out in front, someone had once planted shade trees. They were as out of place in this dry parched atmosphere as she was, yet with an ample supply of water, they'd sent their roots deep, their branches wide. Laurel recognized silver maple and white-barked birch. They towered over the western exposure of the cabin, in summer offering cooling shade, in winter losing their leaves to provide exposure to daytime sun.

"Another flume to water the trees?" Laurel smiled.

Cappy grunted. "River's around the side of the hill. Sammy brings in water every day."

"Something else he hadn't bothered to tell her. "Sammy?"

"Sammy Lee. I'd guess you'd call him a houseboy." He bit the word off sarcastically. "He works the Rebecca."

Leading his mule to a small corral, Cappy pointed to a long building. "That's the Rebecca."

Following the direction of his outstretched arm, Laurel realized that when she'd pictured what the mine would look like, she'd never envisioned this low, crudely constructed building.

Unsaddling his mule and throwing the saddle over the corral fence, Cappy turned to her. He'd be damned if he'd coddle or pamper her. If she was going to get along up here, she would have to do her fair share of the work, or leave.

Returning his gaze, Laurel slipped from the back of the mule. She unbuckled the cinch and pulled the saddle toward her.

Cappy took the saddle from her.

"Go on over to the cabin. We'll eat before I show you the mine."

Opening the door to the cabin, Laurel peeked inside, noting that dust lay on the smooth-planked floors. It was sparsely furnished, with a table, chairs, and large wood stove filling one corner. The doorway at the rear led to another room.

The air inside was cool but musty, as if the paned windows on the far side hadn't been opened in a long time. Fresh air, Laurel decided, would be the first order of the day. She jumped as Cappy entered behind her and threw his hat on a peg beside the threshold.

"I know it's not your fancy houses in Boston, but it's solid. Holds out the snow and wind in winter, keeps pretty damned cool in summer. Jason was the one who wanted to build it into the side of the mountain like that."

At mention of her father, Laurel turned to Cappy. "You must have been very good friends to be partners in the Rebecca."

"Can't say as we were. We just had a mutual understanding, that's all. The mine was his. He needed someone who knew the area to help him work it. So, he cut me in as a partner. There's a pot of stew over there on the cook stove.

"Sammy fills the wood box every night and fires up the stove every mornin'. I'll see if I can find him, but he might be down the shaft!" He disappeared out the door, leaving her to inspect the cabin and the stew. It was a toss-up as to which was in more desperate need of attention.

A thick layer of grease lay over the top of lumps in the crusted pot, and the smell coming from the cold, gray mixture rivaled the dried beef she'd tried to make a meal of. For all she knew, it might have sat there a week.

Straining with the heavy pot, she opened the back door of the cabin, and looked for a place to throw it. A loud squall greeted her. Perched on the back step of the cabin was the most moth-eaten cat she'd ever seen. On its best day, the mottled-gray cat would have stopped anyone in his tracks. And this was obviously not its best day, though the cat was big and obviously a scrapper. One eye was missing, leaving only a narrowed slit where it had once been. And the creature moved with a decided limp as he approached her. Laurel wasn't certain whether she should stand or run. She decided to stand, and the scruffy animal weaved in and out of her denim-clad legs.

"You eat the stew," she told the cat. "Don't leave a drop, and I'll never tell." She poured what was left of the stew into a shallow pan, then moved out of the way as the cat charged at the foul stuff.

Satisfied, Laurel took the pot back into the cabin. Against the far wall was a small sink and cupboards. Mercifully, some-one, probably her father, had had the foresight to put a pump at the sink. Setting the massive kettle on the stove, Laurel began to fill it with buckets of water.

She opened the door of the woodstove and threw in several pieces of firewood. Firing the stove up this time of day would heat up the cabin, but there was no help for it. A good, long boiling was the only way to remove the layers of crusted food from the pot.

Opening every cupboard and a small sideboard, Laurel found a metal platter covered with cotton sacking. She removed the cloth. It was full of biscuits. Then, she found an iron skillet in one cupboard, the lid in another. Breaking the biscuits on the edge of the skillet, she layered the entire bottom. Adding a small amount of water, she covered the skillet and placed it on the stove-top oven to await the reincarnation of edible food.

She opened the windows on the shaded side of the cabin and found the condition of the place worse than she'd thought. Daylight only emphasized its filth and squalor. The cabin might be stout, but Laurel wondered if its walls would collapse if they were cleaned. She had the feeling dirt was holding it together.

"Makin' yerself right at home, I see. Jest like a woman," Cappy grumbled as he came in.

"You find that stew?"

Laurel threw him a hesitant glance. "There must have been less than you thought. There was nothing left, just a few biscuits. I put them in a pan to warm."

"Nothing left? That damned fool Sammy, eatin' all my food. It'll take at least half a day and a toll fee to bring more food in here." Cappy glared at her.

She gave him a long look. She'd endured his rudeness, his anger, and his obvious dislike. She'd put up with a ride that had taken twice as long as it should have because he was trying to discourage her. She'd sweated under the hot morning sun and had come to terms with that damned mule. Now she was going to come to terms with Cappy Burnett. She seized a long handled, wooden spoon from the table, and waved it at him.

"I've put up with your insolence, your aggravation, and your meanness. I've come four thousand miles, the last few hundred on a wagon route. I've been shot at and attacked by outlaws."

She deliberately left out the part about her initial meeting with Ruel Delaney.

"Now that I'm here, you start yelling at me about some damned stew and rock-hard biscuits!" She took a breath. She glanced down at the spoon encrusted with food and heaved it into the boiling water.

"According to my father's attorney, I own the Rebecca, less your percentage. Ninety percent is mine. We *will* get along while I'm here. And, Mr. Burnett," she added for emphasis, "There's no ninety-ten split on that. Do I make myself perfectly clear?"

Hands planted on hips, Laurel stood, eyes blazing. She'd never before lost her temper like that. It was amazing, and she had to admit exhilarating.

"I reckon you make yourself clear, little lady." Stomping across the cabin, Cappy seized his hat. As he jerked it down over his head, a small dust cloud escaped. He slammed the door behind him.

"Good!" Laurel said to the barren walls of the cabin. A deep-throated rumbling brought her from her thoughts. She felt a faint pressure against her leg. The gray cat had come in through the back door after polishing off what was left of the stew. So large were his sides, he could hardly purr, much less walk. He fastened a speculative, if lopsided, gaze on her.

"And don't you start with me," she warned him.

As if silently agreeing, the cat lifted a paw and began to clean itself. Laurel couldn't resist reaching down and scratching it behind a tattered ear.

"Friends?"

He blinked his one yellow eye.

"Good. I wonder if you have a name." The cat responded with a meow that sounded very much like *no*.

After letting the cast iron kettle boil so that all residue rose to the top, she'd drained it and scrubbed it with a coarse-bristled brush and a cake of lye soap. By the time she'd finished, her hands looked like those of a washerwoman. Sighing heavily, she hung the towel up to dry.

Inspection of cupboards and the small storeroom behind the kitchen revealed a lack of supplies. The flour, which should have been sealed in a tin, was full of bugs, and there was no sugar, no beans, and no coffee. She wondered what Cappy and Sammy had been living on.

The aroma of steaming biscuits reminded her she hadn't eaten since early morning. Finding a small jar of honey, Laurel set it out on the freshly cleaned table. She then wrapped the remnants of a burlap bag about her hand for a pad and took the covered pan from the stovetop. The door opened behind her.

"It's ready. There's not much. We'll have to go into town for supplies. But it'll keep us from starving to death." The heat from the oven had made moisture form on her forehead, curling the soft wisps of hair about it. She blew at them distractedly.

"Smells real fine, missy."

Laurel whirled around. She'd fully expected Cappy wouldn't be talking to her after her little tirade, but she was suddenly aware it wasn't his voice she'd heard. Laurel's eyes widened as she gazed at the young Chinese man.

"You must be Sammy." She held out her hand. "I'm Laurel Wentworth."

"I know Mr. Cappy yelling and grumbling all the way down the mine. He always like that. That smells good," Sammy said cheerfully.

Laurel glanced nervously at the door. She'd let Cappy believe Sammy had eaten the remainder of the stew. For her sake and for the sake of a battle-scarred cat, she dared not tell him different.

"She scooped a biscuit from the pan. "I'm afraid it's not

much. We'll have to get supplies. I think you'd better eat it before he comes back."

Sammy smiled as he poured honey over the biscuit.

"He very angry. Not hear him use such words in a long time. Won't be back for long time."

"Won't be back? Where has he gone?" Laurel set the skillet down with a thud.

"Down." Between bites of biscuit, Sammy motioned with his hand.

"Down where? Down the mountain?"

Sammy motioned again as he stuffed another bite of biscuit into his mouth. "He go down in mine. His turn to work."

"When will he be back?"

"Many hours." Sammy smiled appreciatively as he downed the last of his biscuit. He held a large cup beneath the pump and got a drink of water.

"All right. You're coming with me," Laurel said decisively. "Is there a wagon?"

"Sure. Got wagon out behind that." He gestured to the low building across from the cabin.

Laurel smiled to herself. There was more than one way to skin a cat. Giving her gray friend an apologetic pat on the head, she amended that to more than one way to skin a mule.

She still hadn't quite forgiven Lucille for her stubbornness that morning. She'd just see how the mule behaved when hitched to a wagon. "Hitch up the mules. We're going to town."

"Oh no. No go into town, missy." Sammy rose abruptly from the table and backed toward the door.

"Why not?" Laurel demanded.

"Mr. Cappy say no go to town. Shopkeeper right fine thief."

"That may be, but we have to eat. I didn't come all the way up here just to starve to death."

She gave the biscuits a last look. Then she sent Sammy to hitch the mules while she straightened the kitchen. Just in case

Cappy came up early, she left him a half dozen biscuits in the pan.

Three hours later, she and Sammy headed back to the Rebecca, the wagon filled to overflowing with supplies carefully covered with heavy canvas. Sammy had been right.

Everything she'd planned to purchase had been expensive. Upon seeing the prices posted on an overhead chalkboard, Laurel had quickly revised her shopping list. Those had included flour, coffee, dried beans, and molasses. Sugar had been too costly. Cringing as the shopkeeper tallied up the items she'd selected, Laurel had gazed out at the dusty street. A local farmer was unloading his wagon.

Going outside to speak with the man, Laurel quickly learned he'd found his own bonanza growing and selling food to the miners. He had a plot of land nearby fed by a natural spring. A farmer, he'd come to Nevada nearly ten years earlier from Nebraska to find gold and silver. But once a farmer, always a farmer. After bad luck at mining had practically driven him to leave, he'd earned plenty of gold and silver by selling produce, butter, eggs, and grain to the local merchants.

Smiling, she quickly struck a bargain to buy directly from the farmer. She purchased eggs, fresh vegetables, butter, and cheese. Then she negotiated the purchase of a half dozen chickens. The final cost was far less than what she would have paid the shopkeeper.

After leaving the store, they'd circled west of town, and had found the farm. The back of the wagon was filled with supplies and a crate of squawking chickens. Sammy turned the wagon off the road, and guided the mules around to the side of the cabin. He unloaded everything except the chickens. One of the hens had already been designated for supper. It turned out that Sammy was an excellent cook.

"Smell good, missy," he declared as he stood over the cook pot where the chicken simmered. "Almost ready."

She shook her head in amazement as she tried to understand how Cappy and Sammy had survived until now. Laurel filled a plate with chicken, potatoes, and carrots. Sammy's eyes widened as she set the platter in front of him.

"You earned it," she told him.

She liked Sammy. He didn't talk much, but when he did, every word was straight to the point. He reminded her of Soon-Li.

Had she left Virginia City only that morning? It seemed ages ago. Her hand went to the black jade combs holding back her hair. Soon-Li had said Chinese women wore them for their lovers.

She thought of Ruel and just as quickly dismissed the thought. He might have sent word to her before she left. His silence made it obvious that the time they'd spent together was easily forgotten once he'd returned to Virginia City. She tried to convince herself that she could forget just as easily. She fixed a second plate and covered it with a clean cloth for Cappy.

She crossed the yard between the cabin and the long building. Like the cabin, the long building was built into the side of the mountain. Laurel's eyes widened as they adjusted to the meager light inside. Down the center of the building was a series of huge wheels. They were set into an open trough and connected by a web of metal cable.

Windows banked the west wall, while tools of every size, shape and description hung on the opposite wall. At the far end of the building, butted against the side of the mountain, was a huge opening framed in heavy timbers.

Calling out but getting no response, Laurel moved past the wheels to the opening. A single lantern glowed at the entrance, illuminating a shaft that sloped into the mountain. Setting the plate aside Laurel leaned inside the shaft. Cool air brushed her face.

"Just what the hell are you doin' here?" Cappy demanded.

"I wanted to see inside the mine."

"Did it ever occur to you that that could be dangerous?"

Dangerous? She'd been shot at, chased by outlaws, watched men die, and just survived six days in the wilderness, not to mention Ruel Delaney. She wasn't intimidated by him or a hole in the ground.

14

Laurel kept a watchful eye on Cappy as he polished off the food she'd brought for him. He licked his fingers clean.

If it wasn't for that plate of food, he looked as if he might've been tempted to dump her into the mine. As it was, he'd fixed her with a withering glare, ordered her to sit on a crate in the corner near the mine entrance, and treated her to the enjoyable sights and sounds of his eating.

She wondered just how long Cappy Burnett had closed himself off from civilization, other than the trip to the hotel the day before. His appearance was abominable, his manners were worse, and he smelled a lot like the mule she'd ridden in the day before. That comparison brought to mind how she'd finally persuaded the mule to cooperate.

"You don't get down off this mountain very often," she commented.

She thought of the sparsely furnished cabin that looked as if it hadn't ever been cleaned, and the lack of food. She handed Cappy a piece of cloth so he could wipe his hands. He grunted and glanced at the napkin as if it might bite him.

"Got no call to. When I need somethin', Sammy can go into

town for it. I don't imagine I've been in Virginia City more than three times in the last few years. The last time must have been just before your father died." He gave her a long look.

"I don't like most people," he informed her flatly. "I figure the further I am from them, the happier I'll be—them too."

She had the oddest feeling there was more to all this than Cappy was telling her, but she knew better than to pry. For now. He'd only yell at her or say nothing at all. Cappy Burnett was a man of extremes, but she supposed spending most of one's time in a hole in the ground might affect someone like that.

"You're a scrappy little thing," he said, seizing another, piece of chicken. "Could'a got yourself killed going into the mine, not knowin' what yer doin'. Ever hear about curiosity and the cat?" He motioned at her with a chicken leg all but picked clean.

"It's only natural to be curious about the mine. After all, I came..."

He cut her off. "I know—you came over three thousand miles to see it. Well, I suppose you're entitled to that. You are the majority owner now." He refused the napkin she offered and rubbed his hands down the front of his shirt.

"**You ready?**"

"For what?" she asked.

"For what? Hell girl, to go on down in the mine!"

"I'm ready when you are. But I won't be yelled at or ordered around." She informed him, barely reaching his shoulder.

"Yer just like her." Cappy's voice softened as he muttered the words under his breath.

"Who?"

"I'd almost forgotten," he added.

She was learning fast that any conversation with Cappy required keen hearing when he wasn't yelling at her. It also required an ability to pick up whole meanings from only one or two words.

"You mean, Delia?" Laurel replied. Undoubtedly, Jason had brought Delia up to the Rebecca.

"Delia? Hell, no." Emotion caught in his throat. He reached out a gnarled hand and touched her cheek. "You're like her all right—kind, in spite of that punch you landed on my mule. Direct, no nonsense. You got the same way of lookin' at a person, as if you'd like to be friends, and yer pretty like her, not like that other one." Then he added, "Rebecca."

A name she'd carried in her mind since childhood and tried to imagine what she was like.

"You knew my mother?" Laurel asked.

Seizing a rope from a hook on the far wall of the building, Cappy turned toward the mineshaft.

She quickly followed grabbing his arm as he started to descend the wood ladder. "You knew Rebecca?"

For a moment that watery gaze met hers. He shrugged off her hand.

"I knew her," he said, and then he was gone, descending down the ladder with an agility that contradicted his age. Laurel quickly scrambled after him.

The ladder lowered no more than twenty feet into the shaft, ending on a wide wooden platform. A lantern, illuminated the darkness, revealing heavy timbers framing another opening approximately ten feet wide by six high. Another ladder led down from there. Without a word, Cappy headed down.

"Damn." She was not usually given to swearing but the man could be aggravating. "I want answers." Laurel told him as she reached the bottom of the second ladder.

"Stop swearing!" he muttered. "It ain't fittin' for a young lady! She never swore and I won't tolerate it from you. Understand?" Cappy snapped at her.

"All right," she agreed. "We'll both stop, and you'll start answering some questions."

"Damn, but yer bossy! No wonder your uncle shipped you out here."

"He didn't ship me out here. I stowed away on one of his ships." A defiant gleam sparked in Laurel's eyes.

"Bet that went over real good with Edwin Wentworth. He always did think he controlled everything and everybody." Cappy stopped Laurel's foot from landing on his shoulder. "All right. Compromise. No more swearin', except in cases of extreme emergency."

"Agreed. How did you know my mother?"

Cappy started down the next section of shaft.

"This method of putting a shaft in a mine is called the square-set stopping method. As each new level is reached, a framework of supporting timbers is set into place, providin' both a floor for the previous chamber up above, and a ceiling for the next one down below. It's necessary when the ground is real soft and has a tendency to slide right back into the area you just dug out. On the other hand, rock and hard soil tend to form a chamber as you dig."

Laurel heard him step down onto firm footing. They'd climbed down to the third level. Without hesitating, Cappy moved to yet another opening. This chamber, she realized was barely over the level of his head, approximately six feet high. His voice echoed up the shaft.

"I knew Rebecca when she first came to California."

Laurel was breathless from exertion and the heavy, damp air that filled the chambers. "Were you with my father in Sacramento?"

"I knew him then. I was with them when he set up his first claim. He needed someone who knew what needed to be done, and we got on. That was a long time ago." Cappy headed for the next level.

Even though they were going down, she felt she'd been climbing mountains. In a sense she had. Her sides ached from the effort it took to breathe, but she fully expected him to turn on her in anger. Instead, when he turned back to her, something very like concern momentarily filled his eyes.

"I forget how others ain't use to being this far down. We'll rest here a while."

"How much farther down are you working?" she asked.

Cappy handed her a canteen from the wall. She drank sparingly, already realizing that anything used at that level of the mine had to be brought down by hand.

"Sammy and I have managed to clear two more levels. It's slow work, but just about all we can manage without a full crew. What I want to show you is on the last level."

For the first time since he'd barged into her hotel room, something faintly resembling a smile broke the whiskered line of his mouth.

"If yer game?"

"I'm game," Laurel replied, not about to let Cappy Burnett get the better of her.

She took another sip of water.

"I never knew my mother. What was she like?" she asked. "Was she happy with my father? Did she like living in the gold fields? Were you there when she got sick?"

"Whoa! One question at a time." Again, there was silence as Cappy replaced the cap on the canteen. He took an unusually long time replacing the canteen on a nail at one of the wood posts. His voice softened with a memory.

"Rebecca was the most beautiful woman I ever seen. She was small, with hair like warm honey and eyes like a summer sky. She was a lady, just like you. Hardly knew what to expect when she came out here. But she came with love in her heart, and that seemed enough at the time."

Laurel was surprised. These were not the words of an illiterate miner; they were the words of a man who'd once known a great deal more than these remote hills.

Cappy raised his eyes. "You're like her. The same voice, the same way of saying and doing things... the same temper. She could sure get all fired up when she wanted to, but she was the gentlest creature I ever saw. There wasn't any meanness in her."

He nodded. "Yep, yer like in a lot of ways. Oh, your hair is lighter than hers, and your eyes are different. I reckon you got them from your daddy. But you got her fair skin." He reached for her hand, gently turned it over in his.

"Small, but strong." He stroked her fingers as if remembering. "Strong enough to hold on to her faith in the man she loved." Turning Laurel's hand back over, he pressed it gently between his callused hands. Then he released it.

"You knew her well."

Was it possible that Cappy Burnett had once cared for her mother? He'd described the woman she'd known only from old photographs and family portraits. But from the day of Rebecca's wedding there'd been no more photographs. It was as if from that day forward she had ceased to exist. Now Cappy Burnett had managed to give Laurel something no one ever had, the essence of the woman her mother had been.

"I knew her, and your daddy," Cappy added matter-of-factly.

"Were they happy together?" Laurel struggled with the old questions that had sent her on this journey.

Cappy nodded. "I believe they were happy. She gave meaning to everything he did or ever dreamed of doing. And when she went away, his dreams sorta went with her."

Laurel's head came up as she grasped the meaning of his words. "But she didn't want to go away. She was sick."

"Is that what your uncle told you?"

"She was ill after my sister and I were born. My uncle found us in a cabin by a river. He never knew there was another child. I didn't learn about my sister until I reached San Francisco."

"And he just took it upon himself to take you back to Boston," Cappy said bluntly.

"He didn't know when Jason would be back." Laurel tried to defend an explanation even she hadn't understood.

Cappy laughed. "He never tried to find out when your daddy would be back. He just packed you and your mother up and left as quickly as he could."

He rose, slapping the dust from his pant legs.

"From what yer daddy heard afterward, yer mother died within weeks of reaching Boston. Taking her out of that cabin is what killed her," he declared, then moved into the dark end of the chamber, he slowly walked into the tunnel.

It was cool inside the tunnel, and she heard a faint rumbling sound. Cappy secured the lantern he carried on a hook at a post. He looked at her as if to make certain she was still following him. Then, without a word, he entered the next level of the tunnel. It extended farther into the mountain.

Cappy stopped and lit another lantern. The soft glow of light illuminated a large cavern and rock formations at the walls.

"This leads farther back and connects with a series of caves. That sound you hear is water in an underground cavern. What do you know about silver?" Cappy asked as he moved ahead of her, stooping as the ceiling of the passage lowered.

"Practically nothing," she admitted, feeling her way along the damp walls as Cappy disappeared around a bend.

She came to an abrupt halt when she walked right into his back. Without so much as a backward glare, Cappy lit another lantern and picked up a pickax. Pushing her back a good distance, he swung it wide, embedding the sharp end in rock and earth at the wall. He pried away a sizable piece of rock. He crouched low and split it open. He held a piece out to her.

It was heavy, and as she turned it in the light from the lantern, the blue-gray metallic substance streaking through it, glinted back at her.

"Some of the highest grade ore ever found in the Comstock," Cappy announced.

"Silver?"

"Silver. And no damned way of getting it out."

They did not converse on the way up and when Laurel had climbed back up into the surface building, she rubbed her shoulder muscles. They ached.

"I don't understand. Why can't you bring out the silver?"

Cappy replaced the lantern and turned down the wick.

"It's called operatin' capital. In short—money."

"But that's simple enough. Bring out enough ore to set up the operation."

"Not quite," Cappy observed. Reaching onto a shelf beside the door, he took down a pipe. Tamping in an ample amount of tobacco, he lit up, sending streamers of fragrant smoke into the air. As she stepped outside the building, Laurel stared in amazement. The sweltering heat was gone. They had been down in the mine for hours. The night air almost had a chill to it.

"Most of the land around here is owned by a group of investors out of San Francisco. They also own several big mining operations. They're the same ones that set up the toll gate. They own most of the businesses in Gold Hill and several in Virginia City. Right smart set of individuals. They get wealthy off the silver brought out of the Comstock, and then bleed the smaller operations dry selling them equipment and supplies. It eventually forces the smaller mine owners out of business. These fellas step in, offer them one-tenth what their claims are worth, and then consolidate what they bought. Their goal is to own this entire mountain, including the Rebecca." Cappy blew a cloud of smoke into the night air.

"But what about the flume system? Once the ore is brought up, you could by-pass the toll gate," Laurel observed.

Cappy studied her for a moment. She already had a good

grasp of the possibilities. Unfortunately, there were things she didn't know.

"It's a whole lot more complicated than that, Laurel."

It was the first time he'd spoken her name. She felt she'd made it through some sort of invisible barrier. At least he was talking to her, not swearing at her. "Go on."

"The ore I showed you is only the beginning. That vein goes a helluva lot deeper." He flashed her an apologetic look, then continued. "Deeper mining means more levels, more chambers, and more workers needed. You gotta get the ore out before you can send it down the flume."

She wanted to know as much as possible.

"What are those big wheels used for?" she asked.

"As well as being fed by the Sierra runoff, the river is fed by a series of underground springs. Those same springs have a tendency to flood the lower level chambers. Those wheels pump the water out and into the flumes. It provides two things at once. They remove the water so we can keep digging, and it also provides water to the flumes. But nothing works without manpower and materials. And around here those gentlemen I mentioned own all of it." As they passed the corral for the mules, he knocked some of the ash from the bowl of his pipe, then relit the tobacco.

"They can't own everything," she commented. "Who are these men?"

"Ever hear of the Big Four?"

When she shook her head, Cappy continued. "As I said, they're from San Francisco, rich and lookin' to get richer. Jim Fair is one, and John MacKay is another. MacKay probably owns more mines in the Comstock than any other individual. They call him the Comstock King.

"William Ralston's another," he continued. "He's president of the Bank of California that backs several big mining operations. And there's Aaron Talbott. I hear that he's into a little bit of everything—railroads, banking, and one of the local lumber mills. As you may have noticed there's not much in the way of trees on this side of the mountains." He tamped down the tobacco with a stick.

"All the lumber for shoring up the mine shafts has to come in by rail. The Big Four also control the railroads. They own everything needed for a good mining operation."

"What about labor for working the mine?" she asked. Surely there were men who wanted the work.

"Aaron Talbott has a real strong influence on miners in this area. What he says goes. If he doesn't want them working a certain mine, he manages to 'convince' them not to do it."

Laurel gazed up at the moon still low in the sky. It was different from the moon she'd watched from her hotel balcony. There was something almost magical about seeing it from the top of a mountain, here or in the Sierras when she'd been with Ruel. She shook off the memory.

"You're saying that he uses force?"

"Nobody can prove it. The miners won't bring charges against him. If they did, they'd never be able to work in the mines again." Stepping onto the front steps of the cabin, Cappy barely missed the tail of the gray cat.

"Damned fool animal," he grumbled.

She reached down and scratched the cat behind the ears.

"I've decided to call him Captain Kidd, after the pirate. He does resemble him a little."

"Captain Kidd, huh? Well, I suppose that's better than just plain, "Cat."

"We all need a name and a place where we belong." After her tour of the long building, the mine, and the condition of the cabin, it was obvious he and Sammie had been barely eking out an existence at the Rebecca.

"From the look of things. I'd say you don't have anything to work the mine."

"I sneak a small sack of ore out every once in a while and have Sammie take it over to Virginia City. But it's mostly low-grade stuff from one of the higher levels. It's been enough to cover cost of the materials until now, some food for Sammie and me—most of the time," he admitted.

"That stuff I showed you down lower, I've been keepin' quiet about that," he went on to explain. "As soon as Talbott and the others find out about the grade of that ore, there'll be a fight to take the Rebecca from you."

Cappy leaned against a post on the front porch of the cabin. "Of course, you might get them to make you a pretty fair offer for the mine, if you've a mind to sell it," he added with a frown.

So that was it, Laurel thought. His rudeness and angry silences were because he assumed that she'd wanted nothing more than to see what the Rebecca was worth so she could sell out.

Ruel had spoken of Delia's greed. Obviously, Cappy had met her. That explained his attitude toward her. She wasn't her sister.

"What would it take to put the mine in full operation?" she asked.

Cappy stared at her with narrowed gaze. "A lot."

"A thousand dollars, two thousand? How much is a lot?" Laurel asked. She needed to know, not just some wild guess.

He was thoughtful. "A least five thousand dollars just to start up, and another ten or so for operatin' costs until we could get a return. And then there's the shortage of labor to work it."

Laurel inhaled slowly. It was a great deal more than she'd anticipated. "And that's if there's enough ore for a return on the investment," she concluded the obvious.

"There's enough," Cappy replied. "More than enough. Enough to make you a very wealthy young woman."

"How can you be certain? How do you know it isn't just a small vein, that'll soon disappear?"

Removing the pipe from his teeth, Cappy gazed at her thoughtfully. "Because I know the Rebecca. I've spent near the last twenty years down in that hole. It's there."

"I have a lot to think about," she commented.

"Sleep on it," he told her. "You don't have to decide tomorrow or the day after what's to be done with the Rebecca. It will still be here next week, next month."

And so would the Big Four, just waiting to seize it, she thought.

"Take the room in the cabin," he told her. "You don't need more than a blanket this time of year."

"What about you?" she asked. She'd slept on the ground, under a rock outcropping and on a dirt floor more than once the past couple of weeks.

"Sammy and I will bed down in the long building. We've done it before, working shifts down in the mine."

He stepped down off the porch, tobacco glowing in the bowl of the pipe clenched between his teeth, the moon that slowly rose in the night sky casting a silvery glow across the mountain.

EVERY DAY over the next three weeks she went down into the mine with Cappy. While he talked, she listened, learning more than she could have ever learned from someone else. And the more she learned, the more she valued Cappy's assessment of what it would take to put the Rebecca into full operation. He knew these mountains as well, and he knew the Rebecca. It was obvious that his heart was set on keeping the mine open, holding on no matter what it took, but the reality was that decision rested with her.

If Laurel had been told six months ago she'd be digging ore samples from a silver mine in the Comstock, she wouldn't have believed it. Was this the dream, the passion her father had felt?

If so, she'd gained a better understanding of the man. But there was also a practical side to her nature. Mining silver in the Comstock wasn't accomplished by hoping and dreaming. She understood that it took lots of hard work, determination, and as Cappy liked to put it *operatin'* capital," which at the moment was in short supply.

She'd been thinking a lot about that too. She had two choices: sell the mine, or find the money to mine it the way it should be mined rather than picking away at it with a pickaxe and shovel.

"We need to go into town," she announced. "Do you have any other clothes?" Something, she thought, that wasn't covered with grime, dirt, and all sorts of stains.

"Why the hell are we goin' there?"

"We're going to the bank."

"What for?" Cappy rose from his chair.

Laurel turned, dishcloth in hand. "All the banks. As many as it takes to get the loan."

"What loan?"

"You have no money," she explained. "The little money that I have will soon be gone. But I do have an inheritance. I can't hope to persuade my uncle to release any of it, so our best chance is to secure a loan. After all, the Wentworth name is well known."

"Well I'll be damned!" Cappy explained. "Yer plannin' on stayin'?"

She gave him a thoughtful look. "I don't understand why I'm doing this, except that it was my father's dream. It's not the silver. God knows, it would be easier to go back to Boston and forget all of this." She looked around her.

"The Rebecca is all I have of my father. I can't just let those money-grubbing..." she searched for the word.

"Sons-of-bitches?" Cappy suggested.

She smiled. "I can't just let them have it. I don't know how to explain it any better than that. All I know is that I can't just walk away."

She didn't expect him to understand.

"I can tell you what the answer will most likely be." He rose. Coming up behind Laurel, he started to place his hands on her shoulders, then thought better of it.

"But we'll try. All they can say is no."

That is exactly what they did say, every last one of them.

They were polite, the excuses smooth as if they'd had a great deal of practice. As she stepped out of the Bank of Commerce, Laurel couldn't bring herself to meet Cappy's gaze.

"They turned you down?"

Laurel nodded. "I was willing to sign for ten percent profit, but they wanted twenty-five, plus a percentage of the mine. What are we going to do?"

It was late. She was tired, hot, and discouraged. Worst of all, the stays in her corset pinched. These past weeks she'd grown accustomed to the freedom of pants and a loose shirt.

Cappy grinned. "I think this calls for a little celebration."

"Celebration?" He'd absolutely lost his mind. He'd been up on that mountain too long, or he'd just plain gone 'round the bend' as she'd heard someone say once.

"It's too late to go back today. I don't mind being out on the trail after dark by myself, but not with you. It's better if we spend the night in town. We'll get a couple of rooms over at the hotel." He motioned to a small, white clapboard building across the street.

"It's not the International, but it's clean—mostly, and cheap."

They had rooms on the second floor. Her room included a metal hip bath and the owner's promise of hot water. Hearing a light knock on her door, Laurel answered it eagerly anticipating the first hot bath since arriving in Virginia City weeks earlier.

"Miss Wentworth?" A high-pitched, nasally voice greeted her, as lashless, beady eyes inspected her.

"Yes?"

"My name is Tisdale, Walter Tisdale. I'd like to speak with you if I may."

He was dressed in the sort of suit Hiram Turnbull had preferred, and the top of his head was bald and shiny. He clutched a bowler hat in his hands that twitched much like a mouse. She didn't know the man and couldn't imagine what he wanted to talk to her about.

"I only need a moment of your time," he continued when she would have asked him to leave.

"I represent Mr. Aaron Talbott. It is Mr. Talbott's under-standing that you are the owner of the Rebecca Mine. He would like to make you an offer for your interest in the mine." Tisdale waited expectantly.

Leaving the door open so their conversation could easily be heard by Cappy, Laurel asked, "And just what might that offer be?"

"He's willing to make you a most generous offer, Miss Went-worth, and he authorized me to draw up all the necessary papers for the transfer of title to the mine." He cleared his throat. "He's authorized me to offer you twenty-five thousand dollars."

"That is a substantial amount of money," she replied.

Behind Tisdale, a door opened, and Cappy stepped out into the hall.

"But you see, Mr. Tisdale," she continued, smiling sweetly, "I've already had an offer of one hundred thousand dollars."

"One hundred ...?" he stammered. "For an unproven mine?"

She simply smiled back at him.

"Mr. Talbott is a very generous man," he went on to say. "If I were to wire him, perhaps I could persuade him to consider increasing his offer." He was flabbergasted.

CARLA SIMPSON

"You may thank Mr. Talbott for his offer, but I couldn't possibly consider it. That wouldn't be sound business. I'm certain you'll agree. Goodnight, Mr. Tisdale."

"Uh, good night, Miss Wentworth. It was most pleasant meeting you."

Laurel gave him her most charming smile as he turned and disappeared down the stairs. Her smile was replaced by a frown as she glanced up at Cappy.

He nodded, stretching his neck against the unaccustomed feel of a buttoned collar. "One hundred thousand dollars?" He grinned at her.

"I had to tell him something. That's the amount of money I'd like to put into the Rebecca." She shook her head. "He was so sure of himself, I would have told him the moon was blue just to see that disappointed look on his face."

"I'll have to remember that."

"It certainly didn't take Mr. Talbott long to find out we were in town," she commented.

"Like I said, the Big Four own just about everything in the Comstock, and a good piece of this town. What they don't own, they don't want. Except for maybe a few properties they can't buy or steal. And they've got people who keep them informed about what goes on."

She was still thinking about Tisdale.

"Come on," he told her. "Get yerself prettied up. I'm taking you to supper. I only get to town once in a while, and I can't think of anything better to do than to do the town than with a pretty lady."

"I don't feel very much like celebrating. We didn't get the loan, and now we'll probably lose the Rebecca." The misery she'd felt earlier had returned, along with doubts about refusing the offer she'd received.

According to Cappy the mine would yield many times what

was offered, maybe more. But without the means to get it the silver out of the mine, it didn't matter how much it might yield.

They both stepped aside, as a young boy came up the hallway laden with buckets of steaming hot water.

"If I know women, you'll feel better after a hot bath. That always seems to fix a lady right up. I'll call for you in an hour. Don't be late." He turned down the hallway.

"But..."

"When I see you, I want to see a smile. The night's not over yet."

The night's not over yet.

SHE FELT BETTER after the bath. And relinquishing the confining corset had helped.

She hated the idea of taking an offer simply because she hadn't the funds to operate the mine, but more than that she hated what it meant for Cappy. He'd put many years into the mine, had known her father. She couldn't bear the thought that he would end up with nothing. Where would he go? What would he do?

As she answered the knock on her door, she remembered Cappy's parting words, but unless he intended to rob a bank or was particularly skilled at poker, she didn't have much to smile about.

"Where are we having supper?" she asked as she gathered her shawl then turned to the door. She hoped that it wasn't the Bucket of Blood saloon, although she had to admit she was curious to see inside it.

Cappy cleared his throat. "The Comstock House is real nice, just the place for a lady." He passed a hand across his bearded chin.

"Are you all right?" she asked. "We don't have to go there if it makes you uncomfortable. We can eat in the cafe downstairs." Laurel was genuinely concerned.

"Nope." A different expression glinted in his eyes. "I want to show you off. After all, it isn't every day someone stands up to Aaron Talbott, and a lady at that. We're celebratin'." He seized her by the arm and escorted her downstairs.

The Comstock house was elegant, and the food was excellent. It easily rivaled that served in any fine restaurants in Boston, New Orleans, or San Francisco.

Her arm loosely tucked inside his, they walked down B Street toward their hotel. Lights glistened from the windows of the saloons and gambling parlors as they passed.

"I'm goin' to take you on back to the hotel. You must be tired," Cappy observed.

Laurel turned to him. Their hotel was just down the street. "Where are you going?"

He pointed across the street, to where a sleek carriage was pulling up in front of a well-lit building. Brilliant golden lights twinkled from every window, and when the heavy, carved wood doors, opened, Laurel could see a crystal chandelier in the foyer.

"The Crystal Palace. A pretty fancy place, sort of like one of them men's clubs," Cappy explained.

"A gambling house," Laurel stated flatly. "I suppose you're going to try to win. enough money to open the Rebecca?"

"Not exactly. I've never been good at countin' cards." A mischievous gleam danced in his blue eyes.

She immediately thought of Ruel Delaney, though she had no way of knowing if he was still in town. They hadn't parted under the best of circumstances. In fact, he'd seemed relieved to be rid of her. She could hardly go to him and ask for a favor when she was already indebted to him for bringing her safely to Virginia City. No, owing Ruel Delaney favors wasn't a good idea, although it was an intriguing one.

"If you aren't going to gamble then why ...?" Color warmed her cheeks.

Of course, there were other pleasures to be found in a place like the Crystal Palace. It was just that she hadn't thought Cappy would go to such places for those reasons. On the other hand, Ruel Delaney was exactly the sort of man who would.

"I didn't mean to pry."

Cappy chuckled. "Hell, I'm not going for that reason." He scratched uncomfortably at his beard.

"It's purely business, about the Rebecca."

At Laurel's confused expression he went on to explain. "Places like these attract a lot of real rich fellas. Gives 'em a chance to have a few drinks, play some cards, and enjoy some other ...activities. More business deals are made inside a place like this than inside banks."

She glanced at the elegant facade of the Crystal Palace. No signs were posted proclaiming it to be a men's club. A determined gleam deepened the color of her eyes, and lifting her skirt, she started across the street.

"Then by all means, Mr. Burnett, I think we should visit the Crystal Palace."

"Now hold on just a minute! I didn't mean that you..."

She was already greeting the fastidiously dressed doorman, giving him a smile that could have melted the silver right out of the hills. Without so much as a backward glance, she stepped into the gold and blue foyer of the gambling house.

15

Ruel Delaney laid down his bet with the calculated ease of a professional gambler. Then, taking a long draw on the black fragrant cigarette, he carefully scrutinized each player at the table.

The gentleman directly across from him was a well-known banker whose weakness for cards was kept discreetly hidden behind the carved mahogany doors of this exclusive gambling establishment lest he suffer irrevocable damage in the business community. He had often wondered where the man got the money to pay his exorbitant gambling debts, and he made it a policy to maintain his accounts in another bank.

The man to his left was impeccably dressed but had no skill at cards. He'd lost the last five hands, partly because he was completely predictable. He constantly reorganized his cards when dealt a bad hand, as if by reshuffling them, he could change his luck.

Ruel knew there was no magic to gambling. It was a game of skill and shrewdness, and a little recklessness was necessary. He'd always believed if you couldn't afford to lose you shouldn't play. He could afford to lose; therefore he played—a lot, exercising both shrewdness and skill. Others played at cards, Ruel played the players. And he won consistently. That brought others to his table, and drove up the antes.

In New Orleans, San Francisco, or Virginia City, his reputation attracted certain gamblers, and Ruel was more than happy to alleviate their curiosity, not to mention their bank accounts. To his way of thinking, his was a sound operation. He provided a service that his clients paid for, deriving a good amount of pleasure along the way. The stakes in these games were high, usually requiring an opening ante of ten thousand dollars.

Such high stakes quickened the blood, sharpened the competitiveness and, at times—the desperation of some players. But Ruel provided play, pleasures, and passion in an elegant surrounding that was both stimulating and discreet.

A source of one of the pleasures provided, stood slightly behind him at the moment, her hand resting casually on his left shoulder. She was one of several young ladies he permitted to 'occupy' the elegant second-floor apartments over the Crystal Palace. It was an advantageous business arrangement, run by the manager of the gambling house and appreciated by the nabobs from San Francisco when they ventured into the Comstock to oversee their mining ventures.

Ruel's interest shifted as the hum of conversation subtly changed, taking on an edge of excitement. His gaze went to the foyer. Against its heavy blue velvet portieres trimmed with gold braid, a paler, softer shade of gold caught his attention.

Curiosity and excitement raced through him. As the hand draped casually over his shoulder tightened, Ruel covered it with his own. Then, placing an absentminded kiss on the slender fingers, he abruptly released it.

A far more delicate hand came to memory, and with it the memory of blue eyes, pale delicate skin, and a soft full mouth. Pleasure mixed with fascination in his expression as he gazed across the wood and crystal expanse of the elegant gaming room.

Her gown was simple, of the deepest rose color, and matched the high color of her cheeks. Made of satin, the gown sculpted her full high breasts. Her slender waist was accented by the deep V-shaped pattern at the front of the gown, and the full skirt of that same satin overset with rose lace, whispered softly about her.

He imagined the silkiness of her bare skin, and his fingers tightened. Her bodice, cut daringly low, accentuated the creaminess of her breasts, and the sleeves were set slightly off the shoulders. The bare skin the gown revealed hinted at a softness not fully revealed.

Actually, he mused, the gown was quite simply cut, and not one he remembered from New Orleans. The slender, beguiling lady who wore it gave it an air of elegance and sensuality. It was a gown he'd readily purchase, but only if he could have this lady wearing it. No other could hope to match the beauty or fascination of Laurel Wentworth.

"Well, what the hell do you make of that?" the young woman behind him whispered.

"A great deal," Ruel answered. He hoped, giving her a smile of dismissal as he rose.

"Now you just hold on a minute." Cappy grabbed Laurel's elbow, holding her back. He glared at the doorman who'd just caught up with him.

"This just isn't the kind of place for a lady. And I won't have you..."

Laurel cut him off. "You won't have what? Mr. Burnett, this may come as a surprise to you, but I will come and go as I please. And, at the moment, I wish to be here. Unless, of course, you have another solution to our financial problem?"

"You know I don't. It was my idea to come in here in the first place; me, not you. You don't know what kind of place this is..."

He lowered his voice as he took note of the curious stares they were attracting.

Laurel turned a discerning eye on the interior of the Palace. It bespoke understated elegance. Overhead in the foyer, a crystal chandelier winked invitingly. Inside a half dozen more were evenly spaced about the large ceiling, light reflecting off raised frescoes depicting interlocking gilt fleurs-de-lis against a brilliant blue background. At the very center of the ceiling, a glass dome revealed the midnight darkness of the sky. The walls were a paler shade of blue set off by gleaming wainscoting and the floor was covered by magnificent deep, soft carpeting, bordered in gold fleur-de-lises.

"I know exactly what sort of place this is," she replied.

The interior of the Palace was divided into several smaller rooms, some with doors closed. At the center of the main room was a tiled section of flooring. It was set directly below the glass dome to take advantage of daytime light, and filled with ferns.

The long mahogany bar took up one end of the room, and the wall behind it was one long mirror that reflected the entire room, making it seem immense, and each light, including the chandelier sparkled brightly.

The tables accommodating the guests in the main part of the Palace were concealed beneath dark blue linen tablecloths, leaving only the gleaming wood of the legs exposed. About each were six to eight simply designed chairs. Around the perimeter of the large room, for those who chose to partake in conversation or perhaps a drink, clusters of high-backed chairs were grouped. She was absolutely certain the glassware and stemware she saw was the finest crystal.

It was obvious that no expense had been spared in the appointments of this elegant club and she wondered if it was owned by the Big Four. Well, she hadn't come to discuss crystal or linen, she wanted to make a business arrangement, and by the looks of the clientele she'd come to the right place. Recognizing the faces of several of the bankers she'd visited that day, Laurel met their curious stares with a cool aloofness.

"You don't understand!" Cappy argued. "There's only one kind of woman comes into a place like this!"

Laurel smiled indulgently. "This may come as a surprise to you, but I'm perfectly aware of the kind of woman found in a place like this. I'm here on business. Besides, you're here, so what harm could there possibly be?"

Cappy groaned as the manager of the Palace approached them.

"Miss, I'm afraid our clientele is restricted." He chose his words carefully, for he was taken aback by the beauty of the young woman who stood before him.

"That's not posted outside," Laurel calmly informed him.

"I beg your pardon?"

"The restriction is not posted outside. In most cities, restrictions are clearly posted so not to cause patrons any embarrassment." She scanned the room. At the moment she was far more concerned with meeting someone in a position to finance the operation at the Rebecca than she was with etiquette.

"You're right, of course. I have a table over here if you would care for something to drink." The manager was certain she would now be faced with a dilemma. No true lady would drink in public.

"Whiskey, straight!" Cappy announced. At the moment he was badly in need of a drink, or several. Never in his life had he come across a woman so damnably bossy and mule-headed.

"Miss?" the manager inquired.

As she scanned the large room and the elegantly attired gentlemen who plied the gambling tables, Laurel's gaze froze.

"I'll have the same," she said absently, her attention caught by a dark gaze fastened on her.

"Of course," the manager eventually replied. He escorted them to a nearby table.

In the past weeks, she'd forced herself to believe Ruel Delaney was gone from her life. Days had passed with no word from him. Yet he was here, achingly handsome in a black jacket and a shirt almost glaringly white. Nothing could have prepared Laurel for this moment.

"Is there somethin' wrong?" Cappy asked.

"No, of course not!" Shaken, Laurel turned back to him.

The manager sent over a waiter with their drinks. Cappy downed his whiskey. She did the same and gasped as it burned down her throat, and then into her stomach.

"You got no business bein' here," Cappy told her as she slowly took a deep breath.

"Maybe I can be of assistance."

Laurel lifted watering eyes to find Ruel Delaney standing beside her chair. Before she could recover enough to object, Ruel slipped an arm beneath hers and pulled her to her feet.

"You need fresh air, Miss Wentworth."

"I can take care of that. We'll be going now," Cappy informed him, his eyes level with Ruel's when he stood.

"Miss Wentworth and I are acquainted. I assure you, she'll be quite all right. Please stay and have another drink on the house."

Without waiting for Cappy's reply, Ruel escorted her across the room. Ignoring the inquiring stares of customers, he led her through double doors concealing a private hallway, and then took her into a large suite of rooms decidedly masculine in decor.

"Have you taken to drinking now?"

"Please go away." Laurel pushed at his arm.

"I would do anything you ask, except that. I'm afraid if I let go that you'll fall to the floor." He smiled into confused, blue eyes.

He'd forced himself to stay off that mountain. He told

himself that she had to come to him. Now she had. It had to do with the Rebecca, but the reason didn't matter.

He had a point. She took a deep breath, then another one. She would have to remember that about whiskey. As for Ruel Delaney... She didn't need anything from him.

"I need to find Cappy."

"At the moment he's enjoying some of the finest whiskey my ill-gotten money can buy. The man deserves it."

"Your money?" She hiccoughed softly and closed her eyes to stop the room from spinning.

A smile appeared at the corners of Ruel's mouth and she fought the impression of a wolf eyeing its next meal.

"Would you like me to order champagne?" he asked.

"No...! Thank you." she replied.

How could one drink have such an effect on a person, she thought? She gave him a wary glance. She'd come here to find someone who would loan her the money for the Rebecca.

"You were saying?" he reminded her.

What had she been saying? Why did he have to be so handsome, and God forbid... charming. It was not a word she would have used to describe the man she first met. She steadied herself with a hand at a nearby table. And that dark gaze that seemed to see far more than she was comfortable with.

"A lady should never drink in public, Laurel. It starts rumors," he reminded her.

"Rumors? I don't care what other people think!" So far it had been an abominable day, with one refusal after another from the banks. Now she had run into Ruel Delaney. She angled her chin slightly higher.

"I don't care," she repeated, more for courage than out of conviction. And certainly not in a place like Virginia City with a saloon called the Bucket of Blood.

"You should, but you don't. There are people who might get the wrong idea."

"What idea?" she asked. And for him to talk about wrong ideas was almost laughable.

"That you came here for more than just a drink."

The color that spread across her cheeks was her only outward reaction.

Good heavens! She'd never experienced that sort of reaction to champagne and would have to remember that about whiskey. And the man had the arrogance to stand there... with that expression at his face.

That expression? She was used to sarcasm, an occasional grin that seemed to have all sorts of meanings, even anger. But his expression now was different as if there was something far different behind that dark gaze.

"Yes, I suppose it does, even though it was an accident."

"An accident? That's what you can what happened? There is another word for it! Such an easy explanation," she replied.

She could have sworn she saw him wince. It was a small thing, but it was enough.

"Please go away," she whispered. "I came here to find someone."

Regret was sharp. She was right and he knew it. Still, that didn't stop him from... What? Caring about her? Caring what happened to her? It was something new for him, and it didn't go away with the simple explanation that their first encounter had been an accident.

"That's usually why people come to the Palace. Only it's usually the other way around—men come here looking for women."

Laurel's head snapped up at that. "That isn't what I meant."

"What sort of man are you looking for?"

It was foolish to try to talk to him when he was like this. She started toward the door.

"Wait." Ruel's hand closed over her arm, stopping her. "I didn't mean that." He hadn't.

Why did he always become so angry with her? She wasn't like Delia, but the pain he'd suffered because of Delia was there. By hurting her, did he hope to rid himself of the pain her sister had caused him? It made no sense, but it was there, and something more to regret at the look in her eyes as she slowly turned back around.

"I need capital to finance the operation of the Rebecca. The banks have all refused to make that loan to... a woman. Or possibly other reasons. I'm certain they would like very much to see me fail." It was far more than she had intended to tell him.

"Cappy thought someone here might be interested in loaning us the money," she added.

"Then you've decided to stay." He let his hand drop. The feel of her, warm beneath the satin at her sleeve reminded him of that first encounter, something he would like to have undone but couldn't. Regret. It was there again.

She nodded. "Walking away from it would be easy, but..." How did she explain it? It wasn't about the money from silver that could be mined from the Rebecca. It was about so much more—a connection to someone she'd never known, her father's dream... and Rebecca's. And it was foolish in the least, but there it was when it would have been so easy to simply sell the mine and go back to Boston.

He pulled a dark cigarette from inside his jacket and lit it as he sat at the edge of a table. He blew out a stream of fragrant smoke.

"A business proposition?" he said thoughtfully. "Just what sort of proposition are you making?"

"A percentage of profit over the amount of the loan. Cappy thinks we can repay the loan within six months. The banks wanted twenty-five percent interest plus partial ownership. I won't do that. The Rebecca belongs to Cappy and me. I'll close it down before I'll let anybody else have part of it."

Who would have guessed that Miss Boston had such a sharp mind for figures and hustlers—that included himself.

"Six months," Ruel commented. He knew most of the businessmen in Virginia City, had done business with a handful of them.

"I've worked out an agreement," she replied and opened the hand-embroidered reticule she carried. She pulled out the paper on which figures were written.

Was it possible he knew someone who might be interested in investing in the Rebecca?

"The assay report on the mine came back a week ago. Cappy's seen others for the bigger mines, the Consolidated Virginia, the California, and the Crown Point. The ore samples out of the Rebecca are high grade. He insists the vein widens out as it deepens. I've seen it at the two-hundred-foot level, and I know he's right, but we need a way to get it out. It would be a solid investment," she continued.

"You've been down in the mine?" he asked.

"Of course. How could I own a silver mine and not want to know what's down there?"

"So you've decided to be Queen of the Comstock, to throw in your lot with every greedy speculator who can stake a claim."

Taken back by the sudden harshness in his voice, Laurel refolded the paper and the assay report.

"Greed has nothing to do with it. But I don't expect you to understand why it's important that I prove my father was right about the Rebecca." She took a deep breath.

"My aunt and uncle let me believe my father died years ago. My mother left Boston to come with him to the gold fields. I suppose they were afraid I'd do the same thing if I knew he was alive. They were probably right, but I'd have gone for reasons they never tried to understand." Her eyes were bright with unshed tears. She fought them back.

Dear God, don't let me fall apart now, she thought.

"I have no memory of him, only what I was told—that he forced my mother away from her family and brought her here. My uncle tried to make me believe that Jason caused her death by forcing her to live in the mining camps. I wasn't even allowed to keep his name. I want to prove they are wrong." She took another deep breath.

"I have to prove that Jason Cameron wasn't a ne'er-do-well who drove my mother to an early grave. She loved him, believed in him enough to follow him. I want to reopen the Rebecca, for both of them. To prove my uncle was wrong. Can't you understand?"

Ruel knew that she was right. Money didn't hold her here. Wentworth Shipping was known worldwide. If she left Virginia City tomorrow, she'd remain a very wealthy young woman. She chose to stay for other reasons. He believed her. It was in her eyes, and he understood because he couldn't reconcile his own past.

"You've already been to the banks."

Laurel's eyes widened. It wasn't a question, it was a statement. He knew she'd been to every bank in town!

"I tried everything before coming here." And she had. She had even sent a telegram to Andrew, knowing it was futile even as she did it. Andrew's response had been just what she'd expected. He wanted to help, but all his money was tied up in the company. It was impossible for him to lay hands on the amount she needed.

His return telegram had been lengthy. He tried to persuade her to return to San Francisco. He couldn't leave Jessica, not in her condition, and he wouldn't risk bringing her across the mountains to Virginia City.

She had two choices—she could return to San Francisco, or she could do this on her own. She squared her shoulders, the whiskey now only a warm glow in her stomach.

"Since you're obviously aware of everything I've done, maybe you can suggest where I might get a loan."

"There are people who'd be willing to make you that loan, but you couldn't afford their price."

"But there is someone who might be interested in backing you without asking an exorbitant return." He saw the way the expression at her eyes changed—cautious but hopeful.

"Who?"

Ruel smiled. "He's a gambler, and a lowlife. I believe you would call him a scoundrel."

She gave him a suspicious look. "You?"

He watched her. "I've been known to make investments from time to time, and this could be a sound investment."

She'd changed in the time she'd been there on that mountain. She wasn't the naive young woman he'd encountered aboard the *Waverall*.

He was taking a chance—that she wouldn't tell him to go straight to the devil with his proposal. But the more he thought about it, the more determined he was to make an offer that she couldn't refuse.

"You and I both know the big boys in San Francisco would like to force you to sell so they could take over," he explained to her." That's the way it usually happens in this town. Cappy knows it. That's why every banker refused you. They're hoping to close you down before you've even begun."

"And where would a '*scoundrel*' get the kind of money I need? I'm talking about a loan of one hundred thousand dollars."

Without batting an eye, he replied, "I can write you a draft for the money as soon as my bank opens in the morning."

Laurel swallowed and tried to dispel an uneasy feeling. He was bluffing, like the gambler he was.

"Where would you get that kind of money?"

Ruel smiled. "The same place I got it to build the Crystal Palace." His smile deepened as he took in her look of dismay.

"Scoundrels have ways."

Knowing him, she would bet that he did.

"Actually, I get it from men who love to gamble," Ruel explained. "And other business interests." He chose his words carefully.

Her eyes narrowed as she remembered the rumors she'd heard about him.

"Such as Union gold stolen during the war?" she suggested pointedly.

"Over the past several years, I've chosen to change my base of operation from New Orleans to San Francisco," he replied, which was actually no answer at all.

"The South was profitable during the war, in spite of rumors to the contrary, at least for some of us. Now, California is a sound investment, and I've told you a great deal more than most of my business associates. I usually don't discuss past business arrangements with future business partners."

"Is Delia one of your 'business partners?' Or perhaps Dominique?" Having said it, Laurel was immediately embarrassed. It was none of her business who he did business with.

Ruel smiled. "Dominique and I have a unique arrangement. Maybe one day I will explain it to you. As for Delia? No, that was over a long time ago. But now I need to know exactly what collateral you're willing to pledge against the loan for the Rebecca."

Laurel inhaled slowly. She didn't care where he got his money. That was none of her business. Her only concern was getting the loan. And since it appeared this was her only choice.

"It's all drawn up in this agreement that I'd hoped to sign with the bank."

"Let's go into my office," he suggested. "That's where I do all my business."

She expected the office of a gambler, a man who dealt in the business of cards and women, to be opulent, even garish. It was neither. Compared to the bankers' offices she been in that day and Andrew's office in San Francisco, it was quite plain even austere with wood floors, a woodstove, a desk with a chair behind it and two straight-backed wood chairs in front of it.

Laurel laid the document out on the desk.

"The loan will be repayable in six months with interest in the amount of three percent, plus ten percent of the profits of the initial strike."

She'd thought everything through very carefully. Three percent interest was the usual rate for loans made for business ventures. She remembered a loan her uncle had negotiated shortly before she'd left Boston. The ten percent profit was offered as further incentive—obviously not enough for greedy bankers.

Without glancing at the agreement, Ruel nodded. "What if you can't bring in a strike by the end of six months?" He wanted to find out just how realistic Laurel was being about this.

"I've taken the liberty of inserting an extension clause for an additional six months, and compensation of ten thousand dollars."

"It's a big risk," he commented.

"I'm willing to take it," Laurel announced flatly.

"What's your collateral?"

With a surprised look, she pointed to the final clause in the contract. "You would get a ten percent stake in everything that is found." She felt a momentary twinge of uncertainty.

She pushed it aside. If she couldn't realize her father's dream within twelve months... She wouldn't think of that. She would bring in a strike. She had to.

"What use would I have for an unproven silver mine that would require more capital before further mining could be done?" Ruel asked.

"The assay reports are all here. The silver is down there. It's just a matter of bringing it up."

"The Comstock is honeycombed with deserted shafts started by dreamers who were certain a big bonanza was *'down there.'* What makes you think the Rebecca is any different?"

"Every banker I went to declined to make me this loan. Before I left, each of them was making loans to a dozen others without assay reports. The Big Four out of San Francisco have been trying to drive Cappy off Gold Hill since my father died."

She continued with what else she had discovered. "Everybody is trying to drive him out of Virginia City. Someone knows the silver is down there—perhaps the assayer—and wants the Rebecca. I'll get it operating with or without you, Ruel Delaney!"

He smiled. With or without him. He knew she couldn't do it without him. Nobody else in this town would offer to finance the Rebecca. She knew it, and he knew it. But he admired her defiance. There was more honesty in her, more determination, than in anyone he'd ever met.

"I'll make the loan, but I'll need more collateral," he told her.

Laurel stared at him. "If I had more collateral, I would have offered it to the bank. I have a small interest in Wentworth Shipping and an inheritance from my mother, but my uncle won't let me touch them. I don't have anything else to offer."

"Yes, you do." His smile was gone now. He was deadly serious.

"What else is there?"

"I have no use for a silver mine if you can't repay the loan at the end of the contract." He tamped out the cigarette then looked up at her.

"I want you."

She stared at him. "You're mad! Do you really believe that I would accept those terms?"

But he did. She saw it in that dark gaze. He was completely serious. All over her well laid plans suddenly scattered.

"What about Delia?" she demanded. "You're in love with her!" she flung back at him.

He must be mad! That was the only explanation, and he was using her inability to get any other financing for the mining operation in some ridiculous scheme.

"Damn you!" In her anger, she almost choked on the words.

"I'm certain you would if you could. In many ways you already have. But that isn't the issue," Ruel told her amazed at how two people who looked the same could be so different.

He wanted her, had probably wanted her ever since the *Waverall,* but it wouldn't happen here or now. She was too angry at the choice she was being given, which they both knew was no choice at all if she wanted to keep the mine.

"Do you agree?" he asked.

Laurel's eyes blazed anger and humiliation.

"I accept your terms, and I'll repay your loan well before the end of six months. I have only one request."

God, she was furious, he thought. Of all the emotions he's seen in her since that first meeting, this was the one that cut the deepest.

"What is it?"

"You're to stay away from the Rebecca. Once the loan is made, you leave the mining operation to Cappy."

He knew he had to agree, or she'd walk out on everything.

"All right," he agreed. "I won't set foot on the Rebecca until you ask me to."

Until? Of all the arrogant...

Leaning over the table, Ruel signed the loan agreement with bold strokes. Then she turned toward the door. She paused and looked back, meeting his gaze with eyes that blazed blue fire.

"That is something I'll never do," she told him, slamming the door behind her.

"I WILL NOT GO to Virginia City! I hate that town. It's nothing more than a dirty, stinking spot in the middle of the desert. I don't care what little scheme you've got up your sleeve, Aaron Talbott! I won't go!"

"Delia, may I remind you of our little business arrangement. You now work for me."

Hair thinning on top of his balding head, full mutton-chop sideburns flaring over the folds of his cheeks, Aaron Talbott steepled his fingers and, with a cool regard, watched Delia Cameron vent her ire on a chair, a brass cuspidor, and a footstool.

"When you offered me a position, I assumed you were offering me work at the theater. I'm an actress, not a nurse-maid!" Delia ranted.

Talbott was unmoved. He was used to having what he wanted, no matter what the cost. Delia Cameron was his, signed, sealed and delivered. She would do as he asked.

"I never stipulated the terms of your employment, and as I have already invested a substantial sum of money in our 'associ-ation,' for clothes, your suite of rooms and other things, may I remind you of the alternative."

He pulled the satin corded rope that hung at the side of a heavily draped window in his suite of offices in the Bank of California building. Within moments a tall, imposing man entered his office by a side door, and stood motionless just inside the threshold.

Delia shrank back. The man's name was Deaver, and she didn't like him. He was the same man who'd come to her over a month earlier with an enticing offer, from an 'admirer.'

The admirer had been none other than Aaron Talbott, one of the richest men in San Francisco. But Talbott's flattery had turned to ruthlessness after he'd taken her first into his employ and then into his bed.

Deaver was Talbott's henchman, a constant, silent presence who was willing to do whatever he was told and a reminder of the power Talbott wielded by just lifting his finger.

Undaunted, she tried another tactic. "Why is it so important that I go to Virginia City? You must have someone there who can take care of this little matter."

She rounded the desk on the side away from Deaver and slipped her arms about Talbott's neck, allowing him to feel the softness of her breasts through the elegant crimson gown, one of several he'd provided.

"I've arranged for you to travel with the other actors and actresses who'll be appearing at the Opera House in Virginia City. This is important to me, Delia, and you're the only one who can do it. I don't think I need to remind you how generous I can be when I get what I want, or how angry I'd be if you should fail me."

Knowing there was no possible way of refusing him short of leaving the country, Delia's arms dropped from around his neck. She slowly retreated to the safety of the overstuffed chair in front of his desk. Plopping down petulantly, she asked, "Just exactly what is it you want me to do?"

Talbott smiled. Everything had its price. He'd paid a great deal for Delia Cameron, and she wouldn't fail him. They understood each other—greed was a common trait.

"Your sister has chosen to remain in Virginia City, or more specifically at Gold Hill."

"I couldn't care less. I have no interest in what she does."

In spite of her bored expression, Delia couldn't suppress a twinge of curiosity. Laurel. Good heavens, what interest could

Aaron Talbott have in that pathetic creature that just happened to be her sister?

"Shut up and listen. I don't want to repeat myself. Somewhere in that head of yours, I believe there's enough intelligence to understand and follow my instructions," Talbott replied.

Delia fixed him with an icy stare. "Go on."

"Your sister has decided to reopen the Rebecca Mine. She's found financial backing of some kind and has started moving work crews up to the mine. I want her stopped."

"The mine's hers. I have nothing to do with it. Our loving father chose to buy me off and leave her that worthless claim. If you want that hole in the ground, you stop her. But I warn you, you'll be wasting time and money. Nothing Jason Cameron did ever amounted to anything."

"I suppose in a certain sense, you are proof of that," he replied. "Nevertheless, I want the Rebecca. Let us just say that it's a worthy endeavor, and you're going to help me get it. As amusing as you've been, you're going to earn what I've invested in you."

"Why are you so interested in a worthless mine? Unless, of course, it's not worthless." She sat up. "That's it, isn't it?"

Her dark blue eyes narrowed. "You've found out something about that mine. There's silver down there! And you want me to go to Virginia City and convince Laurel to give it up. No deal. At least not for the pittance you've been paying me up to now."

"Don't get greedy, Delia," Aaron Talbott warned. Chewing on the butt end of an expensive cigarette, he raised the fingers of his right hand off the surface of the desk, and Deaver silently came forward. Talbott stopped him just behind Delia's chair.

Always the consummate actress, Delia rose from the chair and leaned seductively across the desk, exposing the ample swell of her breasts.

"We're both greedy, Aaron. The truth of the matter—the

whole truth, is that you need me. Laurel won't listen to anything you have to say. As a matter of fact, I'd be willing to bet you've already tried to buy her out." At the subtle shift of his eyes, Delia smiled with satisfaction.

"She turned you down! Either she's very brave or very dumb. It doesn't matter, because I couldn't care less about her." Reaching out, Delia traced a finger across his lips.

"I'll do it, of course. You knew I would. But the price just went up." She turned her lovely head as Deaver took a menacing step forward.

"Call off your dog, Aaron, and let's talk business. And be prepared to pay dearly. If I'm going to betray my own flesh and blood, it's going to cost you."

"How much?" Talbott snapped.

He did need her. Without Delia, there was no plan, at least no legal plan. And he liked to stay within the bounds of the law as much as possible.

"Two-hundred-thousand dollars, in advance, and a split of whatever you take out of the Rebecca. If that mine is worth enough to catch your interest, you'll never miss any of it," Delia announced with wicked delight.

"You think you're worth it?" Snakelike, his tongue passed over his lips.

Inwardly, Delia shuddered and wondered how she could have let someone like him make love to her, and immediately decided that was hardly what it was called once he finished.

Oh, she'd pretended to enjoy it, but the truth was the man was pathetic at best. She thought longingly of Ruel and of the passion-filled nights they'd shared. Then she smiled. When she had her own money, there'd be a way to get him back. After all, Ruel Delaney liked money.

"I'm worth it, and you know it," she told Talbott.

He conceded, thinking for the time being he'd go along with her demands. Later he would take care of her his way.

Delia smiled. "Good. Now, exactly what it is you want me to do?"

"You're to leave for Virginia City immediately." Waving Deaver from the room, Talbott rose and came around the desk. Slipping an arm about her waist, he pulled Delia against him. She did excite him.

She was intelligent enough to hold his interest for longer than a few moments, and she was pretty enough to make any man's blood warm. His left hand closed over the swell of her bottom pulling her into him.

The perfume, her nearness, and her defiance were already having an effect on him. His right hand splayed across the swell of her breast, pinching cruelly, and a look of satisfaction appeared in her eyes as his right hand dropped to the back of her gown, then lowered over her left hip. With cold brutality he pulled her fully against the hardened shaft swelling painfully against his pants. It had been some time since he'd been able to become fully aroused. His head lowered, his full lips greedily moving over her shoulder.

"My dear, you have a performance to give," Talbott grunted through the haze of lust.

Delia's eyes closed, not with desire, but with disgust. There was a word for what she was about to do and it wasn't nice. She forced herself to remember another man whose touch had filled her with desire as she stroked him then opened the front of his pants.

She'd do her part, and she'd gladly take Aaron Talbott's money. Then, she'd find some way to get Ruel Delaney back.

16

L aurel felt as if she'd made a bargain with the devil.

In the next few weeks, she had plenty of time to think about the agreement she'd made with Ruel Delaney.

At first, she knew she could still back out, forget the loan, Ruel Delaney, and the Rebecca. Knowing it, she put off acting until the day workmen and wagonloads of supplies began arriving from Virginia City.

Then her concentration shifted from doubts about taking the loan to determination to repay it early. She'd take great satisfaction in that and then tearing up the loan documents right under Ruel Delaney's nose.

Stirring the huge pot of stew that simmered on the cook stove, she wiped beads of perspiration from her forehead. It was agonizingly warm in the small cabin, even in the early hours of the morning. Despite Cappy's protests, she'd insisted on cooking the meals for the thirty-man crew that had been sent to work the mine. But she'd soon realized that she was spending almost every waking moment preparing food. Thirty, hard-working men could consume an unbelievable amount of food.

Feeling dizzy, Laurel set down the wooden ladle and went to stand before the window. The last of the cool, early morning breeze stirred the blue curtains she'd insisted on hanging. They lessened the starkness of the sparsely furnished cabin. The breeze helped clear her head.

She'd seen little of Cappy the past few weeks. As soon as the men had started arriving, he'd spent most of his time down in the mine, setting up work schedules, outlining what must be done at the different levels, and familiarizing the men with the equipment.

Sammie helped with the cooking now that they had a full crew to provide for, but it required her help to see that the food was ready when the men came up out of the mine.

Untying the towel that served as an apron, she threw it down on the wooden table. The stew could take care of itself for a while.

She ran into Cappy on her way over the long building.

"You've been lookin' a mite peaked lately. You're spendin' too much time cooped up in that cabin—cookin'. Not to mean we don't appreciate it."

She had a feeling that he was trying to get around the fact that her cooking was barely passable.

"I know of someone over at one of the other mines. I'll have one of the boys bring him on over in the mornin' if you don't mind puttin' him on the payroll. He can make a mean batch of Texas chili, and the best sourdough bread you ever tasted." Cappy's eyes twinkled.

"So that's why you were so anxious to get another cook over here. You're tired of stew and biscuits." She laughed.

"That's not it at all. You're a partner in this mine. I just figured you might want to spend more time involved on its operation."

"You know I would." Laurel brightened.

"Good. Sammy's on his way. He can take over the rest of the

meal for today." His eyes sparkled. "I got somethin' I want you to see. Somethin' I think you'll be real interested in."

Interested indeed. Laurel stared at the spot where light from the lantern glinted off the damp rock of the newest passage. Half a dozen men worked it side-by-side, stripping away rock and dirt. Water trickled through a fissure, pooling at their feet. Pickaxe in hand, Cappy stripped away a layer of black rock, and Laurel's eyes widened upon noting the blue-gray metal underneath—silver ore!

Cappy nodded and handed her a chunk of ore. "This is part of the same vein we've been following the last three weeks, working our way down, shoring up each new level."

"It really is here," she whispered, holding the ore toward the light.

"Of course it's here," Cappy replied indignantly. "Didn't I say it would be?"

"Yes, but it was almost too good to be true. Is there really a chance we'll be able to repay the loan on time?"

"We'll make it. That what's been botherin' you? You've been as touchy as a polecat with a thorn in its paw the past few weeks. I was beginnin' to think it might be that loan you got from Delaney."

Weighing the ore sample in her hand, Laurel nodded. "I just want to make certain we can repay it."

"You did get the extension of time?"

When she remained silent, Cappy's gaze narrowed. "Somehow I get the feelin' you haven't told me quite everythin' about that private conversation you had with him."

"It looks as if we won't need that extension."

"You didn't sign for it, did you?" Cappy pressed, feeling there was a whole lot more he didn't know about the arrangement.

"No," she murmured simply.

"No harm. We'll make it. If this vein continues on laterally, we won't have to go any deeper. I've got a man comin' over to

get the pumps fired up so we can get this water outta here, and
we're gonna start crews round the clock day after tomorrow,
when I'll have more men. We'll need that fry cook."

"Thank you, Cappy."

"What the hell for? I'm only doin' what I agreed to. Besides,
you're forgettin', I'm part owner. Part of whatever I bring up is
mine."

"I know," she admitted with a smile. "But thank you anyway,
for helping me with all of this. My father believed in the
Rebecca, even when others called him a fool. Proving all those
other people wrong is the best gift you could give me."

Cappy cleared his throat. "You're welcome, mighty
welcome."

"Well, I suppose I should get back up to the cabin and see if
Sammy's got everything under control. These men will tolerate
just about anything except a meal that isn't ready on time."

"A bit different than you figured it'd be, isn't it?" Cappy took
the lantern from her as she started up the ladder. "Any regrets?"

Laurel pulled herself up through the opening. "Never," she
stated emphatically. "When I make up my mind to do something, I don't look back."

"Yep." Cappy followed her up to the next level. "You're like
her that way."

Laurel turned around to gaze at him thoughtfully. "My
mother."

He nodded. "I wish you could have known her. There's so
much of her in you. I see it all the time."

A question that had nagged at Laurel once before returned
to plague her.

"Were you in love with my mother?"

The question caught Cappy off-guard. He fixed her with a
scrutinizing glare.

"You sure got a blunt way of puttin' things." He rubbed his
unkempt beard. "Are you in love with Delaney?" he asked.

Seeing the sudden change in the expression in her eyes, he knew he'd struck fairly close.

"I asked first," Laurel insisted.

"So you did," Cappy mumbled uneasily. He decided to retreat to the safety of generalities.

"I suppose everyone who met Rebecca was a little bit in love with her. She just seemed to draw people to her. And she was sure pretty, in a refined, genteel way. A real lady, just like you. She used to get real strong-minded about things, but she never used a bad word or had a bad thought about anybody including this old miner. I appreciated that." He breathed a deep sigh.

"I suppose in that way, you could say I loved her. But she never even so much as looked at another man. She was just plain in love with your daddy. Now, what about you and Delaney?"

"I hardly know the man." In a sense, it was true. "Why would you think that?"

Cappy shrugged. "I hear things." He hung up the canteen that he'd refilled and brought down into the mine.

"What things?" Laurel asked.

"I know he brought you down off that mountain after the stagecoach was attacked. I also know that wasn't the first time the two of you met. I could see it in his eyes. A man carries a certain look about a special woman. Ruel Delaney has quite a reputation, and I was just worried for you."

"Whatever he does, has nothing to do with me," Laurel said sharply, knowing she was lying. "Bring in the vein of silver within six months and you won't have to worry about the loan. After all, I signed those documents, not you. Your part of the mine is safe. I pledged only my portion."

"Delaney's doings might have everything to do with you. He knew your sister in San Francisco. Word has it she was his mistress."

"I try not to listen to rumor and gossip," Laurel replied. Yet rumor had followed her everywhere, everywhere Ruel Delaney happened to be. But Cappy wasn't to blame for her involvement with Ruel.

That was in the past. Now their relationship was strictly business, and she fully intended that it would stay that way. Falling in love with a man like Ruel Delaney promised only heartache.

"Don't worry about the loan," Laurel reminded Cappy. She turned to the ladder that led up to the next level.

"All right, I won't worry about the loan, and you won't worry about Ruel Delaney." He met her gaze knowingly.

A warning shout echoed behind them, and Laurel looked back to see smoke and dust belching up out of the passage below them. The dark cloud stung her eyes, making breathing impossible. Through the thick haze, she cried out for Cappy, knowing he'd been only a couple of feet behind her. Then, as smoke engulfed her, she felt herself boosted—almost thrown up through the opening into the opening of the long building shaft house. It was the last thing she remembered.

She stared through swollen eyelids.

"You be fine. You just breathed too much smoke."

Sammy's voice cut through the fog of in her brain. Smoke?

She struggled to sit up. "Cappy!"

"Right here, missy." A gnarled hand smoothed back her tangled hair.

"You got out all right?"

"It takes more than a little dust and broken beams to slow down old Cappy." He placed a cooling, damp cloth across her forehead.

"The other men?" Laurel tried to moisten her lips and found her tongue was just as parched. Then a strong arm went around her shoulders and helped her sit up. A cool metal of cup was pressed against her lips. She drank greedily, like a person dying of thirst.

"Take it easy," Cappy told her. "A little at a time."

"What about the men?" Her voice now cracked only on every second word.

"We're still trying to dig out down there. It happened at the eight-hundred-foot level. Most got out. Just two were farther down, clearing some of the timbers."

Laurel blinked to clear her blurred vision. Her eyes felt as if someone had thrown sand in them. She smiled when she saw Cappy. His face was smeared with dirt, skin showing through only in the wrinkles at the corners of his eyes. With his bristly beard and shaggy mane, he resembled the great black bear she'd once seen at the zoo in Boston. She wrinkled her nose as she became aware of a faint stench, uncertain whether it was herself or Cappy who smelled so bad.

"There was a small fire, singed my beard," Cappy offered, stroking it thoughtfully. "It was in need of a trim anyway."

He fastened a curious gaze on her. The first question out of her mouth hadn't been about the damage to the mine, or the cost to fix it. It had been about the men. She was more like Rebecca than he'd realized. Delia wouldn't have given a damn about the men, and it would be days before they could know the exact extent of the damage, a costly delay. Only a short while earlier, he'd been assuring her that they'd make the loan payment on time. He couldn't say that now if she asked again.

"Any injuries?" she asked.

"Oh, the usual; a broken leg, some bruises, but we got lucky in that. Now, we just need to get to those two men."

"Dear God, Cappy." Her voice trembled. "Do they have families?"

He shook his head. "Mining isn't the sort of thing that provides a steady income for families."

At least there was that, she thought.

He saw the tears she fought. "It happens, missy. Every miner who's ever gone down a shaft knows the risk. We live with it."

"You could have been down there."

"If I hadn't been with you, I would have. I kinda guess you're my lucky lady." He tried to get a smile out of her. She had to get over this; she had to go on. He breathed easier when he saw the way she squared her shoulders.

"What will it take to get back up in operation?"

"Some extra men to help dig out the shaft, possibly a mule crew to cart the stuff out." That would mean additional cost. "And we should probably let Mr. Delaney know."

"No!'"

Before she had been almost numb, now she was filled with emotion. Cappy frowned. There was a whole lot more to this relationship than she'd told him.

Realizing she'd sounded harsh, she smiled apologetically. "There's no need to concern him with this. We'll take care of everything and put the mine back on schedule."

When he was silent, she searched his face. "We can reopen, can't we?"

"We can reopen; that's not the problem. That's just a matter of digging out and shoring up the damaged areas. Time is the problem. I'll know more when we can get a crew back down there. For now, I don't want you worryin' your head about it. Just rest."

"You need to rest too."

"I'll rest after we get the last of the men out." He pulled the blanket up around her shoulders and tucked her in.

"Everything will work out, won't it Cappy?" There was uncertainty in her weary voice.

He squeezed her hand. "It will. I promise." Gazing at her in the light from the lantern beside the bed, he realized she probably hadn't heard a word he'd said. She breathed evenly and was already asleep. He blew out the lantern.

She was dead set against it, but as he saw it their financial backer had a right to know what was goin' on. He might find a sudden collapse deep in the mine real interestin', especially since they hadn't been using dynamite at that level.

Three days later, when the foreman of the lumberyard refused to ship a consignment of lumber that had already been paid for, Cappy decided it was time to take matters into his own hands. He suspected that the collapse and the sudden shortage of timber were not coincidences.

Cappy didn't know Ruel Delaney, but there were rumors about him. He wasn't at all certain the man could be trusted. But he'd never heard he couldn't be—and there were others he trusted far less. And as he saw it, he and Laurel were partners. His part of that partnership voted to contact Delaney. They had more problems than just a few buried passageways, and it was possible they were going to need not only an extension on the loan but additional money. The only trouble was, a note from Cappy probably wouldn't be enough to bring Delaney out from Virginia City.

RUEL DELANEY WAS HOT, tired, and more than just a little disagreeable. Spending half the night in a high-stakes game had lost its luster. It had gotten to be work and that's when he knew it was time to throw in his hand.

He splashed cold water on his face and snarled at the knock on the door of his suite at the International. He already given his manager permission to extend another two thousand dollars credit to one of their frequent customers, signed off on the order of supplies for the hotel and restaurant, and personally escorted a particularly disgruntled customer out the entrance after telling him that he could return once he was sober.

Now, he stalked across the room, and threw the door open. "What the hell is it?"

"A message arrived for you earlier," Soon-Li informed him, averting her gaze at the sight of his naked body.

"I thought you would want to see it."

At three o'clock in the morning...

Annoyed that he'd lashed out, not to mention his state of undress, Ruel hastily wrapped a towel around his lower body and disappeared into the adjoining room.

"Open it..." he asked, then added, "Please."

His foul temper had nothing to do with Soon-Li or the fact that it was three in the morning and everything to do with a blue-eyed young woman who'd walked out of his office two weeks earlier with not a word since he'd made arrangements to see that Miss Laurel Wentworth had the financial means to expand operation at the Rebecca mine.

"It is marked 'confidential.'" Glancing uncertainly to the door that stood ajar, Soon-Li waited. "From Gold Hill."

There was a curse as he returned to the main room of the suite.

"I apologize," he told her, taking the note from Soon-Li's outstretched hand as she stood with her back to him to avoid further embarrassment.

"Is it the message you've been waiting for?" she asked.

Ruel glanced up, a slow smile replacing the frown. "Yes, and you can turn around. I'm decent."

She cautiously turned around. "Oh no, Mr. Ruel. You're never decent. I learned that long time ago." She smiled impishly.

Ruel read the note one more time. It was indeed what he had been waiting for.

. . .

TROUBLE AT THE REBECCA. *Cappy*

HE REMEMBERED Laurel's angry words the day they'd made the arrangement for the loan she needed.

'I can do this myself; I won't ask for help.'

She'd been more angry and hurt than he'd ever seen her.

What could possibly have made her ask for his help now? *Trouble at the Rebecca...* a cold knot settled in the pit of his stomach. Something had to have gone wrong.

He'd learned days earlier from a loose-mouthed player at one of his tables, that Aaron Talbott had offered to buy the Rebecca.

Laurel's refusal wasn't surprising, but Talbott wasn't a man who would accept that refusal. When he didn't get what he wanted with an unreasonable offer, he used other methods.

Soon-Li read the expression at his face. "You will need work clothes," she said.

He nodded. His usual attire for the gaming parlor wouldn't work for a trip to Sun Mountain. When she would have moved past him to lay clothes out for him out, he stopped her.

"I'll find what I need."

"It pleases me to do things for you." She smiled softly, devotion in her dark eyes.

He shook his head. "No," he said gently. "You do far too much. I won't have you waiting on me or anyone else. You have to think about the baby."

"I do think about my baby," she replied. "You are the reason for everything I have. I owe you a debt that can never be repaid. Please allow me to do small things. It pleases me."

Her gentleness and inner strength reminded him of Laurel.

"It *pleases* me to see that you're happy and safe," he told her. "But, from now on I'm leaving strict orders that you're to rest and delegate your work to others. I don't want anything to happen to him, or you."

"*Him?*" Soon-Li said, a faint smile on her lips. "Everyone is so certain it will be a boy."

"Of course. After all, he has a proud, strong father," Ruel replied. He opened a drawer at the desk that he also kept in his suite of rooms and pulled out a handgun.

She frowned. "Will there be trouble?"

He smiled at her concern. "Ask Cal to have my horse brought up from the stables. And don't worry, I can take care of myself."

"One day, you will run out of luck, and women from everywhere will come to mourn," she scolded.

He shook his head. "There's only one woman I want to come to me, and I have no intention of being in a grave when she does."

"WHAT ELSE DID YOU FIND?" Ruel fingered the frayed piece of line. The fire touched to it had ceased burning before reaching several sticks of dynamite. He followed Cappy Burnett down the passage, dirt and debris blocking their path.

Cappy stopped beside a solid timber. In the passage wall, a notch had been cut into the heavy beam. He held up another stick of dynamite.

"That first explosion would have triggered this one, and three more I found set up. Fortunately, whoever set the explosives wasn't paying close attention when he ran that line or the whole thing would have collapsed and it would have taken months to dig everything out. As it is, we've been able to move most of it by working the crews around the clock in shifts. Only thing is, now I can't get the timber to replace the damaged sections."

Ruel nodded thoughtfully. "And Aaron Talbott just happens to own the lumber yard."

"I reckon there's a better than even chance he's behind this," Cappy replied. "But there's no way of provin' anything, never is when Talbott has a hand in things. If we can't get that lumber, we're shut down. I thought you should know about this, since you financed the operation."

"You're not going to shut down." Ruel examined a piece of ore he'd picked up down the passage. "I'll see that you get the lumber, and anything else you need." He handed Cappy the chunk of ore.

"That appears to be high grade. Does Laurel know what's at stake?"

"She knows."

"Does she know about the explosives?" Ruel wondered how much Cappy had told her.

Cappy nodded. "I couldn't keep her outta the mine. She took the injuries of those men real hard, like she was personally responsible." He shook his head.

"She's stronger than just about anyone I ever met, man or woman, and more stubborn than most. She's hell-bent on going down to that lumberyard and gettin' that shipment of timber herself. That's the main reason I wanted you to come up here. I thought maybe you could talk sense into her. She won't listen to a word I say. She'll only find trouble in Gold Hill, Talbott pretty near owns the whole town."

"What makes you think she'll listen to me any better than she listened to you?" Ruel turned a piece of ore over in his fingers.

Cappy frowned. "She might not, but you hold the note for the loan. That might convince her to listen." He shook his head again. "Never saw anybody who could get so all fired set on somethin' and then come hell or high water go about gettin' it done. First time I saw her handle a pistol, I decided right there and then she had a definite advantage in any argument."

Ruel smiled. "She can handle a gun." And just about anything else she wants to, he thought. "I'll see what I can do."

"That's all I ask."

Lantern in hand, Cappy led the way out of the mine.

"What are you doing, here?" Laurel demanded, as they emerged through the opening into the long house.

"We had an agreement. You weren't to set foot on the Rebecca."

"I've been accused of a lot of things, but not keeping my word isn't one of them. Unless there's trouble."

HER HAIR WAS PULLED BACK and tied at the nape of her neck. She wore a cotton work shirt that was a couple sizes too large and work pants that looked vaguely familiar—from the trail tucked into dust-covered boots that were also familiar.

She was thinner. He could see it in her face, in the slight hollows in her cheeks. He already knew that Laurel Wentworth was a woman who felt deeply but didn't buckle. Her eyes snapping, she glared at Cappy, then turned on her heel and left the long house, the door closing behind her with a loud snap.

Cappy shook his head. "Good luck. Yer gonna need it. And if she gets a look in her eye like she'd like to pound dough, you might want to leave it be," he warned.

Releasing a grim sigh, Ruel headed after her. He shouted across the sweltering, dusty yard.

"I had a right to know."

Laurel stopped abruptly and slowly turned around. "We have an agreement—you wouldn't come out to the Rebecca, and I would repay your money on time. I intend to keep my part of the bargain. The least you could do is keep yours."

He'd thought about that on the ride out to Gold Hill, and knew the best way was to keep this all business.

"As the principal investor in the operation of the Rebecca, I'm entitled to know what's going on," he reminded her. "I have the right to know if there's a problem or setback."

Damn him, she thought. Damn, damn, damn. And damn Cappy, the only way he could have known about the collapse of the mine.

Slowly, very slowly, Laurel turned around, squinting through the sun's glare.

"Now you know," she said. Then she continued her march across the yard to the shed where a horse stood saddled.

Without so much as thinking about it, she flipped up the stirrup and readjusted the cinch strap. Two months earlier, she'd never have believed she'd be out in the middle of nowhere, running a mining operation, helping Cappy organize a work crew of thirty-odd men, or that she'd be going up against someone with great influence who'd decided to close her down.

Close her down! The words came hard, but she refused to accept them.

Ruel slowly came up behind her. "You can't go down there alone."

Jerking the cinch strap tighter, Laurel didn't bother to respond.

He stepped up beside her, and his fingers closed over her wrists, gently but firmly. She jumped as if she'd been branded.

"I can take care of it," she informed him.

"You think you can, but you're going up against something that you've never experienced before. This isn't Boston, New Orleans, or San Francisco. In those cities most people live by rules and laws about things. There's a certain civility about things, polite society. For the most part," he added. "That doesn't exist on Gold Hill or in Virginia City."

"We need lumber and I intend to get it," she announced.

The sun was too bright, the day was sweltering, and she'd almost succeeded in convincing herself that she didn't want to see him again, much less need anything more from him.

There were times over the past three weeks that she'd cursed the agreement they'd made. He was a gambler, a shrewd businessman according to the reputation she'd heard rumored about—was that any different than men like Talbott? And he was a scoundrel. He didn't live by other men's rules and that made her nervous.

The other thing that made her nervous was that for a moment, just a moment, when he and Cappy stepped out of the entrance to the mine, her reaction had been, heaven help her... for just that moment, she was glad to see him.

Ruel reached out, touching her sleeve with his fingertips because he was fairly certain anything else would have had her backing away from him.

Cool logic, keep it all business, he told himself. For now.

"I know these people. I can help. Don't you realize that someone very badly wants you to fail?"

"I thought of that, and I asked myself who stands to gain if I can't reopen the mine, if I can't repay that loan on time?" Laurel countered. "After all, you did see the assay reports."

"And I don't exactly have a sterling reputation," Ruel replied the obvious. "That's too easy, Laurel, think again. Who made you that offer to buy the mine? Who controls most of Gold Hill and the toll road? And who has been trying to shut Cappy down for years?"

"I don't need or want your help!" She jerked away and strode toward the cabin.

"Dammit, Laurel!" Ruel was beside her, grabbing her arm and pulling her around, forcing her to listen to him.

"You're playing a dangerous game, and the deck's stacked against you."

"Then I'll learn the rules, and beat them at it," she angrily replied, trying to free her wrist.

"There are no rules. Don't you know that? They'll do whatever's necessary to take the Rebecca away from you." His fingers tightened as if he could squeeze common sense into her. "It's for keeps, winner take all."

"I intend to win!" she told him.

Heat burned at her skin, but whether it came from the dry, sweltering weather or the man holding onto her, she couldn't be sure.

Surprise, resentment, and something she'd tried hard to ignore—burned inside her. A moment before she couldn't have hoped to break his grasp, now she didn't want to. Her fists tightened as she held onto the anger.

"The stakes are high, perhaps worth millions for a man like him," he warned. "Talbott doesn't lose—ever. Don't you understand?"

"The explosion in the mine was no accident."

17

In the end they compromised. He informed her that he would shut her down himself if she didn't do this his way, and since he held the note on the Rebecca, he had the legal right to do it.

For several moment he was certain she was going to tell him exactly where he could put that legal right, but she didn't.

Instead, she had mounted her horse, turned toward the road that led from Gold Hill, and had simply ridden out. Somewhere on that ride into Virginia City, there was a silent truce.

They left their horses at the stables at the end of the street. Not waiting for him, Laurel headed for the small hotel where she and Cappy had once stayed. Considering their rapidly diminishing finances, she figured it was all she could afford for the night.

Ruel didn't try to catch up with her. Her silence on the long ride from Gold Hill had told him her mood. She was hurt, angry, and scared. It showed in her eyes. Now, he let her walk on ahead, knowing she could be damned stubborn.

"You might consider accepting that suite of rooms at the International," he suggested when he caught up with her at the street corner. "There'd be no obligation. And since finances are important that might be the wisest thing to do."

Laurel stopped and turned. He knew exactly how important they were, especially now with the damage to mine, extra men Cappy would need to hire, not to mention supplies including the lumber to shore up the shaft and connecting passages. Still, she hesitated. In a short while she'd learned a lot about Ruel Delaney—particularly that he never did anything that wouldn't guarantee a return.

"No obligation?" she asked.

"You'll have the only key to the room." He smiled to himself at the doubtful look she angled at him.

Across from the small hotel, Laurel hesitated. Two doors down, in front of the ornate facade of the Opera House, a small crowd had gathered around an elegant black carriage. A woman had alighted, and her laughter could be heard over the conversations that buzzed noisily about her.

"Well of course I'm excited to be back in Virginia City. Everyone is just so hospitable and kind." There was something familiar about that voice. Turning in the glow of a streetlamp that had just been lit, the woman suddenly called out her name.

"Laurel!"

Too stunned to move, Laurel stared incredulously as Delia swept across the dusty street. She stepped up onto the wood boardwalk, scooped Laurel into her arms, and hugged her tightly.

"I was hoping we'd run into each other," Delia said sweetly. Then she quickly added, "Actually, I was hoping for more than that. I had every intention of making certain we had a chance to visit."

Nodding her head prettily and sending an elegant crimson ostrich plume sweeping through the air, she greeted Ruel. "Hello, darling. How are you? I see you made the trip over the

Sierras safely. Such a ghastly, dirty ride. I was fortunate a friend gave me the use of his private coach, otherwise I would probably have refused to make the trip."

Laurel was too stunned to reply. She and Delia had hardly parted on friendly terms, but now she was greeting her as if none of that had happened.

"What are you doing in Virginia City?" she asked.

Delia looped her arm through Laurel's, angling a flirtatious smile over her shoulder at Ruel Delaney.

"It's just the most wonderful turn of luck. When we met in San Francisco, I'd just returned from New York, and my finances were, shall we say, greatly depleted even with my part of the inheritance from Father. It was amazing how much money it took just to pay for my clothes." She gave Ruel long look.

"I'd never worried about such things before. Anyway, I thought it best to pursue my career on the stage. And as luck would have it, a friend put me in contact with a gentleman who knows Mr. Piper." She indicated the sign over the Opera House with a flourish of a gloved hand—Piper's Opera House.

"It seems Mr. Piper was in need of an actress for his next production, and I was fortunate enough to be available. Since it'd been so long since I'd been to Virginia City," she paused, "and I knew that you'd be here," she patted Laurel on the arm. "I just felt it right that I accept the offer." She turned to Laurel and seized both of her hands.

"We started off so badly, mostly due to my bad temper, and other... circumstances." She lingered on the last word, glancing at Ruel. "At any rate, I felt it was time to make amends."

It was the first time Laurel had felt like smiling in days. "I'm glad you're here."

A man called to Delia from across the street. She waved him back with a gloved hand, her golden curls bobbing beneath her edge of her hat.

"I have an early rehearsal tonight. I do hope you'll be able to catch my show. We open tomorrow night."

"I'm sorry, I can't," Laurel thought of Cappy. "I won't be staying in town after tomorrow morning." She hoped.

"I'm only here on business." Laurel felt disappointed. Just when she and Delia seemed to have a chance of getting on together, other obligations pulled her away. But if Delia were going to be in town for an extended period of time.

"You could come out to the Rebecca. There's so much work, I just can't be away from it right now."

"Yes, I can see." Delia brushed at mud on Laurel's shirt.

"How odd, we seemed to have changed places. Here I am, on top of the world, beginning a new engagement here in Virginia City, and look at you. You're certainly not the sister I first met, fresh off the boat from Boston."

Laurel forced a smile. "Yes, things have certainly changed."

"Maybe I can persuade Ruel to take in my show tomorrow night." Delia looked at him invitingly.

"I don't think so," he replied. "I've seen all your performances." He looked over at Laurel.

"We should be going."

Another man called to Delia, but she ignored him and pressed a sisterly kiss against Laurel's cheek. "Of course, you're staying at the International. Ruel can be absolutely a marvelous host, as I know." She smiled.

"Don't look so stricken. It's obvious what's been happening since I last saw you. Actually, it was obvious then. And you must know, I really don't mind. Actually, it's quite entertaining wouldn't you say—twins." Delia flashed him a smile.

She didn't need to explain further. Laurel knew exactly what she was referring too.

It was amazing. With sweet words and polite insinuations, Delia had managed to completely humiliate her, and now she was chatting on amiably. She straightened her shoulders. She was glad to see Delia, but she wasn't about to let her intimidate her. She suddenly changed her mind about her accommodations.

"Yes, I will be staying at the International," she announced, realizing that even with this new cordiality between them, on at least one level she and Delia were still at odds.

"Well of course," Delia replied. "I hope we'll have a chance to see each other before you leave. We have so much to catch up on, and I'm anxious to learn all about Boston." Her sister squeezed her hand.

Laurel frowned as Delia departed in a flurry of crimson skirts, her laughter filling the warm night air as she rejoined her friends.

Reluctantly, she admitted that she was glad she'd decided to take Ruel up on his offer of a suite at the International, even if she had let Delia goad her into accepting.

It seemed ridiculous that her sister had been able to force her to change her mind. She'd been jealous of Delia's casual comments about Ruel, though she knew very well what their relationship was. It had a word, and it didn't sit particularly well— jealousy?

Ridiculous!

Now, as she glanced about the elegant rooms, she realized that she appreciated it. The hot bath, after the last weeks on the mountain, had been absolutely heavenly, and true to his word, Ruel hadn't bothered her, not even with a dinner invitation. He'd had Tibbits escort her to her rooms. Even now, almost two hours later, his cool dismissal puzzled more than she liked to admit.

"Well, just exactly what did you expect!" she had asked her reflection in the mirror when she first saw herself and seeing exactly what Delia had seen on the street in front of the Opera House, in the work shirt and pants.

She was the complete opposite of Delia's velvet and feathered beauty, even with the striking resemblance. It was a bit disconcerting to look at someone and feel that you were looking in a mirror.

During the past weeks there'd been little time to think about Delia, except when Cappy had mentioned her. But Delia was real, and Laurel couldn't help feeling a twinge of emotion at the thought of her. She wanted to know more about her. Maybe this time they could start over with one another.

She was pulled from her thoughts by a knock at the door of the suite, then stared in amazement for the second time that evening at the woman who stood in the hallway.

Delia smiled brightly as she swept into the room with a quick glance at the door to the adjoining bed chamber.

"I didn't catch you at a bad moment, did I?"

Slowly recovering, Laurel stepped back. "No, of course not."

Delia swept into the room, now dressed in a gown in a vivid shade of green.

"The trip was exhausting. We'll rehearse in the morning. But I confess, I couldn't bear to think of you leaving town tomorrow without our having a chance to talk. You're dining alone?" She gestured to the small table and the single place setting.

And before Laurel could answer, "These rooms are lovely, aren't they?" Delia continued to chatter.

"I always stayed here when I was in town, but not alone of course." She gave Laurel an apologetic smile. "I'm sorry. How rude of me to talk about such things. I must have been mistaken. Ruel is always so particular about his... choice of companions. Although, I must say, when I saw you in San Francisco, I was certain you were... involved." Delia stood back, one finger propped beneath her chin.

"I suppose that's almost like paying oneself a compliment, isn't it?" She burst out laughing.

Laurel tried to change the direction of the conversation. "Have you had supper?"

"Yes, hours ago, with a gentleman friend. You know, I really must warn you about Ruel. I feel I can, considering how well I know him. It does seem a little wicked of him, the two of us looking so much alike. Good heavens! The things men will do. I remember a night, right here in this very same bed..."

"Can we talk about something else?" Laurel suggested.

"Of course," Delia smiled with wide-eyed innocence.

For the next two hours, they talked. Delia was very curious about the mine.

"Please try to understand," Laurel explained for at least the third time. "The mine was Jason's. He believed in it. I have to try to get it operating."

"Operating a mine? That's a man's work, not a woman's. Can't you see how impossible it is? I worry about what might happen."

Her concern seemed curious considering they'd only met a few weeks earlier.

"You really should consider selling it," Delia persisted.

"I can't... I won't," Laurel repeated without going into details about the loan, and reasons she'd already tried to explain.

When the clock on the mantel over the fireplace chimed ten o'clock, Delia rose to leave. "Good heavens, where has the time gone? I must be going. My friend is expecting me."

"So soon? You've told me hardly anything about Jason," Laurel objected, disappointment in her voice.

"There's really not that much to tell. He sank every dollar he had into some worthless mine. I finally couldn't stand living in mining camps. When he bought the Rebecca, he finally seemed to come to his senses. He bought the small house in San Francisco and arranged for me to live with a widow woman he knew—anything would have been better than the stinking camps. I just don't know how you stand it up on that mountain. It must be dreadful."

She smiled. "I'm sorry. I keep forgetting that was your inheritance. Poor dear. You really must consider selling it. It'll do nothing but wear you down, just like it wore him down. All that work for nothing. Just look at yourself, so thin and ragged. No wonder Ruel isn't up here tonight. You'd better be careful, darling, or no man will want you." Pulling on her gloves, Delia turned toward the door. She glanced at the door to the adjacent bedroom.

"Good night, dear."

Delia slipped into the private office on the ground floor of the International Hotel. The door to the adjoining room stood ajar.

She could hear the sound of water splashing. A slow smile spread across her face. She knew these rooms, and she knew exactly who she'd find behind that open door. Crossing the office, she peered into the suite.

Ruel stood across the room, his shirt removed as he changed clothes. She frowned at the sight of the bandage low on his side as the scent of cinnamon and oranges filled the room—that scent that she remembered well.

Desire, and regret, tightened inside her. She remembered every muscle, every hardened plane of his body even after more than a year. Approaching quietly, she reached up, her hands covering his eyes.

Would he know the difference, she wondered, as she pressed her breasts against his back?

He reached for one of her hands.

Behind him, Delia shuddered, remembering the touch of his hands on more intimate places. Her other hand lowered and brushed the front of his pants. He turned unexpectedly twisting an arm behind her back.

She cried out, certain her arm would break. "You're hurting me!"

"What, no knife? Did you really think I could be so easily fooled? You forget, Delia," he told her, "I know your scent. It gave you away the moment you came into the room.

"Laurel would never wear such an obvious perfume. But then I suppose that's another difference between you." His fingers tightened over her wrist until she cried out. He pushed her away from him.

"It's me you want, and you know it," she flung back at him, rubbing her wrist. "She's just a temporary fascination—a lady and one that looks exactly like me?" she hissed.

"What did you do to get her into your bed?" she continued. "It's not like you to have an affair with a lady. Too much trouble you once said."

The question cut deep. He'd have to live with that. Not that he would ever admit that to her or anyone else. That was between him and her sister.

"In spite of the fact that you look alike, you are nothing alike in things that matter. Not that you would understand. Get out."

"You just haven't found that out yet," she replied. "We're twins. Remember that." Anger twisted like a knife, Delia turned and left.

'NO WONDER RUEL isn't up here tonight'. Not that it mattered, Laurel told herself. That was the last thing she needed, or wanted. Still, Delia's words cut deep for reasons she didn't want to look too closely at.

Ruel Delaney.

She shook her head. Impossible. Theirs was a business arrangement, nothing more. She looked at her stained work clothes—the borrowed shirt and pants.

Everything would seem better when she had a hot bath,

and miracle of miracles, the hotel had hot water that flowed through brass pipes and into the tub in the bathing chamber at the turn of a faucet. She stripped out of her clothes and stepped into the steaming bath.

She had finished her bath and found a dressing gown in the wardrobe. She looked up at the sound of a knock at the door to the suite. It was Soon-Li.

"I am to ask if there is anything you need," Soon-Li greeted her.

Ruel Delaney again.

"Possibly supper," she replied. "My clothes are not appropriate for the dining room."

"Appro...?" Soon-Li began then smiled sheepishly. "I do not know the word."

"It means that I haven't the proper clothes for eating supper in the dining room." She held up her soiled pants and shirt.

Soon-Li nodded her understanding. "You must dress," she said as she went into the adjoining bedroom.

Thinking the young woman misunderstood her dilemma, she followed her. In the bedroom, Soon-Li had opened the doors to the wardrobe.

"I will be most pleased to help you," the young woman assured her.

"You don't understand, I can't accept any of those," Laurel tried to explain. "If I could just have supper sent up?"

"Very busy tonight," Soon Li replied. "Big game, much money. Players always eat and drink much. No time to send up food."

A big game. Of course. She'd glimpsed the gaming room but there had only been players at one table. It was after all, nine o'clock in the morning. The truth was she was curious to see it again.

"You may choose the gown you like," Soon Li told her. She pulled one out of the wardrobe.

The gown was made of velvet, the darkest shade of midnight blue she'd ever seen. It was so dark it was almost black. The gown was cut low, and instead of the usual full style, the skirt was long and slender, flaring slightly at the floor.

There was a time when she would have chosen something else, something more... proper? But there was a part of her that wondered what it was to wear a gown like that. She smiled and nodded.

Soon-Li helped her dress, including a sheer lace camisole and silk underskirt, and black stockings. Then she helped her with the dress. The neckline was almost indecent and exposed the swell of her breasts, and it was trimmed in a row of tiny seed pearls that glowed against the midnight blue velvet.

She inhaled sharply as Soon-Li fastened the closures at the back of the gown. Then, studied her appearance in the full-length mirror. The transformation from stained work shirt and pants was startling.

There was no mirror at the cabin. She hadn't needed one to remind herself of what she looked like the past weeks. Now, she looked at the change in herself. Her skin was no longer the pale color accepted by proper society. Instead, the sunburn she'd experienced on the trail to Virginia City had deepened into a deep gold color at her face, neck and arms. And the eyes that looked back at her were also different.

They held a confidence and boldness that hadn't been there before. She could only imagine what Jessica would say about the gown and the changes in her.

"Who is the man?" she would have asked.

Who indeed? Laurel thought, refusing to accept that simple explanation.

She was thinner. That was to be expected with the work she'd been doing at the Rebecca. It accentuated her cheekbones. And there was something in her eyes that was different as well—determination.

She had found herself—not some hand-off relation because her parents were both dead, not her aunt and uncle's little niece, not her sister's shadow. And whether or not she succeeded in bringing in a strike at the mine, she knew what she was capable of.

Soon-Li swept her hair atop her head and anchored it with the black jade combs, then stepped back.

"You are pretty lady."

She almost laughed at that. A lady. Perhaps once upon a time. Now? At least she wasn't wearing the boots Cass had given her.

"Has Mr. Delaney gone out?" she asked, certain the young woman would know.

"Oh, no. Big game tonight in private room downstairs. He will be there," Soon-Li replied.

A thought came to her. She took out the leather valise and pulled out the money she'd brought with her to pay cash for the lumber, with Ruel's assistance.

It was all a game. Ruel had told her that.

"Please show me where I can find him."

She followed Soon-Li down the wide, sweeping staircase from the third floor. They had taken the lift to that level. At the front desk, she smiled at Mr. Tibbits, who seemed always to be on duty. She wondered if the man ever slept. As she and Soon-Li entered the dining room, a Chinese man greeted them.

"Miss Wentworth, it is a pleasure to meet you. I am Tommy Chin. Have you decided to have a late supper?" he asked politely.

"Miss Wentworth asked for Mr. Delaney," Soon-Li informed him.

He nodded. "Of course. Ladies are not usually allowed to join the private games, but an exception might be made. If you will follow me, please." Dressed in immaculate formal attire, Tommy Chin bowed slightly.

Laurel followed him across the foyer to a set of double doors that opened onto an elegant carved staircase. They descended the stairs to the lower floor, and Tommy opened the doors to the gaming room.

So, she thought, this is where men came to play. The room was ornately furnished with blue and gold carpet. Overhead crystal chandeliers gleamed with hundreds of lights with a half dozen gaming tables that circled the perimeter.

It was wonderfully cool down here after the heat of the day, the green of ferns and potted trees making the room resemble an indoor garden and in its very center stood an elegant rose-wood table with chairs set around it, each with a man who concentrated on the hand of cards he held.

As she watched, she realized that they seemed to be playing the same game she'd watched at the cabin when *she* had been the stakes. But the room, the clothing, and the sums of money that sat before each player were far different here. In front of each player was a small fortune in sizable stacks of bills and gold coins.

"The Rosewood Room," Tommy Chin announced.

This was Ruel Delaney's world and it fascinated her.

Her gaze swept the table. Two of the men needed no intro-duction. One was one of the bankers who had refused to loan her money for the Rebecca, the other was Ruel Delaney.

Surprise then something else—curiosity, fascination perhaps, darkened his gaze as he looked up. She was stun-ningly beautiful in midnight blue, a lady, and someone else he had discovered these past weeks.

He rose and rounded the table as she descended the half dozen stairs into the gaming area. He took her hand.

"Gentlemen, Miss Laurel Wentworth of Boston."

A waiter appeared, bearing a silver tray, and offered Laurel a glass of champagne. She accepted it and took a sip for courage. Among the comments at the table was an invitation to sit and observe the game.

"Nonsense, gentlemen," she told them. "I've come to play. Unless, of course, there is some objection?"

An amused smile appeared at the corners of Ruel's mouth. The last time he saw her, she was wearing worsted pants and a work shirt with those damn, ridiculous boots Cass had given her.

Where had this bold, dazzling creature come from? And what was she up to?

"Deal me out," one of the players announced, rising from his chair. "I won't take money from a lady, but I would very much like your company for supper."

"You assume that I will lose, sir. Or that I might take your money?" she replied. There were amused chuckles around the table.

"The lady is already spoke for, gentlemen," Ruel announced, exchanging a look with her.

"If there are no further objections, we'll start a new game. Five card draw."

She slipped into the chair the previous player had vacated. He returned to his own chair. A new deck of cards was provided and passed to the dealer. They played the same game he had played at the cabin.

She lost the first two hands, unwilling to ante up as she watched and studied each of the players, what they bid on, the suits of cards, and how many had been dealt. When drinks were served, Ruel approached where she sat. He handed her a glass of champagne.

"In order to win, you have to be willing to lose," he told her. He then gave her several hints about the other players—gestures, a nervous tick or comment, a shift in the chair, the refusal to make eye contact.

"Is that how you beat Dawson?"

He laughed. "Dawson was lazy and stupid. He was easy to read and beat. As I told you, there was never any danger that I would lose."

It was as much a game of bluff as it was skill, and studying the other players. She lacked the skill, but that didn't mean that she couldn't read the players or bluff when necessary.

"It's a game of chance. How much are you willing to lose?" he asked as the other players gathered to begin the next game.

She had come to Virginia City for just one thing, and she was determined to have it. A game of chance he called it.

"I don't intend to lose."

The cards were passed to Ruel as the next dealer. She watched fascinated as the cards were shuffled one, twice, three times, then passed to her to cut them. That dark gaze briefly met hers then looked around the table.

What did she see there? Who was he now? Gambler? Rake? Scoundrel? Dangerous behind that handsome smile and those dark eyes?

"Place your bets."

She watched the others, and she watched him—the casual way he dealt the cards, the almost indifferent bets he made, that dark gaze that flicked to one player then another, never giving away a thought or emotion.

Who was he now behind that cool, flat stare—gambler's eyes that revealed nothing. She could play that game too. After all, she told herself, it was business, nothing more.

Several hands were played. Bets were made, won and lost as the evening grew late. The deck was passed to her, and she caught the faint hint of disapproval from two players.

"I would like to pass the deck. Is that allowed?" she asked. All agreed and she passed the deck to Ruel. That dark gaze briefly locked with hers, then his expression was that of the gambler.

Tommy Chin provided a new deck, bound, and with a wax

seal. Ruel had the player across from him break the seal. The deck was then passed back to him and he shuffled. He passed it to her to cut and then he dealt the cards. His fingers seemed to stroke them, expertly dealing until five cards—two up, two down, lay before each player.

She studied the cards each was dealt, what was discarded, and how many each man drew, including Ruel Delaney.

A game of chance... and skill.

When it was her turn to discard, she kept the three cards in the same suit that she'd been dealt, discarded two, asked for two new ones, and increased her bet. That dark gaze briefly met hers.

Four players threw in their hands. Ruel had thrown in his as well. She calmly waited while the man across from her fidgeted with his cigarette. He was one of the bankers who had turned down her loan, and he was rumored to be Aaron Talbott's man.

"I'll see your bet and raise you... five thousand." He announced.

She had brought money with her from Gold Hill to pay cash for the lumber they needed. Through the game she had managed to keep her losses at a minimum. She would be risking a great deal to meet his bet.

A game of chance... she wanted very badly to beat him. If she failed, it would go badly for the mine. And he knew it.

"Miss Wentworth?" Ruel reminded her that it was her turn or she could '*fold*' as he called it.

What did she see now behind that dark gaze?

"I'll '*see*' your bet—I believe that's what it's called," she added. "And raise you twenty-five hundred dollars."

There was a unanimous sound of surprise around the table, even a chuckle or two, as she placed her raised bet in the center of the table.

The banker smiled. "I'll call that," he replied, placing

twenty-five hundred dollars more in the center of the table. He spread his cards for all to see.

"A full straight," one of the others announced.

She was aware they all looked at her and waited for her to turn over her last two cards.

The banker sat back at his chair, a satisfied grin slowly spreading across his face. Drawing on his cigarette, he exhaled a long stream of smoke.

"It has been a pleasure, Miss Wentworth."

Laurel smiled. "I assure you that the pleasure is all mine." She turned over her last two cards.

Amazement swept over the table as the men stared at the cards she'd turned over.

"A royal flush, all hearts!" one of the men exclaimed.

Laurel rose from her chair. "Thank you, gentlemen. Now, if you'll excuse me, I feel the need for some fresh air."

The men rose from their chairs, all except the banker. He stared disbelieving at her winning hand from across the table. Then color flooded his cheeks as he came out of chair.

"The odds against drawing a hand like that are almost impossible, even for an experienced player."

Laurel turned and met his gaze evenly. "Are you accusing me of something?"

"I'm stating the facts, Miss Wentworth. And I say that it's impossible for someone with no experience to draw a hand like that."

Ruel watched all of the men at that table.

"Are you saying that I cheated, sir?" she asked. "I believe to cheat one must conceal the extra cards."

To Ruel's amusement she spread her arms wide.

"Where on earth could I possibly conceal any cards?" she asked to the amusement of every man at the table, except for one.

"Did you consider that could have been dangerous?" Ruel asked as he signaled for an attendant to bring her champagne.

She took the goblet of champagne. She felt like celebrating as Tommy Chin collected her winnings and walked them over to her.

She took another swallow of that golden courage. "It was wonderful!" she exclaimed, then gave him a long look.

"What are the odds for drawing a hand like that?" she asked. She had her suspicions, but watching him at the game table she wasn't able to discern anything out of the ordinary.

A royal flush, and the queen of hearts was standing before him. His mouth curved in a smile.

"Someone once told me the odds were somewhere around four in one-and-a half million."

"The gambler who took you in as a child?"

"He was a very smart man."

Four in one-and-a half million odds...

She studied Ruel Delaney as he took a glass of whiskey from the attendant who also brought more champagne for her —something she needed to be mindful of. There was nothing she had seen, not that she was experienced enough. Still, she wondered if he might have had something to do with the cards that were dealt. Guaranteeing that she would win?

"Have supper with me," he invited her. "I promise no dried hardtack or beans."

A simple invitation, and she *was* hungry. In fact, she was starving. She wondered if winning over fifteen thousand dollars made one hungry?

"Your very own private dining room?" she asked as he escorted her into the private suite adjacent to his office on the ground floor.

"I don't eat here very often."

"Usually just beans and hardtack?" she replied.

"More often it's something from Soon-Li as I'm leaving."

Soon-Li. One of the women in his life.

The dining room was small and almost... intimate with wainscoting, a wood floor with a wool area rug, a table with two chairs, and a fireplace. Windows looked out to Sun Mountain rather than the lights of a dozen saloons and gambling houses along main street.

Even though it was well into the night and dark, there were campfires that dotted the mountainside—camps as miners settled in for the night and reminiscent on their nights on the trail from San Francisco after the attack by outlaws. She imagined them gathered about those campfires as they had, putting a last piece of wood on the fire, or talking about the day's results and plans for tomorrow. And no doubt a bottle shared around the fire to help stay warm, of course.

She soon discovered that Mr. Chin wore several hats as the saying went—floor manager of the gaming room, overseer of supplies for both the restaurant and the gaming floor, and maître d' when he appeared and announced that a supper of fresh crab from San Francisco and roast pheasant would be served when they were ready to eat.

Ruel asked him to wait thirty minutes and provide wine before supper. To all outward appearances, he was the embodiment of a perfect gentleman. Another mask he wore, Laurel thought.

The wine appeared. He nodded his approval and two glasses were filled with golden wine that was amazingly chilled, something she might have encountered in Boston. But the Comstock in the middle of Nevada?

"Ice is cut and hauled in during winter, then stored in underground cellars to keep certain things cold."

"And you just happen to have a cellar with ice in it," she commented.

"A very ingenious person pointed out the advantages when

I first built the International," he replied. "It serves as a cold box for storing food."

"No hard tack and beans?"

He laughed. "I ate a lot of that when I first came to the Comstock."

This was a different side of him that she hadn't seen before, in familiar surroundings with people he trusted. His world, so very far from the world she knew.

Who, she thought, was the real Ruel Delaney?

Gambler? That was obvious. Businessman? Also obvious. Scoundrel? She had glimpsed that as well, and yet there was another side to him she had discovered on that long, dangerous trip after their coach was attacked weeks earlier—someone she had trusted, put her life in his hands not that she had any choice, and the brief smile she had discovered—unguarded, without the usual sardonic criticism, or sarcasm. A dangerous man, to be certain, and yet... she wasn't afraid of him. And there was something else, something she'd never felt before.

A set of double doors opened out onto a terrace with flag-stones and a rock half wall. She walked out, trying to understand all of it, to understand him. The sort of man who signed a note for one hundred thousand dollars to bring in the mine as easily as if he was signing a chit for a fellow gambler, or the man who brought fresh crab from San Francisco packed in ice?

Gambler? Businessman? Scoundrel?

It was beautiful out on the terrace, the air cool now that the sun was long gone for the day with the sharp smell of sage-brush, something else she had discovered. So very different from Boston or New Orleans. It was almost as if there was room to... breathe, away from the smell of refuse and coal in the air, along with other smells that clogged a city.

This was what her father and mother had both chosen. She understood that now, as raw and dangerous as it was.

Ruel watched her, the subtle angles of her head, the way

she breathed in the night air and slowly smiled. Another surprise about her on a list of them. Along with strength, courage, and a great deal of determination, she wasn't intimidated by the rowdy, crude or challenging life out here. In spite of everything, she seemed to thrive on it, taking hold of it, and that smile...

"We'll move the table and chairs out here," he decided with a nod to Tommy Chin and caught the way her smile deepened.

How was it, he thought not for the first time, that two women who looked so much alike, could be so different?

The crab and pheasant were wonderful, far different from beans and hard tack, and most definitely an improvement over her own meager attempts the past weeks at the Rebecca Mine. She wondered what Cappy would have said of the supper, having chosen to stay at a nearby boarding house.

"It's clean enough and I can get some sleep," he had declared as they arrived in town. It hadn't surprised her that he had declined the additional invitation to stay at the International.

"Too noisy, too many out looking to lighten my pockets. Besides we have business in the morning with the man at the lumber yard."

"Oh, heavens!" she said, sitting back from supper. She caught the amused look Ruel gave her.

"Supper met with your approval?" he asked.

"It was wonderful." She smiled. "And no beans."

He laughed. "I specifically requested that there would be no beans."

He gave her a long look. He liked seeing her smile, the sound of her laughter—genuine, the way she gave into it, and way she tilted her head and seemed almost embarrassed by the amount of food as if it was unexpected.

He had missed her smiles even when they were smudged with dirt and soot from a campfire. He had missed her, something he'd never felt for a woman before.

She shifted against the confines of the bodice of the gown, grateful at least that she hadn't worn a corset.

"Would you like take a walk?" he suggested. "See a bit of the town at night?"

"Yes," she replied enthusiastically.

They stepped out the front entrance of the International, after he handled some bit of business with Tommy Chin.

Virginia City—wild, raw, noisy as a rider ran the length of main street, firing off a handgun, a fight erupted between two men and they tumbled out of the Bucket of Blood onto the wood boardwalk at the same time music from a piano filled the air along with laughter, curses, and women who offered other diversions from second floor balconies.

It was dangerous and exciting at the same time, and she had never felt so safe in the company of a man who should make her feel anything but safe.

A man staggered out of another saloon and approached them, asking for money to buy another drink. Ruel tucked her behind him as the man became insistent.

"I won't give you money, but I know the owner of the Bella Union," Ruel angled a look at the gaming house and restaurant that still provided food at that late hour.

"I'll purchase a meal for you," he told the man.

"What do I want... with food?" the man demanded somewhat unsteadily as Laurel watched the exchange with growing curiosity.

"So, you'll live to gamble another day," Ruel told him.

The man seemed to consider that as he stared at Ruel, then shook his head and staggered off.

"I need a drink, not food!" he shouted over his shoulder.

"You can lead a horse to water..." she recalled the old saying. "But can't make it *eat*..."

"Unfortunately, it's a problem in Virginia City, and the

reason I don't allow the people who work for me to drink on the job."

"And yourself?" she pointed out as they continued their walk.

"I make the rules," he pointed out. "They're for me to break if I chose too."

"What rules have you broken recently?" she asked. It was a natural enough question and she was curious.

He angled a look at her. "None lately."

She smiled. "Then I suppose you're overdue."

He could get lost in that smile... So different from another's that hid things so well.

They had walked half the length of main street, crossed over dodging a carriage, and arrived safely back at the opposite side with the International Hotel just down the way.

"Do you know the risk you were taking going up against a man with the banker's skills?" he asked. "He's owned by Talbott's men. He would have taken great pleasure in winning, taking your money that would have meant a loss for the Rebecca."

"I guessed as much." As Laurel met his dark gaze. "I refused to lose."

It was something he understood only too well.

"I think I understand why you gamble," she commented. "It's exciting."

Ruel agreed. "It can be. I don't like to lose."

Was there something more behind those words? she wondered. With anyone else she would have ignored it as a simple comment taken at face value. But she had discovered there was often far more behind a casual comment with him.

The champagne and the mountain air were an intoxicating combination and she felt reckless and a little bold as well as light-headed as they continued their walk.

She gave him a sideways glance. How different might it have

been if they had met under the different circumstances—a formal introduction through acquaintances, time spent together, and then...

"Are you all right?" Ruel asked as silence expanded between them. She had consumed a great deal of champagne.

"I was just thinking."

"About lumber for the mine, no doubt."

She laughed. He had come to know her so well in a short amount of time.

"No, I am quite determined that the man at the lumber mill will come around to my way of thinking." She hesitated.

From Jessica, she knew that Andrew was not the sort of man who wanted or needed to know what she was thinking. She supposed that most men were like that—not giving a woman the consideration that she had a brain and could think for herself, and might have something of value to add to a conversation. So ridiculous and possibly the reason she had been bored with young men who called on her in Boston.

It might have been the wonderful supper, the champagne, or God forbid, the man. She angled him another look. It was definitely the champagne and she decided to throw caution to the wind.

"I have wondered what might have happened if we had met under... different circumstances," she commented, fully expecting him to change the conversation, suddenly discover that he had some extremely important matter of business to attend too, and then promptly escort her back to the International; something a nervous man who was suddenly confronted with such a personal question might do.

He did none of those, but laid his hand over hers on his arm. He was thoughtful and didn't immediately respond. Then surprised her.

It was something he had thought about almost from the beginning when he realized the horrible mistake he'd made, and then apologized for something that in her world would never be forgiven, a young lady's reputation forever sullied. But, as he had discovered, she had more courage, more determination than many people he knew, and if she hadn't forgiven him for it, she wasn't about to let it define who she was.

What might have happened, he thought as they walked together? What would have been acceptable in her world? A man like him? His fingers stroked hers.

"We would have been properly introduced, by your family or a mutual acquaintance." He would have insisted on it.

"Possibly at a formal occasion or one of those ridiculous fancy balls they give in New Orleans," he continued.

She laughed at that. Jessica loved that sort of thing that she had always found to be boring.

"I would have called on you afterward and you would have dressed in your finest gown." He made a point of looking at her then and the midnight blue gown that emphasized the color of her eyes as they reached the International and stepped into the light at the entrance.

"That is, of course, if I accepted your invitation," she replied.

It was long after midnight by the clock behind the front desk. The night clerk nodded to him, as he escorted her to the elevator and closed the gate after them. The elevator made the long slow climb to the sixth floor of the hotel.

"I would have made certain that you did."

She angled a look at him. The conversation was fascinating. She had to smile at that. It was so like him—self-confident yet not full of himself as other men might be.

He escorted her to her suite, the perfect gentleman that was quite simply so very different from the man she had first encountered aboard the *Waverall*.

"How would you have done it?" she asked, genuinely curious what he would have done if... he was a gentleman and they had met under those *other*, proper circumstances.

"I would have walked you to your door." Nothing he'd ever done with another woman.

"Very proper," she commended him with a smile as he opened the door with her key.

"I would have probably thanked you for a most 'delightful' evening," he continued.

She laughed, impossible to imagine that coming from him." And then bid me goodnight while someone in the family watched from the second-floor window to make certain that you were a perfect gentleman?"

That dark gaze fastened on her. He touched her cheek, his fingers brushing the side of her neck.

"I wouldn't give a damn who watched or what they thought..." His warm breath brushed her lips.

"Not even if you were sent away and told never to return..." She didn't pull back or step away. Instead, she breath in—his scent, that mixture of fragrant tobacco, brandy, and cinnamon, and dear heaven... him.

"I want..." anything more wouldn't come and she closed her eyes against impossible thoughts, impossible things. She heard the breath he took. Still, he no more than brushed his fingers down the side of her neck to her shoulder, feather light, and not nearly enough.

"What do you want?" She had to say it, he thought.

Never in his life, not even his first time when he was fourteen or any time since had he asked. He had only taken. And now?

"What do you want, Laurel?"

If she asked it, he would walk away. He would give her that —choice, her choice. Something he hadn't given her that first time.

It was so simple, and yet not simple at all, and came from that first time, and all the moments since—his care of her, protecting her, his laughter and something in that dark gaze discovered over a campfire in the wilderness, and willing to die for her?

How many times had she wondered who was the real Ruel Delaney? She saw him now in the tenderness of his touch, in the choice he gave her now. What did *she* want?

Her breath caught as that dark gaze met hers.

"I want you to kiss me..."

It was dangerous, reckless, everything she'd been raised to believe was not for her as his lips brushed hers.

She reached up, her hand slipping through the dark hair that hung in waves over the pristine white collar of his suit—dark and light, no shades in between, like him.

Then they were inside the room and his kiss deepened, explored, then demanded until she was breathless, slightly unsteady as if the room spun about them, and she needed to hold on.

What did she want?

Him.

His hands closed around her arms, lightly brushing her breasts through the bodice of her gown, and she wanted more. She wanted to feel his hands on her.

"What do you want?" he whispered again.

"You." She shivered at that one small word as she felt his beard roughened cheek against hers. She knew what it meant, the anger and pain, a memory that crowded her.

"I'm not my sister."

He knew what she was saying, and what she was asking. If this was to happen between them, it would have to be different because she was different, inexperienced, and brave enough to want him.

"I know that," he told her and meant it from that part of him that had been closed off to someone else for so long, he had doubted it even existed any longer. That place someone had once spoken of a long time ago—the old gambler who had taken him in and taught him about the game, life, and surprisingly about caring for another person.

"What I mean is..." She was grateful for the shadows in the darkened room that hid her embarrassment.

"That is, I have never, not before that time..."

He brushed a stray gold wisp of hair from her forehead, those eyes so dark and solemn, and that slipped inside him in a way he could never have explained.

"I don't know how..."

"Yes, you do," he told her, and realized he could never explain it. How the innocence along with her strength and honesty and that damned stubbornness meant more to him than worldly experience.

"It's just that... That is, you have far more experience and I realize that men expect certain things, and I'm not... her."

"I know that," he replied.

Her eyes were dark now in the shadows of the room, narrow bands of blue all that remained as her breathing gradually slowed.

"I want you to show me... how." She couldn't explain it any other way, to make him understand.

He laid his fingers against her lips. The door closed with a faint click behind them.

"We'll learn together," he told her, picking her up and carrying her into the bedroom. He set her on the edge of the bed.

"I won't do anything that frightens or hurts you."

She thought of that first time, the circumstances, the man she knew now. She believed him.

"I want..." she hesitated, embarrassed to say it.

"Whatever it is, you tell me." His promise was there in those few words, in the way he touched her, a simple gesture, his fingers stroking her cheek as if to comfort her.

Good heavens! How must this seem to him, a man of experience, who might have any woman he wanted. But he was there, with her, and she saw something in his eyes, never glimpsed before as if she was truly seeing him now. She took a deep breath.

"I want to touch you." She saw the way his gaze angled away from hers, the way a muscle worked at his jaw, then that dark gaze came back to hers.

He removed his jacket and dropped it to the floor, then the brocade vest. She stopped him when he would have unbuttoned his shirt, her fingers working the buttons until the front of the shirt lay open at his chest.

Heat had an entirely different meaning as she flatted her hand there, suddenly pulled back as if burned, and then touched him again. Her gaze held his as he slowly removed his shirt, her fingers brushing the barely healed wound on his side, then at his taut belly just where that shadow of dark hair disappeared just below the waist of his pants.

She heard him take a sudden deep breath. "I didn't mean... That is..." When she would have pulled her hand away, his fingers wrapped around hers.

"If I caused you discomfort?"

He would have laughed at that, but, deep inside, he knew that he couldn't. This was for her and she had no way of knowing how just the touch of her hand almost undid him.

"No," he assured her. "Just the opposite." Touching her cheek, all that he would allow himself for now, he explained.

"When you touch me like that, I imagine other things, other places." This was so much more difficult than he'd thought and even explaining it had that effect on him.

"Show me," she whispered.

He took her hand in his and pressed it against him. He expected her to pull back in shock. She didn't, as he slowly unbuttoned his trousers. And still didn't when he wrapped her hand around him. Her only reaction was the slight widening of her eyes, and the breathless sound she made.

She felt the hard ridges and the thick veins that wrapped his thickened flesh and something far different than that first time was felt deep inside, something that tightened.

Innocence and curiosity were both there at her eyes. He wanted that for both of them. He had been the first for her, he was certain she had no idea how it pushed him to take her, lose himself in her. He didn't... not yet. This was for her. It had to be, because... The answer was there, but he pushed it back as his other hand tenderly stroked the swell of her breast just there above the bodice of her gown, then slowly turned her.

Show me, she had asked him, and like an innocent school-boy, as if it was his first time, his hands shook slightly as he unbuttoned the first button at the back of her gown.

She removed the combs from her hair and shook it loose, waited expectantly, then felt him unbutton the next button, and the next until the gown opened, then fell to her feet. And she slowly turned, almost terrified at what she would see in his eyes —that she wasn't pretty enough, that she was too like her sister... that he didn't want her?

She saw none of that, only the way the light that spilled through the windows caught in that dark gaze. But if he didn't want her, she needed to know now. She couldn't bear the thought...

His lips closed over hers, and that last thought spun away as his tongue slipped between her lips. Silken heat was all she could think of and then she couldn't think as she wrapped her tongue around his and tasted all of him at the slow invasion— the sweet tang of the cigarette, the whisper of brandy, and him. The demand that flicked then disappeared, and something else, very near her own need as she slipped her arms around his neck and felt the heat of his chest through the sheer silk of that was all that covered her breasts.

This, she thought, taking the kiss deeper. This was what she wanted to feel, that sensation of possession, then the way he released her only to take possession again, as if he was drowning and she was the very air he breathed.

Show me... and he did as he stripped away the silk, pulled her naked body against his, and then slowly showed her with his hands, his lips, with the words he gave her.

"Touch me." Until he thought he would explode, then pulling himself back.

For her, all for her, as he tenderly explored her body until she whispered it again, "Show me".

She grew restlessness as she reached for him, and he slowly joined with her, watching her eyes and the expression on her face, hearing the way her breathing caught, then the way her hands clasped him, pulling him deeper.

Delia sat at the satin-covered settee and poured herself a substantial amount of whiskey.

"I tried to tell you it wouldn't work. I argued, I pleaded. She won't do it," she announced flatly.

"Then you'll simply have to try again." Aaron Talbott was maddeningly calm.

Delia came up off the settee to pace the elegant sitting room of the suite he'd occupied since arriving in Virginia City. He'd provided her with a far less opulent room on the floor below.

"She's determined to bring in that mine. Dear God, she's just like him."

"Who the devil are you talking about?" Talbott thundered, his patience slipping.

"Our father. He had the same stubbornness about that damned mine."

"Stubborn or not, you're going to do whatever's necessary to convince her to sell that mine."

Clasping her hands to hide the anger, Delia shook her head. "It won't work. She's got backing. Ruel Delaney is financing the mining operation. Damn him!"

"How quaint that your former lover is now your sister's business partner," Aaron cruelly replied.

"Damn you, shut up!" When Delia would have slapped him, he caught her wrist and squeezed until she cried out.

"Remember one thing, Delia, I know what you like. You're greedy. I've bought you, and you'll keep your part of the bargain. I don't care what it takes to get her to sell the mine, just see that she does."

She twisted out of his grasp. "She's in town. I'll see her again before she leaves. If necessary, I'll even go up to the mine."

She traced a long, tapered finger along his collar, bending to allow him a full view of her breasts. Then, speaking so that her voice carried to the hallway where Talbott's henchman always waited, she rounded the desk.

"Keep your dog on a chain." The man was disgusting, she thought. Still, there was a certain appeal to that sort...

"I'll take care of my sister."

18

It was barely dawn and the first time in years that Ruel Delaney wasn't already at his desk at the hotel, going over the accounts, gaming receipts, supply orders, the day beginning as any other.

The frown eased into a smile as he looked down at her, asleep, her a slight frown on her mouth. At something she dreamed? He brushed her lips with his fingers and those incredible eyes slowly opened, the frown disappearing.

"Good morning," he whispered. And then a little shy. Or possibly regret?

"Good morning."

There was something at her eyes, something she struggled with.

"What is it?" he asked.

She shook her head. "Nothing."

And that smile again. He wasn't convinced. He slipped his fingers beneath her chin, forcing her to look at him.

"Don't hide from me."

When had it become important to know a woman's thoughts, much less care? The answer was so easy—with her.

"It's just that..."

"What?" he asked.

She bit at her lower lip, something else he discovered that went right through him. Something worried her. He wanted to know and then he wanted to take it away.

"You thought I was someone else—my sister. And last night... "

"What about last night?"

"It's just that," she started again. "I thought that it was possible, since we look alike that you thought..."

He pressed a finger against her lips, stopping her. "Don't ever thing that, not ever. There is only one woman here, Laurel —you. And in spite of the fact that you look alike..." he shook his head. "You are nothing alike."

"But you were..."

He stopped her again. How to explain to her, how to make her understand?

"It was something that ended over a year ago, and it was never..." He hated how this would sound, but she needed to hear it, to understand. For both their sakes.

"I was never in love with her." It came out so easily, as if it had just been waiting for him to say it. He saw the way her slender brows came together.

"But...?" she tried to understand.

"I was never in love with her," he repeated.

He'd never known what it was to love someone. Possibly the man who had raised him? But that was different. It had been about survival, kindness that he'd never known before. Maybe this was survival too, needing something so badly, feeling something so deeply.

"I'm..." It shouldn't be difficult to say what he felt; shouldn't be and making the biggest bet he'd ever made in his life.

"I'm in love with you."

Her eyes widened.

"And I've placed a big bet on that," he added. Everything he had, everything he was, and hoped for.

Her eyes filled with tears as she slipped a hand behind his neck and pulled him down to her.

"I'll take that bet."

"COME IN." Ruel glanced up and nodded at the man who entered the office. "Thank you for coming over."

It was almost noon and the middle of a business day. He appreciated that the man had agreed to meet with him after Tommy Chin had delivered his message. He offered him one of the long, tapered cigarettes, then selected one for himself.

"Do you have something for me to see?" Ruel rounded the desk and perched casually at the corner.

"I've several pieces I think should please you. I was quite surprised at the request," Richardson responded politely, trying to curb his curiosity.

He placed the leather case on the desktop and opened the latch. After opening the velvet-lined case he stood back. Ruel leaned over to take a better look at the stones displayed there.

Arnold Richardson was a renowned jeweler from San Francisco who'd opened a shop in Virginia City to take advantage of the newfound wealth in the mining community.

Ruel was looking for a ring, a very special ring—one that would last a lifetime.

"I brought these settings along merely as a sample of what is available," Mr. Richardson explained. "As you requested, I brought blue sapphires and a selection of diamonds." He displayed several of the diamonds. "They were not white, but different shades of blue. Blue diamonds are quite rare," he went on to explain.

"These are from mines in Australia."

Rare. Ruel took a sketch from his desk and handed it to Richardson. He'd been playing with it since coming into the office. It was a simple design, a large stone in the center with smaller ones circling it. Circles, never ending.

"The center stone is to be a blue sapphire, the finest you have," Ruel told him. he nodded at the exquisite blue diamonds.

"The other stones are to be blue diamonds. I want it set in gold." He caught the jeweler's surprised expression.

"Is something wrong?" he asked.

"Only that this would be quite..." he hesitated, "the cost, at least ten thousand dollars."

Ruel nodded. "I want it by the end of the week," he told him. "In addition, I want a necklace of the same design. However, I won't be needing the necklace for at least a month. The cost doesn't matter. It's to be a wedding gift." That is if he could persuade the lady.

Richardson finally recovered and cleared his throat.

"I'll have the ring by the end of the week. And the necklace by the end of the month. The size for the ring?"

Ruel looked down at his own hand. "The size of my small finger."

He imagined the stunned look on Laurel's face when he gave her the ring. She'd probably accuse him of winning it in a poker game. He pushed back the possibility that her answer would be no. He didn't intend to lose.

Mr. Richardson closed his case. "I'll send word when the ring is ready."

AARON TALBOTT ROSE from a chair in the outer office as Mr. Richardson left. "I hope you'll forgive me for dropping by... unexpectedly," he said with smile that quickly disappeared.

Ruel looked up. Inwardly, he felt that instinctive reaction to Talbott, a man he wouldn't have trusted out of his sight. Outwardly, he regarded him with the expression glimpsed across more than one high-stakes poker game—boredom that hid the curiosity.

"You're not a regular customer at the International," he replied with that same indifference. "What brings you here?"

Crossing the room, Talbott took the armchair across the desk. Without an invitation, he leaned forward and poured himself a cup of coffee from the silver service.

"I've always admired your ambition, Delaney. Five years ago, you came to Virginia City with nothing but a reputation at cards and the rumor of all that stolen gold. Since then, you've built the finest hotel in the Comstock, and you run the best gambling house, along with your other business interests."

"Go on."

"I've come to make you a proposition, one that would be advantageous for both of us."

Senses sharpened, Ruel nodded. Ever since he'd come to Virginia City, the Big Four, headed by none other than Aaron Talbott, had done their best to push him out.

He'd been the one person they couldn't scare, bribe, or buy out. Not that they hadn't tried. But he had learned how they played the game and had used it against them. He'd not only built the hotel and the Palace, he had acquired and started a few prime businesses. He paid his people well, and yes, it had paid off.

The last time Aaron Talbott had stepped foot inside the International, the carpenters had only just finished framing the ground floor. Talbott had threatened to burn him out, and then see him driven out of town along with his Chinese friends.

In the end, Ruel's hotel had been successful and had re-built a good portion of the Chinese section of town for the workers, because he couldn't be bought and he was willing to fight for his place even if the fight became dirty and dangerous.

"I'm listening." He was certain Talbott's little scheme had something to do with Laurel and the Rebecca. The timing was too perfect for it to be otherwise.

"You own the French Lady mine right next to the Consolidated which I have controlling interest in. Everyone knows it would be advantageous to sink a lateral mine from the Consolidated to enable you to open the lower levels of your mine."

Talbott flipped open the box on the desk, helping himself to one of the cigarettes. He paused, almost as if he expected Ruel to jump up and light it for him. When Ruel remained seated behind the desk, Talbott went ahead and lit it himself. He threw the match down into the ash tray almost like a challenge.

Ruel shrugged. "That's no secret."

"No, and you've never bothered to approach me about using my shaft to sink that lateral opening."

"There are new methods of mining being developed all the time," Ruel replied. "Something will be invented that will allow me to sink a deeper shaft. And as you know, mining is not a full-time concern with me. I have other businesses that are lucrative." Leaning back in the chair, Ruel watched Talbott the way he watched other gamblers across a high-stakes table.

"So far, this conversation is a waste of time," he added.

"I'm getting to the reason I'm here," Talbott replied. "Sinking that shaft could make a fortune for you. Everyone knows the assay reports on the French Lady have been worthwhile."

In fact, Ruel thought to himself, the last reports were good, very good.

"As I recall, you tried to buy me out before. When that didn't work, you threatened to burn me out. When that failed, you cut off my supply of lumber and threatened my workers."

Talbott smiled slyly. "You know something, Delaney? You remind me of a cat that always lands on its feet."

"Trial by fire?" Ruel replied.

Talbott was the sort of man who had access to so much money he believed he could buy anyone. The banking was simply a convenient way to move that money and that of his friends around.

Ruel wasn't a fool. Talbott was more dangerous now than he'd been five years ago. These days, he paid his henchmen to keep things in line. Ruel and his people had several run-ins with them. That was the reason most of his people carried weapons beneath their finely cut coats and dinner jackets. Tommy Chin preferred a knife. Ruel had seen what he could do with it.

Shifting in the chair, Talbott leaned forward. "I'm willing to make you an offer. You want that lateral shaft. I'd be willing to allow your people to sink it and take out whatever silver you find down there... in exchange for a favor."

"What sort of favor?"

"Persuade Laurel Wentworth to sell me the Rebecca Mine. You and I both know she can't hope to bring it in with the people she's got up there. And mining can be... risky not to mention expensive business."

"You would know about that," Ruel replied.

Talbott ignored the comment. "I would be willing to make her a very generous offer. I'd be taking my chances on the investment, of course, but that's a risk I'm willing to take.

"She'd make a good profit," he continued. "And not be at any risk if that mine doesn't come in. I'm aware you know the woman. I heard she's staying here at your hotel. You might have some influence with her."

He wondered what information Talbott had about the Rebecca. He had connections all over town, including the assay office. It wouldn't take much for someone to provide him information on the quality of the silver that had been found so far at the Rebecca.

He'd heard Talbott was back in town. Come to think of it, he'd heard it from one of his men just after he and Laurel had seen Delia. And now Delia was scheduled to appear at the opera house. He thought Delia's sudden appearance in Virginia City was suspicious, especially since she'd always hated the town.

Someone with connections in Virginia City had set up the engagement for her. He knew Delia had already tried once to convince Laurel to sell. Now Talbott was asking him to persuade her. It stood to reason that he had put Delia up to it and would try whatever it took to get the Rebecca. That set off a warning and could explain the accident at the mine—any means necessary to get what Talbott and his backers wanted.

He needed time to find out who Talbott's henchmen were. Until he knew exactly what was going on, Laurel and Cappy could be in danger. He needed to buy time.

"That's a very interesting offer." Ruel came out of his chair. "We might be able to work out something that could be mutually beneficial. You know my man, Tommy Chin? I'll send him over to your office when I have something for you." He'd just stacked the deck.

Realizing their meeting was at an end, Talbott rose from his chair and extended his hand across the desk.

"To successful business transactions."

Facing Aaron Talbott was like staring down the barrel of a loaded gun. He merely nodded.

Waiting just outside the door as he'd been instructed to do whenever anyone arrived, Tommy Chin watched Aaron Talbott leave and then slipped into the office.

"What do you want to do?" he asked.

"Have your people keep an eye on him. Let me know any moves he or his men make."

BLENDING the spot of color at her cheeks, Delia gave her reflection in the mirror a critical inspection. Then she glanced out the window at the late afternoon shadows cast by the taller buildings across the street, then looked back at the muscular shoulder exposed above the quilt at her bed.

The man she'd brought back to her rooms last night wasn't a bad lover. Maybe a little quick on the draw, as they say and not as attentive as Ruel Delaney had been, but he was young and strong. She was certain they'd get along just fine while she was in Virginia City. She patted a curl into place then rose from the dressing table.

According to Aaron's plan, she was going to try and see Laurel again today before her sister returned to Gold Hill. She had to convince her to sell that mine to Aaron, then Delia would be comfortable for a long time. Aaron had promised her a percentage, and though he was a lousy lover, he was a good businessman.

Hopefully her meeting with Laurel would go well. Afterward, she'd indulge in a little shopping, even though she considered Virginia City's shops inferior to those found in San Francisco. She seized her reticule then swept past the bed, bending over and kissing the man who barely stirred as she did so. She smiled. She couldn't recall his name, but he definitely had potential.

Delia frowned as she climbed the stairs to Aaron's suite on the second floor of the Gold Hill Hotel.

She would have preferred the luxury of the International, including Ruel Delaney.

At the thought of him, desire sharpened inside her. Yes, she would have to spend considerable time with the man she'd just left. He had a long way to go before he could hope to compare with a man like Ruel Delaney.

Crossing the carpeted landing, Delia walked down the hallway toward the suite of rooms Aaron occupied. As she started to knock, she dropped her reticule. When she bent to pick it up, voices came to her from the other side of the door. One was Aaron's. Pressing an ear against the wood of the door, she recognized the other voice—Charlie Deaver, his right-hand man and the most despicable man she'd ever met.

Deaver took care of things for Talbott. She'd had an encounter with the man and hated him almost as much as she hated Talbott, and didn't trust either one of them. Whatever Talbott asked him to do, he did it. Curious about the conversation, Delia listened at the door.

"I spoke with Delaney earlier," Talbott told him. *"I made him an offer, not that I have any intention of going through with my part of it. But he seemed interested. In exchange he would persuade Laurel Wentworth to sell me the Rebecca."*

"Do you think he'll be able to convince her?" Deaver asked.

"Delaney is no fool. My guess is that he'll try to play both ends against the middle and get the mine for himself."

"What about Miss Cameron?"

"She's to meet with her sister again, but if she fails to get what I want..." The rest went unspoken. Then, *"Do you understand?"*

Understand? Obviously, he intended to do whatever it took, whether she was able to convince Laurel, even double-crossing Ruel.

And if she failed to convince Laurel? With a cold chill she was fairly certain she knew what that meant. She continued to listen at the door. She wanted to know everything Aaron Talbott was up too.

"What about the mine?" Talbott asked.

"Just like you ordered. It's a mess up there now and the manager at the lumber yard has his orders," Deaver replied. *"It will take a lot of work when you take over."*

She could almost see Talbott's reaction to that, a wave of the hand. For Aaron Talbott, money could buy anything, including herself, she thought with disgust.

"Was anyone hurt?"

"Some injuries, enough to slow them down for a while. It would have made it a lot easier if she had been there when the explosives went off."

"Good. One way or the other this will work."

She could almost see the smug expression on Talbott's face.

"Go over to the International. Follow Laurel Wentworth when she leaves. She'll try to persuade Potter at the lumberyard to give her the supplies she needs to reopen the mine. He knows what to tell her —she won't get anything she needs."

"You want me to scare her, boss?"

"I want you to do more than that."

There was a meaningful silence. Delia knew exactly what Talbott meant.

"As soon as it's done, get back here. Their being twins could be useful."

"What do you mean, boss?"

Delia leaned in closer to the door. She wanted to know exactly what Aaron was planning.

"Think how easy it would be to replace one twin with the other. With the Wentworth girl out of the way, we could easily pass Delia off as her. No one would ever know the difference. And Delia will do whatever I ask her to do."

"What if she tries to claim the mine afterward?" Deaver asked.

"We'll take care of that too. Now, get over to the hotel and don't lose sight of the Wentworth girl."

Delia straightened, pain and anger burning inside her as she quickly slipped around the corner, hoping that Deaver would take the stairs in the opposite direction.

She peered around the corner a moment later and let out a of relief sigh as he disappeared at the far end of the hall. Waiting until she was certain he had gone, Delia followed in the same direction.

At the foot of the stairs, she watched Deaver leave the hotel and head toward the International. Aaron Talbott had gotten a little too greedy this time.

A slow smile slipped into place as her plan formed. She was capable of a little double-crossing herself.

If she went along with Talbott, eventually he'd force her to give up the mine, or worse. But if she went to Laurel with the truth but hid her own part in all of this, there was every possibility Laurel might be grateful, very grateful. After all they were sisters. Surely she could convince her that they were both entitled to a share of the mine. After all, she was a very good actress.

Stopping a young boy outside the hotel, she gave him a quick note and a quarter, and sent him toward the hotel. Within twenty minutes he was back. The clerk at the front desk had informed him that Laurel had already left the hotel.

Delia tried to imagine where Laurel might have gone. She knew the Rebecca was in desperate need of supplies because of the "*accident*."

LAUREL FROWNED as she stepped down from the boardwalk in front of the lumberyard. The manager had just given her the same answer she'd gotten at the one in Gold Hill—there were no heavy shoring timbers available. Yet she was certain that she'd seen stacks of them in the huge yard in back of the building. She'd offered him twice the going price. But the answer had been the same. According to Cappy it would cost a great deal more to have them brought in all the way from Reno.

She shielded her gaze from the glare of the sun.

She was at the far end of town, near the stables. She squinted as a small, wiry figure walked toward her.

Sammy! What on earth was he doing in town?

"Miss Laurel, you must come back to mine. Big trouble!"

"What is it?"

He gestured and talked at the same time, but she was able to make out just one thing—there was some sort of explosion at the Rebecca.

"Were any men hurt?"

"Bad missy, real bad."

Everything else could wait until she found out how bad the damage was.

"I'm going back to the mine. I want you to go to the International Hotel. Ask for Tommy Chin. Tell him I sent you for my winnings last night. Then, get back up to the mine as soon as you can," Laurel told him.

She had no experience with mine explosions but just the words alone she knew they were going to need help, a great deal of it. She needed to find out if there was a doctor in town.

DELIA WAS HOT, tired and thirsty, and there was dust all over the hem of her skirt as she carefully picked her way across the street. Glancing up, she almost collided with a young Chinese man who was obviously in a big hurry, head down, running as fast as his legs would carry him.

"Watch where you're going!" Delia told him.

"Sorry." He ducked his head several times, then looked at her directly. His eyes widened, then an uneasy look appeared at his face. He turned, hurried on across the street.

"Wait!" Delia hitched up her skirt and ran after him. Her gloved hand closed over his arm.

"Sammy?" She remembered the boy from the last time she'd been to Virginia City when Jason had still been alive.

His nod told her she was right. "I'm Jason's daughter."

"Yes, yes. Work for Mr. Cameron before he die," he replied. "Must go."

Delia refused to let him go. Something had obviously happened for him to be in such a hurry.

"What are you doing here in Virginia City?"

Sammy turned, his expression now very serious. "Big trouble up at the mine. Had to find Miss Laurel."

"Have you seen her this morning?" Delia held onto his arm when he tried to pull away.

"She already gone."

"Gone? Where? It's important that you tell me," Delia insisted.

"Back to mine." He gestured in the direction of Gold Hill.

"How long ago? Was anyone with her?" She described Deaver.

Sammy shook his head and Delia sighed with relief. At least Talbott's heeled dog wasn't with her.

"How long ago did she leave?"

"Maybe hour," he guessed. "You want me to give Miss Laurel message when I get back to mine?"

"No," Delia replied, a new expression at her face. If she hurried, she could still beat Talbott at his own game.

"I'll give her the message myself."

"HAVE YOU FOUND HER YET?" Ruel looked up as Tommy Chin entered his office, ignoring that nagging voice inside his head that said it was more than a coincidence that Laurel was gone shortly after his meeting with Aaron Talbott.

"No, sir," Tommy replied. "But there's someone you should see."

"Who?"

Stepping outside the door, Tommy pulled Sammy into the office.

"He came for the money you had me put in the safe for Miss Wentworth," Tommy Chin explained. "There's something you need to hear."

"I've seen you up at the Rebecca," Ruel said. Sammy nodded. "What are you doing in town? Is Cappy here with you?"

"Oh, no." Sammy shook his head. "Mr. Cappy is at the mine. There is big trouble."

"What kind of trouble?" Ruel's demanded as he nodded to Tommy to close the door for more privacy.

"Men come last night, big explosion, many injured. Come to find Miss Laurel and Cappy."

"Did you find her?"

Sammy nodded. "She go back to mine to help."

Ruel would have bet who was responsible for the explosion. So much for his meeting with Aaron Talbott. The man was determined to have the Rebecca and it didn't matter what it took. Laurel had no idea what she was going to find up there. he turned to Tommy Chin.

"They're going to need help up there. Have Cal arrange for wagons and supplies, and a doctor." He returned to his desk and pulled out the revolver he kept in the top right drawer.

"Send word over to the French Lady that the extra crew I arranged should get up to the Rebecca as soon as possible. And I'll need you and some of your men, armed. I don't want those wagons ambushed. If they hit the mine once, they may try it again."

And Laurel would be caught in the middle of it.

19

Laurel made the ride alone from Virginia City to Gold Hill.

As she approached the toll gate, she didn't even bother to skirt the guards as she had before. She needed to reach the Rebecca, and it would take almost double the time to take the high trail around the mountain.

The guards were Aaron Talbott's men. She paid the toll and spurred her horse up the dirt road that wound around the mountain, looking back to make certain she wasn't followed.

At first glance, the damage at the mine didn't seem so bad with thin wisps of smoke hanging in the air above the camp. She walked her horse slowly through the encampment, her eyes widening as she took in the full extent of the damage.

The long house had been reduced to nothing but a pile of smoldering cinders, and bare skeletons of steel pump wheels stood idle in the shimmering heat. The hot midday air carried the acrid smell of burned wood. The barn and corral had fared no better than the shaft house. Nothing remained but collapsed timbers. Horrified, she saw the charred remains of one of Cappy's mules.

She searched the perimeter. The two wagons they'd brought to haul supplies were gone, probably dragged off or pushed over the nearby embankment. One of the chickens she'd purchased lay dead in the middle of the yard, crushed under the hooves of a horse. Its feathers ruffled faintly on a lifeless wing. Aggravating creatures, yet in the span of a few weeks, she'd developed an affection for them, always there to greet her in the morning.

She scanned the yard, almost afraid of what she would find and wondered if Captain Kidd had survived. As if in answer, the cat hesitantly rounded the corner of the cabin. He gave her a lopsided look with his one eye. His moth-eaten fur was in even worse condition now, singed in several places. Obviously, he'd barely escaped the fate of the other animals. She slipped slowly from the saddle and called to him.

He ran to her, winding in and out of her legs as usual. She scooped him into her arms as she continued her search of the camp.

Where was everyone?

The afternoon breeze gusted across the yard. Somewhere at the back of the cabin a loose shutter banged. Then another sound brought her around sharply. A lone figure slowly walked toward her from what remained of the long house.

"Cappy?"

She set the cat down and slowly walked toward him. Covered in dust and soot, he frowned amid the tangled beard. She ran to him and threw her arms around his neck. She had no idea when he'd returned, but was relieved to see that he was safe.

Completely taken aback, Cappy stood for a moment. Then his arms came up and closed around her.

"Sammy said there'd been trouble," she told him.

He nodded. "He found me right after he spoke with you. I came up the back way, wasn't about to pay a nickel to

Talbott's men at the toll gate, and it was quicker." He looked at her sharply. "Sammy's not with you? You came all that way alone?"

"I sent him on an errand. I thought we'd probably need all the money we could lay our hands on." She looked around the yard. "Everything's gone."

"Not quite everything," Cappy replied gruffly. "Oh, the shaft house is burned, and the barn. And we lost one of the mules. But it's a little hard to burn dirt and rock. We've still got the mine, although the first and second levels collapsed from the explosion. We're going to need a helluva lot more lumber now. I don't suppose you were able to do much about that in Virginia City."

"I got the same answer you got in Gold Hill."

He nodded. "Aaron Talbott owns just about everything, even the lumberyards. It's his way of keeping a tight rein on the smaller operators. We sure could've used that lumber."

Pain twisted inside her as she realized the depth of the loss for both of them, but especially for Cappy. He'd put in years of back-breaking work, living off the small amounts of silver that were found. Then, to find that rich vein and have it all destroyed. Only a miracle could reopen the Rebecca.

What did it matter what money they had if they couldn't buy lumber to shore up the mine shaft and the tunnels. She glanced around. It was quiet, too quiet.

"Where are the men?"

"When Talbott's men hit the camp and then after the explosion, they lit out. There was no one down in the mine at the time. Can't say as I blame 'em for taking off." His shoulders sagged and he suddenly seemed much older.

"Come inside where it's cooler," she said. Taking him by the arm, they walked to the cabin.

The inside, the cabin was mercifully cool after the heat from the sun and smoldering fire at the long house.

"Talbott is determined to run us out," Cappy muttered as she handed him a cup of water.

"Why is the Rebecca so important to Talbott?" she asked. "Doesn't he have enough mines that are producing?"

"Greed," Cappy said simply. "And revenge."

"For what?"

He took a long drink from the metal cup. She refilled it. He was thoughtful as if considering what to tell her.

"Jason won the Rebecca in a card game, bet you didn't know that," Cappy said with a faint smile. "Oh, he won small pots occasionally but nothing like the Rebecca. He won it fair and square. It's likely that Talbott had a fairly good idea what the mine was worth at the time and he didn't take losin'.

"When Jason died," he continued, "Talbott was certain he'd be able to find a way to get the Rebecca back."

"He hadn't counted on my claim and reopening the mine," she added.

Cappy nodded. "That's the long and the short of it. You see, if a mine lays idle for a certain period of time or the owner dies with no heirs, anyone who files an assay report can lay claim to it. And Talbott was confident he could work around any interest yer sister had in it."

"Can we reopen?" she asked.

"You asked me that once before, and the answer was yes. This time, I'm not so certain. Without that lumber we can't move a lick, but even if we had it, we haven't got the men to work it. There's not a man on Gold Hill who'd come up here now after this, and with Talbott's men keeping a watch on things and likely comin' up here any time."

Laurel rose from the table and gazed out at the yard, the burned timbers that were all that remained of the long house, and the gaping hole in the ground where smoke from the explosion and fire filled the air. Then a different sound.

"Someone's coming," she told Cappy.

"Riders?" He was immediately alert, his hand reaching for the shotgun by the wood pile next to the wood stove.

"A carriage." Laurel shaded her eyes as she stepped out onto the covered porch. Cappy stepped out beside her.

"It's Delia." She stepped off the porch and crossed the yard.

Pulling the horse to a stop, Delia stepped down from the carriage.

She slowly surveyed the damage.

"Talbott is thorough," she exclaimed.

"What are you doing here?" Laurel asked.

"I ran into Sammy in town. From what little I was able to get out of him, I got the impression things were pretty bad up here. I thought you could use some help. I can see I was right. By the way, where's Cappy?"

Help them? Only the day before a team of wild horses couldn't have dragged Delia up there. And not to forget, the way she had pressured Laurel to sell out. What was the real reason for her sister's sudden appearance?

"What about Talbott?" Laurel asked. She wanted to find out exactly what Delia knew about what had happened.

Delia moved past Laurel to the shaded porch, fanning herself against the heat.

"Hasn't changed," Delia remarked with a bitter laugh. She untied the silk ribbon of her hat as she looked about the inside of the cabin.

"About Talbott," Laurel reminded her again.

"That's what I came here to tell you. I heard... from someone," she thought of the man she'd spent the night with, "...that he planned this if he wasn't able to talk you or Ruel into selling out."

Cappy brushed past her at the door.

"I see you managed to survive," Delia commented. "You and this damned mine."

"You here to gloat?" he asked and kept walking to what

remained of the long house. Delia turned from the doorway, and Laurel was struck by the resemblance between them.

"Talbott won't stop," Delia said with a thoughtful frown. "He and his partners, are determined to own all of Virginia City and the surrounding mines, including the Rebecca."

"Why are you telling me this?" It made no sense, Laurel thought. From the beginning Delia had made it clear how she felt about her and the mine.

"Maybe I did it out of sisterly love," Delia replied. "Maybe, I wouldn't want it on my head if you ended up dead because of this damned mine."

She brushed the dirt from her hands as if it was something contagious.

"This place was our father's dream," she commented, the words cold. Then she looked over at Laurel.

"Maybe I did it because I don't like Talbott." That was closer to the truth. "He uses people. And when he's finished with them, he throws them away." She'd had too much experience with that.

Laurel frowned at the bitterness in her voice.

"Or maybe..." Delia turned and her gaze met Laurel's. She smiled. "Just maybe, I thought you'd be grateful for my information and cut me in for a share of whatever's down in that damn hole. After all, part of the profits should be mine.

"Jason gave me that cash to buy me off." Delia entered the cabin and looked around. "He knew how much I hated this place." She turned. "After all, we are sisters, it only seems fair that we should share in whatever Jason left."

She shook her head. "I was raised in a cabin like this until I was twelve years old on the banks of the Sacramento River. Anybody with a whit of sense knew the gold fields had played out by then, but Jason had his dream.

"After a while, I started planning how I could get out of that cabin." She turned to Laurel.

"I suppose after a while he felt guilty about dragging me through all those gold camps. He bought that little house in San Francisco."

"You must have known some happiness there," Laurel commented.

Delia laughed. "It was better than a mining camp. I had a roof over my head and went to school. When there was enough money from the odd jobs he worked, I even got a dress from one of those charity stores."

She turned then. "I knew about you, all those years. Jason, used to tell me about our mother and the Wentworth family. I remember walking downtown San Francisco with Mrs. Chamberlain, the widow woman Jason left me with when he was gone.

"We walked past those tall office buildings with names lettered on the outside. Wentworth Shipping was one of them. I remember looking at those letters. That was my family. I didn't understand about twins at first, then Mrs. Cartwright explained and I used to wonder if we truly looked alike."

Laurel smiled sadly. "You were luckier than me. I knew about mother, but she died when I was only a few months old. I never knew about you. You were richer in memories that I was."

"Richer?" Delia laughed at that. "Poor in everything else. I wanted more. I wanted a big, grand house, and nice clothes. And I wanted a man to love me, to tell me how beautiful I was, and take care of me the way Jason never did."

She sighed. "I came close to getting that once." She turned to Laurel, and their eyes met, the same and yet different.

Laurel knew who she was talking about. "Ruel Delaney."

Delia nodded. "There were all sorts of rumors about him, he had the most awful reputation. I suppose, being with him was like I was getting back at Jason in a way. He always said that I deserved more.

"I was sixteen when I left this place," she continued. "Ruel was older, a gambler, and he bought me nice things. He was supposedly a blockade runner during the war. It was said that he stole a shipment of Union gold, but I never saw any of it."

She frowned "We were two of a kind, both looking for something. You know what I mean?" There was a bitterness in her voice. "Then I did something that drove him away, the one thing he never put up with was cheatin'." She laughed.

"Imagine that, a gambler who won't forgive someone who cheats." She continued. "I tried everything to get him back, but he didn't want me."

Delia looked at her then. "Did you know you were born first? Jason told me. So, you see, you were the original." She laughed again, a painful sound.

"I was just a cheap imitation. So I figure that maybe you owe me. And if that mine is worth anything near what Talbott thinks it is, a small share wouldn't be any great loss to you."

"It doesn't matter who was born first," Laurel told her. "All I ever wanted... I had hoped we could at least be friends. We were both cheated in a way. I came up here because the mine was a link to Jason and Rebecca. The silver never mattered to me." She shook her head. "I was angry when I first found out all the things that'd been kept from me.

"Somehow that doesn't seem important anymore." Her own smile was a little sad. "If we'd found nothing but worthless rock, I could have walked away, but I had to understand about Jason's dream, the reason he stayed." She squeezed Delia's hand, surprised when she didn't pull away.

"I suppose we both have the right to be angry," Delia admitted. "I'll tell you what," she offered, "you cut me in for a share of the mine, and I just might consider staying up here. It would be worth it if there really is silver down in that damned hole. And, it would give us a chance to know each other."

"It's there, I've seen it," Laurel replied. "And there's more

than enough to share." She smiled. Maybe there *was* a chance
for them to be friends. It was a place to start.

Delia pulled her hands from Laurel's, as if suddenly
uncomfortable. The most she'd expected was a payoff for
information.

"This place could use some straightening up. And maybe
Cappy won't throw me out, he never had much use for me." She
picked up a pair of Laurel's pants from the back of a chair and
looked at her with raised brows.

"I wear them when I help out or when I went to go down in
the mine," she explained with a shrug. "A dress gets in the way."

Delia shook her head. "The proper lady from Boston
wearing men's pants and boots."

Laurel smiled. She could imagine Cappy's reaction when
she told him that Delia would be staying, at least for a little
while.

"You'll ruin your dress."

Delia laughed. "All right, I'll wear an apron. Is there one
around here?"

"By the stove." Laurel turned toward the door. "I'll see if I can
find Cappy," she headed out of the cabin.

"Wait!" Delia wanted to tell her about Deaver. It was
possible he was on his way to Gold Hill at that very moment.
But Laurel was already across the yard and heading for remains
of the long house.

As soon as she returned to the cabin, she'd tell her about
Deaver, she thought. Turning back to what served as the
kitchen, Delia rolled her eyes at the stack of dishes, pots, and
pans. A one-eyed cat looked at her skeptically.

"I know," she told the cat. "It's a little hard to get used to, but
there really are two of us."

"SHE CAME HERE to tell us about Talbott," Laurel argued.

"What the hell does she really want?" Pickaxe in hand, Cappy continued chipping away at the debris at the mine entrance.

"She's never done anything that didn't mean somethin' for herself." He paused, a different expression at his eyes. Then, he continued with the pickaxe.

"I think she wanted to make amends," Laurel began hesitantly. It would do no good to explain her conversation with Delia. Cappy was too stubborn, his dislike of Delia too deep.

"I'll just bet she did! Chances are she and Talbott are in this together." Refusing to slow his pace, Cappy heaved a timber out of the way, then picked up his axe once more.

"She's my sister. I want to believe her," Laurel said softly.

"Did it ever occur to you that her appearance in Virginia City coincided with Talbott's?"

"Even if you're right, she had no reason to come here. She didn't have to tell me the truth. Please, come back to the cabin. You can't do anything here by yourself. Somehow, we'll get men up here and we will reopen this mine. Talbott's not going to beat us."

"There's work to be done," Cappy muttered under his breath. "You know something, Delia was always complaining about her lot in life, always whining about having finer things. Well she got them when she was hooked up with Delaney and what did she do? She stole from him. Did she tell you that?"

"No," Laurel replied.

"Trouble with Delia is she tells you what she wants you to know," he continued. "But there's usually a whole lot she isn't tellin'. Delia always takes care of Delia—no one else. She never had one lick the courage Rebecca had, comin' out here, not knowin' what she'd find, not even havin' a decent roof over her head that first year." He gave her a long look.

"A lot like yerself."

. . .

LAUREL FROWNED, putting that conversation aside.

"We'll work together," she said. "Two can move twice as much rock and debris as one." She met Cappy's glare evenly, her dark blue eyes filled with determination, and his paler gaze narrowed with grudging reluctance.

"Damn-fool girl! Hasn't got a lick of sense!" he grumbled. But he put a shovel in her hand.

Laurel smiled. Sometimes battles, were won with small victories. Reaching for a timber, she helped him move it to the side of the shaft. They would rebuild, and they would beat Aaron Talbott at his own game.

Ruel avoided the toll gate as he guided his horse through the brush and scrub oak that covered the mountainside. The last thing he wanted was to alert Talbott's men.

He'd given Tommy Chin strict orders to have the drivers of the wagons he'd arranged for to wait before approaching the toll gate until they got word everything was clear.

He wound his way up the mountainside, keeping off the wagon path. If any of Talbott's men were still around, they'd be watching that road. He reached the crest of the hill, then turned east where the mine lay.

The sharp crack of a rifle shot scattered the birds from a nearby tree.

He rode hard the rest of the way, then reined to a stop when he was within a hundred yards of the cabin. Then, he saw her, laying in the dirt at the yard, and the stain that spread at her back.

20

R ifle in hand, Ruel scanned the rocks that surrounded the cabin.

There was no movement, no sound. Whoever had fired that rifle was already gone. One shot...

He ran across the yard, then knelt beside her. He slipped an arm beneath her shoulders and gently lifted her.

She was still alive, but he'd seen wounds before. This one... Then a scream from across the camp.

"No!" Laurel cried out as ran toward them and fell to her knees beside them.

Ruel stared at her. They were identical, the same—the woman who knelt beside him and the one in his arms who lay dying.

Laurel reached out and took hold of her sister's hand. Her tear-filled eyes, so like Delia's met his.

"No!" she whispered again as Cappy came up behind her.

And then, a sound that Ruel knew too well as Delia looked up at them. She tried to laugh, but coughed up blood instead.

"Ruel?" Laurel pleaded even as Cappy laid a hand at her

shoulder. And she knew what neither of them said as Delia tried to say something.

"Don't try to talk," Laurel told her. "It will be all right." She thought her heart would break when Delia smiled back at her and she struggled to draw a breath."

"Talbott," she whispered.

"What about him?" Cappy asked as he knelt beside them, something unreadable in his gaze.

"He said that he would stop you..." Delia looked up at Ruel Delaney with a faint smile.

"... only a cheap imitation," she said with a faint smile, then looked at Laurel. "I wanted all of it, but I couldn't do what Talbott wanted..." That smile slowly faded.

Tears spilled down Laurel's cheeks.

Ruel wrapped an arm around her shoulders and held them both.

"I'll take her to the cabin," Cappy said with that same unreadable expression, his voice unexpectedly quiet. He loosened Laurel's hand from Delia's then slipped an arm beneath Delia's shoulders and gently lifted her.

"Delaney." Cappy gave him a parting glance. "She's gonna need you, even if she doesn't know it yet," he said with a nod toward Laurel.

She sadly shook her head as she knelt in the dirt. "It was supposed to be me, wasn't it?" She shook with the raw emotions she felt inside.

"What was Delia doing here?" Ruel asked as he stood and held onto her.

Cappy's words came back. He had said it—Delia and Talbott were somehow connected. She hadn't wanted to believe it. She didn't want to before now.

"She came here to warn me about Talbott."

"The only way Delia could've known what he intended was

if he'd told her," he pointed out. "He was using Delia to get to you and the Rebecca."

The truth was painful. Tears filled her eyes. She'd learned long ago in her uncle's house that truth could sometimes be harder to accept than a lie. And she'd learned a lot more about truth and deception these last months.

"I thought that we could be friends and maybe..."

He pulled her against him, tucking her head into his shoulder. "I know how hard it is to want something so badly, and then lose it."

"How did you know to come here?"

"I followed you; I didn't know Delia would be here." His fingers lightly brushed her cheek. "There was so much unsaid after last night. And then Talbott came to see me and I knew he would do whatever it took to have the Rebecca." Even if it meant killing her.

Cappy sat at the steps of the porch, staring out across the purple-shaded slopes of Gold Hill as Ruel crossed the yard in front of the cabin. He'd spent some time with Laurel.

"She'll be all right. She's got a lot of Rebecca's strength. Delia never had that kinda strength. It was like there was somethin' missin' inside her." He looked up at Ruel.

"You're in love with her?" Cappy asked.

Ruel nodded.

"Go to her then. She's hurtin', but the hurtin' will pass in time."

"You talk like you know something about that." Ruel squinted into a late afternoon sun.

Cappy nodded. "Make her understand. Then she's gotta make a decision about the mine. Talbott will be back."

Ruel stepped up onto the porch and entered the cabin. He expected the tears and the look at her face. He wasn't prepared for the anger as she looked up.

. . .

"I WANT Talbott to pay for what he's done." Laurel told him

CAPPY'S FIST came down hard on the table.

"Hell no! It's a damned fool idea. You'll end up getting your-self killed, just like her. Is that what you want?" He came out of his chair, sending it over backward.

"I won't have it! Do you hear?"

Ruel watched from across the cabin. He saw the look in her eyes and knew there was nothing either he or Cappy could say that would change her mind.

"Nevertheless, I intend to do it," Laurel announced.

"I'll be damned if I'll let you." Cappy replied.

"There's nothing you can do to stop me. Besides, we both know there's only one way to get to Talbott legally. He controls everything except the law. And I want him brought to justice for Delia's murder."

"There's no way of provin' it. Don't you understand? No one would ever accept the words of a dyin' woman against those of Aaron Talbott. All he'd have to do is prove he was somewhere else at the time, and he can get just about anyone to say that."

"Then we have to play his game."

Cappy leaned across the table. "And just how do you plan to do that?"

She refused to meet Ruel's gaze as she slowly stood and paced the cabin. Talbott had to pay for Delia's death. She turned back to the table.

"Talbott has no way of knowing it was Delia who was... killed instead of me. By now, he believes I'm dead." She rushed on, aware of the disapproval on both men's faces.

"I want to take Delia's place. All I need is to get Talbott to admit that he ordered his man to come up here."

"I won't allow it!" Cappy roared, running a gnarled hand

through his mane of hair in frustration. "He'd see through it. It's too dangerous."

"It's the only way," she argued. "And it is my choice."

"I agree with Cappy," Ruel told her. "If Talbott recognizes the difference, it would be too dangerous."

"You know as well as I do that it's the only way to get him to admit to it."

"Damn!" Ruel swore softly. "The two of you... as much as you looked alike, there is a difference. He knew it, had seen it in an expression, in the softness of her smile so different from Delia's. He shook his head again. He could tie her up, he could take her back to San Francisco, anything to stop what she was suggesting...

"I have to try." When Laurel raised her gaze to his, she was herself. There was none of Delia in her, except for that resemblance that had fooled him.

"Can you understand that?"

The damned truth was, that he did understand. It was who she was, someone brave and honest, and stubborn, and he was in love with all of those.

Ruel stared down into the deep blue of her eyes, knowing that he'd never refuse her. It had to be over, once and for all, and unless he gave her this. He slowly nodded, knowing she'd do it even if he hadn't agreed.

"You're damn fools, both of you!" Cappy declared, then stormed out of the cabin.

"I know," Laurel whispered. "I know."

LAUREL CROSSED to the dressing table in the hotel room for the third time to check the wig that was part of the costume she was to wear for the evening's performance at the Piper Opera House.

The evening before she'd been brave enough to carry out her plan, but her courage slipped when she entered Delia's suite at the Silverado Hotel.

It had been so easy at first. She'd nonchalantly walked up to the desk clerk and demanded the key to Delia's room. She hoped the smile she gave him was convincing.

The clerk had handed over the key without a comment. Giving Cappy as reassuring smile as he waited outside, she went upstairs to Delia's room and let herself in.

Laurel had looked about the suite, fascinated by what she was learning about the sister she'd never known. From Delia's assorted gowns, hats, jewelry, and stage make-up, she learned a sad truth.

Running her fingers over the brushes, combs, and small glass containers of makeup, Laurel stood before the dressing table, feeling more sadness than grief. She had never known her mother or her father, but Delia had been a lost soul, hiding behind wigs, make-up, and the things men bought her.

Now, Laurel stood back from the mirror, studying the image that looked back at her. The likeness to Delia was uncanny. In a wig, heavy makeup, and the daringly low-cut costume, she was indeed Delia.

What would Ruel Delaney think when he saw? She pushed that thought away as she smoothed the fuchsia satin of the gown, then jumped as the small porcelain clock at the table chimed the hour—eight o'clock.

She'd sent word to Aaron Talbott's suite that she needed to see him. And twice the maid had returned, informing her he wasn't in his rooms. Realizing their meeting should be in a public place, she'd hoped to arrange to join him for supper after the performance, but without a response she had no way of knowing if he would be in attendance at the theatre that evening.

She took a deep breath to calm her nerves, then picked up

the script, she'd tried frantically to memorize that afternoon. She knew the three songs she was to sing. Two were from plays she'd seen in New York months ago. The third was an old favorite her aunt had taught her. But there was the matter of the play itself. Being alone all afternoon in Delia's suite had played havoc with her confidence. She wondered how she could have imagined that she could take Delia's place?

Giving the clock one last glance, Laurel gathered up fan, script, and sheet music. The Piper Opera House was conveniently located next to the hotel. As she descended the stairs, she glanced about the lobby wondering if she might catch sight of Talbott, or Cappy. The old miner had steadfastly promised that he or Ruel would be close by at all times. But she saw neither of them.

"Hello, Delia."

She'd have known voice anywhere. Laurel turned, her gaze meeting his dark one as Ruel stepped from the shadows beside the hotel entrance. He'd used her sister's name, in keeping with their scheme, but a warm glow spread through her, as Ruel looked at her as he had that night they'd shared.

She wanted to say how glad she was to see him. But something prevented her. even under the assault of that steady gaze that seemed to see into her so easily. She wanted to melt into his arms and forget the next few hours. But even as she thought it, she knew what she had to do, no matter how dangerous it was.

She smiled faintly, desperately in love with a man she should never have met.

"I couldn't let you give your first performance in Virginia City without extending my wishes for every *success.*" Emphasizing the last word, Ruel took her hand and looped her arm through his. "And I'd hoped I might see you after the performance."

It was a conversation he might have with any woman, or

with Delia considering their past relationship. But the look he gave her was for her alone.

"Are you all right?" Ruel whispered.

"Yes." Laurel smiled as an attendant at the entrance to the opera house greeted her.

"Good evening, Miss Cameron." Then she stepped into entrance, the attendant waiting to escort her backstage. There was nothing by either look or gesture that he thought her to be anyone other than Delia.

"I know you have to do this," Ruel told her. "Don't meet with Talbott alone. You have to draw him out where there are witnesses. And I'll be close by."

His fingers wrapped around hers, his touch warm, strong. Another couple passed by. When they had gone, he touched her cheek.

"I love you," he whispered. Then, for the benefit of those arriving for the evening's performance, he bowed with a gentlemanly bow.

She had no time to contemplate those three words as she approached the dressing room door.

"Evenin' Miss Cameron." A tall man stood just beside the doorway.

"Hello," she replied, hoping it was something Delia might have said.

The man was dressed in a dark suit that seemed completely out of place, the sleeves too tight, the front left open on that muscular body. He hardly seemed the sort who would be part of the other performers considering the play as a musical, nor did it seem he was part of the theater staff with the bowler hat he wore.

Was this Deaver? Talbott's man, who took care of things, possibly Delia's murderer?

"Mr. Talbott got your message," he gruffly informed her. "He'll meet you in your dressing room after the performance."

The mention of Talbott set every nerve in her body on edge.

She nodded. "I want to go over my lines one more time before the performance." She looked at him then with an expression she could only imagine Delia might have used—she had despised the man. A leer spread across the man's face as he stepped aside.

"Sure thing. And I want to give you a friendly little warning from Mr. Talbott. Keep away from Delaney."

She didn't answer but quickly entered the dressing room, then slammed the door in his face.

How much did he know? Had he seen her and Ruel on the boardwalk outside the theater just now?

"Good evening." A soft voice greeted her from the shadows.

Laurel practically jumped out of her skin. Walking away from the door, she peered across the dimly lit room. A small figure stepped from the shadows.

"Soon-Li! You scared me half to death."

The young Chinese woman quickly came forward. "I am sorry. I didn't mean to frighten you."

"What are you doing here?" Laurel tossed aside the script.

"I asked to help."

"Please go back to the hotel," she told her. "It could be dangerous for you and for the baby."

"Tommy says it is all right. So, I stay. I can take message to Mr. Ruel."

She stubbornly refused to leave. "I am of no importance," she said. "No one will think it strange that I am here."

Laurel was grateful for someone to share the next hour with her until it was time for the play to begin.

Soon-Li had known Delia. Perhaps she could tell her about her. There was so much she didn't know.

"I know when they first together," Soon-Li replied to her question, smoothing a strand of hair as Laurel sat in front of the dressing table. "And when he sent her away."

"Why did he send her away?"

"It was after he found out about baby," Soon-Li solemnly replied.

Laurel's thoughts tumbled. A year ago?

"What baby?" Laurel asked. Was it possibly Ruel's child?

Soon-Li nodded. "Your sister go to Mr. Delaney and tell him she going to have baby."

Laurel felt as if the floor had suddenly dropped out under her.

"Mr. Delaney thought the baby his," Soon-Li continued. "Next thing, there is no baby."

"What happened?" Laurel asked, horrified.

"She go to woman in San Francisco and get rid of child. When Mr. Ruel find out, he was like wild man. I was afraid he kill your sister. They say horrible things to one another. Then she tell him it was not his child. He told her to leave and not come back.

"We hear later she go to New York. I see you at the hotel here. I did not understand there are two—you and Miss Delia. When Mr. Delaney explain, I see something in his eyes, something I never see before, and I know you are very different to him."

"In many ways, we were very different," Laurel replied, slowly grasping everything Soon-Li had told her. It explained so much, but left other questions.

"Thank you for telling me." She looked up at Soon-Li's reflection in the mirror.

"You care very much for Mr. Delaney."

"Oh, yes. My life is very good because of him. I have a home, good husband, and soon I have strong son to make Tommy Chin proud."

"Tommy? But I thought ..." Laurel stared at the girl. "It's just that you seemed to care for each other. He takes care of you." Laurel added.

Soon-Li's eyes widened. "You think Mr. Delaney father of my baby?" She shook her head. "I am very grateful to him for many things. He bought me in San Francisco and then gave me freedom and bring me here where I meet Tommy Chin. He is a good husband."

Laurel smiled. "Thank you for sharing this with me."

There was a knock on the dressing room door.

"Five minutes, Miss Cameron," the stage manager called through the closed door.

Miss Cameron. She was about to set her deception in motion, and God knows what would happen.

"I have to go." Standing, checked her appearance in the mirror. The resemblance between her and Delia was startling. She just hoped that it was convincing enough with Aaron Talbott. She gave Soon-Li a last message.

"Tell Mr. Delaney that Mr. Talbott will come to my dressing room after the performance."

Ruel waited in the shadowy aisle as the last few people passed him and took their seats in the theatre. He couldn't see him, but he knew Cappy was across the theater, watching, waiting to spot Aaron Talbott when he arrived.

The longer he stood there, the more he doubted Laurel's plan. Watching the stage, listening to the musicians in the orchestra pit, he knew that he should have talked her out of this —forbid it. There was too much risk. If Talbott sensed the deception she would be in a lot of danger.

He preferred his original plan. Putting a bullet in Talbott's head the next time he saw him was far more appealing. Except for just one thing, something he'd learned long ago. If you killed a man, you had to be ready to face the law, or run from it.

He'd done a lot of running in his life. He'd had no real family, no roots, no home. And he'd never had respectability, nor any need for that. He wanted all those things now, with her.

For the first time in his life, Ruel wanted something that

couldn't be bought or stolen. He'd realized it when he'd held Delia in his arms as she lay dying, and thought she was Laurel.

Afterward, discovering the truth, he felt as if he'd been given another chance—something that was laughable for a gambler.

He scanned the faces of those in the audience as much as possible through the dim lights in the theatre. Then the footlights came up and the curtains parted. Ruel knew nothing about the play. He watched, waiting for the moment when Laurel would step out onto the stage, his hand brushing the comforting bulge of the revolver inside his coat.

He'd seen Delia countless times at the Tivoli in San Francisco, and private engagements at the Golden Empress. Watching Laurel, he saw how very different they were in spite of the fact that they looked alike. On that stage, even in costume and makeup, the woman he watched was real, more alive than Delia had ever been.

The performance ended and the curtain lowered. He had Soon-Li's message and Ruel moved down the side aisle before the audience rose to leave. He glimpsed Cappy across the theater and nodded. Then both men blended into the darkness beyond the footlights and headed backstage.

Laurel stood with the other actors, watching those around her, watching for Aaron Talbott.

What if he didn't come? What if all of this was for nothing? she thought.

"Miss Cameron?"

Laurel felt the pressure of a hand at her elbow.

"These are for you," the tall man in that brown suit handed her a bouquet of flowers.

"Mr. Talbott is waiting."

Laurel glanced back over her shoulder, trying to spot Cappy or Ruel, then turned toward her dressing room. He took her by the arm.

"You're to come with me."

Taking a deep breath, she forced herself to remain calm. Obviously, Talbott had no intention of meeting her in her dressing room. She had to stall for time. Ruel and Cappy were somewhere in the theatre.

"I'll just be a minute," she told him. "I want to put these flowers in water."

"You're coming with me now!" His hand tightened painfully at her arm and she was dragged toward the back entrance of the theatre.

She caught a fleeting glimpse of Cappy as she was dragged out into the alley behind the theatre, then down the boardwalk, past the darkened windows of businesses and shops closed for the day. Reaching a small office beside the bank, he opened the door and pushed her inside.

"Come in, my dear."

Aaron Talbott was just as Laurel remembered him from that day weeks earlier when he'd approached her about selling the Rebecca. The lamp at the desk cast long shadows into the small office. This man had ordered *her* death.

"Let me congratulate you on a stunning performance."

She took a deep breath, the role she was about to play far more important than the one she'd just performed.

"I hoped we'd have a chance to talk," she fought to remain calm. "I sent several messages." She angled a look over her shoulder at the man who'd *escorted* her from the theatre.

"Was it necessary to send him?"

"I thought it best that we meet here," Talbott replied. "I didn't want you to lose your way or leave with some other... distraction."

Dear God, had he seen through her little act?

"Did you like the play?" She rounded the desk, leaning casually at the corner in what she could only hope was a convincing act.

"You are a creature of many surprises," he replied. "I wouldn't have thought you capable of such a fine performance," Talbott complimented as he picked up a cigarette from a nearby ashtray.

He was disgusting, so sure of himself and his power. How could Delia have been with this man?

She forced a smile. She couldn't wait for Cappy or Ruel. She had to draw Talbott out, make him talk about what had happened at the Rebecca.

"I understand there was a bit of trouble up at the mine," she began casually, leaning over his desk with the hope of distracting him enough to get him to talk.

Talbott's smile deepened. "Trouble for some."

"Then you're pleased with the way things went?" Leaning farther forward, Laurel lightly brushed his shoulder. The glare of Talbott's heel hound was making her increasingly uneasy.

"Surely we can have some privacy." It was dangerous in the least, foolish at best but she needed to learn as much as possible, without the threat of his man standing there.

Talbott nodded at his man. "I'll see you later at the hotel."

Waiting until she heard the click of the door closing, Laurel turned back to Talbott.

"Did everything go well?"

"Well enough. I told you, if you couldn't get that sister of yours to sell out, I'd take care of it myself. Well, I took care of it," he announced with a certain amount of bravado, then inhaled at the cigarette.

"By the way," he added. "Where were you last night? Deaver said you weren't in your rooms at the hotel."

She should have known Talbott would have Delia's rooms watched. Her thoughts raced. This was something she hadn't know or counted on—that Delia and Talbott were lovers, if it could be called that.

"With the opening of the play tonight, I wanted to celebrate." She switched the conversation back to the mine as she rose from the desk and went to stand behind Talbott, draping her arms about his neck. Just that brief contact made her flesh crawl.

"However, did you manage to get my sister to sign over the mine?" she asked. "The last I spoke with her, she was absolutely determined to mine it herself."

"I didn't convince her," Talbott replied, his fingers closing around her wrist. "I sent Deaver up to the mine. He took care of it. She's dead." He pulled her down to him.

She fought to remain calm, giving into fear or anger now would ruin everything.

He had admitted having her sister killed. She ached at the thought that it meant no more to him than dusting the dirt off his boots.

The movement of a shadow beyond the glass-paned door caught her eye.

Was it Deaver or someone else? Dear God, she prayed it was Ruel. She forced calmness into her voice as she tried to pull away.

"Now, my dear," he added, pulling her around from behind the chair. "The Rebecca is mine."

"You mean the Rebecca is now mine," she corrected him as she thought Delia would have, and with a painful twist of her wrist, slipped out of his grasp.

Talbott started out of the chair. "Yours, mine, it's all the same."

"Not quite." Rounding the desk, Laurel put a safe distance between them. Pretending to smooth her gown, she brushed the comforting bulge of the revolver Ruel had given her.

"There's no reason why I should let you have any part of the Rebecca. It's rightfully mine."

"Why you lying little whore." Talbott started toward her.

She pulled the pistol from the pocket at her gown and

leveled it at him. "I don't need any partners," she calmly announced.

Talbott laughed. "Put that down, you little fool. You don't have the guts to pull the trigger." Taking a quick step forward, he struck out at her.

As she fell back across the chair, her finger closed over the trigger. A loud report filled the office, smoke bursting from the barrel of the pistol. Aaron Talbott's enraged scream was filled with pain. He lunged at her. Before she could react, his other hand came up and closed around her neck, choking her. The pistol fell to the floor as her hands closed around his and she clawed as his hold.

The room exploded, glass shattering, and Cappy charged into the room, rifle in hand. Seeing Laurel crumpled on the floor, his reaction was a moment too slow. He saw the look on her face and spun as Talbott came up behind him.

Ruel shouted a warning. Cappy fell back, blood spreading across his shirt from a knife wound, and Talbott was already out the door.

Ruel knelt beside Laurel.

"Did you hear?" she asked, rubbing her bruised throat.

"We heard, everything. You little fool, you could've been killed!"

"What about Talbott?" she asked.

Ruel pulled her to her feet.

"Take care of Cappy," he told her now that he was certain she was unharmed. Without another word, he slipped into the shadows.

He knew Talbott, knew his habits and his hiding places. He figured there was one place where he would go. Ruel slipped down a back alley and cut across the street toward the Liberty Bank.

Money was the only thing more important to Talbott than his own life. And a great deal of Talbott's money was in that bank. Coming around behind the bank building, Ruel knew he'd guessed right.

A shadow separated from the other shadows at the back of the building, moving toward the back door.

"Hold it right there." Ruel told him. "Step away from the building where I can see you."

"Delaney!" Talbott's breathing was labored. "You're in this with her!"

Ruel nodded. "Yeah, only not for the reasons you think. You sent your man up to Gold Hill to kill Laurel Wentworth. He killed someone all right, he killed your only chance to ever get your hands on the Rebecca."

"What are you talking about?" Talbott demanded as he moved toward him.

"Stay right where you are," Ruel told him. "I have no problem killing you, Talbott. To me, you're nothing but a snake, dangerous and deadly. And stupid. You didn't even know you'd killed the wrong one."

"Delia?"

"That's right. Shot by your man up at the mine."

"I don't believe you. Back there ..."

"A convincing performance by Laurel Wentworth. Delia could never have given a performance like that. It's over, Talbott."

There was a shout from the end of the alley as the sheriff arrived.

Desperate, Talbott sprang toward him, knife in hand.

Ruel fired twice. The first bullet tore through Talbott's chest, the second one snapped his head back. He staggered, then slumped to the ground in the alley.

The sheriff knelt beside Talbott's lifeless body. "You took a chance," he said, taking the knife from Talbott's hand, and a small pocket gun from his other hand.

"Damn, this is gonna cause all sorts of problems." He looked up at Ruel Delaney.

"I'm gonna need you to answer a few questions," the sheriff told him.

"There were two witnesses. He ordered the death of Delia Cameron," Ruel told him.

"Oh, my God!" Laurel cried out as she ran to him from the crowd that had gathered.

"I heard gunfire...! You're not hurt?"

She discarded the wig she'd worn for the performance, and her hair was streaming down her back. He stroked a loose strand back from her tear-stained face.

"When you ran out of there, I was afraid. I thought..."

"It's over." He wrapped an arm around her and held her against him as they left the alley. He saw something in her eyes just then, mixed with the fear. Was it love?

Even when she'd come to him that last night, a part of her had held back. He didn't want part of her, he wanted all of her.

WHEN RUEL and Laurel got to the doctor's office, his wife greeted them at the door.

"Mr. Burnett?" Laurel asked.

"The doctor's with him now," the woman explained. Then she disappeared into a back room.

They waited. Ruel knew Laurel was fond of Cappy, and since she'd lost so much, he didn't want to think of her losing someone else she'd come care about.

The doctor's wife returned. "You can see him now."

The doctor met then at the door of the private room. "He lost quite a lot of blood before he got here, so he's a little weak."

"Will he be all right?" Laurel anxiously asked.

"If it were anybody else, I might be concerned, but living up on that mountain either kills you or strengthens you. He'll be fine. Don't be alarmed when you see him. He took another cut at the side of his face. It looks worse than it is." He smiled as he washed his hands in a nearby basin and then left.

Cappy seemed to be dozing, his face was turned to the wall. He slowly turned his head.

The scraggly beard had been shaved away so that the doctor could tend the wound there. The face she saw now was strangely familiar.

There were lines of hardship around his mouth and eyes, but she knew that face from that old daguerreotype. It had been a wedding picture. Her mother was the bride, small, slender, and beautiful. And standing beside her was a man Laurel had believed dead.

"Father?"

21

"Damn you!" Laurel turned on Jason Cameron.

She'd been too stunned to be angry by the revelation that Cappy Burnett was actually her father days earlier. However, this morning when he was much stronger and moving about, was an entirely different matter.

"Why did you let me believe that you were someone else?" She paced the suite he'd occupied since leaving the doctor's care.

He eyed his daughter warily. She really had her temper up, and with good reason if one was inclined to view things from her point of view.

"Will you stop that infernal pacing and sit," he told her. "Somewhere! Anywhere!" he bellowed, setting off the aching in his head.

There wasn't an ounce of pity in Laurel. In fact, she derived a good measure of satisfaction from causing him a little discomfort.

"Never mind that I thought you were dead. Never mind that I came out here grieving the loss of my father. Oh no, you wanted to play your little games." Laurel vented her anger on the upholstered footstool.

"If you'll just give me a minute I'd like to explain," Jason tried to get in a word.

She whirled on him, hands planted at her hips. "I'm listening."

"I know I caused you some bad moments. But you have to believe I didn't know it would turn out this way when I first had the attorneys in San Francisco write you that letter about my death."

"Didn't know?! Just what did you think I would do when I got that letter?"

This was the part that he hadn't planned on. "You need to understand that I'd tried to reach you for years. Every letter I ever sent you always came back or just went unanswered. I knew your uncle was behind it, just as he was responsible for taking you and your mother from me in the first place. But money can buy a lot of things, and silence is one of them. I knew he'd never let any letter get through to you."

"So, you sent the letter about your death and the inheritance."

"I didn't lie about the mine. The Rebecca *is* yours."

"What about Delia?" she asked, her voice softly breaking.

His head went back against the chair back. He suddenly seemed drained of all strength.

"I know that I made mistakes, raising her in the gold fields was one of them. She hated that kind of life, and I suppose I robbed her of many things little girls should have. But I always believed I was providing for her as well as I could.

"The Rebecca was my hope for the future, for both of you." He smiled sadly. "She didn't want any part of it. Said it was like all the other times, nothing but a worthless hole in the ground. To her I suppose I was a failure, but I knew better.

"Two years ago, Delia came to me, wanting more money,"

he went on to explain. "I gave her what I could, but she wanted more. It was like she was always trying to make up for the things she'd wanted as a child. That's when she met Delaney."

At the mention of Ruel's name, Laurel's head came up. "He told me."

"Did you know she stole money from him? It was a pretty good amount too, almost twenty thousand dollars."

Jason watched her. She was so different from Delia, a lot like her mother in her quiet, thoughtful ways. That is, when she wasn't squaring off at him like an angry cat that got its tail caught in a door.

"She said I owed her," Laurel said sadly.

Jason nodded. "She knew about the Wentworth family. I guess she figured you'd had a lot more advantages than she ever had. I hoped the two of you could be together someday. But, as I said, I figured the only way I could get you out here was to make Edwin Wentworth believe I was dead."

"He tried to stop me." Laurel smiled, remembering her scheme to get aboard the *Waverall*.

Jason's eyes softened. "I loved her in spite of herself, and I loved your mother. We came here together to build a dream. You and Delia were part of that dream for a short time. And then you and Rebecca were taken from me. So many years." His voice broke.

"Why did you keep everything a secret?" she asked. "Even after I came here?"

He answered with that name. "Talbott. I knew he wanted the Rebecca, would do anything to have it. After all this time, I had no idea you would come here. I had to protect you."

It was all still too new. Laurel needed some time to absorb everything he'd told her.

"Where you going?" Jason asked as she turned toward the door.

"I need to get back up to the mine. There are decisions that need to be made about the mine. It'll be a while before you're in any condition to go back up there."

"Are you going to shut it down?" he asked.

Laurel shook her head. "That should be your decision. After all, the Rebecca is actually yours, since you're still..." She had started to say since he was still alive.

"The assay reports and the claim are in your name now," he replied. "It's your decision." He shifted in the chair.

"I made the arrangements for Delia," he continued. "I thought it best that she's buried in San Francisco. God knows she hated this place."

Laurel was silently grateful that everything had already been taken care of. She didn't think she had the strength to return to Gold Hill and face an undertaker.

"I'll look in on you when I get back into town," she told him in parting.

"Sammy will be there to help you. He's reliable and a hard worker." His mouth worked with something else he struggled to say.

"I love you, daughter." The words stopped her at the door. "I always have, even when you were far away."

SHE SPENT the next four days at the Rebecca with Sammy, going over the full extent of damage to the mine shaft. Each morning found her deep inside the mine, groveling along on her stomach, crawling through chambers that were still intact from another opening, or digging out cluttered passageways.

By evening she was too exhausted to even think, much less eat, and she fell into bed when she couldn't put one foot in front of the other.

On the morning of the fifth day, the first of the wagons rounded the hill and pulled into the yard. The noise the men made as they unloaded supplies and materials brought Laurel up out of the Rebecca. For several minutes she stood staring at the commotion that had churned up dust clouds in the yard. Sammy ran about, chattering in that odd mixture of English and Chinese, arms waving wildly as he directed where the supplies should be taken.

Laurel spotted Tommy Chin in one of the wagons.

"What is all of this?"

Tommy shrugged. "New supplies ordered for the mine," he announced.

"I didn't order any more supplies."

Laurel's eyes widened as more wagons pulled into the yard, several filled with lumber and heavy timbers for shoring up the passages, along with several Chinese men.

"Work crews," Tommy informed her.

"Wait." She rounded a wagon, trying to make herself understood to the workers who had scrambled to the ground and now stood watching her with expressions that were a mixture of amusement and patience.

They didn't understand a word she was saying, or if they did, they were politely ignoring her.

"You have to tell explain," she told Tommy. "I didn't order any supplies or workers for the mine." She watched with growing frustration as crates of chickens, sacks of flour, and fresh vegetables were unloaded.

"I have no way of paying for this!"

"Everything is paid for."

"By whom?" Laurel demanded. Tommy handed her the sales bill.

Ruel Delaney's signature was scrawled at the bottom.

Glancing across the yard, she spotted Sammy. He came running when she called to him.

"How much money did you bring back from Virginia City?"

At Sammy's wide-eyed expression, Laurel's voice rose an octave. "Sammy!"

"Very sorry, Miss Laurel." He bowed from the waist. "Mr. Delaney say he hold money against note you owe him."

"Of all the...!" Laurel groaned. All she had was the money that she'd won in that card game. The loan had covered the original expenses that had gone up in smoke, literally.

She hadn't seen Ruel since the night he'd killed Aaron Talbott. Most of her time had been spent with Cappy—her father. An inquiry she'd made at the sheriff's office revealed only that Ruel wasn't going to be held for Talbott's death. For his part in her abduction and various other crimes, Deaver had been tracked down and arrested. It seemed that there was some law and order in Virginia City.

She had planned for the money she'd won in that game to get them through until she could figure out how to re-open the mine. She needed Cappy—Jason's help to do that, but until he was well enough to travel to the mine that would have to wait.

What angle Ruel Delaney was playing by sending those supplies, not to mention the timber that had been so badly needed. And paying for them?

Arriving back in Virginia City, Laurel went straight to the International Hotel. Her attire—the pants, shirt and boots she usually wore at the mine, drew the obvious attention as Mr. Tibbits asked her to wait.

Pacing the lobby, she caught sight of her reflection in a window that fronted the street. Her hair was in complete disarray, its thick waves controlled only by a string of ribbon. She hadn't realized how she'd neglected her appearance the last few days. But, straightening her shoulders, she decided it would just have to do. After all, one didn't usually wear satin and crinolines when crawling around in mine shafts.

She waited. And waited. By the time Tibbits informed her

that Ruel would see her, her anger after cooling on that ride down from the mountain, was back. She entered Ruel's office, forced to wait as he finished discussing some matter with an employee.

She thought of the man she'd first encountered aboard the *Waverall*. It was still difficult for her to believe that Ruel was a respectable businessman. All this time she'd thought him nothing more than an itinerant gambler. And she'd fallen in love with him anyway.

"Good morning. This is a pleasant surprise." Ruel smiled. He suspected that Tommy Chin had arrived with the supplies she needed up at the mine. It was the only thing the past several days that would have brought her down off the mountain.

Laurel waited until his employee was gone, and the door was closed. "Perhaps not when you learn the reason I'm here," she said tartly.

Ruel rose and walked around the desk, that dark gaze fastened on her. Laurel was immediately wary. But he leaned back against the edge of the desk.

"You're looking well." He commented, when what he wanted to do was drag her into his arms and kiss her.

She didn't want pleasantries, she wanted her money, and she didn't trust that look in his eyes.

"This isn't a social call; I have a business matter to discuss with you."

He'd deliberately stayed away, figuring she needed time to sort through her feelings after everything that had happened. And he'd assumed she'd spend some time with her father. After all, there was a lot for them to catch up on. But she'd gone back to that mountain and buried herself inside the mine.

"There are things we need to talk about," he agreed.

She looked well enough. In fact, she looked beautiful, even in faded pants and shirt. Anger or summer heat had put color in her cheeks, and those blue eyes... Laurel Wentworth was the most desirable woman he'd ever known.

His thoughts went back to the first time he'd seen her, when he'd hauled her out of that trunk in the hold of the *Waverall*. He'd wanted her then, and he wanted her now.

Laurel ignored his obvious meaning. "I came here for my money. Sammy told me you refused to give it to him."

So that was it. Ruel fought back a satisfied smile. He'd deliberately refused to let Sammy have the money, knowing what her reaction would be, fairly certain it would bring her back down off the mountain. And now she was here.

"Your money?" A dark brow arched. "I think you have that just a little wrong."

"Wrong? I won that money fair and square in a card game right here in your hotel."

"That is correct, as far as it goes." He saw the way her eyes darkened, the same way they'd darkened that night when he'd gone to her.

If getting her angry was what it took then so be it.

Laurel relaxed. He seemed to agree with her, but there was that last thing—*as far as it goes.*

"Just what is that supposed to mean?" she asked.

Ruel flipped open the ledger on his desk. "There is still the matter of the loan," he reminded her.

"The loan is a completely separate transaction. It has nothing to do with the money I won in that game. Please instruct Tibbits to give me my money," she replied.

"I can't do that."

"What do you mean, you can't do that?" Her eyes narrowed. She didn't trust him. He was up to something.

"It wouldn't be good business. And I'm certain you can appreciate sound business decisions."

Laurel's lips thinned. "Either you give me my money this minute, or..."

It was then he moved, reaching out, and grabbing her by the waist and pulling her against him.

She tried to pull back. There was a lesson in all of this, she thought. She had to remember not to stand too close to Ruel Delaney when she was trying to make a point.

"Or what?" he whispered against her throat. "What will you do?"

He bent over her until his mouth was a fraction of an inch over hers. The tantalizing heat of his breath, whispered over her lips. For a long agonizing moment, Laurel was certain he was going to kiss her and her body betrayed her. She wanted him to kiss her, wanted him to touch her.

Ruel's eyes darkened. So close and yet so far away. Her lips parted as if she would have said something, then her lashes lowered, for an instant shielding the smoky heat in her eyes. Not yet, he told himself. Not yet. With maddening calm, he set her from him, rounded the desk and sat down once more.

At the creak of the chair, Laurel's eyes flew open, and anger sparked in the depths of her eyes. His answer echoed in her mind—what would she do?

"What do you mean?" she asked, having learned that it was dangerous to bargain with Ruel Delaney.

"It all comes back to the matter of business, Laurel."

Taking a cigarette from the box on his desk, Ruel lit it, then sent a fragrant streamer of smoke into the air.

"I hoped that you brought money with you."

Anger exploded. "I don't have any money. That's why I came here, to get what *you* owe me."

Ruel stared thoughtfully at the glowing tip of the cigarette. "That is only partial payment for what you owe."

"Owe for what?"

He'd timed the conversation perfectly. A slow smile spread across his face as the clock on his desk methodically announced the noon hour. Then he sat forward in the chair and pulled a piece of paper from the ledger. He turned it toward Laurel.

"According to the terms of the note you signed, full payment was to be made by noon of the eighth." Glancing at the small calendar on his desk, he declared with aggravating calm, "It is now noon, September eighth. Your note is due in full. I'm afraid the money you won in that game will cover only part of what you owe, and as I said partial payment isn't good enough."

Laurel stared, open-mouthed, as his words sank in. Then her control snapped. "You know very well I can't repay that loan now!" she protested. "Damn you, Ruel Delaney. I needed that money to repair the damage to the mine. I have workers to be paid, equipment to replace." She stamped her foot angrily. "You can't do this to me!"

"Oh, but I can. Unless you'd like to try to change your luck."

"Luck has nothing to do with it, unless you're referring to my misfortune in having met you," she flung back at him.

"I was referring to that original card game. You were willing to play for pretty high stakes. That takes courage."

Laurel glared at him as she remembered all the champagne she'd consumed that night, and what that had led to after she'd won. How was it possible to love someone and be so angry with them at the same time.

"Would you be interested in another friendly wager?" he asked.

"What kind of wager?" Laurel looked at him suspiciously.

"One hand of cards, you pick the game."

"I have nothing to bet, remember?" Tiny flashes of fire darted from her eyes.

Undaunted, he continued. "If you win, the debt is canceled. I'll gladly tear up the note and the money in my safe is yours."

"And if I lose?" she asked. She wanted to know exactly what was at stake.

"If you lose, I collect on the note according to our original agreement."

The Rebecca, Laurel stubbornly thought. She'd already pledged it. Actually, she had nothing to lose. But if she won... And she had won when she'd played before. She'd won big.

The look at her eyes changed. "One hand, five-card draw," she announced.

Ruel smothered a smile of satisfaction. Opening a desk drawer, he drew out a fresh pack of cards.

"If you're prefer, I can call in one of the dealers from the gaming room," he offered. "And have him bring a new deck."

She agreed and they waited. When one of his dealers arrived, he handed Ruel one of those bound decks with the seal. Ruel handed her the deck.

She broke the seal as she had seen that previous evening, then handed the deck back to him. He dealt the cards.

He dealt the first round of cards. "I'll cover your bets," he told her. "Since you don't have any money."

"What will that cost me?" she flung back at him. He smiled, always dangerous she thought.

He dealt two more cards. A ten of hearts joined his king in the same suit, and a four of diamonds went to Laurel.

She held her breath. The cards they'd both been dealt were in the same suits. She discarded, then waited as he dealt two cards to cover the two she'd rejected.

Laurel watched him carefully, reminding herself that in spite of his easy manner he was still a gambler by profession. He hadn't taken any cards.

"What is your bet?" he demanded.

This was ridiculous, she thought, as she looked at her cards then smiled to herself. Assuming an expression that was completely unreadable, Ruel reached for his last three cards. With deliberate slowness he turned over one, then another, then the last.

Laurel stared, unable to believe what she saw. It was impossible! And yet, face up on the desk, along with the ten and king, were a jack, a queen, and an ace—all hearts.

"It would seem I've won," Ruel announced.

Several emotions raced across her face—disbelief and anger and panic.

"That's impossible! No one could draw a hand like that. You said yourself the odds were impossible. Damn you, Ruel Delaney, you cheated!"

He slowly rose from his chair. "May I remind you that you also drew the same kind of hand, a straight flush, all in the same suit before."

"But..."He was right. She had drawn that exact hand.

"Now, regarding the matter of the loan, I'll want to collect immediately," he calmly told her. "It's a matter of good business."

She'd lost. How could she ever explain to Cappy... Jason? She shook her head.

"I'll see that the papers are drawn up accordingly."

"That's not good enough."

Her head came up, and her confusion showed at her eyes.

"It's just not good enough," he repeated. "I explained the terms of the loan when I gave you the money in the first place. I have no use for another silver mine." He gestured to the map and diagram hanging behind his desk. At the bottom was inscribed the name French Lady.

"I already own three. And the Rebecca *is* unproven."

"I don't have anything else."

"Yes, you do," he told her. "I want... you."

"But you can't mean...?"

"Those are my terms."

"I won't do it!" Her eyes snapped with renewed anger. "I won't be your whore. I don't care what deal we made. No court in the world would force me to do it."

"That's true. But I'm confident you'll regain your figure after the baby arrives. Actually, I'm looking forward to a family," he informed her nonchalantly.

"A family?" Laurel exclaimed. Ignoring the dangerous look in Ruel's eyes, she rushed on. "No child of mine is for sale, Mr. Ruel Delaney, nor am I. Forget your damned bet! Somehow I'll get the money to reopen the Rebecca." She headed for the door.

Ruel was across the office, barring her way. "It's not that easy, Laurel. Didn't I tell you that before?"

He pulled her into an embrace that drove the breath from her. His mouth found hers and in that one blinding, fraction of a second, all resistance was obliterated. His lips parted hers and his tongue plunged inside while his hands worked their way down her back and closed over her bottom in those damned pants.

"So beautiful," he whispered against her throat, then pressed kisses into her hair, and then his mouth took away the last of her anger.

It was madness, she thought as her arms came up around him. "I don't want this," she cried unconvincingly. "I don't want you..."

"Say it again," he teased, his lips whispering down the column of her neck. She tasted of sun and wind, and fire. "Tell me that you don't want me."

"I don't..." Her denial was cut off as his lips hungrily found hers again.

"Tell me..." he demanded, his fingers unfastening the buttons at the front of her shirt.

"I don't—"

He kissed denial from her mouth, drinking her in.

Laurel shuddered as he pushed away the thin cotton shirt, finding bare flesh beneath.

"I do want you," she whispered. Her fingers went through back through his hair, holding him for her kiss.

Carrying her across the office, he kicked open the door to his private suite. If it took a lifetime, he would convince her that he loved her—her, not some illusion.

He lowered her onto the bed, his lips leaving hers to tenderly trace the exposed breast. Her eyes closed with pleasure and she held him against her.

Slowly, Ruel undressed her, pulling off boots, then removing her shirt and pants. That dark gaze glowed.

She wore absolutely nothing underneath the pants or shirt. She lay before him, soft, pale and golden, her hair shimmering across the pillows as he bent over her, trailing kisses, slowly learning her, the way her breath caught as he wandered lower.

His name caught in her throat as his hands played a maddening game down the length of her body, remembering the softness, the hidden places he'd discovered before. He traced tiny circles on her skin, stroking, tasting, all of her. Slowly his hand caressed her stomach and a roundness that hadn't been there before.

Those dark eyes fastened on her. With just that look, she realized that he knew what she had only guessed at the past weeks.

"Were you going to tell me?" he asked.

"With everything that's happened..." she started to explain.

He saw it at her eyes. There had been enough pain at the secrets people had kept.

"If you don't want a child, I understand..." she started to explain. "I'm perfectly capable of raising a child by myself, and with Cappy..." She still found it difficult to call him by his real name, her father—Jason Cameron, she would do it.

A child, his child with her, not a mistake to be gotten rid of, Ruel thought.

"I want you and our child," he told her and tenderly kissed her there.

Then, she asked the question that had haunted her for so

long. She needed to know that he wasn't simply replacing her with her sister.

"What about... Delia?"

He laid his head just there, holding her, holding his child. How to make her understand? What could he tell her that wouldn't hurt her?

"It happened, but it was never... And from the beginning, I knew there were other men."

It was never what he had with the woman who lay beside him now, what he felt when she walked into a room, the sound of her voice, a look that was there in her eyes even when she was angry, and what he felt knowing she was going to have his child.

"It was over a long time ago," he said, trying to remember something, anything about that. But there was nothing, only time spent together for a while and always with the understanding that it would never be anything more.

Silence filled the room. Then he whispered, "I remember every moment I've had with you."

He recalled every detail of the gown she'd worn that first day aboard the *Waverall*, the first time she wore the shirt and pants Cass gave her, her stubbornness, strength, and courage.

"And Dominique?" she asked, needing to know.

"I was fifteen, she was older... and more experienced. And she was there when the man who raised me was killed, then introduced me to a man who saw the advantage of having someone to handle some of the contraband shipments he ran through the blockades during the war."

"What about the stolen Union gold?"

Ruel smiled. "I could tell you that I won it in a card game. There was this stranger who came to town..." He grunted as Laurel drove her fist into his stomach.

"The truth."

"Would you believe me if I said I was on a special assignment for the Union Army?"

She looked at him suspiciously.

"The gold was actually stolen by a band of Confederate soldiers," he explained. "They were trying to get it to Jefferson Davis during the last months of the war. The South was desperate for money to buy weapons and supplies. The Union wanted it back."

"Would this be the same sort of story you'd tell me if I asked about those crates aboard the *Waverall?*"

Lying across him, she pressed her fingers against his lips. "No, don't tell me. I can wait to hear about that later."

"If you're certain...?" He suspected that she didn't believe him for a minute about the gold.

"Positive," she replied, then pressed kisses down his neck and across his chest.

It didn't matter. She knew *who* he was, someone who believed in her, had protected her. It was all that mattered.

Then, slowly, very slowly, and with great tenderness, he began to tell her all the ways he loved her, and then showed her.

Her breath caught as he traced a path down her thigh with his lips, desire burning deep inside her.

"It's not decent!" she protested. "The middle of the day?"

Then he parted her, tasting the heat inside her until she shattered in wave after wave of pure sensation.

Afterward, she lay across him, her hair spread across his chest, and decided it was a very pleasurable way to spend the day after all.

He lifted a golden strand of her hair, breathing in its fragrance. "How do you do it?"

"Hmmm?" Laurel replied.

"How do you manage to wear a man's clothes, and still smell so desirable. You could wear burlap, and I'd still want you."

She ran a finger through the silken hair at his chest. "How did *you* do it?"

"What?"

"How did you manage to draw that hand of cards?"

He smiled and pressed a kiss at her forehead. "Luck," he replied.

Laurel leaned over the edge of the bed where she'd thrown his clothes. She raised her hand and showed him the three cards that she'd picked up off the floor.

"How did you manage to cheat without my seeing it?"

There was nothing to do but confess his sins. "The stakes were high. I had to be certain I'd win." He pulled her against him, shifting her body over his.

"And... I have quick hands."

It was impossible to be angry with him. Especially when he was doing such things to her with those hands. There was one more thing she wanted to know.

"Are you planning a trip?" She angled a look across the room at the steamer trunk that sat against the wall.

"My back-up plan."

At her confused expression, he gently pulled her under him. His leg moved between hers.

"Back up plan?" she asked, very much liking the feel of his long legs against hers.

"I decided that if you didn't see things my way, I'd simply lock you up in that trunk until you did."

"Kidnapping," she replied.

"Kidnapping in the case of my unborn child." His dark eyes teased. "In your case, I think they'd call it wife-napping."

"Wife?"

He rose from the bed and crossed the room to a tall chest of drawers and opened a drawer. He pulled out a small leather case. He had run blockades, calmly stared down other men with unknown cards in their hands, and done other things that had earned him the reputation he had. But he'd never been this uncertain, nothing had ever been this important.

He returned to the bed and opened the case, then took her hand in his and slipped the ring on her finger. Brilliant diamonds and a huge sapphire winked back at her.

"I could go down on one knee and propose like a true gentleman," he offered.

She dissolved into fits of laughter at the thought of Ruel Delaney, completely naked, proposing marriage on bended knee.

"That won't be necessary, and you won't need the trunk."

That gaze met hers—dark, intense, and refused to let go.

"Is that *yes*?"

EPILOGUE

Laurel turned in the bed, trying to find a comfortable position. In spite of the cool, blue sky beyond the windows, the room was unbearably warm.

The nurse moved around her, periodically replacing the cloth at her forehead. Laurel batted at it away, aggravated by pain, the nurse's dour expression, and her growing suspicion that Jessica might not have told her the complete truth about childbirth.

Dear Jessica. In spite of all the months of early morning sickness and the later months of confinement, she'd delivered a healthy son, and Andrew was absolutely ecstatic, boasting that he'd like another child as soon as possible. But Jessica had remained strangely noncommittal on the matter, saying only that she wanted sufficient time to enjoy her firstborn.

She had given Laurel somewhat vague answers to her countless questions about what to expect when childbirth began, and she felt there was a great deal that might have been left unsaid.

How different everything was now than when they'd first returned from Boston months earlier. She had insisted on returning to Virginia City for a few weeks to see Jason, and she had aggravated Ruel by insisting on moving up to the cabin on Gold Hill to await the strike at the Rebecca. She was so close to her time that everyone working at the mine had begun to take bets on which would happen first—the strike or the birth of the baby.

As the weeks passed, she'd even placed some small wagers herself. A small person, she'd been astounded at how rapidly she'd outgrown the gowns made for her. But the Rebecca hadn't disappointed them.

True to Jason's prediction, the main strike came in at the third level. There was a big celebration at the mine, and the next day, Ruel packed her off to San Francisco. Jason had followed a few days later, determined to be there when his grandchild was finally born. Andrew and Jessica had been overjoyed to see her and hear about their trip to Boston. Andrew had sent word about the strike to his father. Everything was perfect.

Almost.

Laurel reached for a glass of water only to have it taken from her by the nurse.

"That does it!" she muttered, her patience gone. She hurt, she was scared, and she wanted Ruel with her.

"Please have my husband come up," she instructed the nurse.

The woman turned to her with uplifted brow. "It's most unusual for fathers to be present. We're most efficient in these matters. After all, women have been having babies for centuries. We'll send word as soon as the baby arrives."

"No! You'll send for him now! I want my husband. I want him here!"

"There, there, my dear. You're merely distraught. It's usually this way the first time. Just leave everything to me."

Her hand closed over the metal bowl on the stand beside her. Her knuckles whitened as she lifted it.

"If you don't summon my husband immediately, I will throw this at you."

The nurse backed away as if she'd had a gun waved under her nose instead of a wash bowl, then disappeared through the door.

Laurel slumped back against the pillows. She breathed in slowly, gathering her strength for the next wave of pain. Jess had very definitely neglected to tell her about this part—pain low in front, and at her back.

As another began, she threw back the covers and swung her legs over the edge of the bed. She'd be damned if she was going to lie in this bed and suffer in the most uncomfortable position imaginable.

She didn't care how many centuries women had been having babies. She wanted to move around, to stretch and draw an even breath, to move with the pain instead of against it. The next one drove her to her feet.

She grabbed the footboard and leaned into it, breathing in slowly, exhaling just as slowly. It actually seemed to help, and being on her feet eased the pain at her back.

"Laurel? What the devil...!"

She turned around and met Ruel's startled gaze. She smiled. He was beside her in an instant.

"What the hell are you trying to do?" His arm immediately went around her. He took her hand and started to lead her back to the side of the bed.

"Trying to have a baby, I think," she retorted. "No, please," she begged. "I can't stand that bed. Let me walk."

He gave her an uncertain look. "What about the baby?"

"From what I've learned from Jessica, a baby just doesn't pop out. It takes a great deal of effort to give birth. I will admit, they're much easier to make than to get here."

In spite of his worry, Ruel couldn't help but laugh.

She tried to smile, her fingers tightening over his as another one began.

"It's really not so bad." She bit at her lower lip as the pain grew stronger and she breathed her way through it.

"I'll get the doctor!" He headed for the door.

Laurel reached out to him as she sat on the bed. "Stay with me."

The doctor arrived, the nurse right behind him, as Ruel helped her into the bed and another pain began. The doctor proceeded to examine her.

"Your baby's almost here, Mrs. Delaney," the doctor assured her, and glanced over at Ruel.

"It's unusual for the father to remain..." he started to explain.

With one look at her, Ruel announced, "I'm staying."

"Very well," the physician replied.

As the next pain began, he told her to push.

She felt as if she were being split apart. Biting her lower lip, she silently cursed and squeezed Ruel's hand.

"Jessica lied about this part!"

"And again," the doctor instructed. "And once more."

Their son burst into angry squalling as soon as he suddenly appeared.

"My God!" Ruel whispered as he stared down the tiny infant.

The cord was quickly cut, the afterbirth disposed of, and the nurse wrapped the infant in a blanket.

Ruel's hands tightened over Laurel's.

"I want to hold him," she whispered.

"That's highly irregular." The nurse glanced from physician to new mother. "He hasn't been properly cleaned."

"I want to hold my son!"

Seeing no harm in the request, the physician nodded to the nurse.

"He's so little." Ruel stroked his son's tiny fingers. They closed around his larger one.

"I might argue that with you," Laurel told him. Dark hair curled damply about the baby's head, eyes already dark stared into darker ones.

"He's the most beautiful baby in the world," Ruel whispered, as he bent to kiss his son's forehead. "Perfect."

"Boys aren't supposed to be beautiful," she told him. "They're supposed to be handsome. And he's not perfect, he's a scoundrel, putting me through all of this."

"But worth it." Ruel sat on the bed beside her, ignoring the disapproval of the nurse.

"How soon will he be able to hold a hand of cards?" he commented.

Laurel laughed softly. "I'm not so certain about cards." Her eyes widened and she cried out in alarm.

"What is it?" Ruel asked. The expression at her face terrified him as nothing in his life ever had. She clutched at his hand with almost deadly strength.

"It can't be!" She tried to breathe. "I thought the pain went away as soon as..." The words were cut off as another pain seized her.

Ruel came up off the bed and called for the doctor.

The nurse slipped between them and took his son. Then the physician quickly checked Laurel. Fear twisted inside Ruel. He'd heard there were women who died in childbirth with bleeding that wouldn't stop.

He'd never been a man who prayed, and he suspected that it wouldn't sit well if he tried to bargain with God.

"Are you ready, Mr. Delaney?" The doctor's gaze briefly met his, then he called for the nurse.

"Ready?" Ruel asked. "For what?"

Laurel smiled through the pain. "I think what the doctor is trying to tell us, is that we're not quite through."

Reality finally dawned on him. "Twins?"

"So it seems." The physician nodded. "This one seems more impatient than the first." The doctor had time for only one hastily given instruction to the nurse.

Impatient, strong-minded, defiant.

All those words and more filled Ruel's thoughts as he stared with disbelief at the tiny, squirming form of his daughter as she entered the world as if she'd had enough of waiting.

Her eyes were not the dark ones of her brother, but much lighter. And her hair was the softest whisper of downy gold.

He felt none of the boastful assurance that he'd felt with their son. This tiny creature, promised to be completely unpredictable.

"Twins!"

"Is that really so surprising?" Laurel smiled up at him, then she gasped.

"Oh my!"

Seeing his startled expression, she laughed as the nurse placed their son in the curve of her arm, and Ruel continued to stare down at their daughter.

"I think two are quite enough for one day, don't you?" She took hold of his hand and pulled him down beside her.

"Want to make a small bet?"

He pressed a kiss at her forehead. He'd never known what it was to have a family. She had given him all of that, and more.

"What kind of bet?" he asked.

"On the next time?" She glanced up at him.

"Twins again?"

She smiled. "It could happen."

"Doctor?" Ruel asked.

"I would say it's not very likely. I usually see only one set of twins in a family. It's rare you know."

Ruel looked down at her. "Yes, *she* certainly is."

ALSO BY CARLA SIMPSON

Angus Brodie and Mikaela Forsythe Murder Mystery

A Deadly Affair

Deadly Secrets

A Deadly Game

Merlin Series

Daughter of Fire

Daughter of the Mist

Daughter of the Light

Shadows of Camelot

Dawn of Camelot

Daughter of Camelot

The Young Dragons, Blood Moon

Clan Fraser

Betrayed

Revenge

Outlaws, Scoundrels & Lawmen

Desperado's Caress

Passion's Splendor

Silver Mistress

Memory and Desire

Desire's Flame

Silken Surrender

Ravished

Always My Love

Seductive Caress

Seduced

Deceived

ABOUT THE AUTHOR

"I want to write a book... " she said.

"Then do it," he said.

And she did, and received two offers for that first book proposal.

A dozen historical romances later, and a prophecy from a gifted psychic and the Legacy Series was created, expanding to seven additional titles.

Along the way, two film options, and numerous book awards.

But wait, there's more a voice whispered, after a trip to Scotland and a visit to the standing stones in the far north, and as old as Stonehenge, sign posts the voice told her, and the Clan Fraser books that have followed that told the beginnings of the clan and the family she was part of...

And now... murder and mystery set against the backdrop of Victorian London in the new Angus Brodie and Mikaela Forsythe series, with an assortment of conspirators and murderers in the brave new world after the Industrial Revolution where terrorists threaten and the world spins closer to war.

When she is not exploring the Darkness of the fantasy world, or pursuing ancestors in ancient Scotland, she lives in the mountains near Yosemite National Park with bears and mountain lions, and plots murder and revenge.

And did I mention fierce, beautiful women and dangerous, handsome men?

They're there, waiting...

Join Carla's Newsletter

www.ingramcontent.com/pod-product-compliance
Lightning Source LLC
Chambersburg PA
CBHW020010120726
47903CB00004B/1226